W9-BUE-575

THE
EXPLORER'S
CODE

A Novel

KITTY PILGRIM

SCRIBNER

New York   London   Toronto   Sydney

SCRIBNER
A Division of Simon & Schuster, Inc.
1230 Avenue of the Americas
New York, NY 10020

First Scribner hardcover edition July 2011

SCRIBNER and design are registered trademarks of The Gale Group, Inc., used under license by Simon & Schuster, Inc., the publisher of this work.

For information about special discounts for bulk purchases, please contact Simon & Schuster Special Sales at 1-866-506-1949 or business@simonandschuster.com.

The Simon & Schuster Speakers Bureau can bring authors to your live event. For more information or to book an event contact the Simon & Schuster Speakers Bureau at 1-866-248-3049 or visit our website at www.simonspeakers.com.

Designed by Carla Jayne Jones

Manufactured in the United States of America

1   3   5   7   9   10   8   6   4   2

ISBN 978-1-4391-9719-6
ISBN 978-1-4391-9727-1 (ebook)

To Maurice

The tension of life has tilted dangerously towards the material side of the watershed, disabling the balance of our soul; so that we are constrained at intervals to leave the social structure of our time, and turn away for our stability to breathe in quiet, hoping for the Unexpected.

—FREYA STARK, EPHESUS, *IONIA: A QUEST*

Under Roman law the Latin expression "terra nullius" meant "land belonging to no one," or no-man's-land. In international law the term refers to territory that is not under the sovereignty of any state. Sovereignty over terra nullius is achieved through occupation of the land.

London, England

Peter Stapleton sat with his feet up on the leather ottoman. A light rain misted the dusk outside the window; evening was just setting in. He had done nothing all day except work on his portfolio. While everyone was piling into financials, he had moved into the safety of cash and a couple of choice investments. He flipped through his broker's reports. It looked like he got out in time. The whole world was in a credit meltdown, banks collapsing like bamboo huts in a tsunami.

He looked past his monogrammed velvet slippers propped up on the ottoman. The fire was just dying down again. He would ring for more wood in a moment. Oh, on second thought, Magda would have left for the day. It was time to get dressed for dinner. Sara and David had a great cook, and meals at their home were always a delight. Not that he needed it, five stone overweight and still gaining. He really should get a grip on the weight; the doctor just kept shaking his head every time he went for a checkup.

He looked back at his financial documents. The Packton Fund was the ticket; that fellow in Chicago was a genius. And, of course, there was that little deal that Andrew had put him on to. The return on that was almost criminal. He took a sip of his highly sugared Earl Grey, but the tea had gone cold.

There was a noise a floor below. Magda must still be here. He rang the electronic bell beside his chair. Nothing. Only the sound of the clock on his desk. Must be his imagination. No, there was the noise again. It sounded like things falling to the floor. Peter Stapleton got up, heaving his enormous bulk out of the leather chair. Better check that out. It could be a window open, things blowing about.

He started down the stairs, feeling a little light-headed after sitting all afternoon. He had tried to stave off his indigestion after lunch, had drunk some tea. Lamb chops were always a bit heavy, nothing to be alarmed about. Of course, the sticky date pudding wasn't really necessary, but Magda did it so well. The heaviness had sat on his chest on and off all afternoon. Walking about now, he started to feel a bit nauseous and clammy.

As he moved down the stairs he heard the unmistakable sounds of the contents of his living-room bookshelf being pulled to the floor. What was going on?

He glimpsed the intruder as he stood in the doorway. *What in the bloody hell?* The man was slight, dark, wearing a sweat suit and Windbreaker, still wet from outdoors. Peter Stapleton looked at the spots of rain beaded on the nylon. It must be raining hard. He must have just come in.

That was his last real thought. Suddenly he felt very short of breath, his face flushed hot. His vision blurred and he was racked with a searing pain in his left arm. The man started toward him. Dark, foreign-looking. Not English. Peter Stapleton reached out to him, a perfect stranger, as he fell.

Ephesus, Turkey

For the last hour, John Sinclair had been crouched over a fragment of bone sticking up from the earth. With a small camel-hair brush he flicked away grains of soil.

"Karl, take a look at this," he shouted over his shoulder. There was no reply.

Sinclair stood and looked around the site. Ephesus was strangely deserted. The silent ruins stretched out for miles in the sunshine, and not a soul was moving among the white chunks of marble. Even the few off-season tourists had left. He glanced at his watch, dustproof, shockproof, and well suited to his work. It was noon.

He spent most of his time in Ephesus on his hands and knees in the dust, breathing it, smelling it, and—truth be told—worshipping the ground of the ancient city. He loved the palpable heat that beat down on his back every day as he worked, baking the soil, warming the ancient marble ruins. Sinclair experienced Ephesus through his senses: the smell of the dust, and the feel of the warm stones beneath his hands. The carvings were as clear to him as if they had been done yesterday. He would trace, like a man reading Braille, the Greek and Latin inscriptions on a wall, or the secret Christian symbols carved into the marble pavement.

In the ancient graveyard he would handle every bone fragment with a deep reverence, because for him these people were real, and this was a living city. When he walked among the crowds of tourists along the ancient streets, he had no problem imagining that he was walking in the Ephesus of Roman times, along a broad marble avenue trod by leather sandals and resounding with a polyglot of archaic languages.

Sinclair realized his passion for the ancient city bordered on the irrational. If he were a superstitious man he would attribute his obsession to the power of ancient ghosts. If he had a strong belief in reincarnation, he might conclude he was influenced by the memory of a past life. If he were a religious man, he would say God was calling him. But Sinclair was neither superstitious nor very religious; he liked to think of himself as a man of science.

Sinclair wiped his forehead, streaking a smear across his temple. His dark hair was coated with dust. The intense blue eyes swept around the archaeological site. No sign of Karl. He sat down, leaning against a warm marble slab, and closed his eyes to the Turkish sun. There wasn't a sound.

He drowsed, and his mind roamed freely: first he reviewed his find of the day, a new femur, and the utter thrill of lifting it out of the ancient soil. As he relaxed, he recovered the sense-memory of a pair of beautifully curved buttocks cupped in his hands, and the way he could slide two of his fingers between them as he pulled the woman's body toward him. Then he felt her beautiful legs as they wound around his back, her head tilted, goading him, her eyes half shut with desire.

The shrill pierce of a cell phone sounded. Without opening his eyes, he worked it out of the pocket of his cargo shorts and flipped it open.

"Sinclair."

A voice on the other end began speaking at a rapid pace. The pitch was feminine. He listened for a moment in silence, and his eyes finally opened and focused on the distance.

"Sure, I can work it out."

The woman's voice continued.

He answered. "I was planning on coming at the end of the week for the award ceremony, but I can come today if you need me."

He consulted his watch.

"I'll get a flight this afternoon."

The BMW R1200GSA Adventure was parked under the tree where he left it this morning. He put his notebook in the Zega side pannier, climbed on, and started the engine. The sound of the bike roared over the silence of Ephesus. Sinclair swerved sharply out of the dirt parking lot onto the macadam and followed the road uphill through an olive grove. As he left the dig, he scanned his cherished site. Random bits of marble stuck up from the grass like giant teeth, irregular and gleaming white. Only about 15 percent of Ephesus had been excavated, and the remnants of marble scattered around the fields were hints of more treasure to come.

Sinclair pushed the bike faster, and the wind cooled his face. He loved this ride. The road climbed steadily up into the arid hills for several miles. Across the landscape there was nothing but scrubby vegetation, mostly silver-leafed olive trees and narthex, a plant used in ancient Ephesus as a torch to light early church gatherings.

At the summit of the mountain, Sinclair pulled into the courtyard of a modest stone house and cut the engine. No other vehicles were in the yard. He walked to the door, unlocked it, and pushed it open. Inside, the single room was nearly empty: a neatly made bed, armoire, writing desk, and a couch by the window. He punched the sound system on the desk as he walked past, and the Baroque melody of Arcangelo Corelli's *La Follia* filled the air. As he walked to the shower, he stripped naked, his uncovered flesh gleaming white in contrast to his deep tan. Throwing his clothes in a bin, he stepped into the shower and let the hot needles of the water sluice away the dust. He had to bend his knees to rinse his hair.

Sinclair stood at an impressive six feet four inches; his legs hinted of some extreme form of exercise; the muscles of his thighs were striated. An obvious guess would put him as a triathlete or competitive cyclist. But a closer look would reveal one thigh was slightly thicker, the telltale mark of a champion fencer. His broad shoulders had some bulk, but he carried no spare weight.

He finished his shower and walked to the phone naked, a towel thrown over his shoulder, dialed, and waited for the beep.

"Karl, it's Sinclair. Sorry, but I have to leave for Monaco this afternoon. I'll be back in a couple of days to help with the new quadrant. I think I just found a very nice femur there. Take a look and let me know what you think."

The second call was to Charles Bonnard. Voice mail again.

"Charles, I'm heading to Monaco a few days early. If you're still in Capri, don't worry. There's no rush; we can still meet at the end of the week if that works for you."

He dialed again, and this time someone answered.

"Malik, it's John Sinclair. Can you come pick me up right away? I need to get to the airport."

Sinclair listened and then continued.

"It's not a scheduled flight; I need a charter. Can you arrange it? Yes, for Monaco. Thanks, Malik, I'll be waiting."

Then he walked to the armoire and pulled it open. Nothing in the modest room would have given a hint of what lay inside: six immaculately tailored Italian suits, crisply ironed English-made shirts, dozens of silk socks, a rainbow of exquisite ties, and two rows of custom-made shoes. Sinclair pulled on a pair of Egyptian-cotton boxers and started to dress. Five minutes later he was tying his tie. When he heard the van rumbling up the hill, he scooped up his keys and tossed them into an earthenware bowl over the sink and walked out onto the terrace. If all went well, Sinclair would be in Monaco by evening.

Guaymas Basin, Gulf of California

Cordelia Stapleton unzipped her full-body dive skin, peeled it off, and flung it on the deck in a sodden black heap. Underneath was a blue tank suit. She could feel the ocean water evaporate instantly from her back, leaving the sensation of dried salt on her shoulder blades. Her dark hair was still wet, splayed like tentacles over her shoulders.

Dripping, she walked over to the bin of towels. She took one and rubbed her limbs vigorously, conscious of the deep tiredness that comes after swimming for hours. She massaged her leg muscles to warm them up. Cordelia was long and lean, and her body was well toned. The ocean currents served as her personal trainer, and the workouts were daily. She tied the towel around her waist into a sarong.

That was a good morning's work. She had volunteered to be one of the two swimmers to retrieve the submersible. She and another diver had attached the tag line, to pull the Alvin to the stern of the vessel. The crew was now in the process of raising it up to secure it in the hangar.

She was not happy about the manipulators. The check of the robotic arms turned up multiple issues. They would need extensive repair. The whole thing was frustrating; those arms had just been installed two years ago.

"Hey, Delia," Joel said, coming out on deck. "You have a phone message. The Herodotus Foundation called."

"Never heard of it," she said, taking another towel and drying her long hair.

"Well, they heard of you. They said they've been e-mailing you about an invitation for the last six months and you never replied," Joel said, padding over in L.L.Bean flip-flops. His red shorts were faded to pink, and the logo on his shirt read WOODS HOLE OCEANOGRAPHIC INSTITUTION.

Cordelia took the pink message slip, trying not to drip on it: *Charles Bonnard, Herodotus Foundation. 377 92 16 4738.*

"Where is this? Where is three seven seven?"

"Monaco. Too late to call them back now; they're nine hours ahead. I'll remind you tomorrow."

She didn't answer. She tried to hand the message back to him, but Joel ignored her and walked away.

"They want you to come to Monaco to accept an award in honor of your great-great-grandfather," he said.

Cordelia said nothing, staring at the pink message slip again.

"Hey, I had no idea you were related to someone famous. How come you never said anything about it?" Joel challenged.

"Most people haven't heard of him."

"What did he do?"

"His name was Elliott Stapleton. He was a polar explorer."

"Are you kidding me? You are related to *that* Stapleton. Delia, he was *huge*, in what . . . the Victorian era?"

"Yes, but he made his most important expedition later, after the turn of the century—in 1906."

"That is incredible! I had *no idea* you were related. So I guess the Herodotus Foundation wants you to accept *his* award. You *have* to go!"

Joel hoisted himself up to sit on a gear locker but didn't break his gaze, which was magnified by his thick lenses. His skinny legs dangled down, and his flip-flops fell onto the deck and lay there like dead fish. He was the only man she knew who could spend his life on a ship and still look white and anemic. So typical for him to push his point like this. She ignored him, hosing off her flippers and mask, and setting them up against a gear locker to dry. When she looked back, he was still staring.

"Joel, I can't go to Monaco. I have too much to do here."

Cordelia didn't want to tell him that she had been invited to lecture on the cruise ship the *Queen Victoria* directly after the award ceremony. The Cunard company had called her only last week, inquiring about her schedule. Cordelia had put them off, unable to decide whether or not to take them up on their offer.

"You have plenty of vacation coming to you," Joel persisted. "Anyway, we are taking Alvin to the high-bed area for maintenance in another two days."

"Yes, and I need to be here for that."

"Don't be silly, I can supervise that. You should get out of here."

Nothing doing. She was always around for the repairs—both major and minor. The maintenance schedule on Alvin was critical. The Woods Hole Oceanographic Institution's deep submergence vehicle had regular three-month, six-month, and annual maintenance, which was done during the regular operational cycle while the vehicle was in use. But there was a major overhaul and strip-down every five years.

Cordelia always stood by as the engineers went over every bolt, filter, valve, and circuit. The lights were especially important. There was no natural light at the depths the Alvin descended, so the quartz-iodide-and-metal halide lights were critical in lighting up the ocean bed. Alvin couldn't function without them.

"Joel, you *know* I want to be here for the overhaul," she said, finally facing him down.

Just then Susan came out on deck and handed Cordelia an oversized mug of lentil soup. Cordelia immediately wrapped her hands around it for warmth and inhaled the fragrant steam. Thank God for Susan; she was always the voice of reason in any discussion. But today Joel sensed that Susan would not favor Cordelia's argument.

"Susan, back me up here. Delia is telling me that we can't take care of the overhaul."

"Of *course* we can. What's the big deal?"

"No big deal, I just want to be there when they do it, that's all," said Cordelia, starting to feel a bit cornered. What damn business was it of Joel's whether she went or not?

"Delia, you should go," Joel insisted.

"Go where?" asked Susan.

"Monaco," Joel said to Susan. "She's been invited for an award ceremony two weeks from now."

"An award? You *have* to go if they're giving you an award. Anyway, it's perfect timing; the overhaul and strip-down will take at least a month."

"The award isn't for me. It's for my great-great-grandfather."

Cordelia handed the message back to Joel, put her soup mug down on a gear locker, picked up her skin suit, and walked to the railing to wring it out. She squeezed it extra hard, out of frustration with Joel.

"Delia, you've been working seven days a week for ten months straight," said Joel, as he jumped down and reattached his flip-flops to his feet, hopping on one foot and then the other.

"So have *you*, Joel."

"*I* haven't been invited to Monaco." Joel looked determined.

"Come on, Delia. You can't refuse to go if it's an award for your great-great-grandfather," Susan added. "Unless there is someone else who can accept it?"

"No . . ." said Cordelia. "I'm the only one left in the family. Except for a distant cousin in England."

"You really should go. It's not like Monaco is that hard to get to. You could be back in less than a week."

"I guess I could check the dates . . ." Cordelia wavered.

"Look," said Susan, "I know what you're worrying about. I can take care of the manipulators."

The clawed pincers on the sub were not extending to their full seventy-four inches. A critical component of the submarine, they were used like hands to deploy instruments and pick up marine samples.

"That one stern thruster is not right either," Cordelia added. "We can't turn the way we should."

"I know. I'll check all six thrusters. I promise," said Joel.

"You have to *swear* to call me if there is anything major."

"Hey, you can count on it," Joel agreed, hastily.

"And, Susan, the pumps for the seawater need to be checked; the variable ballast has been sluggish."

"Right. I'll check it."

"It's decided then," Joel said, walking away quickly, his flip-flops flapping against his heels. Cordelia glared after him. She wanted to clobber him.

He stopped and turned back. "Oh, I just remembered, you have another message. I forgot to write it down. Your lawyer in New York—Jim Gardiner. He says to call him, it's urgent."

Villa San Angelo, Anacapri, Capri, Italy

Charles Bonnard looked away from the majestic view of the sea and saw the light blinking on his cell phone. He retrieved it from the stone parapet and sat down in the alcove. After looking at the water, his eyes had to adjust to the shade. It took a moment to register the number of the missed call.

John Sinclair's international cell number—that was odd. They weren't supposed to talk until the end of the week. He pressed the voice-mail retrieve button and listened.

"Charles, I'm heading to Monaco a few days early . . ."

Sinclair was going back to Monaco already? There could only be one reason: a five-foot-eleven, 118-pound bundle of destruction named Shari. What stunt could she be pulling now? Poor guy. Sinclair sure knew how to pick them—each one worse than the last.

Charles sighed and walked back into his house. He had better go meet Sinclair. But he really didn't want to go back to Monaco and leave this little piece of paradise.

Villa San Angelo was built high into the hills of Capri and stood apart from the mayhem of the fashionable and famous down below. While the glitterati enjoyed their international watering holes in town, above them on the hillside Charles gloried in monastic isolation. Three hundred meters above the sea, his villa claimed the spectacular views that had been enjoyed by the ancient Romans when they built upon this spot. Charles had planted the Mediterranean garden out back. With his own hands, he had unearthed bits of Roman artifacts buried in the soil. Those marble fragments now held places of honor on the walls of the villa.

He walked into his bedroom to pack. The Villa San Angelo's beautiful whitewashed rooms had the pure décor of a monastery. It dated back to the late nineteenth century. When he first bought the house, the locals had repeated the legend of an angel who had been seen sitting on the cliff side looking out to sea. It was his favorite place in the world, and the parapet was built on that spot, with a glorious view of the Bay of Naples.

He sighed. It was always hard to leave. He finished putting a few things in a duffel and looked around the room one last time before closing the door. In the town square, Charles just managed to catch the local bus down to the harbor. He took a seat for the death-defying ride along the cliffs and considered his plans. He had better get to Monaco as soon as possible. He had a strong suspicion it wasn't going to be pretty.

The bus had nearly reached the village below when he remembered Brindy's luncheon tomorrow. He'd have to make a quick stop to apologize. The contessa Giorgiana Brindisi wasn't going to like it that he was not coming to her little party. And she would be furious when she found out the reason he couldn't come—it was because of John Sinclair.

Hotel Metropole, Monaco

John Sinclair leaned over the balustrade of the Hotel Metropole. It was a gorgeous day. The breeze was blowing, the megayachts were bowing to one another in the marina, and the sunlight was sprinkling the sea with diamonds. At 1 p.m., Sinclair was still in his robe and unshaven. His head was pounding from a massive hangover, and the sunlight was searing his corneas.

God damn it, Shari. He remembered how she had looked last night. The breathtaking beauty of her as she walked into the terrace restaurant. Her white silk dress flowing around her magnificent body. She was ethereal. Golden hair was piled on top of her head, wound around with silver ribbons like an ancient Greek deity. He had become accustomed to her beauty. But last night he had been staggered.

What a fool. He had been kidding himself for months. Actually, he should have known it wouldn't work out a year ago, when she turned up at the dig wearing those ridiculous shoes. Shari had teetered on four-inch heels along the ancient marble street, trailed by paparazzi. It had been a surprise visit. He had been supervising the excavation with Karl and Fabian. The three of them had been thunderstruck when she turned up. Fifteen screaming photographers kept shouting, "Look this way, Shari!!!! Look this way!!"

Sinclair was disgusted with himself. He had always been annoyed by the headlines: "Beauty and the Geek," "Supermodel Digs Archaeologist." He had lied to himself about it. Told himself it wasn't all that bad. He had ignored the telltale signs the whole time.

At first she had seemed to like the way he lived. She even tried to read his archaeological articles and academic papers. After all, she wasn't stupid. He was flattered. So he had made the effort to adjust to her world. Gradually he had become used to the idea of her celebrity. He had come to enjoy going out with her, spending time on a friend's yacht or lounging by the pool and having lunch in one of the lavish Côte d'Azur villas. Her friends were silly and amusing. It was always perfectly pleasant, and a great diversion—even if he sometimes felt he didn't always get the jokes, or didn't seem to enjoy them as much as the others did.

Sinclair turned toward the beautiful coastline. The view was lost on him. He was consumed with introspection—trying to be realistic, and honest with himself.

He leaned on the railing of the balcony to ease his back. Come to think of it, being with Shari hadn't been all that great lately. They had been irritable with each other. Not always, but plenty of times. And she did demand a lot. Of course, the sex was incredible. He could put up with a lot to keep that going. He closed his eyes, remembering her lithe body under his, her gold hair splayed all over the pillow.

But last night had been the last straw. What an awful scene. Never in his life had he fought in public like that. He had lost all control. And God knows she did too. Sinclair winced at the thought of it.

He could see where he had made his big mistake. It was thinking he was in love with her and would eventually marry her. He had believed she was going to tell him good news when she had called yesterday.

"I have something very important to tell you," she had breathed over the phone in that tiny little voice. He had been in the middle of the dig, but he had left immediately at her call. No questions asked.

He actually thought that when he got to Monaco she would tell him she was expecting his child. He had spun quite a pretty picture as he sat on the plane from Turkey. Sinclair shook his head in disgust. He had even been hoping for a boy.

Well, that conversation had turned into a disaster. Oh, she had a new baby all right, but the Brazilian Formula One driver wasn't quite what Sinclair had in mind.

Fifth Avenue, New York City

Cordelia Stapleton smiled to herself as she stood in the doorway of Jim Gardiner's office. Her lawyer was seated at his desk, doing what he loved to do more than anything in the world—eating. Gardiner was looking over about a half dozen New York deli containers, his white plastic fork poised, ready to swoop. He glanced up and saw her standing there.

"*Cordelia!* Come in, come in," he said, and put down the fork, and hauled himself to his feet. Gardiner walked to the door and gave her a bone-crushing squeeze. She knew it was coming and braced for it. Gardiner ushered her in, and then hastily returned to his desk.

"'Scuse me," he said. "I didn't expect you for another half hour."

He took one last bite of French bread and chewed rhythmically, fat-cheeked like a squirrel, while he crumpled up the wrappers and closed up the containers.

"Don't let me interrupt your lunch, Jim," she said as she took a seat. "Sorry, I'm early. I never know how to gauge New York traffic."

"Not at all—I'm finished, anyway," he said, neatly stacking the plastic containers.

She let him get settled while she looked around. Fifteen years she had been coming here. The room was still pretty much the same. The cases of leather-bound law books insulated the office from sound. Heavy drapes cloaked the windows. The dark-wood paneling also dampened the outside noise. A grandfather clock in the corner ticked as if counting time from another era. Only faintly could she hear the taxi horns on Fifth Avenue.

She surveyed her lawyer. Even *he* was almost exactly the same. His paunch had turned into a basketball and his hair was nearly all gray now. But he was still the big bear of a man he had been when she first met him.

It was she who had changed. Cordelia had met Gardiner just days after her parents had died. Gardiner, the executor of the will, was the one who had to tell her the bad news: no one wanted her.

Her closest living relative, in England, Peter Stapleton, now had *legal* custody, but he had no interest in seeing her. It would be boarding school for Cordelia. There was no other choice.

That was a lifetime ago. Now Cordelia looked at the corner of the desk and pictured her young hands holding on to it. She had gripped the oak as if clutching a life raft. Jim Gardiner had reached across and held her cold twelve-year-old fingers in his big warm mitts.

She thought about touching the wood of the desk again in the same spot, but her hands stayed in her lap. It was the same wood. Her hands were different.

"Jim, it's really good to see you," she said.

"Cordelia, I have to say, you look great. You look great." He was beaming at her.

"I'm glad I could get a couple of days free to stop off in New York. I wanted to see you before I head to Monaco."

"Monaco? *Very* fancy. Well, you deserve it, honey, you work hard enough."

"Oh, it's not a vacation. It's an award ceremony, to honor great-great-grandfather Stapleton. And after that, I have been invited to give a lecture on the *Queen Victoria*."

"The *Queen Victoria*! That is wonderful! I've always wanted to take a cruise. You have to tell me all about it when you get back."

"I'm pretty excited to go, although I am a little nervous about the award ceremony. I might have to give a speech or something."

"You'll do just fine," said Gardiner. "What an honor to accept an award for Elliott Stapleton! Now *that's* something."

"It's the Herodotus Foundation Award."

"No kidding. I've heard of that. It's a big honor. You know, come to think of it, you're a chip off the old block, aren't you? Being an oceanographer and all. He'd be proud of you, Delia."

Cordelia basked in his approval. Gardiner was the closest thing to a parent she had. It was Gardiner who, all these years, had sent the checks, received the report cards, and enrolled her in schools. He had paid the tuition and living expenses from her small inheritance.

His legal work for her had always been pro bono. Awhile ago, she figured out he probably chipped in his own money to help her make ends meet. After all, her parents hadn't left her *that* much.

But it was more than that. He had also supported her emotionally. He had always been there on the other end of the line when she called from the phone booth in the dorm. She had called him hundreds, thousands of times. And he was always available, offering encouragement, help, support, and love.

And then there were the presents; he had spoiled her atrociously. The boxes would come to school wrapped in brown paper, her friends crowding around. Always sent with the card signed: *Love, Jim Gardiner.* The fancy prom dress from Bergdorf Goodman for the senior dance. The red velvet box of Valentine chocolates every year. The tartan skirt from Scotland, and a very grown-up bottle of perfume from Paris. So many gifts.

When she was very young, she had often fantasized that someday Jim Gardiner would adopt her himself. She often wondered why he hadn't. It was only when she became an adult that she learned about Tony, Gardiner's domestic partner. And then she realized that adoption by a gay couple was not possible when she was a girl.

She looked at Gardiner closely. Tony had died last year. This was the first time she was seeing Gardiner since the funeral. At the grave site, they had clung to each other under an umbrella in the pouring rain. He had been unspeakably sad. Even today he looked a bit forlorn.

"It's really great to see you, Jim. It's been too long," she said.

Her comment sounded formal, as she often did when she tried to express her love for him. He never seemed to notice, and he didn't notice now.

"I know, Delia, I know," he said briskly. He shuffled some papers on his desk, and seemed as if he were in a great rush to tell her something important. "Listen, I needed to see you because we got this notification from England, and I wanted to talk to you about it in person."

"England?"

"Yes, your *distant* relative." He said *"distant"* with derision.

"Peter Stapleton? You haven't really mentioned him since my mom and dad died."

"Yes, well, he didn't exactly step up to the plate, if I recall."

"Well, who could blame him: a twelve-year-old kid from the States . . ." Cordelia said.

"Well, it wasn't right. He should have done *something*," Jim said, his face flushing in anger. "But all that is water under the bridge." He fussed with the papers to hide his irritation, but the gesture only amplified it.

"So what about this letter from England?"

"Well, Peter Stapleton's wife died five years ago."

"I remember. I wrote him a condolence note."

"Geez, Delia, you're too nice."

"Well, it seemed like the kind of thing most people do."

"Well, that note may have paid off. Peter Stapleton just passed away himself. It turns out you are his sole heir."

She swallowed and nodded. She knew they were both thinking of that other day, long ago, when they had sat there together after her parents had died.

"Delia?"

She nodded again, more vigorously, to let him know she was all right, and took a breath.

"How did he die?" she asked.

"Heart attack, at his town house in London."

She nodded again, mutely. She felt slightly faint, and a little tingly in her fingertips. Was she feeling shock? Certainly it was only because this talk of death conjured up such bad memories. After all, she didn't really *know* Peter Stapleton.

Jim Gardiner said nothing. He looked down, leafing through his papers.

"This inheritance doesn't make sense to me," she finally said. "I thought there wasn't any more money."

He looked up, surprised.

"There *wasn't* any money left from your parents," Gardiner assured her. "This is his *personal* fortune, which he never felt inclined to share with you. Until now."

"So this is his will?"

"Yes, in fact you are his *sole* heir. He probably didn't have anyone else. Or maybe he wanted to make amends. Who knows?" Jim Gardiner's tone was still bitter.

"How much did he leave me?"

"Let's see, Delia, he left you . . ." he said, riffling through a sheaf of documents. He stopped, and paused dramatically, looking at her over his glasses with a bit of a smirk. "It's actually quite a lot."

"A lot? Like, how much, a lot?"

"At least twenty million pounds in stocks, investments, plus the town house in London and all its contents. That has to be worth at least eight to ten million pounds more."

She sat back, stunned. The leather chair creaked.

"That's a fortune! That would make me *rich*."

He said nothing. He sat still, his glasses halfway down his nose.

"What am I going to do with all *that*?" she asked him.

"Keep it, honey. Keep it. And don't let me hear one word of gratitude for the son of a bitch. He wasn't there for you when it counted."

She looked at him in shock.

"God rest his soul," he added hastily, and smiled at her over his glasses.

Cordelia walked out into the cacophony of New York City. It was a warm morning, about to get a lot warmer. Traffic was gridlocked, noxious, and loud. After the quiet of Jim Gardiner's office, she felt disoriented. She should do something, or go somewhere. The prospect of going back to her hotel room and sitting there alone was unappealing.

She glanced at her watch. It was too early to call Susan and Joel and tell them the news. California was three hours behind.

There were streams of people passing by. Some were bellowing into cell phones, shouting above the street noise. She stood in the alcove of the doorway and watched them. They were like schools of fish, yielding to objects in their path. Cordelia laughed a little to herself. Imagine thinking of fish right now. She felt very shaky, and considered getting a cup of coffee, but the caffeine would decidedly make her feel worse.

She tried to get her bearings. Across the street was Saks Fifth Avenue. It might be nice to go there and buy something. Shop a little. A woman walked by in high heels and a black designer suit. Cordelia suddenly felt dowdy in her best sweater, a peach cashmere twinset. She pretty much stuck to a classic grad-student wardrobe. She dressed that way on purpose; it was her safety net, her camouflage in the world of science and academia. She didn't want to stand out, and these clothes didn't draw unwanted attention. But it was time to grow up, wasn't it? Just look at her purse. Who carried a shoulder bag these days? A new handbag would be a start.

She had money now. Life had moved on. This was not the time to be timid. Besides, she would need some clothes for the cruise ship. Cordelia stepped out onto the sidewalk with the rushing crowd.

The Hotel Sussex on the Upper East Side of Manhattan was cozy and quiet, the lobby decorated in beautiful French toile wallpaper. On the reservation desk, a bowl of yellow roses perfumed the air. Cordelia handed her seven shopping bags to the porter and let her aching arms drop.

"I'll send them right up, miss," he promised.

"Miss Stapleton," called the desk manager. "You have a message."

He handed her a thick-milled envelope. There was her name in black calligraphy on the front, and on the back was engraved the word CUNARD.

In her room she kicked off her shoes and fell on the couch. Her muscles ached, but she was feeling much better. Choosing a new wardrobe had given her confidence. She had redefined a look for herself, picking out a few smart suits and several dresses as well as formal gowns to wear on the ship. She had a half dozen pairs of new shoes to replace the flats she always wore. Cordelia had never shopped like that in her life.

It wasn't too hard in the dressing rooms, when the admiring salespeople told her she looked gorgeous and she should buy, buy, buy. She had even gone up to the café on the eighth floor and picked her way through a salad, alone. But that's when her confidence had waned, when she sat watching mothers and daughters lunching together.

"Are you alone, miss?" the waiter had asked, as he handed her the oversized menu. "Or will someone be joining you?"

"Nobody's joining me," she said, refusing to say the words "I am alone."

She had eaten her salad without really tasting it. Just chewing seemed too much of an effort. She had forced herself to stay. Cordelia knew deep in her heart that it was important to leave the comfort of work, and the ship, and to try to do things that were normal and healthy. Maybe someday in the future she would actually enjoy a life outside work. Maybe there would come a time when she would not have to do everything alone.

Cordelia started to open the envelope the concierge had given her. The paper of the envelope was so thick she could barely slide the letter out.

Dear Miss Stapleton,

We congratulate you on accepting the Herodotus Foundation Award in Monaco on September 5. We would like to extend our official invitation to have you join our cruise on the Queen Victoria *as it travels on its maiden year. The itinerary "Legends of the Mediterranean" will take you to Livorno and Naples, Italy; Valletta, Malta; Aghios Nikolaos and Piraeus, Greece; Izmir, Turkey; and Civitavecchia, Italy, near Rome. The ship departs Monaco September 7th at 5:00 p.m.*

We are happy to offer you a suite, all expenses paid, for the duration of your stay with us. As discussed, Cunard would also like to offer you the opportunity to lecture on your recently published paper, "Oceans, Our Most Precious Resource." We hope you will join us.

Best regards,

Greta Havens

Executive Manager, Queen Victoria. Cunard.

Cordelia dropped the letter onto the coffee table. There was a sharp rap on the door. The porter. She had almost forgotten about him.

"Your packages, miss."

Hôtel de Paris, Monaco

John Sinclair escaped from the glare of the Place du Casino into the old-world elegance of the Hôtel de Paris. The grand lobby was hushed, cool, and dim. Sinclair stopped to let his eyes adjust, taking in the sumptuous dark-wood paneling, the sheen of the Persian carpets and crystal chandeliers, silk-upholstered armchairs sheltered by potted palms.

He looked around for his colleague and didn't see him at first. Charles Bonnard was almost horizontal in a chair, a touch-screen phone inches from his face. Sinclair walked over, noticing that Charles was conspicuously overdressed as usual: cream silk slacks, Italian driving shoes, and a blue blazer of such fine wool it draped off his body.

"Look at you," said Sinclair. "I hope you didn't dress up for me."

"Hey, Sinclair, how are you doing?" Charles never lifted his eyes from the phone.

"Charles. Put the damn thing down. You're addicted to it."

"Sorry. You want a drink?" Charles sat up. He flagged the waiter.

"Iced tea," Sinclair ordered. "Lemon, no sugar."

"Late night, was it?"

Sinclair didn't answer, looking away.

"How's Ephesus?" Charles tried.

Sinclair shifted his eyes back to Charles and brightened.

"Great. We're really making some good progress."

Charles studied him closely. Sinclair looked exhausted. Blue bruises under his eyes. Puffy eyelids from drinking, and his skin was sallow and dry. Clearly he was hungover.

"*Bad* late night? Or *good* late night?"

"Argghhh," Sinclair exhaled, with the ghost of a smile. "Let's just say it wasn't all that good."

"Do you want to talk about it? Or should we stick to business?" Charles ventured.

"Business. Definitely business."

"I hereby call this meeting to order," Charles said.

But Sinclair derailed all formality.

"Before we go into all that, I should tell you about Shari. You introduced us, after all."

"Shari? What's *she* up to?"

"Hector Corillo—the number-one driver for Team McAllister."

"The race-car driver?"

Sinclair nodded, his face drawn.

"Did you break it off with her?" Charles asked.

"She did it."

Sinclair sounded depressed. He looked around the lobby, and took a long sip of his iced tea. He looked down at his glass as if surprised at its contents, and then took another long swig.

Charles fussed with his monogrammed cuff links.

"You knew," Sinclair accused.

"Yes, I knew." Charles stopped with the cuff link and slid a magazine out from under him.

"You were literally *sitting* on the story!" exclaimed Sinclair.

"I didn't want to be the one to tell you."

He handed over the rolled-up magazine. Sinclair unfolded the *Paris Match*. Shari and Corillo were entwined on the cover.

" 'The Fast Life,' " translated Sinclair. "I guess I'm the last to know."

"Well, unless it's carved on the marble in Ephesus, you're not likely to read it."

Sinclair thumbed through the article, his brow furrowed, and handed the magazine back to Charles. Then he looked away, watching people walk through the lobby.

"Listen, we have to talk about tonight," Charles finally said.

"So what's the deal?" Sinclair's voice was dispirited.

"The usual." Charles struck up a brisk tone, rummaging through his brown crocodile folio.

"Six p.m. cocktails. Seven p.m. sit down for dinner. The program starts

after the main course is over, and runs through dessert and coffee. Dancing afterward."

Sinclair winced. "I don't suppose you could take care of it, could you,
Charles? I'm really not up to it."

"Sinclair, I *can't*. It's *your* foundation. It's your award. You *have* to come."

Sinclair took a deep breath and blew it out in exasperation. There was
a long moment as he decided.

"OK," he said resignedly. "Who does the opening remarks? The prince?"

"Exactly," Charles said, reading his notes, "His Serene Highness Prince
Albert the Second will award the Monaco Prize to the Ocean Surface
Topography Mission for their climate-change work. And right after the
main course, during dessert, you're up."

"Damned if I can remember who we are giving it to. I got the letter, but
I don't remember where I put it."

"It's in some pile of bones on your desk in Ephesus, no doubt."

"Probably."

"We gave the award to Elliott Stapleton. American. Polar explorer
and scientist. He was on expedition with Prince Albert's great-great-
grandfather Albert the First—he made quite a few expeditions, from
about 1898 to about 1910."

Charles was again referring to his notes. "Accepting is . . . here we go,
Cordelia Stapleton. Great-great-granddaughter. A big deal in her own
right. Oceanographer at Woods Hole Oceanographic Institution in Mas-
sachusetts."

"Hometown girl," said Sinclair approvingly.

"Yup. Quite a babe, from what I hear."

"Oh, sure she is," said Sinclair. "A real nature girl, I bet. Wears L.L.Bean.
Swims five miles a day, dates ichthyologists. Do you have the speech?"

Charles handed over the cream envelope with the Herodotus Foundation logo.

"Don't be bitter, Sinclair. Get even. Plenty of fish in the sea."

Sinclair looked over at Charles skeptically.

"Are you aware that last year Shari was voted the most beautiful woman
in the world?"

"What do they know? You're going to believe *People* magazine? Besides,
those glamour girls are a dime a dozen."

Sinclair ignored the remark. "Why's it heavy?" he asked, weighing the
embossed envelope in his palm.

"The people at Monaco's Oceanographic Institute are returning Sta-pleton's diary from 1908. Somehow it ended up in their archives here in Monaco, with a bunch of other documents from the expeditions."

"Why do *we* have it?"

"They want us to give it back to the great-great-granddaughter when you present the award. Somebody over at the institute called me and dropped it off yesterday at the office. It's all in the speech."

"OK, sounds good." Sinclair finally said with some energy, "What's her name again?"

Charles looked at his notes. "Cordelia."

Port Hercule Marina, Monaco

In the Monaco marina, yachts were lined up one next to the other, and music from the deck parties floated up into the night. It was an array of wealth and luxury that was almost beyond comprehension. Only the most fabulous of the Mediterranean yachts converged at Monaco.

Each had its own style. In the early evening, as the sunlight faded and the interior lights were turned on in the main salons, the activities of the inhabitants were clearly visible from the dock. On some boats, the interiors were festive, people having cocktails, sitting on the couches or standing out on deck. Other boats were the picture of domesticity, children sprawled before the television, with sodas and pretzels, their parents relaxing with a glass of wine before dinner. Still others were dark, silent, their wealthy occupants pursuing other pleasures in other parts of the world.

On the enormous megayacht the *Udachny,* five people sat in tense silence. The room was sleek, luxurious, and well designed. A discriminating yacht owner might quibble that there was a little too much gold in the details of the décor, but despite the glitz, the artwork on board was above reproach. A bronze Rodin nude posed in a recessed alcove by the bar, and a Jackson Pollock hung on the wall.

The only nonhuman occupant of the yacht—a Russian Blue cat—walked across the bar, leapt to a chair, and finally made a deft spring into its master's lap. During its tour of the salon, the animal avoided touching the floor.

Evgeny, the yacht owner, wondered why the cat did that even when the seventy-one-meter Benetti was docked. It probably hated the vibration of the twin marine diesel engines. The cat always spooked when they were running. Evgeny pulled its ears in a rough kind of massage, and the cat settled down.

He looked at the two couples across from him. There were two Russians: Vlad and Anna. Sitting across from them were two Americans: Bob and Marlene. Vlad returned his gaze belligerently, while his wife, Anna, sat staring at Evgeny with compressed lips and darting, nervous eyes. Evgeny scanned her up and down. She was an expensive-looking woman, all plastic and designer—like most expat Russian women these days. But she looked like she knew the score and would keep her husband in line. Vlad was only about thirty-five or so, and too much of a hotshot for his own good. Too vulgar, too flashy. Oligarch wannabe, with none of the talent. But Anna, she could kill. He stared at her ripe breasts, half exposed like fruit. She saw him looking and didn't flinch. Yes, she would do what was necessary if given the chance.

The Americans, Bob and Marlene, were sitting together, with absolutely bovine expressions, seemingly upholstered into the white leather sofa, in pools of their own flesh. Only Americans could get big like that. It must be the corn diet. Evgeny liked fat people. Appetites like that could be counted on. They were weak and greedy—the best possible combination. Bob and Marlene would be no problem.

It was a weird crew: two high-rolling Russians and two fat Americans. Strange bedfellows, but it might work. They were all in it for the money. No high principles to get in the way. Vlad and Anna could do the legwork; the Americans could get cozy with the young woman. Disarm her with their friendliness. A young American girl on her own might be drawn to them.

Evgeny picked up the phone and dialed a number, then punched the speakerphone button.

"We're all here," he said. "What have you got?"

Vlad, Anna, Bob, and Marlene all leaned forward, as if they could discern who was on the other end of the line. But there would be no names used. Russian politicians like to keep their hands clean. And a wild card was always good in every game. It kept people on their toes. No one in Moscow could be identified if things went wrong, and that would make for an easier mop-up in the end. Evgeny would be the eraser on the chalkboard, so to speak.

The voice on the phone was factual, calm, the accent thick.

"We got the journal. They found it in the old storeroom of the Arctic

Coal Mining Company up in Svalbard. We read every word of it and only found a few references to the land deed. There is not enough information for us to go on."

Vlad looked sideways at Anna. Staring at the phone, she didn't move. The voice continued.

"There is a guy digging around up in Svalbard, in the old graves. He appears to be a scientist looking for medical specimens. But he also might be looking for the deed. We are following him to see if he turns up anything."

"So what do you want us to do?" asked Evgeny.

"We'll keep an eye on the guy up in Svalbard. You need to keep track of the journal."

"Where is the journal now?" asked Evgeny.

"We planted the journal in the archives of the Oceanographic Institute of Monaco. And, good little researchers that they are, they found it already," said the voice from Moscow.

"Then what?" asked Evgeny.

"The Oceanographic Institute is going to give it back to Cordelia Stapleton, Elliott Stapleton's only living relative. She will read the journal. It will make more sense to her. It's her family, after all."

"What makes you think she will look for clues in the journal?"

"We will send her an offer for the land. Big money. So she will start to look for the deed. She will lead us right to it."

"So we follow her, right?" interrupted Bob.

Evgeny gestured with a dismissive chop of his hand for the American to shut up.

"Who is giving the journal to her? The Oceanographic Institute?" asked Evgeny.

"No. They are going to pass it to the Herodotus Foundation. The American philanthropist John Sinclair runs it. He doesn't know anything about the significance of the journal. He thinks he is just returning it as part of the foundation's award ceremony—as a courtesy."

"Good," said Evgeny. "When do we expect the girl?"

"She'll be there at the gala tomorrow. And then she will go to the cruise ship after that."

"Good, so we will start surveillance tomorrow night, when she gets the journal," Evgeny said, and looked over at the two Americans and the two Russians sitting on the couches of the yacht. "It shouldn't take long."

Monte Carlo, Monaco

As she stepped out of the Hôtel Hermitage, Cordelia checked her reflection in the glass of the lobby doors. The fabric of the midnight blue column dress was heavy and silky against her legs. The slight train gave her movements a new, stately glide.

"The Sporting Club," she told the limo driver. "But can you drive around a bit, take the long way, so I can see Monaco?"

The driver held the door for her.

"Of course, mademoiselle."

Cordelia slid onto the seat and had the ridiculous feeling that the car was way too big for just one person. The Herodotus Foundation had hired the limo and chauffeur for the evening. The driver took his place behind the wheel and looked at her in the mirror.

"Where shall we go, mademoiselle? Anywhere you wish."

"Just around. Whatever you think. I don't have to be there until six thirty."

They started off at a slow pace and Cordelia looked out the limo windows. Monaco was magical. The floodlit pink palace was glowing against the deep blue sky. They drove past the Place du Casino and the harbor. Many of the yachts had lights strung along their masts. The car turned, and they drove through the charming cobblestoned streets of the town. Then, farther away from the casino, they followed the highway along the ocean to the Monte Carlo Sporting Club. Inside, the enormous Salle des Etoiles was the venue of choice for many large galas and events. The limo pulled up and stopped.

Cordelia felt a twinge of nervousness as she waited for the driver to walk around to open the door. She looked at the red carpet going up the stairs and the line of photographers waiting for arrivals. Real paparazzi. This was heady stuff. Well, Monaco was certainly all it was cracked up to be. She was going to be the center of attention accepting this award. Her heart pounded, and she felt a surge of adrenaline.

For the briefest flash she wished she had never come. It would be so much cozier to be having pizza and beer with Susan and Joel on board the research vessel rather than champagne and caviar at this award ceremony. But there was no choice; she *had* to accept the award. The car door opened and she gathered her skirts to step out.

Inside the Salle des Etoiles, guests were milling around sipping cocktails. The cavernous hall was hung with royal blue and silver banners in commemoration of the 1906 Arctic expedition of Elliott Stapleton and Prince Albert I—great-great-grandfather of the reigning monarch. She looked at Elliott Stapleton's name on the banners and suddenly Cordelia felt a burst of family pride. He and Prince Albert I had mapped half of the Norwegian Arctic together. She walked around, looking at the huge hall filled with people, and suddenly realized what a monumental figure her great-great-grandfather had been. Of course, she had always known about the expeditions, but to see all these people gathered tonight to commemorate his work was astounding.

Cordelia noticed the reigning prince of Monaco, Albert II, in the center of a group. Middle-aged, handsome, he certainly looked royal. Look at that red-and-white sash and all those impressive medals. He was laughing. She tore her eyes away from him. She really shouldn't stare. God knows she didn't have the nerve to walk over and introduce herself.

She walked a few paces, took a glass of champagne from the waiter, and looked around. How sophisticated everyone looked in their evening clothes. This was really very exciting! She relaxed and started to enjoy the buzz of the room. Cordelia walked toward the middle of the crowd and stopped again, taking another sip of champagne.

Standing in front of her was a Russian undersea explorer. What was his name? She studied him and his group. They were clearly all Russians. The explorer was booming forth in his pompous way. What a fool. Her team had laughed at him last year, when he planted the titanium capsule with a Russian flag in the seabed at the North Pole, claiming it as Russian territory. Things got even more ridiculous when the Russian TV station Russiya reported on the expedition. The new show *Vesti* had spliced in undersea footage from the movie *Titanic,* saying it was from the expedition. They had labeled the footage "Northern Arctic Ocean," but a thirteen-year-old Finnish kid had recognized the footage from his DVD at home and talked to his local paper.

Cordelia took another sip. Alexandrov. That was it. How weird Alexandrov should be at the gala. He was the first to descend the fourteen thousand feet to the Arctic seabed by submarine. Technically pretty difficult, but Russia had then preposterously declared the region "Forever Russian." Canada and the United States immediately accused Russia of a crude attempt to grab the Arctic.

At the jingoistic press conference, Alexandrov had brandished the Russian flag and carried a stuffed polar bear, the symbol of United Russia, President Vladimir Putin's political party. He had shouted, "Russia has what it takes to win! The Arctic has always been Russian."

Suddenly the group of Russians turned and looked in her direction. One of them was talking about her. She could tell by the way they pretended *not* to notice her. Why were they all so interested in her?

Sporting Club, Monte Carlo

John Sinclair circulated through the crowd at the Oceanographic Institute Ball, greeting as many guests as possible. If he was going to be here, he might as well do it right. Don't let them see you down. Not this crowd. He smiled even harder. Shari who?

Prince Albert II, surrounded by a mob, reached around to shake his hand. They exchanged a word, and the prince was drawn off to talk to another guest. Sinclair turned to work the other side of the room and realized too late he was on track to cross paths with the contessa Giorgiana Brindisi. After an imperceptible hesitation that showed only in his eyes, Sinclair moved confidently ahead. To avoid her would be a sign of weakness.

"John," she called, as she saw him approaching. She air-kissed him, brushing his face with her dark mane of hair. He caught the familiar scent of her intoxicating perfume, the one she had designed herself. It got him every time—even tonight. Sinclair stepped back with a tight smile.

"Lovely to see you, Brindy."

"John, darling. You look marvelous."

Sinclair was aware of her escort, a tall, smoldering fellow about fifteen years her junior.

"May I introduce Giancarlo Grimitti."

Sinclair's eyes widened. It must be the son, not the father. The father would be, what, seventy by now? This man was not even thirty.

"Delighted," said Sinclair, shaking his hand. The young man made a small half bow, more of a nod, but did not reply. Sinclair stepped to the side of the couple, as if to continue through the crowd. "I'd love to stay and chat, but duty calls. I'm searching for Charles. Have a great time!"

Sinclair walked slowly away, listening to the chatter build to a crescendo in the large space. Brindy. The last person he wanted to see. Now all he needed was for Shari to show up with her race-car driver. And he couldn't even have a drink until after his speech. The gloom came over him like a pall. It was going to be a real trial to get through this night.

He walked to the enormous two-story windows of the Salle des Etoiles and looked out at the night view of Monaco. Right now he could use a nice sunset, an excellent whiskey, and a good book.

"Nice night, isn't it?" Charles appeared at his elbow.

"Hmm . . ." said Sinclair.

"Oh, don't let Brindy get you down," Charles said. "Who is that with her, the Principe de Parma y Bologna?"

Sinclair barked a laugh in spite of his dour mood. He translated: " 'The Prince of Ham and Baloney.' Good one, Charles."

"Seriously, who is that? Look at him—he's a kid. How old is he? Brindy is risking charges of pedophilia."

"It's the Grimitti heir."

"Are you joking!" said Charles in disbelief. "Wow, Brindy is really trolling for the next big one. How much you figure he's worth?"

"Charles, please. I can't. Not tonight."

"Oh, sorry, sometimes I get carried away. Listen, do you have the speech?"

Sinclair patted the lapel of his tuxedo. "All set."

"You're at table two," Charles said. "Did you remember to bring the journal?"

"Yes, I have it." Sinclair held it up in his other hand.

"OK. Well, don't forget to take it up with you to the podium."

"Charles, please stop harassing me."

"OK, I'm done. Cheer up, Sinclair. Go find somebody pretty to talk to."

Charles gave him a wink and drifted away, his glass of Perrier in hand. People were starting to sit down. Sinclair found table 2 and shook hands with a portly Italian industrialist and his wife. Thank God, here were his old friends from New York: the director of the World Wildlife Fund and his wife, Jody. He continued around the table, looking for his place card. What luck! Charles had done him a good turn in the seating arrangements. He was right next to Jean-Louis Etienne, the director general of the Oceanographic Museum in Monaco. The conversation would be bearable after all.

"Mr. Sinclair, I have been hearing about your foundation for years. A pleasure to meet you," Jean-Louis said, shaking his hand.

"The pleasure is mine."

They took their seats and fell easily into conversation. When the appetizer of lobster thermidor was served, Sinclair realized he was hungry after all.

"How did your expedition go?" Sinclair asked, sampling a forkful, which was rich and delicious.

Etienne looked surprised.

"We just got back. I am astonished you know of it. Your field is archaeology, is it not?"

"Yes, but the foundation is looking at polar exploration next year. It seems like the right time to fund some research on the melting ice cap."

"That is great news! We usually go in April, when the pack ice is at its maximum thickness."

"That late?"

"Yes, the ice is actually solid enough to land a plane on at that time of year. The air is stable then."

"I had no idea."

"The cold gives good buoyancy to the EM-Bird. We use that to measure the ice."

"So the air is less stable when it's warmer?"

"Absolutely. In April, you really only get turbulence over the ice fracture zones. That's where the water evaporates into the air."

Sinclair felt someone brush his shoulder and take the seat next to him. Etienne looked past him and perked up the way Frenchmen do when a woman arrives.

"Cordelia Stapleton." A woman reached around him to shake Etienne's hand. "A very great pleasure to meet you."

Sinclair turned to make his own introduction.

"John Sinclair," he said, shaking her hand and looking into a pair of very beautiful green eyes. Charles was right, she was a stunner. She smiled politely at him, but then her eyes moved past him to Etienne.

"Are you talking about your expedition? I have been dying to hear about it."

"Yes, we got back last week," said Etienne, clearly charmed.

"What was your route?" she asked.

"Up through Tromsø, then straight up Norway to the Barents Sea and Svalbard."

"Have you analyzed the data yet?" Her voice was firm and confident.

Etienne was talking to her in the lingo. It was all Greek to him, so Sinclair inched his chair back. That way they could talk, and he could observe her. Young, a bit nervous. Great figure. Not much makeup, but didn't need it. She clearly was not used to wearing an evening dress: she kept fidgeting with the long skirt.

"We went over the polar drift current to the North Pole and then made radial trips to the latitude of eighty-five North," Etienne explained. "Then we went to the Magnetic North Pole and the Beaufort Sea. We made about ten thousand measurements."

"Where did you land?"

"Alaska."

Now they were talking over him as if he weren't there. Sinclair found himself thinking he had never been so charmingly ignored in his life. The room quieted and the program began. Prince Albert began his opening speech.

"We cannot go back in time," the prince was saying. "It is essential to rise above political divisions and ask ourselves what measures we can take today for the development of our planet that are sustainable and respectful of nature."

Sinclair felt in his pocket for his speech. This was going to be good. Cordelia Stapleton had no idea she would be accepting her award from the man she had ignored through the first two courses of dinner. Well, she couldn't ignore him now.

"Presenting the Herodotus Foundation Award for Historical Contribution in Science and Exploration is John Sinclair, founder and chairman."

He rose and walked to the podium in a crescendo of applause. Sinclair waited a moment for the audience to settle, looking over the crowd. He started.

"Elliott Stapleton was one of the great scientists of our time. His scientific discoveries outshone those of many of his peers. Several explorers gained more notoriety at the time because they were masters of publicity. But we at the Herodotus Foundation believe Elliott Stapleton was head and shoulders above the others. He was not only an explorer but also a dedicated scientist. He met Prince Albert I in Tromsø, Norway, in 1898, and that collaboration continued until 1910. During the prince's expedition to Spitsbergen, the area now known as Svalbard, in the summers of 1898 and 1899, aboard the *Princess Alice,* they conducted a series of groundbreaking experiments. Together, these leading oceanographers made inroads in discovery we all still recognize. We are delighted to honor the expedition, the glorious collaboration of talent, and the historical contributions of the esteemed scientist Elliott Stapleton. Here accepting the posthumous award is his great-great-granddaughter, Cordelia Stapleton, one of the preeminent oceanographers in the world. She has come all the way from the Woods Hole Oceanographic Institution. Please welcome Cordelia Stapleton."

Sinclair watched her walk up to the stage. A spotlight found her and followed her through the tables. The midnight satin dress flowed around her slender figure. He noted the simple elegant lines. Her dark hair fell shining to her shoulders. He was struck by her poise. She reached the podium and accepted the plaque, thanking him with regal grace. A flash went off.

"Would you please hold for some additional pictures?"

"Of course." Sinclair stepped closer to her. There was a swarm of photographers at their feet. Cordelia looked around, searching for a place to put down her jeweled minaudière while she held the plaque.

"I didn't realize I'd brought my bag up with me," she said to Sinclair. "Where should I put it?"

"Allow me." John took the small purse and slipped it into his tuxedo pocket so she would have both hands free.

Cordelia faced forward on the dais with the spotlight still in her eyes. She was suddenly very conscious of all the people in the vast hall watching her; there were so many more tables than she had realized. She shot a quick look over to Sinclair for an indication of what to do. He gave her an encouraging smile.

He seemed very comfortable. He stepped right behind her, and she could feel the wool of his tuxedo jacket against her shoulder. Then he reached around her to take hold of the plaque, encircling her with one arm. As he folded his hand over hers to support the plaque, his touch was warm and strong. She reacted to his nearness, intensely attracted to him. He smelled of lemon verbena and soap—some kind of aftershave that evoked the scent of Mediterranean sunshine.

"Look at the plaque," a photographer called out.

She looked down at their hands together on the dark wood. His hand was tan, and almost twice as large as hers. She was aware of how tall he was, standing behind her. She felt incredibly awkward as she stood still for the camera, almost holding her breath. How long did this take? How many pictures did they need?

"Earlier, at dinner, I didn't realize *you* were the head of the Herodotus Foundation," she apologized as they held the pose. "I was corresponding by e-mail with someone named Charles Bonnard."

"I know," John said. "It's my foundation and Charles is the director. I should have mentioned that when I met you, but you were so interested in talking to Etienne, I didn't want to interrupt your conversation."

There was a hint of teasing in his voice. She flushed, and let go of the plaque, turning to face him.

"We were talking about his *work*. We're in the same field."

"Of course."

His eyes were laughing at her.

"I'm going to hand this to you again, for the cameras," he said, and handed the plaque to her. She took it. A couple of flashes went off.

"Thank you," she said.

"You're welcome."

His smile was devastating, and his eyes seemed to take in everything, intelligent and full of laughter. The irises were blue, light in the center, dark around the edges; and the color gave them an intensity that was startling. As their eyes made contact and held, the entire room faded away. She kept staring, a little too long. Then she looked away and began gathering the folds of her gown to walk down the steps.

The photographers were packing up, starting to leave. The crowd was ignoring the activity on the dais; the noise level picked up, and the waiters were serving dessert; Sinclair stepped closer and put a hand on her arm, speaking quietly.

"Please, stay a moment. I have another announcement."

Sinclair stepped to the microphone.

"Ladies and gentlemen, another moment of your attention, please." Sinclair waited as the room settled down.

"We have something else for Miss Stapleton—something quite special. The Herodotus Foundation has the great pleasure of returning part of her very prestigious heritage."

He seemed quite pleased with something. Almost as if he had been planning a surprise.

"We are pleased to return the journal of Elliott Stapleton from the year 1908. It was discovered in the archives at the Oceanographic Institute here in Monaco. We return it now, to his direct descendant, Cordelia Stapleton, a woman of considerable distinction in her own right."

Sinclair presented her with a battered leather journal. He did it with great formality, holding it out to her with both hands. She didn't speak. She could not stop staring at the brown leather journal in his hands. Finally she took it, clutching it to her along with the plaque. The room grew quiet, sensing something highly charged in the exchange. The silence lengthened in the vast ballroom. She had no idea what to say. Sinclair felt her awkwardness and spoke into the microphone as if continuing his presentation.

"Perhaps you will come to know your great-great-grandfather in more detail as you have the opportunity to read his personal observations in that momentous year."

"Thank you," she finally managed.

She looked up at him. There was a lump in her throat and, to her horror, tears welled in her eyes. How could he know what this meant to her—to recover just a tiny fraction of the family she had lost? Suddenly she thought about her parents, and emotions took over. They would have *loved* to be here. They were always very proud of Elliott Stapleton, and talked about him often. She missed them more at this moment than she had in decades.

She looked up at Sinclair, her eyes shining with tears. Sinclair looked startled. For the first time all evening, he seemed uncertain what to do. Realizing her emotional distress, he took a small step toward her, as if to take her arm, but stopped. His eyes questioned her. She couldn't answer. They stood frozen on the dais as the people at the tables watched. Cordelia dropped her eyes, tucked the journal and the plaque under her arm, gathered her long skirt, and fled the stage.

Cordelia stood outside the Salle des Etoiles waiting for her limo. The gala was still going on, people were dancing and talking, but she was ready to leave.

It had been an exciting night. After the award, the press representative of the Royal Palace had appeared, inviting her to join the prince at his table. In awe, Cordelia had followed the palace official and suddenly found herself conversing with Prince Albert. He abandoned small talk and immediately began questioning her about her work on the submersible Alvin. The prince was passionate about preserving the marine environment around Monaco, and Cordelia was surprised at his expertise. She told him about her work in deep-ocean biodiversity and the marine-life census project she had been involved in. He described a similar project that was going on in the Mediterranean. When she left his table, he promised to contact her about collaboration between the Oceanographic Institute and Woods Hole Oceanographic Institution.

Cordelia was then surrounded by people who wanted to congratulate her. She nodded and responded for nearly an hour, until suddenly jet lag caught up to her. It really was time to go.

As she walked to the entrance of the Salle des Etoiles, she felt happy, but relieved that the pressure of the evening was over. It had gone well, except for her gaffe while accepting the diary. How long had she stood there just gaping? It felt like ten minutes. Thank God John Sinclair had filled in the awkward moment for her. The audience might not have noticed, but Sinclair certainly had. She could still see his blue eyes looking at her in absolute confusion.

She felt cowardly sneaking out like this, without saying good-bye to him. But it was better to leave quietly. She couldn't think of a thing to say, and certainly didn't want to explain why she had been so moved when he gave her the journal.

She looked down at the leather book in her hand. To her, this was the most valuable thing she could ever own—her great-great-grandfather's journal. The famous polar explorer had captured her imagination since she was a child. She had modeled her work and career on his life. Here was his legacy, her heritage, right here in her hand.

Her dark limo broke out of the pack and moved forward to pick her up. Her driver smartly stepped around to the back of the car to open the door for her. Just then she heard her name being called.

"Miss Stapleton. A moment, please."

She turned in the direction of the voice and saw an attractive man sprinting over to speak to her. Light-blond and in his midthirties, he moved with incredible speed. She would swear his feet didn't touch the flight of stairs as he flew down them. He was like a beam of light incarnate. She had never seen anyone move like that in her life.

"Charles Bonnard," he said, offering his hand. "We spoke on the phone. Sorry I didn't catch up with you until now. I had a lot of last-minute things to sort out. I had planned to find you before dinner, but somehow the time got away from me."

"Oh, hello," Cordelia said. "Thanks so much for everything. The entire evening has been perfect."

"Leaving us so soon?" Charles said. "Could I entice you to stay for an after-dinner drink?"

"Oh, thank you, but I really am tired," she replied automatically.

It was her standard excuse. How many times had she said it in the last year? But this time, as she said the words, she regretted them. He looked so charming; she found she really wanted to stay after all. Maybe he would press her to stay, and she could pretend to reconsider. She hesitated a moment to see what he would do.

"Oh, don't worry, I understand completely. These things drag on for hours," assured Charles.

"It has been lovely," Cordelia said uncertainly, but she didn't move toward the car.

"Well, I am so glad you had a nice time. It's great to finally meet you. I know John Sinclair was delighted to be seated next to you at dinner."

He didn't move either, as if to prolong the moment.

"Oh, gosh, I hate to tell you what I did to John Sinclair. I feel like a perfect fool," Cordelia admitted.

"What?" asked Charles.

"I didn't realize who he was," she confessed. "I ignored him during dinner and talked to Jean-Louis Etienne instead."

Charles threw back his head and laughed.

"Oh. Well, don't worry; Sinclair's ego is strong enough to take it. But personally, I would be in tears."

He stood in front of her, perfectly still. He seemed to be waiting for her to make a suggestion.

She hesitated. He was adorable. Why couldn't she just reverse her decision to leave? She searched for a way to say it.

Charles, sensing her reluctance, misunderstood and stepped over to open the car door. He gave the driver a nod of dismissal as he held the door for her.

"Allow me."

She reluctantly slid in, folding her dress away from the doorframe.

"Thank you."

Charles lingered still, holding the car door handle.

"I'm sorry, I'm holding you up. You must be tired from traveling."

"Not really, it's fine," Cordelia assured him.

"I understand you will be around for a day or so. You must promise to call me if you want some company, or need anything." He handed her his Herodotus Foundation card. She took it.

"Congratulations on the award, and thanks again for coming," Charles said, finally shutting her door. He waved with a smile as the limo pulled away.

She sat back in the luxurious interior of the car and looked at his card. He clearly wanted her to take the initiative and call him. She looked up and saw the limo driver observing her in the rearview mirror. He gave her a respectful nod and looked back at the road.

Maybe she *would* call Charles tomorrow. She was in Monaco, after all! He offered to show her around. What harm could there be in that? It was time to live!

She reached for her evening bag, to put away his card. Her bag wasn't there! On the dark leather seat were only the diary and the Herodotus Foundation plaque. She frantically searched the seat and the floor of the limo for her minaudière. It was then she realized it was still in the right-hand pocket of John Sinclair's tuxedo.

Udachny Motoryacht, Monaco

Evgeny stood on deck and watched Anna walk along the quay toward his yacht. This was perfect. Her husband, Vlad, was at the Oceanographic Institute Ball. Alexandrov and the rest of the Russians were probably all drunk by now, celebrating their claim on the North Pole.

He ogled her as she tottered up the aluminum walkway. Magenta silk shirt unbuttoned to reveal deep cleavage. Hip-hugging little white skirt already hiking up as she ascended the steep incline of the *passerelle*. The tide was in and the Benetti rode high in the harbor. She had to hold on to the handrails to manage the climb.

She was wearing very high platform espadrilles, with laces that crisscrossed up her legs almost to the knee. Those laces might be interesting later in the bedroom. He had an exciting mental preview of what he would do to her.

Evgeny had known she would come. She had intelligent eyes and understood, even from that first meeting, what he wanted. She hadn't seemed surprised when he called her this afternoon. He didn't think anything would surprise this woman, but he was going to try. He felt the deep stir of excitement at the thought of making her his toy for the evening.

She bussed him on the cheek as she reached the top of the gangplank. What a great little piece. Her scent was sweet and heavy. Expensive. He felt a stir again. He wanted to smell it mingled with sweat, fear even. It was going to be one hell of a night.

London

British researcher Paul Oakley picked up the phone on his desk and dialed a long-distance number. As he waited for the ring, he surveyed his office and ran a hand through his mop of hair. He really had to sort out some of this mess. Stacks of paper stood in piles as high as his head. His office at Queen Mary's School of Medicine was the epicenter of internationally renowned research on the deadly pandemic of 1918, but right now it looked like the epicenter of an earthquake. It was time to clean up. But he didn't have the emotional focus right now; he was nervous. For the first time, he actually was involved in something clandestine, and it didn't suit him.

The person he was calling didn't answer, but the voice mail clicked on. He spoke quietly.

"Miles, it's Paul Oakley. I hope you have been able to find what you were looking for. Give me a call."

Paul Oakley was maintaining deniability about the expedition. The story was, his friend Miles was acting on his own. Oakley's department head at the hospital would never approve of what they were doing, and if something went wrong he would have to play the innocent. Miles had offered to take the blame, if it came to that; he was retired, wealthy, and had no organization to censure him.

To maintain secrecy, they were both paying for the expedition out of pocket. Oakley had the money. He had patented a popular ulcer drug early on in his career and had been living off a princely income ever since. With his money and Miles's dedication, they had decided: no paperwork, no grants, and no funding proposals. They hadn't said a word to the press, had not even indulged in any lunchroom chat. Scientific competition had torpedoed many a worthy project. And Oakley wanted to be the very first to crack the gene sequencing of the apocalyptic pandemic virus of 1918.

The problem was finding tissue samples of victims who had been stricken ninety years ago. There were only a half dozen cadavers in the world preserved under the kind of conditions necessary to generate a good tissue sample.

His cell phone was ringing. It was Miles, calling back.

"Paul, we are good to go here."

Miles sounded ramped up and energized, and the connection from Svalbard was surprisingly clear, despite the fact he was in the most remote spot on earth.

"Did you find enough people to help you do the digging?"

"Yeah, I got a couple of guys who can do the heavy lifting. I will call you when we get closer to the . . . samples."

"Great. Talk then."

Svalbard, Norway

Miles flipped his cell phone shut and watched the exhumation. They had been digging for three hours now, thawing the earth with a steady jet of steam, shoveling out the muddy gruel, and piling it to the side of the pit.

He remembered when he first considered exhuming the grave in the Svalbard settlement of Barentsburg, forty years ago. Back then, he had been a young scientist with lots of ambition. But he hadn't timed his expedition properly, just went on a whim, with only a pickax and determination. It had been a complete failure. The season had been wrong, the ground frozen. There were no samples.

Miles had learned a lot about permafrost since then. In very cold climates, permafrost can tolerate a considerable amount of heat, water, or steam without thawing, making a steam generator a critical piece of equipment. And even then it wasn't easy because the amount of energy needed to melt the ice was intense. Normally it took one calorie to raise one gram of water a degree, but it took 80 calories to melt a gram of water from ice, and 540 calories to make one gram of water into steam.

Luckily the ground in Barentsburg was ideal for this. This grave was in thaw-stable permafrost, well-drained and coarse sediment. It was mostly glacial outwash that contained a mixture of soil, sand, and gravel. Because there was so much rock, the settlement of the ground after it thawed would be minor.

Miles was also lucky the mass grave was well below the active layer of earth, not subject to annual thawing and freezing. It was permanently frozen.

The great problem with cemeteries in the Arctic was that if the graves were not deep enough there would be frost heaving. Shallow graves were often subject to the phenomenon of frost jacking—the thawing and freezing gradually pushing the ground surface upward. Any object buried in this active layer of soil would be constantly rising with each season. So coffins buried hastily in shallow earth were continually heaved up after a few thaw cycles. It was a macabre sight, and unnerving to many who had placed their loved ones in what they thought was a final resting place only to have them reappear after a few seasons.

This, however, was a very, very deep grave—a mass grave. It had not thawed since it was originally dug in 1918. The bodies would not have decomposed as rapidly as they normally would. Now Miles would try again to collect the tissue samples frozen into a pile of cadavers all buried in a common pit.

Miles had contacted the authorities before he began work. The magistrate was in the town of Longyearbyen, a village six hundred miles from the North Pole, one of the northernmost pieces of land in the world, on the edge of the ice pack. Longyearbyen administered the smaller hamlet of Barentsburg, where he was digging. It was an old mining camp, which for three-quarters of the year was frozen wilderness. Even during the peak of the summer season Barentsburg had only some four hundred residents. But the residents Miles was interested in were long dead.

The magistrate's answer to Miles's question lifted his hopes. No one had been near the mass grave of the 1918 flu victims in Barentsburg in nearly forty years. The last person who had examined the site was Miles himself. Back then, he had traveled the fifty-five miles to the village by dogsled. Now he would take a Land Rover. When he went to Barentsburg that winter long ago, the little village had been clad in the romance of the Arctic ice and snow. Now, in early autumn, the place had lost most of that romance. Barentsburg was a desolate dump. Coated with coal dust, it stood ramshackle and depressing on the edge of a bleak sea.

When Miles arrived this time, there had been a great willingness to help. It was almost as if unearthing a pandemic might liven the place up a bit. Six young diggers, coal mine workers, had stepped forward to help, for the modest fee of a hundred dollars each.

Miles knew the grave held seventy-two people. The history was grim. In 1918, a village celebration had turned into a death sentence. A ship had put into Advent Bay, and two men on board had brought the deadly contagion with them. They had arrived in Barentsburg by dogsled, ready to work in the coal mine. They had been lavishly welcomed: the village had prepared a feast for the newcomers and everyone had turned out to celebrate. There was grilled fish, blueberries, griddle cakes, and whiskey consumed in the largest structure in town, a church, with people crammed cheek by jowl on the wooden benches in the overheated room, talking, laughing, eating. That proximity had been their doom. Within a day the first had fallen, in extreme distress.

First came the high fever, facial discoloration, deep brown splotches, and purple "heliotrope" rash. Next came the telltale cyanosis, victims blue-faced from the lack of oxygen. The feet turning black was the indicator of eventual death. The victims were a horror show of symptoms, with blood-colored saliva foaming out of their mouths and rectal bleeding from the intestines. Some died within hours, delirious with the high fever, gasping for air as they drowned in their own blood.

The whole village had been wiped out. Only five adults survived. The rest were buried hastily in a deep pit. What a tragedy, Miles allowed himself to think, as he watched the generator pump steam into the permanently frozen ground.

Miles took a deep breath to quell his excitement. There was a good chance they would be able to biopsy the tissue if it had been frozen all this time. This deadly pestilence was all but extinct, but he would seek it out, resurrect it, bottle it, and send it back to the civilized world, to Paul Oakley.

Miles and Oakley had been comrades-in-arms for decades against the new influenza strains that were emerging in the world. Most recently, they had been conducting clinical trials using new vaccines and antiviral drugs.

Paul Oakley had already tried to get samples from the high Arctic. He had funded a team last year to try to get tissue from the old miners' graveyard in Longyearbyen. The mission had been only partially successful. This year they might succeed in Barentsburg.

This was not a mere ego trip, or the resolution of an unfulfilled scientific quest from decades ago. Miles and Oakley knew it was a critical race against time. Tissue samples were essential to discovering the genomic connection to the avian flu that was ravaging Asia. The pandemic of 1918 would be the key to stopping the new avian flu outbreak from spreading.

"We're almost there," he encouraged the men who were digging.

They were covered in mud. The steam helped, but the diggers still had a hard time, their strong young arms wielding picks and shovels.

The slurry was heavy with water, rock, and mud. The rectangle they dug was six feet wide and twenty-eight feet long. As the ground melted, and the earth warmed, the powerful grave stench came up. They dug steadily despite the retch-inducing smell.

Now the remains of bodies came to their muddy hands, as if longing to be resurrected. First badly decomposed skeletons, no soft tissue, but bits and pieces mixed with the gravel and dirt. As they dug deeper, there were chunks of protoplasmic goo. Suddenly Miles felt the hair lift on his head.

Eight feet down, there she was. And he knew she would be a good sample. A fully preserved cadaver. Her blue parka crusted with mud, the Arctic fox-fur trim still intact. Clearly the young woman had been obese in life, and for that reason her remains were astonishingly preserved in death. The extra adipose had insulated her remains in the frozen grave.

Miles gestured for the men to stop digging and knelt in prayer. The diggers removed their caps and fell silent. His prayer was inchoate, distracted by intense elation.

Without delay he began to slice her up. Kneeling in the thawed mud, he set to work. The lungs were still frozen as he cut into them with his autopsy instruments.

Monaco

John Sinclair walked through the golden district, the Carré d'Or, of Monaco in his shirtsleeves with his jacket slung over his shoulder. His tie was undone, and he had the measured pace of a man who was out too late, with one glass of whiskey too many.

The streets of Monaco were quiet. The gala event was long over. He had stopped for an after-dinner drink with his friends from New York. He had chosen the famous La Rascasse bar, which was popular during race time in Monaco with the Formula One fans. Situated on one of the most difficult turns of the course, it gave spectators a perfect view of the cars as they came around the bend. In addition to its Formula One fame, it was an exceptionally good restaurant. Off-season, as it was now, Sinclair would frequently go there to spend an evening with friends. This evening had been even longer than usual. It was three o'clock in the morning.

After saying his good-byes, Sinclair was glad to be walking. The distance back to the Hotel Metropole was just enough to sober him up from the long evening. It was a gorgeous night, and the town was quiet. For the first time since he had so publicly fought with Shari, he felt good. He had no idea why, he just felt better.

He looked down on the harbor, leaning on the stone parapet above the yacht basin. There were a lot of boats this year. It used to be that two hundred feet was big enough for a yacht, and three hundred feet was vulgar. Now four hundred feet didn't raise an eyebrow. And the lines were god-awful, all angles and smoked glass. Some even had helicopter landing pads, Jet Skis, minisubmarines, all kinds of tow toys and rafts.

He rested his arms on the stone wall and looked over the boats. The

Udachny was one of the gaudiest down there. *Udachny* meant "good luck" in Russian. Owned by some superstitious oligarch, no doubt, who was looking over his shoulder counting on luck as he counted the coin.

Back in the late 1920s the British author Somerset Maugham lived in nearby Cap Ferrat, and had called Monaco a "sunny place for shady people." Of course, nowadays that was not the case. Now a very progressive prince was determined to make Monaco into a shining example for the world. Prince Albert II had become an outspoken leader on environmental issues, and also initiated a real effort to make Monaco's banking operations more transparent. His work was paying off, earning Monaco the reputation of being above reproach in major international circles. Consequently the real estate was more desirable than it had ever been. Monaco was now seen as a glittering backdrop for corporations and new entrepreneurs, as well as for its more traditional reputation as a playground for the fabulously wealthy, famous, and beautiful.

Nevertheless, Sinclair would hazard there were still crooks, money launderers, and oligarchs mixed in with the superrich in this sunny tax haven. People like that were always drawn to extreme wealth, like flies to a picnic, and they continued to be a scourge, from Dubai to Dubrovnik. Monaco was no exception.

Sinclair draped his jacket over the wall, and something clanked against the stone. He picked up the jacket again and felt in his side pocket. A lady's purse. He looked down at it in his hand, a small jeweled oval. How did that get there? He searched his fuzzy mind for an explanation. The last drink didn't help him much. Then it struck him. He had taken it from Cordelia Stapleton as they had posed for photos. He had a quick flashback of offering to hold it for her. She had fled the stage soon after. The bag was small enough not to notice for the rest of the evening. He held it in his hand as he leaned on the wall and considered what to do. He would return it tomorrow. Charles would know where she was staying.

Pretty girl. He had a mental picture of her walking up to the podium in the spotlight. Why did she leave so fast? He didn't see her after giving her the award. Why did she leave without saying good-bye?

The *Udachny* caught his attention again. The oval windows of the Benetti looked sinister, like eyes watching the night. Very flashy, that Jacuzzi on deck, and a bar on the sundeck, a thirty-six-foot Hinckley speedboat, two Yamaha Jet Skis, a trampoline, two kayaks, and a fourteen-foot Novurania tender. A bloom of satellite gear, three domes, sat on the upper structure. Not too many people on board from the look of it, just the light on in the master cabin. Sinclair picked up his jacket and headed back to his hotel.

Cordelia slipped off her shoes as soon as she stepped inside the hotel room and closed the door. The room was neat, cool, silent, the air conditioner whirring. Had it been only a few hours since she had left for the gala? It felt like her entire life had changed, not in a dramatic way but in an organic shift—the way the introduction of a nonindigenous species into a natural setting will ultimately alter every living organism in that environment.

She laughed at herself. That was a bit complicated for this time of night. She stepped out onto the hotel balcony. The cool tile floor was soothing to her bare feet. They absolutely *ached* from the unaccustomed high heels.

The view was stunning. A couple of hundred meters away, in Monte Carlo's *avant-port*, she could see the *Queen Victoria*. The dark gray hull was easily recognizable, as was the black-and-red smokestack. Cordelia admired the lines. It was much more elegant than the white cardboard-box cruise ships. The berth was a semifloating mole attached to the shore on the southern end. The northern end was held in place with eight very large anchor chains, probably about sixty meters deep to the bottom.

She would board the day after tomorrow. Cordelia stepped back off the balcony into the cool stillness of the hotel room. Her laptop was open on the writing desk. She pulled up the chair and started a new message.

> Susan. I'm here in Monaco. Do me a quick favor. Send me anything you can find on John Sinclair—Chairman Herodotus Foundation. Thanks a million. Delia.

There was an unopened e-mail in her in-box. She clicked on it.

> Dear Ms. Stapleton,
> We are writing to you to inquire about a possible sale of land rights in Svalbard that have passed into your ownership as a result of your recent inheritance. We would like to know if you would consider selling or donating this land to our nonprofit organization, Bio-Diversity Trust, which administers the International Seed Vault.

The International Seed Vault is now located on the site of the former Arctic Coal Mining Company owned by Elliott Stapleton. The government of Norway constructed the seed vault on your inherited property without a proper title search. Therefore, the land on which the seed vault is built belongs to you. The government of Norway will undoubtedly contact you in the near future to ask you to sell the rights to the land. We urge you not to do so.

We believe that no sovereign nation should be in possession of the vault. It should remain in trust to protect the common interest of humanity, and its benefits should remain outside the conflict of national interests. We respectfully request that you contact our solicitor at your earliest convenience to discuss this matter.

Yours sincerely,

Thaddeus Frost, Executive Director, Bio-Diversity Trust

She hit the Forward button and sent it to Jim Gardiner in New York. What on earth were they talking about? Jim could figure it out.

She was absolutely exhausted. With the time-zone shift, even her bones were tired, and her head was spinning. She walked to the bathroom, dropping her gown to the floor. She'd pick it up later. Cordelia had barely enough energy to splash water on her face and brush her teeth. Her nightgown felt light and cool. She pulled down the coverlet, slipped into the silkiness of the Frette sheets, and closed her eyes.

But even as tired as she was, Cordelia was not at all sleepy. Her mind was racing through a montage of all the spectacular scenes from the event. She kept hearing the speeches, and replaying the long walk to the podium in the spotlight with John Sinclair looking at her. The scent of his lemony, herbal cologne, and the feel of his hand next to hers. His jacket sleeve brushing her shoulder. What an unnerving man. She reviewed her conversation with Prince Albert II and marveled at how much knowledge he had about environmental matters. She remembered her conversation with Charles Bonnard. She really *must* have jet lag, to refuse a drink with him.

The whole evening had been sensory overload, and she couldn't find the off switch to her brain. After forty minutes of listening to the soft whir of the air conditioner, Cordelia sat up, turned on the bedside lamp, and picked up the battered leather journal of Elliott Stapleton.

JANUARY 1, 1908

IN THIS LEAP YEAR OF 1908, I MAY WELL NEED THE EXTRA DAY TO RECOVER FROM THE FESTIVITIES OF LAST EVENING. I SPENT MUCH OF THE EARLY EVENING AT RECTOR'S ON BROADWAY, WHERE LANGDON HALE HAD ASSEMBLED A DOZEN OF HIS COMPATRIOTS. WE CONSUMED QUANTITIES OF CHAMPAGNE ALONG WITH OYSTERS THE SIZE OF SAUCERS. ALMOST AN HOUR BEFORE MIDNIGHT WE ASSEMBLED IN THE BROAD PLAZA, TIMES SQUARE, IN FRONT OF THE TIMES TOWER BUILDING, THE SECOND TALLEST STRUCTURE IN THE CITY.

ON THE SUMMIT, THEY HAVE ERECTED A 70-FOOT FLAGPOLE AND A LARGE SPHERE, ENTIRELY COVERED IN ELECTRICAL LIGHTS. WE WERE TOLD AT MIDNIGHT IT WOULD DESCEND. THE ROWDINESS OF THE CROWD INCREASED AS THE HOUR DREW NEAR. SEVERAL OF LANGDON'S FEMALE FRIENDS WERE CLINGING TO ME IN THE HOPE OF KEEPING WARM. SUDDENLY THE CROWD BROKE INTO A THROBBING CHANT, AND THE LIGHTED GLOBE STARTED MOVING SLOWLY DOWNWARD UNTIL BRIGHT LIGHTS PULSED THE YEAR 1908.

A GREAT CHEER WENT UP AND MY COMPANIONS WERE EMBRACING EACH OTHER. ONE WAS EMBOLDENED ENOUGH TO PRESS HER LIPS TO MINE IN A CELEBRATION OF THE MOMENT. WE THEN REPAIRED TO THE FAMOUS MARTIN'S, BUT BY THREE IN THE MORNING MY ENTHUSIASM FOR THE COMPANY HAD WANED AND I SENT MYSELF OFF TO BED.

The sunlight was blazing in from the balcony. Her reading light was still on and the journal was lying across her chest. Cordelia put the journal gently on the night table and walked outside. It was breezy, her cotton batiste nightgown billowed around her limbs, and the sun warmed her body through the thin fabric. How could she have slept so long? Time to get moving. She wanted to sightsee in Monaco today. She dialed room service and her breakfast arrived within minutes. Hot coffee, croissants, beautiful strawberry jam, and the lovely sweet butter—the kind found only in Europe. She gorged herself on three croissants and fruit, washing them down with the aromatic coffee.

On the way to the shower Cordelia checked her e-mail. Susan had replied.

Delia, I have attached John Sinclair's bio. It looks like he founded the Herodotus Foundation just after leaving Wharton. He sold his Internet

business at the height of the tech bubble and is now involved in archaeology. I also attached the newspaper account of his wife's car accident.
She died six years ago. John Sinclair is single, but he is currently dating
Shari (yes, THAT Shari). I would steer clear of him. He seems like quite a
player. I hope you are managing to have some fun. XX Susan.

P.S. Joel asked me out last night! Can you believe it! I almost died of
shock. We had Mexican food.

Cordelia smirked and closed down the computer. No wonder Joel
wanted her out of the way. She picked up her cup, but the coffee was
already cold. She checked the thermal pot and there was none left. As she
reached to call room service, the phone rang under her hand.

"Miss Stapleton, a gentleman has returned your handbag to the front
desk, and we are sending it right up."

"Is he still there?"

"No, mademoiselle, he has left."

Cordelia was relieved she didn't have to face Sinclair. She didn't want
to explain or apologize for her behavior and her abrupt departure.

"Can you send up another pot of coffee with the purse?"

"Certainly, mademoiselle."

The waiter came with the coffee and the handbag on a silver tray. She
poured a cup and picked up her purse to tip him as he left. There, wedged
into the clasp of the handbag, was a personal calling card. The name John
Sinclair was engraved in plain black script, and handwritten underneath
was his international mobile number. Interesting that he didn't use his
Herodotus Foundation business card. OK, she got it. He wanted her to call
for social reasons; it had nothing to do with the foundation or the award
ceremony.

She put the card back on the tray and sipped the coffee, looking over
at the newspapers. They had been delivered to her door earlier, and she
had read them thoroughly already. But she picked up the *Monaco Times*
again and looked at the write-up of the ball. She scrutinized a picture of
the prince talking to Sinclair, and another of Sinclair standing next to her,
holding the award. She didn't look nervous at all; in fact, she looked very
composed. But that moment with him on the podium had been electric.
He certainly was a very handsome man. She looked over at his card lying
on the room service tray.

In the paper, the caption under the photo read: "In addition to the Herodotus Award, Miss Stapleton was given the missing journal of her great-great-grandfather from the year 1908."

Cordelia looked over at the journal on the nightstand, still open to the page she read last night. She walked over, picked it up, and read another entry.

FEBRUARY 19, 1908

THE MOST INGENIOUS APPARATUS I HAVE SEEN IN THE ARCTIC IS THAT WHICH IS FASHIONED FOR AERIAL BALLOONS. WHEN BALLOONS ARE NOT FEASIBLE, BIG KITES ARE SENT UP FOR THE SAME PURPOSE. ALL THE DATA IS RECORDED ON THE GROUND, INCLUDING TEMPERATURE, HUMIDITY, AND RAINFALL, AND, MOST INTERESTINGLY, EARTHQUAKE VIBRATIONS THAT ARE ACCURATELY LOGGED ON A SEISMOGRAPH. THIS METHOD IS ALSO USED TO RECORD THE VIBRATIONS OF ICE FALLS FROM THE GLACIERS.

Cordelia closed the journal and gazed out at the harbor, thinking. Elliott Stapleton was describing the first version of the kind of Arctic ice survey Jean-Louis Etienne was doing with his team now.

Longyearbyen

The excavation had gone well, and the common grave was interred again. Miles was elated, and paid the young men twice what he had promised. The diggers had been so grateful, they had insisted on shaking his hand all over again; his departure had taken another half hour. Miles looked at his watch as he headed for the Land Rover. He needed to send the tissue samples out on the flight from Longyearbyen, fifty-five miles away. But first he needed to pack them properly.

Arriving at his hotel about two hours later, he knew the timing would be tight. He pulled into the gravel parking lot in front of the door and unloaded his Styrofoam coolers of samples. The hotel was an old mining barracks that had been converted into a very snug guesthouse for about twenty visitors. He claimed his key from the desk and headed up the wooden stairs.

Inside the room, Miles put the Styrofoam coolers on the table. He had assembled all the packing materials on the bed before he left, and now he began to wrap and tape the package with care. The courier label from Global Delivery Express was filled out and ready.

The cadaver had given him more than forty perfectly intact samples of lung, kidney, brain, and liver. The 1918 pandemic virus would certainly be recoverable in one of them. Miles checked his watch again. He had an hour before the last flight from the small airport in Longyearbyen.

As he packed, he thought about that call to Paul Oakley. The scientist had been characteristically subdued on the phone. Of course, that was just British sangfroid. He was probably wild with anticipation. Oakley was one of the most talented young virologists in the world. And for Miles, it was a pleasure to do his dirty work, so to speak. He was glad to help crack the sequence of one of the deadliest viruses in history.

Miles had only one other thought as he packed the small Styrofoam crate. He also wanted to check out the Arctic Coal Mining Company graveyard in Longyearbyen. There were nine miners who died of the pandemic buried in the company plot. The company had done right by them. They had been buried in good wooden caskets, deep into the permafrost. The American company had treated its employees well, even in death.

The company burial plot was a mile or so outside the town of Longyearbyen. It would be a short drive after he dropped off the package at the airport. There would be time before dark. Of course, Miles would take his rifle in case of polar bears. They roamed freely in this area, and anyone leaving the perimeter of the town was required to carry a firearm.

Miles looked at his watch and panicked. Forty-five minutes until the plane would leave, and it would be the last one for the day. From his present location, halfway up the mountain, he would have at least a twenty-minute drive. He couldn't miss that plane. He scooped up the tightly wrapped package and headed for the door, doubling back for his cell phone. He needed to hurry.

On the way to the airport, Miles remembered he had left his rifle back at the lodge. But if he wanted to make the plane there was no time to turn back. He continued to drive down the rutted track to the small airport. Should he continue out to the burial plot tonight? At this latitude, and at this time of year, the daylight would last well into the evening.

He decided he could do it. He would make a quick trip tonight, just for a look, and then go back tomorrow. It wouldn't do to be out too late by himself in the middle of the Arctic without a rifle. He'd have to keep a sharp lookout for bears.

The stink of jet fuel was terrible; the purity of the air made it even more acrid and nauseating than it normally was. Miles watched the SAS MD-82 take off from Svalbard Lufthavn, Longyear, the single scheduled flight each day out of the world's northernmost full-service airport. His package of tissue samples was on board. The pilot headed into the bright sky for the three-hour flight to Oslo and, from there, on to London.

Miles watched it for a while, then started up his vehicle and took the airport road, turned left, and headed west along the dusty track to the outskirts of the town. The oblong shapes of the town buildings, made of concrete and tin, soon blended with the landscape and faded into the distance. This was certainly desolate country. He drove for several miles without any sign of human contact on the lunar terrain.

Then suddenly, farther ahead, he could see the Arctic Coal Mining site and the remnants of the workers' housing. The group of buildings stood abandoned but resilient, a testimony to the courage of the few dozen men who had eked out their livelihood here in 1918, when the pandemic hit.

He drove through the ghost town. The graveyard was not hard to find. The small chapel, identifiable by its steeple, was padlocked and boarded up, but the wrought-iron fence around the cemetery stood, gate open, unhinged and hanging by one rivet. Inside, the tombstones listed terribly, and many were down flat on the earth. The stones had shifted during the past century of thaw and frost.

Miles put his vehicle in Park, deciding to keep the engine running in case he needed to get out quickly. Especially in late summer and spring, polar bears were all too prevalent, and he didn't want to take any chances.

He walked among the stones, looking for the names of the nine miners who had been stricken in 1918. He knew their names by heart, so often had he fantasized about doing just this. It was a long shot, but he wanted to get permission from the magistrate in Longyearbyen to take more samples. Paul Oakley had exhumed three of these graves last year, but there were six others. Why not take a few more days to see what other possibilities might turn up? The samples Oakley had taken a year ago were of mixed quality because some of the graves had repeatedly thawed over the decades. But some of the other six graves might have more intact samples. Tomorrow he would petition the local officials in person.

As Miles walked, he bent over each grave to decipher the worn stone, completely absorbed in his quest. Three rows down, he saw one of the graves had been disturbed. The tombstone read PERCIVAL SPENCE 1918. He looked at the earth; it bore the rough surface of recent digging. This grave had been exhumed. Very recently. The dirt was barely tamped down and still stood in a slight mound over the site. Percival Spence had died in the 1918 contagion. Who would have dug up the grave? He bent down to look at the plot, his knees protesting as he held the squatting position.

"You're getting old, my boy," he said to himself.

Those were his last words. He never heard the rifle shot. His cranium was blown away and his brains were splattered all over the headstone in a bloody mass.

His assailant lowered his rifle and walked over to the Land Rover, turning the ignition off with a gloved hand. Then he approached the inert body. Extracting the cell phone and the wallet from the parka pocket, he left as silently as he had come. The gunman drove away in his own vehicle, past the churchyard, and checked to make sure the body of the scientist was not visible from the road. Much was hidden by the filigree of the wrought-iron fence that surrounded the tombstones. Only the small iron gate tilted open on its broken hinges.

The bear was a big one, a male weighing more than nine hundred pounds. It sniffed the air as it came down the mountainside, and made tracks in the earth. The searchers found the tracks later and measured them at thirteen inches long, nine inches wide, and estimated the bear would have stood about ten feet tall. Its fur had the cream color of a mature male, and when it opened its mouth the gray tongue was a stark contrast to the yellow-white teeth. The bear had smelled the kill.

It didn't take long to find the body. The scent of blood called across the hard ground. After a long winter the animal needed food to satiate its cravings for flesh. And the human had been so freshly killed, the polar bear found it acceptable for feeding. The little iron gate was open. The parka offered as much resistance as a candy wrapper to its massive claws. The bear feasted messily on the carcass of the slain scientist, obliterating any evidence of how Miles had met his death.

The assassin walked into the courier office at the airport hangar and looked around. The Norwegian kid at the desk was reading a dog-eared thriller in English.

"Good evening, I'm sorry to bother you, but I just wanted to check that my package made the plane. My colleague was supposed to bring it. An older guy in a black parka?"

The kid looked up. His mottled complexion revealed he still suffered the hormonal upheavals of youth.

"Yeah, he made it." The boy looked unwilling to put down the Clive Cussler novel. "He made it, but just barely. I think there was only three minutes between the time he arrived and the time the plane took off."

"Wow, that's a little close. Would you mind if I checked the paperwork to make sure it was sent to the right place?"

"Sure," said the kid. "Take a look. It went to Professor Paul Oakley, Institute of Cell and Molecular Science, School of Medicine, Queen Mary University of London, Mile End Road, London E1 4NS."

The assassin held his hand out for the clipboard of receipts for the day's courier packages.

"Let me just check to see if he put down the right phone number."

The kid handed over the clipboard and went back to his novel. The assassin riffled through the dozen package receipts, deftly palmed the one he wanted, and gave the clipboard back.

"Good book?"

"Yeah, it's really interesting." The kid took the clipboard without looking at it.

"Well, enjoy it. Thanks a lot."

"You're welcome," the kid said, still looking down at the novel and finding his place.

Oceanographic Institute, Monaco

Cordelia walked through the large Victorian hall of Monaco's Oceanographic Institute and breathed in the fragrant, dusty smell of an old library. The sun was pouring through the large two-story windows, painting the wooden floors with light. The huge room was lined with standing exhibit cases. The original Victorian specimen cases had been in place since the day the exhibition hall had been built, and the floors and tables of the room had the beautiful patina of age. In the cases, the materials had been chosen to coordinate with the theme of the gala, artifacts from the voyages of Prince Albert I and Elliott Stapleton from 1898 to 1910.

Cordelia looked at the sepia-toned photos depicting every type of activity, from whaling to lab work. A film clip flickered in the corner of the room. She walked over to watch the historical travelogue. It was from 1908. There was the whiskered prince, dressed in a naval costume aboard his ship, the *Princess Alice*. The old film jerked and wavered, the movement too fast, but the excitement of the expedition was captured: the enthusiastic crew waved as they displayed their marine trophies—a large fish was caught in an old-fashioned conical net. There was the prince on deck leaning over to examine a small whale. The loop on the film was short, only a minute or so. She watched it several times.

Cordelia's footsteps echoed in the empty hall, and her body relaxed in the warmth of the Mediterranean sun streaming through the windows. Her mind drifted. These exhibits spoke to her in a very intimate way; this was as close to home as she had been in a long time.

"I need you," she said aloud to the empty hall. "I need you."

She felt the crushing loneliness.

"Please, I need *somebody,*" she whispered to herself. She didn't know whom she was talking to.

She suddenly remembered her father's old coat, in the cardboard box in the back of her closet. For years, she would take it out and bury her face in the cloth, trying to catch the scent of him. But after a while, it had no more power for her. Life moved on. The answers she needed became more complex. In the past few years she could no longer hear her father's voice in her mind. She forgot what he sounded like.

But now, after reading the journal, and walking through the museum, the yearning came back. Her great-great-grandfather's voice was the one she heard now, calling out from the faded pages. She desperately sought some communion with her own flesh and blood—an elemental urge.

She stood and walked across the cavernous space to the next exhibit hall, identical to the one she had left, soaring, sunlit, and Victorian.

As she walked into the room, standing there in a shaft of sunlight was John Sinclair. He was totally absorbed in reading the documents in the case before him. She felt a twinge of embarrassment for her behavior last night. But there was also the flush of sudden confusion, and deep attraction to the man. Her reaction was so strong she thought it must be visible to anyone watching her.

Just then he looked up, noticed her, and smiled. Standing there in the sunlight, with strongly chiseled features and a deep tan, he was very much the Victorian explorer. His white linen shirt was crumpled and rolled to the elbow, and he wore a rumpled pair of khakis.

"Cordelia, how nice to see you."

"Hello, Mr. Sinclair," she said, and walked over.

"Don't make me feel a thousand years old. Call me John."

"Of course, John."

"Fascinating exhibit. Have you been here long?"

"Yes, I woke up early, with the jet lag. I read some of the journal last night and I wanted to see if there was anything about Elliott Stapleton in the exhibit. I was just finishing up."

"It's fascinating stuff. I stop by from time to time when I'm in Monaco. I'm just heading out. Can I interest you in lunch?"

"I hadn't made plans."

"Well, now you have."

✳

Sinclair pulled the silver Audi R8 up to the portico of the Hôtel Hermitage and leaned across to pull the handle and pop open the door.

"Hop in, we are going to drive down the coast a bit."

"OK."

Cordelia folded her tall frame into the passenger seat. She had changed into one of her new wrap dresses, and as she slid into the car her skirt unfolded just enough to reveal well-toned thighs. Sinclair had to force himself not to stare. She closed the panel of her skirt automatically, without noticing his look.

He put the Audi into gear and tried to get his mind off her body. It was going to be a rough afternoon if she was going to play like this. He headed for the lower route to Cap Ferrat. Hotel du Cap might be the right place to take her—exclusive, secluded, the venue of choice for the jet set and Hollywood royalty during the Cannes Film Festival every year. The food was the best on the Côte d'Azur, with only a few exceptions. She might just enjoy a nice, romantic little lunch. He knew *he* would.

Sinclair looked in the rearview mirror.

"I don't mean to get personal, but you don't happen to have a jealous boyfriend with a Ferrari, do you?" he asked.

Cordelia shook her head, not comprehending.

"This guy seems to be following us," said Sinclair, flooring the Audi in a sudden burst of speed. The Ferrari Enzo, running on twelve cylinders, followed easily, keeping the same distance, turn after turn, as if on an invisible tether. Sinclair pulled to the right several times to allow the car to pass. The red Ferrari stayed put.

Sinclair frowned, and took the next sharp turn up the corniche. "I know a back way," he said as the Audi accelerated. Cordelia clung to the armrests, startled.

"Sorry," apologized Sinclair. "I want to shake this guy. I don't like these kinds of games." He kept checking the rearview mirror as he carefully executed the hairpin turns.

"Is the car still there?" asked Cordelia.

"No, we seem to have lost him," said Sinclair. "It might just be me, but I could swear we were being tailed."

What on earth for? she wondered.

⊛

Sinclair relaxed into his chair at the Hotel du Cap, studying the menu. Cordelia looked at him surreptitiously over the top of hers. Yes, he certainly was handsome; probably the most gorgeous man she had ever seen in her life. She looked at his face; it was severe in repose. He had a sensual mouth—but one that closed with a firm line, dispelling any suggestion of weakness. What would it be like to kiss him? She kept thinking about it. He was in wonderful shape; even his tanned arm resting on the white tablecloth was sculpted.

He looked up and caught her staring. She smiled back at him.

"I've followed your work. It's really impressive, especially for someone your age," he said, putting down the menu. His eyes seemed to register everything she was feeling.

"I'm not so young. I've been doing this now for nearly fifteen years." She kept her voice detached, professional.

All the selections on the menu were swimming together. She needed to focus. The dishes were described in French and she didn't know half the words. He drew her attention away again.

"Do you ever take any time off?"

"Well, it's not easy with Alvin. The submersible has to go out to sea for months at a time, and, of course, I stay with it. We have to do long expeditions in order to make it worthwhile, in terms of cost."

"Your work is truly impressive, but what do you do for fun?"

"Go to France for lunch."

He looked at her and laughed.

"Glad to hear it." He smiled.

Suddenly he seemed younger, not so imposing.

"Shall we order? I'm having the langoustine with drawn butter and fresh basil."

She chose quickly.

"I'll have fish, the *loup de mer* . . . but it's served with '*pois mange-tout.*' What's that?"

"Tiny peas in a pod. You eat the whole thing. Very tender."

"Sounds great."

He took a chunk of French bread and coated it with sweet butter.

"You seem to work very hard, from what I am reading about your research. Do you ever relax a bit, just loaf around or travel?"

"Have you been talking to my team? They set you up to say that, didn't they?"

"Not a bit." He smiled.

She could hear the softest of accents in his speech. What did it remind her of? Yes, that was it, what phonologists would call the broad Boston *a*. Could he be from Boston?

He seemed absorbed in thinking about something. The silence lengthened. She noticed he had the same ability to sit in silence as people who spend a lot of time alone—a trait common in scientists. She did it herself. But now she could tell he was weighing some line of conversation.

"What do you want to ask me?" she broke in. "Clearly you have something on your mind."

"Oh, yes, excuse me. I was lost in thought there. I wanted to ask you to help me with something I'm working on in Ephesus."

"Ephesus? In Turkey? What use would I be at an archaeological dig?"

"We are trying to date some marine artifacts that we found in the earth there. Some of the carbon dating is turning up interesting results."

"Marine artifacts?"

"Yes, Ephesus was a port until the harbor silted up."

"I had no idea."

He warmed to his subject, leaning forward.

"That is what is so interesting; the ruins are four kilometers inland. But at one time ships anchored right at the base of the main street."

"What a great place for a dig."

He flashed a brilliant smile. "It's incredible. Cordelia, could I talk you into coming down there?"

She turned slightly away and pretended to look at the view. Was he really saying he wanted her to come to Ephesus with him? For what? They were talking about dating, all right, but it had nothing to do with carbon.

Was he really this fast? He would invite a complete stranger to Ephesus with him? Susan had said in her e-mail to stay away from him. And he was romantically linked with Shari, the supermodel, wasn't he?

He was eating steadily, buttering the bread, as if unwilling to look up and gauge her reaction. But she knew he was entirely focused on her response.

"John, I can't."

Even before she could finish, he waved his hand in a dismissive gesture, still chewing.

"No problem. Just a thought."

He seemed to expect a rejection. He was light about it, but she sensed an undercurrent of disappointment. She had a strong impulse to spare him any discomfort.

"John, I really *would* like to come. But I'm sailing on the *Queen Victoria*. The ship is leaving Monaco tomorrow evening."

He looked up in surprise, his bread suspended.

"Oh, that is *wonderful*. How long are you going to be on the ship?"

"I guess about a week—it goes all through the Mediterranean."

"That sounds like a great trip."

"I am really looking forward to it. I'm scheduled for a lecture the first day. Then I can disembark at any port I want."

"What are the ports of call?" he asked.

"Down the coast of Italy, Livorno, Naples, then Malta, Crete and then to Izmir, and the—"

"*Izmir?* That's less than fifty miles away from Ephesus. I could pick you up."

"Oh, I didn't realize . . ." She faltered.

"It would be great," he urged.

Evgeny picked up the yacht's phone and dialed Moscow. With a new Ku-band satellite, he could do business twenty-four hours a day, call anywhere in the world, whether he was docked or at sea. Bulletproof windows in the guest area on the main and upper decks increased his confidence in the yacht's security. The connection clicked through to Moscow. He didn't identify himself, but began speaking immediately.

"We believe we can locate the deed," Evgeny said. "If the girl has it, we'll offer ninety-seven million U.S. dollars for the land rights. If she will sell, that will be easy. No problem. Straight legal sale. But if not, we'll wait until she finds the deed and then take it. After that you can do what you want with it."

Evgeny listened for a moment, then replied, "I think it's pretty simple. If you destroy the deed, you can make a Russian claim on the land. Russian miners settled in Spitsbergen in 1900 and that claim would hold in a court of law."

The cat came into the main salon of the yacht, drawn by the sound of its master's voice, and wound through Evgeny's legs as he talked. "No, no need for violence," he explained. "We don't want to attract attention. We have four people sailing on the *Queen Victoria*. They will cozy up to her and find out about the deed." Evgeny stroked the cat as he explained. "We have to keep the Norwegians away from her. We can't let Norway talk her into giving up the land."

The voice on the other end of the phone was harsh and spoke at length.

"No, I understand," said Evgeny levelly. "We will get the deed first. Everything is in place, I assure you."

London

The dark-haired man sat in a car in the parking lot of the Queen Mary College in London. He took a lab coat with his fake ID out of the backseat of the car and slung it over his arm. The white coat was a subconscious clue, a badge of legitimacy that showed he belonged in the research building. It was good camouflage to any observer, but more convincing if he carried it casually and didn't put it on.

Walking toward the locked service door, he took his time, trying not to look rushed. It was five thirty at night and few people would still be around. The researchers at this facility kept early hours. At least that was what the head office in Moscow told him. The back door opened, and a middle-aged scientist came out carrying a large briefcase overstuffed with papers.

"Please hold it," the dark-haired man called in a passable Scottish accent. He jogged up to the open door. "I forgot something."

"Sorry, you still need to swipe in," said the scientist. "Regulations."

He stepped aside to allow the other man to scan his ID card.

"Thank you," the dark-haired man said. "I must dash back inside. My wife would be upset if I forgot the wine for tonight's dinner party."

"I totally understand," the scientist said, and continued toward the parking lot.

The dark-haired man found his way through the maze of corridors and oddly shaped offices. He located Paul Oakley's office on the second floor, cracked the standard lock, shaking his head at the pathetic security. The door creaked open. The office was empty. He looked around the lab—a squirrel's nest of academic papers and documents. Only the lab counter and sink were clear. He opened the door on the far side. Oh, this was nice—an office suite with its own loo. That would make the overnight stay more comfortable.

The man hung his lab coat up on a hanger on the back of the door, sat down at the desk, and took out his newspaper. He had a twelve-hour vigil until the courier was due. He would be here to sign for it. The package had been sent to Oakley from Svalbard yesterday, and Moscow wanted to know if it contained a land deed.

At 8:30 a.m. the next morning, Paul Oakley was reading the *Financial Times* and eating toast with marmalade. He chewed and looked out over his back garden. The rain dripped depressingly from the rhododendrons. He was not feeling all that sprightly. He had to stop falling asleep with the telly on. It ruined his REM sleep when he woke up at 3:00 a.m. with the TV blaring. Abominable habit, but living alone encouraged indulgences like that. A domestic partner would have put a stop to it, but it had been awhile since there was anyone to account to. He hated living alone, but somehow he never made the time or effort to meet anyone new. Some weeks he barely acknowledged his housekeeper as she crept around trying to clear up his mess. Paul feared he was going to turn into a recluse if this continued.

By the time he backed his vintage Bentley out of the garage, it had stopped raining. The forty-minute drive to London was always a pleasure—he enjoyed driving his beautiful car. But today his mind was on the flu samples that would be arriving by courier this morning. He was sure Miles had found a good tissue specimen and he could start working. As he backed out of the driveway, he looked carefully both ways before swinging out into the narrow roadway.

The sound of the other engine took him completely by surprise; the silver car appeared out of nowhere. He tried to reverse gear rapidly and pull back into the drive just before impact. As he heard the bone-jarring smash, he found himself wondering why in the devil the driver didn't even touch the brake. It was a full-steam-ahead smash, as if his Bentley were invisible.

Oakley's head wrenched backward and then there was silence. He exhaled. His hands were still gripping the steering wheel as if to lessen the impact. When he took them down they were trembling, and damp with perspiration. His mind searched for an explanation. Was it his fault? Why did the car just jump up into his mirror suddenly like that and smash him? He was clearly visible.

Oakley opened the door and stepped out of the car, his knees weak. He put one hand on his beloved vintage car to steady himself. He didn't feel injured, but just *look* at his car! It was crumpled up like tinfoil.

"Didn't you see me?" he called back to the other driver. "What in the bloody *hell* is your problem!"

A well-dressed young man came toward him.

"Are you all right?" he asked in a heavy Russian accent. His solicitous demeanor infuriated Oakley.

"No, you stupid fool, I am *not*. Just look at my car!"

"I didn't see you, you pulled out so fast," the Russian explained.

Suddenly Oakley realized that this accident was going to be a major problem. He had no time for this! The tissue samples were arriving at his office this morning. He needed to sign for them. By the time he finished with this mess, the police report and insurance and all the paperwork, the courier would be gone. He quickly calculated that he would have to call Global Delivery Express to see if he could pick up the tissue samples at their package center later that afternoon. Those were not samples he wanted lying around for very long.

At Queen Mary College research laboratory, the dark-haired man stood up from his makeshift bunk under the cubby of Paul Oakley's desk. Research reports do not make a good pillow, he noted, and ran his hands over his clothes to smooth them out. He unlocked the office door and put on the lab coat with the fake identity pin on the lapel.

He was seated at the desk with a Paul Oakley ID tag on his lapel when the Global Delivery Express courier knocked briskly at 9:30 a.m.

"Dr. Paul Oakley?" the courier inquired, holding a large Styrofoam package in his hands, secured with the Global Delivery Express logo packing tape.

"Yes."

The dark-haired man could keep a good Scottish accent for a while. For a Russian émigré child, watching James Bond films was useful language training. The only thing was, his voice had always sounded a little like Sean Connery's.

The delivery guy watched him sign, completely disinterested in the process.

"Thank you."

"Thanks," the dark-haired man said with studied gruffness.

When the door closed, he stripped off his lab coat, crumpled up the receipt, and put it in his pocket. He tucked the package under his arm, draped the lab coat over the package to conceal it, and walked briskly out the back corridor. Within minutes he was unlocking his rental car in the empty parking lot.

He put the package on the passenger seat and backed up out of the parking space, a little confused by the size of the package. Why would a document be packed like this? Moscow had said it would be an envelope, a document—a "land deed." He rechecked the label. Yes, this was the package they had been expecting. The sender's address was Longyearbyen, Norway.

The dark-haired man pulled his rental car out of the parking lot and into traffic at 9:45, and started driving along the roadway. He wanted to get out of London-proper as quickly as he could. He was starving, and the deep ache in his stomach had been torturing him for hours; now hunger was gnawing into his brain. Twenty-four hours without any food.

He was driving on the seedy side of town. Houses were interspersed with cheap snack bars and fast-food restaurants. He turned into the Chesterton Kebab and Fried Chicken House. The parking area was at the back, near the chain-link fence, out of the line of sight of the windows. A blind spot. Trash, waxed-paper cups, and discarded chicken wrappers were blowing around in the early-morning wind. The area was pretty run-down and no one was around.

The dark-haired man took a penknife out of his pocket and began slashing open the package, making a mess all over the front seat with tiny balls of Styrofoam and pellets of packing material. Inside the package, he found very heavily packed glass vials, three dozen or more. They were sealed. His eyes widened with surprise. This was no document. What was this?

The dark-haired man took one of the vials and pried off the plastic double-lock cap. It required downward pressure, like the childproof caps on medicine bottles. It was hard to turn, but eventually came off. He took a deep sniff of the dark, greasy substance inside. It certainly didn't smell very good. It had the dark brown, fudgy look of opium chunks. He stuck his index finger into the vial and lifted out some of the goo. He smelled and touched the tip of his tongue to it. No real taste. He licked it harder to be sure. No. Not opium. He wiped his finger on the plush car seat and then on his slacks, and closed the vial.

Moscow would be angry. This was not what they were looking for. They wanted some kind of legal document. The dark-haired man wondered for a moment if the package would have any commercial value, and decided it did not. On the way into the kebab-and-chicken restaurant he dropped the vials in the Dumpster.

Inside, the smell of food cooking reminded him how hungry he was. He ordered hastily and sat in the far booth. Only two other people were in the restaurant, hunkered over their breakfasts and not interested in him. They had the gray pallor of night-shift workers, from the look of them: a nurse and a security guard.

The dark-haired man took a huge bite of his fried chicken and chewed as he dialed his cell phone. The other line picked up, and he began in Russian.

"Package intercepted. Not documents. Looks like some kind of medical samples, or possibly chemicals for medicine. Not what we are looking for."

The person on the other end of the line spoke for a long time. The dark-haired man held the phone cradled against his shoulder while he continued to eat, pulling apart his food into bite-sized pieces. He put small pieces of chicken in his mouth quietly, surreptitiously eating as he listened.

"No." He swallowed his food and answered more emphatically. "It was *not* a document. I told you, it looked like worthless stuff. Just some glass vials of medicine or some kind of samples. Your document must be somewhere else."

The other person stopped talking and the dark-haired man snapped the phone shut. Now he could concentrate on his meal. He might just get some chips after this, and another coffee with sugar.

⊛

Outside the Chesterton Kebab and Fried Chicken House, a vagrant rummaged through the bin. Morning was the best, because they would toss out the breakfast food that hadn't sold by ten o'clock. He always found a few good egg sandwiches this time of day. He put his hand into the bin and pulled out a Styrofoam container. This sure wasn't a sandwich wrapper. It was large and bulky. A bit heavy. He opened it. Inside were glass vials.

Monaco

Cordelia stretched out on her bed at the Hôtel Hermitage for an afternoon nap and listened to the sounds of the marina from the open windows. Lunch with Sinclair had been divine, and, in fact, the whole day had been exciting, and strange. The chemistry between them still sizzled in her blood. Of course, he was a terrible flirt. She had expected that. But she had to admit she was very attracted to him.

She lay there and thought about the strange incident with the Ferrari. Sinclair had been convinced they were being followed, and even more so when they discovered the Ferrari in the Hotel du Cap's parking lot. His eyes had narrowed suspiciously. She had watched him take in and memorize the license plate number without saying a word to her. And she had liked the way he had protectively taken her arm on the walk back to the car. It was a small gesture but it had pleased her.

She lay on the bed and looked at the pink-striped wallpaper. The sounds from the harbor were a pleasant backdrop—the slap of the stays against the masts, the faint murmur of an outboard motor, voices calling across the water.

She was sluggish, but her mind would not give her rest. After a while, she sat up and started to read her great-great-grandfather's journal.

August 4, 1908
What joy! Today I finally received my Pierce Arrow motorcar. I know it is a luxury most can't afford, but average families may soon be able to purchase motorcars for their own use. I talked with Mr. Ford about his plan to begin production of the Model T automobile by the end of this year. After hearing

OF HIS INNOVATIVE MANUFACTURING—WHAT HE CALLS "ASSEMBLY LINE PRODUCTION"—I WILL CERTAINLY INVEST IN THE COMPANY. AS COMMON AS THESE FORD AUTOMOBILES MAY BECOME, THE PIERCE ARROW IS A REAL THOROUGHBRED. LIGHT GRAY IN COLOR, WITH AN OPEN BODY AND A SIX-CYLINDER ENGINE, THE SOUND OF THE CAR'S MOTOR AS IT TEARS THROUGH THE QUIET OF THE COUNTRYSIDE IS A DELIGHT OF WHICH I WILL NEVER TIRE.

She flipped ahead several weeks. Here was her great-great-grandfather meeting her great-great-grandmother.

SEPTEMBER 5, 1908

AT THE PALATIAL HUDSON RIVER MANSION OF MRS. OGDEN MILLS THIS WEEKEND IN STAATSBURG, I WAS THE WITNESS OF A DELIGHTFUL TABLEAU VIVANT. THE CURTAIN WAS PULLED ASIDE TO REVEAL ASSORTED PEOPLE COSTUMED AND POSED TO RESEMBLE A PRE-RAPHAELITE PAINTING, THE NAME OF WHICH ESCAPES MY MEMORY. I AM AFRAID MANY OF THE DETAILS OF THE ELABORATE SCENE WERE LOST ON ME, AS MY ATTENTION WAS DRAWN TO A MISS ISABELLE VAN TASSEL. SHE WAS MORE CHARMING IN HER FROZEN POSE THAN THE ARTIST'S MODEL COULD HAVE BEEN WHEN THE ORIGINAL WAS PAINTED. I VOWED ON THE SPOT I WOULD FIND AN OPPORTUNITY TO SPEAK TO HER DURING THE WEEKEND ACTIVITIES.

Here was something about his business. Cordelia read on.

DIPLOMATIC CORRESPONDENCE SEEMS TO BE THE BEST METHOD TO ADDRESS THE NUMEROUS CONFLICTING CLAIMS ON OUR PROPERTY IN SPITSBERGEN. FOR SOME TIME THE GOVERNMENT OF THE UNITED STATES AND THAT OF NORWAY HAVE BEEN IN HEATED DIPLOMATIC CORRESPONDENCE OVER THE TITLE OF THE LAND OF THE ARCTIC COAL MINING COMPANY. HOWEVER, I FEAR THE TITLE MATTER ULTIMATELY WILL HAVE TO BE SUBMITTED FOR ARBITRATION. BUT I TAKE HEART THAT UNTIL THE DECISION OF THE ARBITRATORS OCCURS, NO ONE BUT MYSELF OR MY PARTNER, SIR JAMES SKYE RUSSELL, CAN HAVE TITLE TO ANY OF THIS PROPERTY.

Monaco Fencing Club

Sinclair was late. He bounded up the steps of the Fédération Mone-gasque d'Escrime. Charles was already lounging on a couch. The main hall was all dark wood, leather furniture, and polished marble floors—it was a real Victorian men's club, the same as it had been at the turn of the century.

"Hey," said Charles when he saw him, and started to get up.

Sinclair simply tilted his head in the direction of the changing rooms and kept moving. Inside, he pulled open his locker and surveyed his gear. Wire-mesh masks, heavy canvas jackets, sabers, rubber-soled shoes with a special tread on the heel. The club kept everything in good order for him.

Charles came in and selected sabers from his collection, checking the fit on his mask. He seemed totally absorbed, and disinclined to talk.

Sinclair remembered the first time they had met at the club. Charles had been tearing up opponents for an hour or so when Sinclair had approached. Charles had beaten him in seconds, the start of a good friendship.

"Hey, I tried to get you earlier," Charles said, testing the grip on his saber.

"I turned off my cell. I went to lunch at Hotel du Cap," said Sinclair. Charles looked over at him.

"Why, you like the burgers?"

"No, I ran into Cordelia Stapleton and asked her to lunch."

"No. Really? I was going to ask her out myself, but you beat me to it," Charles admitted. "So . . . what do you think?"

"Lovely girl," said Sinclair, checking the fit of his jacket.

"I *told* you she was fantastic," said Charles.

"No, it's not like that. I was just being hospitable. I wanted to show her the neighborhood."

"Sure," said Charles.

"Seriously, I'm not interested in anything right now. I can't stand another go-around. I've had it."

"Look, don't let a coked-out boozer like Shari put you off women."

"Shari's not a coked-out boozer. A lot of other things, but not that."

"OK, you would know." Charles changed the subject. "But seriously, what do you think of Cordelia? I talked to her after the gala. She said she ignored you during dinner and was worried about it."

"Good. Serves her right for flirting with Jean-Louis Etienne right under my very nose."

"She did?"

"No, actually they were talking about the ice pack."

"Very romantic. You must be slipping if you couldn't break up that kind of chatter. So what do you *really* think of her?"

"I don't know. We just had lunch. She seems smart. Great-looking, of course, but sort of reserved. Almost shy."

"Anyone would seem shy after Shari."

"Agreed," said Sinclair with a wry smile. "Shari *was* a bit of an exhibitionist."

"I would say so," said Charles. "Remember that time on Yanni's yacht?"

"God, how could I forget? The papers had a field day."

"So what about Cordelia. Going to see her again? She doesn't leave for a day or so."

"Well, you won't believe it, but I invited her to Ephesus."

"To *Ephesus*!!" Charles was staring.

"Yeah, to show her the dig."

"Are you *insane*? What woman would like that? It's a pit!"

"Literally," said Sinclair.

They both laughed.

"Great move, I'm sure she'll love it."

"Oh, hell. I don't know. She's going on the *Queen Victoria* down through the Med. It ends up in Izmir. So I tried to convince her to join me."

"Well, here's a thought. Why don't you just jump on the ship and ride down there with her? You're going there anyway."

"What? No, that's really too much."

"Are you kidding? She would probably find it very romantic."

"Charles, no. Forget it. I'm finished talking about this."

"OK. See you out there."

Sinclair picked out his jacket and mask, and slammed his locker shut. She hadn't been that interested. She made that clear at lunch. Why chase her?

The fencing salon had floor-to-ceiling windows. The brilliant Mediterranean light poured in. The room was the size of at least two American basketball courts. Approximately thirty fencers were now laboring up and down their individual pistes. Squeaks and squeals of the rubber fencing shoes, grunts of extreme exertion, were the only sounds. It was a temple of concentration; not a word was spoken. Only now and then a particularly fierce flurry would culminate in a sharp cry of victory or defeat.

Charles was at the far end, warming up. He had been one of the top-ranked fencers in Europe for nearly a decade. His technique and skill had been well chronicled. Extremely thin and light, he had such flexibility his arm appeared to bend in places that were physiologically impossible. He had his own distinct style, which was now emulated widely in the international fencing world. The point of his saber was impossible to see when in motion. In saber fencing, a touch can be scored with the blade as well as with the tip. In technique, Charles was the best Sinclair had ever encountered. Sinclair learned early on that despite his affable appearance, Charles had a competitive nature that was truly revealed only in the fencing lane.

Charles stepped into place on the strip without a word. Sinclair faced him. There was a slash of impatience in their mutual salute; blade to the mask and down to the floor.

"*En garde.*"

"*En garde.*"

Sinclair had fenced Charles so often he knew the opening moves like a chess game. Charles would hold back, taunting, drawing Sinclair out. He would pull him further into his trap, tempting him to risk more and attack closer. Sinclair, with his left-handed advantage, used every device. He had unique combinations, but Charles had fenced Sinclair often and was wily enough to recognize all the obvious moves. In their bouts Sinclair could always sense when Charles would be about to coil for a final spring. It was the way a naturalist instinctively senses when a snake is going to strike. But today Charles had not yet pulled back for an attack.

Sinclair fought on, breathing heavily—parry, riposte, parry, riposte. Sinclair was grounded and strong, and much taller. But as the bulkier of the two, and a decade older, he worked harder to keep his movements quick. Charles's feet flew across the floor barely touching it. He was—as the reviews claimed—miraculous.

Sinclair gritted his teeth, spoiling for a fierce exchange. Charles kept delaying his attack. He could hear Charles laughing behind the impenetrable mesh face mask.

"Come on," Sinclair growled. "Come *on!*"

His blood was up and he craved battle.

Charles ignored him, teasing back and forth, advancing and withdrawing. Sinclair felt his muscles starting to rebel. They were beginning to tire, dragging down his strokes.

Then Charles sprang, out of nowhere, with an assault so rapid and fierce Sinclair would have been astonished if he had not experienced it before. Sinclair fought like a man possessed. Blazing fast, the sabers connected again and again. It was beyond training, practice, or even experience. It was a contest of pure skill, and their talent was almost evenly matched. Charles attacked like a dervish for what seemed an endless amount of time. Sinclair tried to take over the attack, advancing almost the entire length of the strip in the process, and Charles let him come at him.

But then Charles drew back, and a moment stretched and suspended, defying the normal physical rules. Time stood still. Charles was about to strike.

Sinclair felt the survival surge of adrenaline and executed a classic disengage. He ducked his blade under the other weapon. Charles attacked, but Sinclair executed a lightning parry, riposte. Charles parried clumsily, leaving his right shoulder open. Sinclair sprang and scored with a triumphant shout.

They both ripped off their masks, streaming sweat and breathing heavily.

Charles looked at him and smiled.

"You got me."

Villefranche-sur-Mer, France

Evgeny looked out over the lawn of La Villa Alberta and savored the commanding view. The legendary French estate sat on twenty acres of manicured gardens filled with hundreds of cypresses, lemon trees, and a parterre garden of boxwood filigree. This morning the ocher stucco mansion was in full sail, with striped awnings and pendants flying in the brilliant sunshine. It was questionable if Versailles in its heyday had been more meticulously groomed. In the gardens, a legion of thirty workers never let a leaf linger for more than an hour on a gravel pathway.

Throughout the decades, the villa had passed from hand to hand, with an elite ownership of European monarchs, industrial tycoons, and idle rich. It now belonged to Oleg, the son of Russian peasants from Yegoryevsk. Oleg was one of the endangered Russian superrich. In the current tough financial times, he had neither the peace of mind nor the culture to enjoy what he owned. Oleg knew the property was a work of art, but he valued it only as a marquee possession. Without an audience of admirers, the villa would be worth nothing to him.

Oleg came out onto the terrace, and Evgeny turned to greet him, rising out of respect for his immense power and wealth.

"*Dobro pozhalovat,*" Oleg greeted him, waving him back into his seat.

Oleg's wicker chair creaked ominously when he flopped onto the cushions. He wiped his face with a linen handkerchief, sitting under the striped canopy, and looked at the sparkling Mediterranean. His white linen guayabera hid his vast flesh, but his fat toes were visible in his sandals. His Cohiba polluted the beautiful morning, as foul-smelling and unexpected as the sudden whiff of a sewer drain.

Oleg's corpulence was legendary. Most oligarchs had earned monikers because of their tastes or habits: "the curator oligarch," "the football oligarch." In the tabloids Oleg was "Obese Oleg." His girth was the focus of public criticism, but the real cause of animosity was his vulgar display of wealth. He had drawn international outrage last year when his housekeeper leaked to the tabloids that guests had amused themselves one idle evening by throwing five hundred euro notes into the air and setting them on fire.

From the looks of things now, Oleg wouldn't be igniting banknotes any time soon. And it wasn't because he was worried about the press.

Only two years ago, Oleg had been estimated as the third-richest oligarch. His vast wealth was built on commodities dug out of the hard Russian earth, but with liquidity problems and plunging share prices his net worth had been devastated. His fortune was now one-eighth of what it had been. The Vnesheconombank, the Russian state-owned bank, had bailed him out with a $6 billion loan last year, to be repaid to the Royal Bank of Scotland. In turn, he had to transfer 50 percent of his shares of his company to Vnesheconombank.

As he sat on the terrace of his legendary estate, Oleg was now technically bankrupt—his assets did not cover his obligations—but things were fluid. He was working on it.

Just then Shari came through the French doors and walked over to Oleg. "Good morning, Oleg. Is everyone else at the pool?"

"*Da*," he grunted.

Because Oleg barely acknowledged her, she turned her attention to Evgeny. "Lovely day," she said.

Her blond hair was pulled up into a sleek chignon. She wore a yellow string-bikini top and an Emilio Pucci pareu that revealed her left leg all the way to the hip. Evgeny stared and nodded, but didn't engage her in conversation.

"I'm going for a swim," she said, tossing the words over her shoulder as a taunt and wiggling her magnificent bottom down the gravel path through the garden.

"Isn't she . . . ?"

"*Da*. The fashion model." Oleg nodded.

"Very pretty," said Evgeny.

"Have you found the deed?" Oleg asked as he watched Shari walk away.

"No. We are looking for it. So are the Norwegians, the CIA, and, of course, our benefactors."

Oleg and Evgeny were creatures of the Kremlin. They both desperately needed a bailout. The recovery of the land deed of the Arctic Coal Mining

Company was the price the Russian government was asking. Monetarily the deed was worthless to the Russians. It had been made out to Elliott Stapleton. But if it were destroyed the Russians could claim ownership of the land. Their claim would be based on the land grants to Russian miners in Spitsbergen in 1900. That would give them a foothold in a bid for territorial sovereignty.

"When are you meeting with your bank?" Oleg asked. Evgeny blanched.

"I have a meeting in Florence in a few days. I got Raiffeisen Bank to refinance the five-hundred-million-euro loan from Deutsche Bank."

"That's chickenshit," said Oleg dismissively. "Listen to me, we have to think bigger than that."

"Believe me, I want to think bigger than that. I need two point six billion dollars for my syndicated loan."

"I'm looking at the same thing, so here's my plan." Oleg, despite his thick features, had a mind like surgical steel.

Evgeny leaned forward. Oleg's voice had a low timbre that indicated he was about to impart something important.

"Let's merge."

"*Merge?*" Evgeny was stunned.

"Yes, we will merge most of our assets, the mines and factories, and turn them into a state-controlled conglomerate. And in exchange the Russian government could refinance the bank debt."

"What are we, Soviets? That would be like reversing the privatizations that set up our companies in the 1990s."

"Who cares? We would be first in line for the Kremlin money. There won't be enough for everybody."

"The government promised fifty billion," Evgeny said.

"And froze it after the first eleven billion," said Oleg, looking out over the lawn. "The faucet is closed. If we go in together, they will take half our companies, but we could both survive."

"Not bad," said Evgeny, thinking hard. "But what about the deed? They want the deed. And they expect us to produce it. We haven't got it."

"We could always kidnap the girl. She has got to know where it is," said Oleg.

"I have people following her. She's here in Monaco right now. If she doesn't lead us to the deed, we'll grab her."

Oleg gave a curt nod, replaced his cigar in his mouth, and looked out to the sea below.

London

The nurse on duty in the emergency room at the Royal London Hospital could see that the man was very ill. He was chalk white and sweating, his eyes bloodshot. You really didn't see that kind of pallor except in intensive care. With deep edema under both eyes, he was barely ambulatory. He walked up to the glass booth and stared at her, dazed, swaying.

"Your name please?" she asked.

He rallied and began talking urgently, but she didn't understand the language. Then he fell in a heap on the floor.

The phone on Paul Oakley's desk rang only once before he reached for it. It had been a hell of a day. First the motor accident, and now the tissue samples were missing. He had called this morning right after the accident and Global Delivery Express told him it was fine, someone had signed for them. When he got to the office they weren't there. But that was hogwash. The courier had clearly lost them. Oakley had put out a blast e-mail to everyone in the building, asking for his lost package. No luck.

Global Delivery Express was sorry. *Sorry.* Not as sorry as he was. That package was deadly! They kept promising to check the tracking number. There was no way to decipher the illegible electronic signature on the driver's hand-carried device. Maddeningly they kept asking for his receipt number. Oakley had explained repeatedly that he did not *have* a receipt because he had *not signed* for the package.

"Paul Oakley," he said, picking up the phone. He listened for three horrifying moments before answering tersely, "I'll be right there. I'm about five minutes away."

Oakley grabbed his jacket and raced to the back entrance of the parking lot. A patient at the Royal London Hospital was showing severe flu-like symptoms. The Health Protection Agency thought it might be avian flu. Paul Oakley knew more about avian flu than anyone else in England. Avian flu was lethal in more than 50 percent of the cases. It was tantamount to a death sentence. But so was another virus, and that was what he was worried about. The symptoms of avian flu looked identical to the symptoms of the flu of 1918.

Paul Oakley looked through the double-thick glass at the man under the oxygen tent in the ICU. He was being held in a private self-contained negative-pressure room in the Royal London Hospital. There were no drapes and it had only minimal equipment: one bed, one chair, one bedside table, a hamper for discarded linen, a garbage bin for contaminated equipment. Outside the room was a table that held personal protective gear for the staff entering the room: N95 respirators, goggles, face shields, hairnets, gowns, protective gloves, and protective scrubs. Going in and out required an entire change of clothes and extensive scrubbing.

Oakley could see through the glass that death was hovering. It could be hours or days, depending on the man's resistance and the virus he was fighting.

"Who is he?" Oakley asked the doctor from the Health Protection Agency.

"We don't know. No wallet. He just walked in and collapsed. One of the nurses thought he was speaking Russian. Or some kind of Eastern European language."

Oakley shook his head, looking at the charts. It was very much the kind of symptoms he would expect—high fever of 105 degrees and extreme respiratory distress. He needed test results to be sure, but it didn't look good. Oakley was nearly paralyzed with a horrifying thought.

"We cleared the floor," the doctor was saying. "Lucky for us the SARS scare put this hospital on the map. They have two infection-control practitioners who monitor this operation at all times. It's impressive."

"Great," said Oakley.

"We may have to evacuate all the other patients. I am afraid of nos-ocomial transmissions—other people in the hospital being infected," explained Oakley. "So I ordered the droplet precautions in all clinical areas and airborne precautions in the unit."

The staff was now using N95 respirators, which covered mouth and nose, to protect against splatters of fluids: blood, respiratory secretions, vomit, or any other bodily secretions.

Oakley surveyed the ventilation specs. The room met a standard contagion-control requirement of six air changes per hour, upgraded recently after the swine flu scare. The engineering department routinely tested the negative-pressure status of the unit and reported to the hospital administration. An external company conducted regular assessments of the air circulation within the room.

"Did you call World Health?"

"Yes, they're all over it."

"Good," said Oakley. He felt sick. What had happened to his package? And what had happened to this poor soul who seemed to be dying of the very virus he had been expecting just this morning in a courier box?

Monaco

John Sinclair handed a ten-euro note to the valet and slid his lanky frame into the Audi R8. He was feeling restless.

He ran his hand over the steering wheel and it was like meeting an old friend. He missed driving this car, but there was no use abusing such a beautiful machine in the dusty ruts of Ephesus. His motorcycle was enough for the dig.

But he truly loved gorgeous cars. Sinclair had always been attracted less to flash than to performance. He found that on the test track the R8 had performed better than the Lamborghini Gallardo and the Aston Martin DB9. He turned the car out of the courtyard of the Belle Epoque hotel, past the royal palms along the driveway, and out onto the streets of Monaco.

In the old section of Monaco, the narrow alleys were crowded with the late-afternoon tourists. He steered carefully around them as they crossed back and forth to the souvenir shops. When he was clear of the roads of Monaco Ville, he opened up and floored it, following the signs toward Nice. For a moment, he thought about taking the Moyenne Corniche straight to Eze, but he wanted the challenge of driving the long route along the coast.

He needed to think. Sinclair had a quick memory of Cordelia sitting in the seat next to him, crossing and uncrossing those fabulous legs as they drove to Cap Ferrat. He frowned remembering the Ferrari following them. Who was that? And what did they want? There was no doubt in his mind they had been trailing him.

Sinclair pressed Start on the Bang & Olufsen sound system. The voice of Bizet's *Carmen* grabbed his heart and squeezed. *"Si tu ne m'aime pas . . .*

je t'aime. Mais si je t'aime . . . prends garde à toi!" He thought about the line: "If you don't love me . . . I love you. But if I love you . . . you'd best beware!"

You can say that again, sister. He followed the serpentine route along the coast to Eze sur Mer. He turned off the main route and headed straight up the side of the mountain. He boosted the opera louder and hunkered down for the challenge, driving the switchback fast enough to push his skill.

He loved this network of roads along the coast, trimmed with narrow stone walls, at each turn a sheer drop-off on the other side. A plunge off the cliffs was usually fatal. It didn't matter who you were. God rest poor Princess Grace.

He tangoed the car back and forth up the mountain through a few hundred turns. Don't think, just drive. Carmen egged him on in her seductive voice. About twenty minutes later, he was at the summit.

Built into the cliffside, the village of Eze was a medieval fortress, with high stone ramparts and narrow streets. Sinclair parked and started walking up the steep cobblestones of the village. He turned right through a twisting alleyway. Then, next to the glass shop, there was an ancient portal. Through it was the lobby of the Château de la Chèvre d'Or, one of the most beautiful hotels on the Riviera. He walked out to the terrace.

The view was stunning. The full panoply of the Mediterranean spread below: Cap Ferrat, Cap d'Antibes, and the Gulf of Saint Tropez. And his timing was perfect. It was what photographers call the "magic hour," when late-afternoon sun casts a golden glow.

"Monsieur Sinclair, we haven't seen you in quite some time."

"*Bonjour,* Guillaume. How about that table by the railing? I'm alone today."

Sinclair looked around. There were only a few other diners on the terrace—by the affluent look of them, Americans, probably, from the luxury cruise ships.

"*À votre service.* What can we offer you today?"

"I'll have your porcini mushroom ravioli and a green salad. And that incredible white wine we had last time, chilled."

"Very good, monsieur."

Sinclair sat and looked in the direction of Saint Jean Cap Ferrat. Good time to think. No pressure of conversation.

Finally he snapped open his cell phone and dialed his office in Ephesus. The voice mail kicked in. His assistant would get the message tomorrow.

"Malik, it's Sinclair. I'm going to be away a couple more days. I'm thinking of taking a ship back instead of flying. Can you tell Karl? Oh, and give
my love to Kyrie, and tell her I will be home soon."

Guillaume was shaving white truffle over his ravioli. The dusky scent
blended with the fragrant Mediterranean air. He felt his appetite rise.
Damn, it was good to be alive. The waiter withdrew.

Sinclair took a sip of wine and thought of the lyrics again.

*"If you don't love me . . . I love you. But if I love you . . . you'd best
beware!"*

Both diesel engines on the *Udachny* were rumbling as Evgeny stood on the
foredeck. The yacht's stern lines had been cast off the dock, and the *passerelle* was up. His crew stood on the deck, anxious and attentive, as they cast
off the Mediterranean-style mooring. The boats were lined perpendicular
to the dock, stern to, with the anchor chains extending out into the port,
which made pulling out a delicate operation. As the windlass reeled in the
anchor, the captain held his breath and prayed to Neptune that the anchor
chains would not get tangled with those of the neighboring boats. If that
happened, the only solution was for a diver to go down and untangle them.

Evgeny watched the seventy-one-meter yacht float free of the dock.
Slowly it slid forward into the harbor, with the crew carefully manning
inflated fenders along the railing to avoid colliding with yachts on either
side.

Evgeny's crew were terrified of him. He fired his people regularly, to
keep his movements secret. No one had any real knowledge of his operations.

He was headed roughly in the same direction as the *Queen Victoria*
except he'd continue on to Cyprus. Half the Russian mob based their
financial and banking operations there. Officials never even raised an eyebrow when Evgeny's yacht came in.

Evgeny looked at the trademark black hull and red funnel of the
majestic *Queen Victoria* as they passed it to starboard on the way out of
the harbor. The ship would leave at 5:00 p.m. that night with Cordelia
Stapleton on board, carrying her precious journal in her luggage. Vlad,
Anna, Bob, and Marlene should be in their staterooms by now. It was one
of the strangest teams he had ever assembled for a job. But it was going

to work: the Americans were there to befriend her; Vlad and Anna were there to do the tough stuff, if necessary. Of course, they were all in it for the money. There would be plenty to go around. But Evgeny was thinking of giving the Americans less. After all, who could they complain to? They had five days to get her to talk.

Nothing like a nice relaxing ship to make friends and spill the beans. Cordelia was alone, and she'd open up pretty quickly to friendly strangers. Especially Bob and Marlene. Mom and Pop types who could cozy up to the girl. She was an orphan, probably susceptible to that type of thing. It just might work. By the time the *Queen Victoria* reached Turkey, they should know enough about the deed to find it. Either that or Miss Stapleton would have to deal with a lot rougher stuff than a cruise on a luxury liner.

Bob and Marlene looked as if they were hosting a cocktail party in their suite on deck 7 of the *Queen Victoria*. Marlene held her flute of champagne, and was choosing a morsel from a plate of canapés. Bob sat stolidly with both feet planted on the floor. His plaid Ralph Lauren shirt pulled tight at the buttons over his vast stomach. From time to time he took a long swill of champagne, bumping his nose with the flute. Champagne clearly wasn't his usual libation.

Vlad and Anna sat on the couch across from them, wearing miserably pained expressions. On the low table, the hot appetizers and the cheese tray went untouched. The champagne in their glasses was going flat. From time to time they looked out the glass doors to the private balcony as if gauging a route for escape.

The ship was about to move. The ship's horns had just bellowed, and soon the *Queen Victoria* would glide out of the harbor. Outside in the corridors, they could hear a lot of thumping as the luggage was delivered and guests found their staterooms.

"Are y'all going to attend the lady oceanographer's lecture this afternoon?" asked Bob.

Vlad and Anna exchanged glances as if it were a trick question.

"*We* are," said Marlene encouragingly.

"I thought I would check the seating for dinner. We've requested that she be seated with us," Vlad answered.

"She's traveling alone?" asked Bob.

"Yes, I checked her stateroom. It's a suite just down the corridor. She's by herself," said Vlad.

"Good. We don't want anyone near her, screwing this up," said Bob, and he took another gulp of champagne.

Quite a few people were already seated in the Queens Room when Cordelia walked in. The ballroom swayed slightly; the long curtains waltzed at the windows, and Cordelia could see the ocean streaming past as the ship moved. The Mediterranean Sea was churned into a froth by the bow. As she walked to the podium, she noticed the placard:

CUNARD PROUDLY PRESENTS
DR. CORDELIA STAPLETON
GREAT-GREAT-GRANDDAUGHTER OF FAMOUS EXPLORER
ELLIOTT STAPLETON
CELEBRATED OCEANOGRAPHER
WOODS HOLE OCEANOGRAPHIC INSTITUTION
"THE SEAS, OUR MOST PRECIOUS RESOURCE."

A uniformed Cunard steward stepped forward.

"Miss Stapleton, thank you for being so prompt."

Cordelia shook her hand.

"It took me a minute to find this room. I kept getting lost."

"It is a big ship," the steward agreed.

"It's huge. And it's so *luxurious*! I am not used to this. Chandeliers, carpets, paintings, a casino! Nothing like our exploration ships, that's for sure."

"I hope you enjoy it."

"I *love* it. I can't wait to see the rest!" Cordelia exclaimed.

"Excuse me," a male voice said right behind her. "I hope you won't mind if I join the audience."

She recognized the voice. She whirled around and looked up at him. "John! What . . ."

"I heard you were going my way," said John Sinclair. His blue eyes were laughing, as if he had played a great joke on her. She felt a flash of annoyance.

"I had no idea you were coming. . . . You never said anything," she said in an accusatory tone. She hadn't invited him. How dare he just presume to tag along?

"I just decided at the last minute." Sinclair looked amused.

Cordelia just stared at him. He continued, "I'm headed back to Izmir. I asked myself, why not travel in style and pick up a good lecture along the way?"

Cordelia didn't know if she was flattered or annoyed. Now what was she going to do with this man—just the two of them on a ship?

"I hope you don't mind," he added. He was smiling, but less confidently now.

She shouldn't get involved with him. He seemed like such an operator. And where was his supermodel girlfriend, anyway? Why wasn't *she* with him?

"I'm . . . just a little surprised," she said.

"Miss Stapleton, forgive me for interrupting. We're about to start," said the steward.

Cordelia walked to the podium and looked down at her prepared notes. She felt off base, irritated. Now she was nervous with Sinclair out there. For the first time since the seventh-grade science fair, her hands were shaking.

She looked out at the crowd. It was hard to focus, now that he was in the audience. She looked at a cluster of well-dressed women, who gave her a group smile. That helped. Her voice came out strong and confident: "By 2050 most physical oceanographers believe there will be very little year-round ice cover in the Arctic. It is very hard to tell what are permanent changes and what is natural variability. But the Arctic is one area where any climate change is very visible."

She didn't look, but she could feel him sitting there on the left, in the back. She was conscious of his presence, and it made her awkward. The flow of the speech never came, and it felt too long, and lifeless.

Finally it was over, and the applause was enthusiastic. Several guests came to the podium, but Cordelia could barely concentrate on their questions. As she answered, her eyes searched the ballroom. Some people were leaving. Chairs were being rearranged. Small tables were being set up as waiters started afternoon tea service. They shook out the white linens, flowing over the tables. A phalanx of gloved busboys streamed in, carrying trays at shoulder height. Soon the room was filled with the buttery scent of scones and pastries. More people came in and took seats at the little round tea tables. Then waiters came around with china pots and poured the tea, as the harpist began to play. There was no sign of Sinclair.

Cordelia sat in her teak lounge chair, looking out at the Mediterranean and enjoying the beautiful September weather. Sinclair was on her mind, but she was trying to avoid thinking about him. She was going to stay on her private deck. She would deal with Sinclair later, when she had figured out how she felt about him. She adjusted her cashmere throw and picked up the journal.

> OGDEN MILLS ESTATE, STAATSBURG, SEPTEMBER 6, 1908
>
> I HAD THE OCCASION TO SPEAK TO ISABELLE VAN TASSEL AS THE LUNCHEON PARTY WAS DISPERSING FOR THE AFTERNOON. SHE EXPRESSED AN INTENTION OF WALKING DOWN THE LAWN TO THE BANK OF THE HUDSON RIVER, AND I OFFERED HER MY COMPANY. AFTER A MOMENT'S HESITATION SHE ACCEPTED, AND WE RISKED THE DISAPPROVAL OF THE ASSEMBLED COMPANY BY VENTURING OUT UNACCOMPANIED. SHE IS VERY BEAUTIFUL, EXTRAORDINARILY WELL-READ, AND EXTREMELY SPIRITED. I HAVE NEVER MET ANY WOMAN QUITE LIKE HER, BEING MORE ACCUS- TOMED TO YOUNG WOMEN WHO ARE RETICENT AND SOCIALLY CONVEN- TIONAL IN THEIR REMARKS.

When Cordelia looked up, the sun was setting and it was time to dress for dinner.

Sitting at the table in the middle of the soaring Britannia dining room, Sinclair looked at his watch. It was fifteen minutes into the second seating for dinner, and her place was still empty. That was cause for worry. She hadn't seemed at all pleased to see him. If she was avoiding him, he was now stuck at this table with a very strange lot. He reviewed his dinner companions.

Across the table, Vlad and Anna had the look of fast money. Anna's jewels and clothes indicated they had managed to get a lot of cash out of dear Mother Russia. The Americans, Bob and Marlene, had waistlines as broad as their accents. They introduced themselves as televangelists from the Church of the Enlightened Gospel, but they clearly enjoyed the material world. Bob wore a gold Rolex on one wrist and a platinum Atlas bracelet on the other. He had the shifty eyes and jovial manner of a double-dealer. Next to them was Joyce Chin. The young Asian woman was a really high-strung New Yorker. Any guy would be nuts to go for her—a perfectionist, by the look of her designer dress and impeccable coiffure. And watch out for those hard, calculating eyes. Gjertrud Flagstadt was a real Norwegian grandma type, and the mousy clothes spoke of a modest background. She must have saved up for the trip.

Sinclair took a place next to Bob, making sure the seat next to him was open.

"Where you from, son?"

"The States originally, Boston," Sinclair said, keeping it simple.

"Did you hear the talk by that lady oceanographer?" asked Marlene. "She was just terrific this afternoon."

"She was? No kidding," Sinclair deadpanned, hoping like hell she would turn up.

Another few moments went by in aimless chitchat. Suddenly Sinclair noticed Bob shift into a more artificially jovial manner. Although Sinclair was facing the back of the restaurant, he could tell from the expectant look on Bob's face that Cordelia was approaching. How curious that Bob seemed to be waiting for her as anxiously as he was. Sinclair looked at the others. They also seemed to be aware that she was approaching the table; their expressions were anticipatory. Cordelia seemed to have quite a fan club on this ship.

Sinclair resisted the impulse to turn around until the last moment. When he did, he was astounded at how beautiful she looked. She was wearing something formfitting and elegant in a silver blue color. He met her eyes, and fought with himself not to look her up and down.

Her pupils flashed recognition, but her gaze slid past him to the others, taking the introductions with easy grace. He stood as the waiter held her chair for her, and then sat down.

A string quartet was playing dinner music; at the moment, Pachelbel's Canon drowned out the sound of cutlery.

"That was a fascinating lecture this afternoon, Cordelia," Sinclair said, reaching for his napkin and unfolding it slowly.

"Thank you."

There was a tense silence. She didn't look at him as she unfolded her napkin and put it in her lap.

"Are you angry with me for some reason?"

She turned to him, and looked him in the eye.

"I'm not mad at you. But you *could* have let me know. Why are you following me?"

"I assure you I have no intentions other than . . ."

"Miss Stapleton, would you mind if Bob took a picture of our table?" the middle-aged woman, Marlene, was asking, a small camera in her hand.

Cordelia looked away from Sinclair, and answered with a gracious smile.

"Oh, of course not. That would be fine."

They spent a moment arranging themselves for the picture.

"Could you move closer," Bob asked, waving his hand to indicate that Cordelia should sit closer to Sinclair.

"One, two, three." Bob took the picture, and then sat down all smiles and compliments. "Great shot."

"That was good, honey," Marlene said.

Cordelia moved back away from Sinclair and settled her chair a chilly distance from his. Just then the waiter came with the menus. Cordelia accepted the leather folio and began to study the selections without further comment. Joyce Chin interrupted her perusal.

"I don't know if you eat seafood or not, but the Alaskan crabmeat risotto and the lobster bisque with tarragon are incredible. I highly recommend it. It's better than they make it at Daniel in New York."

"I had the chicken cordon bleu with sherry cream sauce last night," suggested Gjertrud.

"I'd like to propose a toast," said Vlad. He poured the bottle of Krug he had ordered for the table. His wife picked up her flute with a heavily ringed hand.

"To our planet, and the people who protect it," Vlad toasted, pronouncing it "PLAH-nyet." He raised his glass to Cordelia.

Anna smiled. She was wearing a very elaborate black chiffon dress with ruffles all along the neckline. Nestled in between the two mounds of her breasts was a dark green emerald the size of a jawbreaker. Cordelia couldn't stop staring.

Anna caught her gaze and smiled.

"I love your necklace," Cordelia felt compelled to say.

"Thank you, dahling." She fingered it with her very long French manicured nails. "Vlad gave it to me for our anniversary."

"Hey, that is a real beaut," said Bob, and it was not entirely clear whether he was referring to the necklace. Then, for the benefit of his wife, he added, "What *is* that, an emerald?"

"Yes, it's called the Star of Jaipur, and was once owned by Empress Eugénie," Vlad answered. He sat back and took a long swill of his champagne.

No one at the table said a word. Sinclair cleared this throat and held his champagne glass high.

"Your beauty does it justice, madame."

Anna beamed, and Vlad looked gratified. The others broke off into small conversations and Sinclair turned back to Cordelia.

"So, Cordelia. Just so you know, I am not stalking you."

"I didn't—"

He held up his hand.

"I think you are a genuinely interesting young woman. Who has many charming qualities."

He made a small half bow from his chair. It was almost like the Japanese bow of respect and submission. She still didn't reply. He leaned toward her and explained confidentially, "I actually hadn't planned on coming. But when you mentioned it, I realized I could take a few days off."

"I see."

"In any event, you won't have to put up with me for long. I will be disembarking in four days at Izmir. And, by the way, you still have my sincere invitation to visit the dig."

It sounded like an apology. She took a sip of champagne. Complicated man. His intensity was so utterly *attractive*. She supposed she knew he was nearly irresistible. She looked over his impeccable dinner jacket, his flawless physique. He was leaning slightly forward, his hand resting on the back of her chair. An inch or two more and he would be close enough to kiss her. She looked at his mouth, and a quick image of their lips touching flashed through her mind. She looked away.

"Why are you inviting me to Ephesus? I don't know anything about carbon dating."

It sounded like a rebuff. She regretted it as soon as it came out. His pupils flared in surprise, but he didn't flinch.

"Because it will change your life," he said. "It is the most interesting archaeological site in the world. It means a lot to me. And when I met you,

I had this impulse to share it with you. I thought you would appreciate it, and I wanted you to see it."

She took another sip of champagne, thinking fleetingly that in the presence of such a man she should not consume it so rapidly.

"I see. I will consider the invitation."

He smiled through his eyes.

"Thank you."

The truce held through dinner. They talked of everything under the sun: archaeology, art, music, science, marine biology, astronomy, technology, exploration, history, religion, philosophy, and literature. As she talked to him, her guard came down. She *knew* she was being deliberately charmed, but she couldn't help but be impressed by him. Never in her life had she met a man as well-read or interesting as John Sinclair. Of course, his physical attractiveness also captivated her, his conversation was nothing short of brilliant. By the time dinner was over, she was entranced.

The coffee was cold in their cups, the petits fours were gone, the champagne was flat when Cordelia realized the Britannia dining room was nearly empty. Vlad and Anna had left right after dessert, Gjertrud and Joyce were standing up to leave.

"We're going to call it a night," Bob said as he held Marlene's chair out for her.

"What are you two up to?" Marlene made it sound like they were a couple.

"Oh, it's late. I should go too . . ." Cordelia started to rise.

"I'll walk you out." Sinclair was immediately on his feet.

"Hey, why don't you kids go to the theater? I hear it's good." Bob checked his gold Rolex. "The show starts in ten minutes."

"Shall we?" Sinclair asked her.

"I don't know. What is it?"

"It's a musical review based in the Victorian era."

She had consumed just enough champagne to abandon her earlier caution. She looked at him and smiled.

"That sounds wonderful. Lead on," she said, daring herself to resist his charm.

Vlad and Anna were already seated in the upholstered chairs of the Commodore Club on deck 10. The jazz pianist was playing "Putting on the

Ritz" with an exaggerated beat. Couples were doing a quickstep around the dance floor. Bob and Marlene plowed through the dancers and walked over to the seats near the window. The broad panes looked out on the dark ocean. Vlad's expression was darker.

"You want to tell me who that guy is?" Vlad growled.

"Son, how the *hell* should I know," said Bob in his best Texas accent. "*You* said she was alone."

"She is booked into her room alone. But they clearly know each other. Did you catch that conversation?"

"Only a little bit," said Bob. He reached into his dinner jacket and pulled out the digital camera. "But I got his picture. I'll e-mail that to my folks in Texas and have them do a search on Mr. Sinclair's identity."

"Can your 'folks' be trusted?" asked Anna.

"Yes," said Bob. "They want this deed more than you do, Vlad."

"Why do *they* want it?" Vlad demanded. He was holding on to his drink as if someone would take it away. His entire body was tense.

"Because my church board believes the International Seed Vault goes against God's will. If the end of the world comes, and Armageddon is under way, it just won't do to have all those survivors with their own little hoard of seeds. End of Days, brother, it's all about End of Days."

"I have no clue what you are talking about," spat Vlad.

"The officers of the church want to shut down the International Seed Vault. The Russian government doesn't care about the vault; they just want the land. So there is no reason why we can't work together."

"I think it's a great plan, honey," said Marlene, patting Bob's knee.

"Well, you two better get on Cordelia Stapleton's good side if you want her to tell you anything," said Vlad, and tossed down his Belvedere.

"But now we're going to have to work around that guy Sinclair. He doesn't look like he's going to leave her side," said Marlene.

"Leave it to me," said Anna. "There are places men can't go."

"Where?" asked Vlad.

"The ladies' treatment rooms in the spa," said Anna.

The *Queen Victoria*'s Royal Court Theater was a little jewel box, all red velvet and rococo. Cordelia picked up the train of her dress to walk down the steps of the theater. Well, this certainly was a far cry from her nights on the research vessel.

A week ago she was curled up in her bunk, dressed in a hoodie and sweatpants, watching television. She really should face it; her social life was a disaster. From time to time she endured a halfhearted date with Roger, a self-involved academic who tried to dominate her intellectually. He believed in his own brilliance with a passion. In the past year, she had listened to his whining litany of perceived academic slights over too many meals of chicken tandoori. After tonight there would be no more Roger, and she was never going to eat Indian food again.

"Would you like one of these?" Sinclair was handing her a small Union Jack flag and a handful of rolled serpentine paper streamers. "I understand the show requires some audience participation."

They took their seats. Again there was the novelty of being so close to him, his leg alongside hers. It felt suddenly like a date. The lights lowered. She found herself wishing he would take her hand in the dark theater. He didn't.

As the opening number began, Cordelia realized she hadn't been to a musical in decades. The last time she had seen one was on a college break when she had gone to New York to visit Jim Gardiner and his companion, Tony. They had gone to a Broadway show, and afterward a big Italian dinner in Little Italy. It had been a wonderful time.

Tonight's show was a classic vaudeville review about Victorian times. There were rousing pub songs and saucy little ditties by singers dressed as barmaids. A cute song-and-dance number involved Victorian explorers in pith helmets with butterfly nets. An elaborate dance number was set in Hyde Park. The finale was a rousing rendition of "Rule, Britannia." The audience was enlisted by the singers to wave their Union Jacks and launch the red, white, and blue streamers. Cordelia and Sinclair threw their serpentine streamers with gusto, singing at the top of their lungs. When the curtain came down, the theater was a jungle of streamers trailing down from the boxes and balconies.

"That was *wonderful*." She laughed.

"Yes, it was just great," he agreed.

"You have a pretty good throwing arm, John. The people in front of us are covered."

She started pulling streamers off her clothes.

"Here, let me help you." Sinclair pulled a blue paper ribbon that had become entangled in her hair, his face close to hers for a moment. She looked up at him, and again thought about kissing him.

"Well," she started, "I should—"

"What? Go to bed early, Little Miss Muffet? You can't do that on this ship. Its only ten thirty."

He stood smiling at her, looking dashing in his beautifully cut dinner jacket. "There are parties going on all over this ship."

"I have to check my e-mail."

He made a face. And she laughed.

"Fair enough, so do I," he admitted. "Let's go to the computer center. And then figure it out from there."

Not many people were at the consoles. Sinclair headed to a station with the European keyboard, and Cordelia took a U.S. keyboard farther across the room. Her first e-mail was from Jim Gardiner.

> Dear Cordelia,
>
> I hope you are having fun on the Queen Victoria!
>
> I am writing about the property matter concerning the International Seed Vault. It has been built on the former site of the Arctic Coal Mining Company formerly owned by Elliott Stapleton. That land is now your property. The title search was botched, and Norway constructed the seed vault on your land, under the impression it was their sovereign territory.
>
> The nonprofit organization that has contacted you—Bio-Diversity Trust—operates the vault, and would like you to donate the land to them. They do not believe any country, not even Norway, has the right to own the International Seed Vault.
>
> No action is necessary at this point. I will investigate further. I merely wanted to let you know I have contacted them regarding this matter.
>
> Love, Jim Gardiner

Cordelia wrote back.

> Dear Jim, all this is so new. I have no idea what to do. Could you send me more information on the International Seed Vault as soon as they get back to you? Please advise. XX, Cordelia

Next Cordelia opened a message from Susan.

Hi, Delia.

We got Alvin in a hangar. The inspection is under way and all is going well. We are checking manipulators, which should take at least two more weeks.

I got your e-mail about the ball in Monaco. I bet you looked like a princess in that new dress of yours.

Joel says hi and don't come home anytime soon. He's kidding, of course. He misses you a lot, and so do I.

XX Susan

P.S. Joel asked me out again! Do you think I should say yes? I'll keep you posted.

Cordelia replied:

Susan,

I will be on the Queen Victoria for a few more days and then will travel to London to take care of some family business. Did you ever think you would hear this Little Orphan Annie say the words "family business"? Miss you. I will write again soon. Cordelia

P.S. I always wondered when Joel was going to figure it out and realize the best girl in the world was right under his nose. He seems to have come to his senses. Keep me posted.

As she signed off, she turned to see the handsome John Sinclair standing, waiting for her.

Sinclair held the heavy door for her as they found their way to the promenade deck. She squeezed past him, brushing him lightly with her dress. Outside, the night was clear and warm.

"There's no wind," observed Sinclair as they started walking.

"Actually, we are moving at fifteen knots, but the wind is from the stern so we don't feel it with the forward movement of the ship."

Sinclair nodded, suppressing a smile. This woman was *incredible*! How refreshing after Shari's tiresome posturing. They began to walk, and

Cordelia kept up a good pace despite the fact she was on an open deck in high-heeled sandals.

"I'm glad we went to the show," she said. "I didn't realize they had entertainment like that on board."

"Isn't it great? And there's a different show every night."

"This one was perfect," Cordelia said, smiling. "I just *love* the Victorian era."

They lapsed into silence, listening to the sound of the breaking waves alongside the ship. As they circled the promenade deck, Sinclair noticed how evenly their strides matched. She was a fabulous girl; how had he ended up with her?

"You know, I hadn't noticed it before, but I just realized that there is something about *you* that's very Victorian," he said out loud as if thinking to himself.

Cordelia turned and made a face at him. "*Really?* Why do you say that?"

"No, don't get me wrong. I mean it in the best possible sense." Sinclair laughed. "You have a wonderful air of elegance about you, yet you are very adventurous at the same time."

"I'm just kidding," said Cordelia. "I know it's a compliment."

"Oh, well, that's a relief. I thought I had offended you." Sinclair laughed.

"Actually, you are very perceptive," Cordelia said, taking his arm to walk across a slippery section of the deck.

"Careful," he cautioned.

"I'm not used to doing this in high heels," Cordelia admitted, tiptoeing through the area where seawater had sprayed onto the wooden deck.

"Don't worry, I won't let you slide off into the ocean," said Sinclair, tucking her arm tightly under his.

"You mean the sea," Cordelia corrected.

"Right. It's the Mediterranean Sea," Sinclair agreed. "You were say-ing . . . about the Victorians."

"Yes, well, the Victorian age of exploration has always interested me. There were spectacular achievements in science, medicine, botany . . . And, of course, it saw the birth of modern marine science."

"And the birth of Elliott Stapleton."

She smiled up at him.

"I'm glad you know him too. Thank you again for giving him that award. By the way, the journal is fantastic! It's wonderful to finally meet him through his writing."

"That *has* to be very moving."

Cordelia turned to him. "I can't thank you enough for returning the journal to me. It means more than you can ever know."

"I noticed you were very emotional when I gave it to you."

"I am sorry about that." Cordelia turned away. "I really shouldn't have left the gala without saying good-bye. It was rude of me."

"Not at all. But I wondered why you did it." His voice showed concern. He was looking at her intently.

"I should explain," she said slowly, searching for a way to begin. She looked up at him and blurted out her painful story.

"I am an orphan. My parents died when I was twelve. My lawyer, Jim Gardiner, took care of me because I had no one else."

She stopped walking and was looking out to sea. The powerful bow wave churned below the railing.

"So the journal was like recovering a family member," Sinclair prompted.

"Exactly." She looked up at him, grateful for his quick comprehension. "My parents' property was liquidated after they died in the car accident. Everything was sold for the money to send me to boarding school. They only let me go into the house one last time to take a few things." She stopped talking for a moment, looking at the sea. "I was just a kid. I took my dad's favorite tweed jacket, my mom's silver hairbrush. A few random things. All the rest was sold."

"That is so tragic," said Sinclair, turning his back to the wind and stepping in front of her to block it.

"So this journal is very precious. It represents a lot to me."

She was facing the beautiful nighttime coastline of Italy, but Sinclair could see she was not looking at the view. She was seeing a dark place, deep in the past.

"I can't take credit for finding the journal," Sinclair admitted. "The folks at the Oceanographic Institute discovered it in their archives a few months ago. They asked us to return it at the gala."

"Was it there all those years?"

"I guess so. Nobody knows how it got there. Maybe it was mixed in with some papers."

"Well, I heard stories about my great-great-grandfather when I was really young. I idolized him. He was everything I ever wanted to be."

They stood for a moment in silence, looking at the water churning on the side of the ship. Sinclair didn't want to break into her thoughts.

"This journal . . . it almost feels like he's communicating with me."
Sinclair stayed silent.

"The oddest thing is, I just inherited Elliott Stapleton's house in London. It was a complete surprise. I've never been there before. So after this cruise I'm going to London to take care of all that."

"How did you inherit it just now?"

"A distant relative, Peter Stapleton, died. He owned it up until now."

"And you inherited it?"

"Yes. You see, Elliott Stapleton was English. He married in England in 1889, and a descendant from that marriage inherited the house. It was my great-uncle Peter Stapleton—my only relative after my parents died. He was my guardian on paper, even though I never met him."

"OK, I follow you."

"So when he died last month he left everything to me, including the Stapleton family's house in London."

"So how did your side of the family end up in America?"

"Elliott Stapleton divorced his first wife in England and ran off with my great-great-grandmother, who was American. He walked away from everything in London—the house, the wife, the child—to start over in Boston. I am the sole surviving heir on the American side."

Sinclair was looking intently at her. She seemed so young and fragile standing there in her pretty formal gown, the slight breeze blowing her hair behind her. The wind pressed the light fabric against her slim body. What a lovely girl.

She gave a slight shiver; Sinclair took off his jacket and placed it over her shoulders. She accepted it with a smile.

"Thank you."

"You looked cold. Do you want to go inside?"

"Not yet."

"Cordelia, I am so sorry to hear all of this. Having no family is awful. I can't imagine how hard it was for you. But you have turned yourself into a success; you are at the top of your field. Your great-great-grandfather and your parents would be proud of you."

She gave him a wistful smile.

"I wish I could have met him. I swear I could feel him with me at the Oceanographic Institute that day when I ran into you. I had this incredible feeling of being so close to him."

"I expect he *was* there," Sinclair said.

There was a moment of companionable silence. The stars were becoming brighter in the night sky. She clutched his jacket around herself and suddenly felt happier than she had in years.

"What about you?" Cordelia asked. "What about your family?"

Sinclair turned to look back out at the ocean. His white shirt was glowing against the dark sky.

"I stopped seeing them. Sometimes family can be a problem. It's not easy either way—having them or not having them."

Cordelia turned to him. He looked hard as he stared out at the dark waves. He started pulling his tie loose as if to remove shackles.

"*Any* family is better than nothing," she said.

"Well, I went for years without seeing my family," he said, rolling up his tie and putting it in his pants pocket.

"Why?"

"I could never live up to what my parents expected of me," Sinclair admitted. "I was a big disappointment to them, so I avoided them."

"How could you possibly be a disappointment? You are so successful. You have a foundation; you're a well-known archaeologist. What could they possibly disapprove of?"

"My dad was in business—Sinclair International—and he wanted me to join the family firm after college. But I wanted to be a doctor."

"Did you go to medical school?" she asked.

"Yes, I got through the first year, but someone very close to me had a fatal car accident. I was there, riding in the car, at the time. I didn't have any real injuries. But I was trapped in the wreckage and couldn't save her."

His voice faltered slightly. Cordelia waited while he controlled his emotions. He spoke slowly and haltingly.

"It was my . . . well . . . she was my wife."

"How *awful*. I am so *sorry*," said Cordelia.

"I was devastated. I dropped out and spent a year in Europe avoiding my family, mostly visiting archaeological sites. Then I came back, caved in to the pressure, and agreed to do a business degree."

"Where did you go?"

"My father is on the board at Harvard, so he tried to shove me into their business program. With the little bit of rebelliousness I had left, I chose Wharton."

Cordelia smiled. "Did you like it there?"

"I don't mind business. I got my degree. But while I was there, I spent most of my free time at the University of Pennsylvania's Archaeology and Anthropology Department. They have a large museum with pretty decent Greek and Roman collections. And the Egyptian artifacts are also excellent."

"Is that how you got into archaeology?"

"Yes. Not at first, though. I had a big breakthrough in business. I started an Internet company based on the premise of sharing scientific data internationally. It was a huge success. I called the system Herodotus, after my favorite ancient historian. Of course, the company I sold it to *immediately* changed the name." He laughed.

"Is that when the Herodotus Foundation started?"

"Yes. I sold the company for a ridiculous price, and I started the Herodotus Foundation with the money."

"What happened with your father?"

"I told my father I was leaving, and walked out on Sinclair International."

"So what did he do?"

"Well, he never forgave me. He always thought I was playing around, wasting my life. And I'm afraid I haven't done much to dispel that impression."

Cordelia said nothing. She just stood at the rail looking out to sea with him. Eventually he continued.

"Anyway, that is why I live here." He waved his hand at the coastline. "Avoiding my family was part of the reason. There are other reasons, too, complicated to go into right now."

"Are you ever going home?"

"No point. Both my parents are dead. Dad died of a heart attack, and Mom six months later of a staph infection at the hospital where she was being treated for duodenal ulcers."

"I'm sorry to hear you lost so many people you love." Cordelia looked at his face, closed and inscrutable. "Will you ever go back to the States?"

"Never," he said, and his tone was final.

On deck 7 at that very moment, Bob had a new plan. He picked up the phone in his suite and dialed the Church of the Enlightened Gospel in Grand Prairie, Texas. It wasn't much of a church—just a studio and back office—but the phone lines were always open for viewer donations.

"Francine, honey, is that you?"

He waited a moment.

"Can you put Lance on the phone? Thanks a lot, hon."

"Lance, this is Bob. I need you to do something for me. There is a ship in San Diego. It's the ship that runs that minisubmarine for Woods Hole. Yes, that is what I said. You know that itty-bitty submarine they have? I need you to go get something off that launch ship."

Bob listened.

"Yes, it's a bit hush-hush . . . if you know what I mean. I'm trying to find that deed to the seed vault. I want somebody to check Cordelia Stapleton's stuff."

Bob waited for the reply.

"Yes, she lives on board. We're looking for some papers. A deed. She might have it in her desk or something. Take a look for me, will you, son? Much appreciated. Oh, and, Lance, don't get caught."

Bob laughed heartily at the reply and hung up the phone.

Vlad and Anna were wolfing cheeseburgers in the Golden Lion Pub on deck 2 when Bob and Marlene came in. Bob looked at their frosty mugs of beer and signaled the waiter. Marlene slid onto the leather banquette next to Anna and picked up the menu.

"Well, it turns out our John Sinclair is quite the man," said Bob, pulling out his notebook. "I got his bio this morning from the folks in Texas."

"He sure is a pain in the ass," agreed Vlad. "So what's the deal?"

"First of all, he's a multimillionaire. Not quite Forbes list but no slouch. He's from Boston but hasn't lived there in more than a decade. Left the States after his wife died in a car accident. Came back and went to Wharton for business."

Bob skimmed his notes. "He runs an archaeological site in Turkey and has a foundation based in Monaco. He doesn't run the day-to-day on the foundation—that's handled by a Charles Bonnard. Sinclair just shows up from time to time."

"Sounds like the CIA."

"Nah. That kind of money wouldn't bother with a chickenshit outfit like the CIA. What for? He has all the dough he needs."

"They *are* chickenshit," said Vlad, taking another bite of cheeseburger. He wiped the burger juice off his chin. "Weapons training?"

"Nope. No military, nothing that I can see. Looks like a pussy to me."

"He doesn't look like a pussy to me," chimed in Anna. They both ignored her.

"I think I'll have the club sandwich with extra bacon," said Marlene, looking up from her menu.

"OK, honey, I'll call the waiter."

Later, on deck 3, Vlad opened his cell phone and dialed Evgeny.

"We have a major problem here," he said. "The girl's not alone."

He listened for a moment.

"John Sinclair. Archaeologist, American. He lives in Ephesus. That's in Turkey. Yup."

Evgeny spoke for quite awhile, and Vlad listened.

"I don't know where, but he must live close to the dig. I'm guessing he is going to get off the ship either at Kuşadası or Izmir. We're stopping in both ports in a couple of days."

Vlad listened again, nodding as he held the phone to his ear.

"Exactly, that's the question. If he gets off, does she go with him? We'll keep our eyes open for that."

He snapped the phone shut. Goddamn Sinclair.

The morning dawned clear; the ocean was teal blue and flat. The wake was streaming off the back of the ship, forming clearly marked parameters that fanned out into the ocean as broad as an interstate. Cordelia was aft, in a lounge chair on the Lido Deck, sunning, dozing, and occasionally looking out over the water. There was nothing to see except the horizon and her beloved sea. She felt Sinclair standing there before she even opened her eyes.

"Hello, Delia."

He was wearing a jogging suit and had a white towel around his neck. She put her hand up to her eyes to look at him as he stood silhouetted against the sun.

"Oh, it's you. Hi, John."

She tried to sound casual, but her heart was pounding. Why did he have this effect on her?

He sat down sideways on a lounge chair next to her, his eyes registering the journal in her hands, but he said nothing about it.

"Are you going in for lunch?"

"I thought I would get something to eat here on deck, it's so beautiful out," she said.

"Not a bad idea. Well, I won't disturb your reading." He stood up.

Why on earth did she say that? Clearly she was trying to keep herself from falling for him, to keep him at a distance. But there was no reason for her to rebuff him like this. Maybe she didn't trust herself.

Just then Bob and Marlene waddled up on deck and came right over, with expectant smiles on their faces.

"Hi, y'all. Do you mind if we join you?" Bob and Marlene were toting books, towels, sunblock, hats, and all kinds of paraphernalia. They eyed the vacant deck chairs beside Cordelia and Sinclair.

"Oh, so sorry," said Cordelia. "John and I were just going in to lunch."

"Yes," said Sinclair, picking up Cordelia's tote bag. "We were just headed in."

"Oh, honey, that's a shame. We could have had a real gossip session. Well, we'll see y'all later," said Marlene, looking disappointed.

As Sinclair and Cordelia walked away, Bob muttered under his breath, "I'd like to throw that guy overboard."

Marlene's eyes widened.

"Bob, you wouldn't do that in a million years."

"The hell I wouldn't," he replied.

When Cordelia and Sinclair went through the doors of the Lido Lounge, Sinclair turned to her.

"Close call." He smiled.

"They seem harmless, but I wanted to read." She smiled back at him.

Sinclair handed her the tote bag.

"Happy reading." He gave her a warm smile. "I'll catch you at tea, perhaps? I'll be there at four."

"Great. See you then," said Cordelia, and headed to the library.

The ship's library was a gorgeous two-story room lined with bookshelves, connected by a beautiful wooden spiral staircase. Writing desks faced out to the ocean. At midday, it was quiet, and many of the large upholstered chairs were empty. As she passed the glass doors of the bookcases, six thousand titles whispered to her imagination. But she had her journal. She settled into a chair and read a passage.

NEW YORK, SEPTEMBER 8, 1908

THE FINANCIAL PANIC OF 1907, I AM AFRAID, IS STILL WITH US. NEARLY SIX MONTHS LATER, IT HAUNTS THE GREAT MANSIONS OF NEW YORK. THEY DO NOT SUFFER GREATLY, HOWEVER. I AM STRUCK BY THE FACT THAT IN THIS SOCIETY ECONOMIZING CONSISTS OF THE ORDERING OF A *VIN ORDI-NAIRE* RATHER THAN FRENCH CHAMPAGNE. THE EVAPORATION OF WEALTH ON WALL STREET BEDEVILS BOTH THOSE WHO SOCIALIZE IN TOWN AND THOSE WHO ARE INVITED TO PARTAKE IN WEEKEND DIVERSIONS IN THE COUNTRYSIDE. WORRY ABOUNDS. THE PHANTOM OF BANKRUPTCY SITS AS CLEARLY AMONG THE COMPANY AS IF IT HAD COME TO JOIN US FOR A CIGAR.

Cordelia looked for another passage about her great-great-grandmother, and found one almost immediately.

SEPTEMBER 9, 1908

I HAD THE OCCASION TO MEET ISABELLE VAN TASSEL AT THE OPERA LAST NIGHT, IN BETWEEN THE FIRST AND SECOND ACTS OF *LA BOHÈME.* DID I IMAGINE HER EXPRESSION OF DELIGHT UPON DISCOVERING THAT HER COUSIN HAD BROUGHT ME, LIKE SOME EXOTIC TROPHY, TO THE DOOR OF HER OPERA BOX? I RECALL WITH PLEASURE HER HAND CLASP-ING MINE THROUGH HER KIDSKIN GLOVE. AS I WAS LEAVING, I WAS BOLD ENOUGH TO WHISPER TO HER THAT HER APPEARANCE WAS PARTICULARLY ENCHANTING. SHE LOWERED HER HEAD, AND I WATCHED THE TIPS OF HER EARS FLUSH PINK AS SHE ACCEPTED THE COMPLIMENT.

Cordelia found another reference to raising funds for the expedition.

SEPTEMBER 10, 1908

FIFTY YEARS AFTER CHARLES DARWIN PUBLISHED HIS *ON THE ORI-GIN OF SPECIES,* I FIND THAT NATURAL SELECTION IS VIGOROUSLY AT WORK IN THE RAISING OF EXPEDITIONARY FUNDING IN THE METROPOLIS OF NEW YORK. AS MR. DARWIN POINTS OUT, ONLY THE VERY STRONG AND TENACIOUS CAN SURVIVE. IN THE COMPETING EFFORTS TO RAISE MONEY FOR THE OUTFITTING OF AN EXPEDITIONARY PARTY, I COUNT MYSELF AMONG THOSE WHO WILL SUCCEED IN THE CURIOUS PHYSICAL TRIALS OF SUCH AN ENDEAVOR. THE GRUELING TEST OF STRENGTH INVOLVES MANY GLASSES OF CHAMPAGNE IN OVERHEATED SALONS, AND THE ENDURANCE OF ENDLESS HOURS OF CONVERSATION. IT IS REMARKABLE THAT THE SUC-

CESS OF AN ARCTIC EXPEDITION DEPENDS ON THE POSSESSION OF SUCH
SURVIVAL SKILLS.

The mention of aviation in another entry was thrilling.

SEPTEMBER 14, 1908

I HAVE BEEN FOLLOWING THE EXPERIMENTS IN AVIATION OF WILBUR
AND ORVILLE WRIGHT. A JANUARY HEADLINE IN THE *TIMES* PROCLAIMED
"MAN MAY FLY IN 1908," AND I DO BELIEVE WE ARE ON THE VERGE OF
ACCOMPLISHING IT. ORVILLE WRIGHT HAS IMPROVED ON HIS FLYING
TIME OF MORE THAN AN HOUR, YESTERDAY CLOCKING SEVENTY-FOUR
MINUTES ALOFT, SPENDING MUCH OF THAT TIME 100 FEET ABOVE THE
EARTH. I AM TOLD HE ACCOMPLISHED FIGURE EIGHTS WITH THE EASE
OF AN EAGLE, AND HAS THE ENTIRE WASHINGTON PRESS CORPS AGOG
WITH HIS DEMONSTRATIONS, DRAWING FIVE THOUSAND SPECTATORS AND
ENTICING CABINET SECRETARIES AND THE DEPARTMENT OF THE NAVY
OFFICIALS TO THE AIRFIELD TO WITNESS HIS SUCCESS.

There was even social commentary.

OCTOBER 4, 1908

I HAVE BEEN THINKING ABOUT MR. UPTON SINCLAIR'S NEW WORK
THE METROPOLIS, WHICH I HAVE JUST RECEIVED FROM MY BOOK DEALER.
CAN WE ALL BE AS VULGAR AS HE DESCRIBES? AFTER READING THE VOL-
UME UNTIL TWO IN THE MORNING, I AM TIRED AND DISPIRITED. WILL
ALL THIS ABUNDANCE OF RICHES LEAD TO A LIFE OF INDOLENCE? I AM
PARTICULARLY REPULSED BY THIS NEW BREED OF WHAT IS BEING COM-
MONLY CALLED "THE AMERICAN COUNTESS," NEW YORK MILLIONAIRES
MARRYING THEIR DAUGHTERS OFF TO THE ARISTOCRACY OF EUROPE
ONLY TO REPATRIATE THEM, GOWNED AND BEJEWELED, TO PRESIDE AT
FASHIONABLE EVENTS ON THIS SIDE OF THE ATLANTIC. HOW I LONG FOR
THE CLEANSING PURITY OF THE ARCTIC AND THE SOCIAL STRATA OF THE
WILDERNESS, WHICH REWARDS COURAGE, HEART, AND STAMINA. I HAVE
BEEN TOO LONG IN THIS PLEASURE-LOVING CITY, AND I MUST PURSUE THE
GOAL OF SECURING MY FUNDING FOR THE EXPEDITION WITH ALL SPEED.

Time for lunch. She closed the journal. As she was walking past the
periodical table, she noticed *Paris Match*. The name Shari caught her eye.

Sinclair was dating Shari, wasn't he? That's what Susan had said in her e-mail. She picked up the magazine, tucked it under her arm, and found a secluded chair in the corner of the library. Cordelia flipped through the magazine until she found the article. It was titled "Shari's Big Blowup."

Shari's antics sold more magazines than those of any other star in the world. It was always headline stuff. She managed to look fabulous as she crashed her Lamborghini, fell down drunk in nightclubs, stole other women's boyfriends, and romped with her friends and hangers-on at wild yacht parties on the Côte d'Azur. But, of course, she never lost an opportunity to audition for sainthood: visiting terminally ill babies in hospitals, serving in a soup kitchen, or flying off to a third world country to look concerned and chic—all done in a size 2 safari suit. The whole world knew that Shari was a joke but couldn't take their eyes off her. From time to time, even Cordelia followed her adventures.

This article was more salacious than usual. Cordelia couldn't understand most of the French, but the pictures told the story. It was a knockdown, drag-out fight between Shari and her "archaeologist boyfriend," John Sinclair.

It was a shock to see him in the photos. Cordelia thumbed through the article eagerly. Truth be told, the limelight was not so flattering for John Sinclair. At first the pictures were romantic, and Cordelia felt a little pang of envy as she looked at the photo of them holding hands across the table.

Next, the conversation between Sinclair and Shari had turned ugly—into a real screaming match. It had reached such a pitch, they had been asked to leave the restaurant. There was Sinclair looking pained and Shari struggling with the mâitre d', clearly a little too deep into the champagne.

The most dramatic photo was Sinclair holding up his hands in a STOP gesture as Shari hurled her Chanel bag at him. Outside now: Shari was calling for a cab at the door of the restaurant, her mouth open in a snarl, and Sinclair running to catch up. The most pathetic photo was of Sinclair running after the cab, palms open in entreaty. In the murky interior of the cab, Shari wasn't even looking at him.

Cordelia examined his face in the grainy photo. He looked more vulnerable than she had ever seen him—with his tie askew and his hair rumpled. Cordelia closed the magazine and slid it under the cushion of the chair. No wonder he wanted to sail away from Monaco.

Porto Mediceo, Livorno, Italy

Evgeny stood on deck and surveyed the anchorage. It looked all right. Livorno was a working port in the Tyrrhenian Sea, and the *Udachny* was docked among all kinds of vessels. The ugly harbor was crammed with fishing boats, modern cargo ships, and passenger ferries that serviced the local islands of Corsica and Sardinia.

It was a gray day, extremely windy and not good for sailing. They would stay put for now. The *Udachny* crew were scrambling all over the structure for routine maintenance, swarming like an army of ants. They wore black polo shirts with a gold crest on the breast pocket and khaki shorts.

The yacht would head out to sea tonight, after Evgeny's dinner with the bankers in Florence. About 11:00 p.m. they would push farther down the west coast of Italy, passing through the Canale di Piombino, a strait separating the island of Elba from mainland Italy by about five nautical miles. Evgeny liked cruising at night and staying docked by day. There were fewer eyes to track his movements.

Evgeny went back into the main salon to look over his financial statements. The documents were spread out all over the bar, with his usual twin paperweights, a bottle of SKYY vodka, and a Baccarat glass filled with ice.

He dreaded this evening's meeting with his bankers. The Raiffeisen Bank in Austria had refinanced a €500 million Deutsche Bank loan to save him from a margin call on his mining operation. That was last fall. Evgeny was hoping for another two-month reprieve to restructure his debt. Right now he wanted a moratorium on payments until he could get the Russian government to provide state support for his operations. He needed about $2.6 billion to repay a syndicated loan from major international banks. Sure, when he gave the interview to *Fortune* magazine he had appeared confident, saying, "We do not need any financial aid from the Russian state." But he needed it badly. The Russian government would bail him out for a steep price. He had to come up with the deed—a deed to a *defunct* coal mine in the Arctic. To think his company was being held hostage for that!

Evgeny pounded the bar in frustration. A steward came in with cautious eyes.

"You needed something, sir?"

"Get out."

Evgeny gathered his financial documents together and put them in an envelope. There was not much choice. He was going to have to team up with that fat bastard, Oleg, and go begging the Kremlin for the money. Either that or find the deed to the mine in Svalbard. If he could find the deed, he didn't need Oleg. He would get the money on his own.

Why not snatch that American bitch and get it out of her? She would know where the deed was. Why have Vlad, Anna, Bob, and Marlene shadow her? It was taking too much time.

The cat walked in, swishing its tail, and stopped, crouching down, sensing the dangerous mood in the salon.

"Get out!!" Evgeny screamed. The cat hissed at him, then took off into the galley at top speed.

The Britannia Restaurant was emptying out after the eight-thirty dinner seating. Joyce Chin, nursing her cognac, told Vlad, "There is just no liquidity, it's nearly impossible to get credit."

Vlad was concentrating on his chocolate soufflé, listening to her with half an ear.

"So how *did* your hedge fund do, Joyce?" he asked.

"No worse than some others—actually a lot better, because I avoided the mortgage securitizations. But it's no picnic out there."

Joyce was dressed in black satin for the Black-and-White Ball, a traditional event on every cruise, and one of the most spectacular nights of every voyage. Guests were asked to dress in a combination of black and white for the formal evening. Joyce looked absolutely opulent in her black satin, with the requisite touch of white—a silk camellia pinned in her décolletage and a platinum necklace encrusted with diamonds and pearls.

Anna was also dressed sumptuously, in a black beaded dress. She leaned across Vlad to put her spoon into his soufflé.

"Dahling, let me have a bite, it looks divine." Anna's dress was precariously low-cut, and the maneuver with the spoon tested the laws of physics.

Bob looked on with a pleased smile. Marlene, engaged in conversation with Gjertrud, missed the show.

"What about your business, Bob?" asked Vlad. "Are you having any problems because of the economy?"

"Not a worry," said Bob, picking up the plate of petits fours and crystallized ginger.

"God is recession-proof." He bit into a small pink-iced square of cake and palmed a second petit four before passing the plate to Marlene.

"What do you mean by that?" asked Cordelia.

"Oh, he doesn't mean to be so flip about it," Marlene said, looking over the cakes, "but the Church of the Enlightened Gospel is doing really well. Everyone is turning to God."

"And away from their brokers," Joyce interjected with a laugh.

Marlene took three petits fours, one at a time, and put them on her plate.

"Our viewership is up twenty-nine percent since last year. We broadcast right into people's living rooms, so they don't have to go anywhere, or spend money on gas, to hear Bob preach."

"Praise the Lord," added Bob.

"Do you *charge* for that?" asked Vlad.

Bob darted a sharp look at him.

"No sirree. The broadcast is free. But we're on cable, so viewers have to subscribe to get the channel. We're being listed in more and more markets, so there's ad revenue. And then people can donate to the church if they want."

"And then they can also order the DVD Bible for twenty-nine dollars and ninety-five cents. We've sold half a million in the last six months and there's no sign of that slowing down," said Marlene.

"You're *selling* the Bible?" asked Gjertrud.

"Yes, Old and New Testament. Plus a tour of the Holy Land, on two DVDs. They're going like hotcakes. Ninety percent profit," said Bob.

"God bless America," observed Vlad.

"You own the channel?" asked Sinclair.

"People just send you money in the mail. Incredible," mused Vlad.

"The Church of the Enlightened Gospel owns the channel. I am the founder and CEO of that corporation."

"I worry, being on a fixed income," chimed in Gjertrud. "My late husband put it all in very safe investments, but everything is down."

Cordelia noticed she was wearing a rather tired-looking black velvet skirt, not quite right for the Mediterranean.

"If you want me to take a look at your portfolio, give me a call," said Joyce, sliding her business card across the table. "This is my New York office number, and you can get me at the Westport, Connecticut, number on weekends."

"What business are you in, Mr. Sinclair?" asked Gjertrud.

"I am an archaeologist. Our dig has been underwritten by an Austrian foundation for the next five years, so we're in good shape."

"Enough about these *boring* things, why are we talking about business?" said Anna, looking at Cordelia and Sinclair. "Let's talk about *love*."

Everyone else at the table collectively raised their eyebrows.

Hundreds of black and white balloons were floating on the ceiling of the Queens Room, with their silver streamers dangling down to make a shining forest for the Black-and-White Ball. The streamers wafted gently with the movement of the ship. Cordelia had chosen a white gown— a dress slightly Grecian in design. A silver cord bound the waist, and the folds of the beautiful silk chiffon fell straight to the floor. Her tan, deepened from the last expedition in the Guaymas Basin, was her only accessory.

"Would you like to dance?" Sinclair asked.

She slipped easily into his arms. As they danced, she had a little trouble at first finding her footing on the moving dance floor of the ocean liner, but after a few moments she found her balance. Dancing with Sinclair was easy. He moved with incredible lightness and grace.

She relaxed and thought how nice it was to be dressed up and dancing. How glamorous. Dancing so closely together, she was again reminded of how tall he was. Her hand looked very small against the black wool of the tuxedo jacket. A memory came to her and she was transported back to another lifetime. At a father-daughter dance in seventh grade, she had danced with her father just like this. He had worn a satin-lapelled tuxedo. The image of her small hand against the black satin came back to her. The memory hit her hard.

She closed her eyes and savored the image. It was the spring before the accident. She was all dressed up in a white organdy party dress and her first pair of high heels. She remembered the slightly citrus smell of his aftershave and the way his strong fingers had closed over her entire hand. She remembered the way he had to lean forward slightly to dance with her, even though she was tall for her age, a gangly girl on the edge of becoming a teenager. She felt tears prick her eyes.

Suddenly it was too much, to be thinking about this while she was dancing with Sinclair. She felt the tears spilling out from under her closed eyelids. She kept her head down so he wouldn't see. He didn't seem to notice at first. But then he stopped dancing, and felt in his pocket for a handkerchief and handed it to her. He didn't say a word. Neither did she. The dancers around them glided to the Cole Porter song. She and Sinclair stood still in the forest of silver streamers. She finished blotting her eyes, smiled, and handed the handkerchief back. He put it in his pocket and pulled her tight into his chest. They continued to dance.

Her suite was on the port side; his stateroom was on the same deck, starboard. They were quiet on the walk back. At her stateroom, he took her card key from her, opened her door, and handed it back to her. She murmured good night and started to go inside.

"Cordelia." His voice was low.

"Yes?"

She met his eyes. He looked very kind. She thought he might kiss her.

"Good night. Sleep well."

He leaned forward and kissed her on the forehead.

Sinclair had brought his KWV 20 Year Old brandy out with him onto the promenade deck, and its fumes were strong in the open air. As he stood at the railing and looked at the dark sea, he rolled the brandy over his tongue. The deep amber liquid had a spicy aroma, rich with the essence of dried fruit. It brought back pleasant memories of Cape Town.

His mind drifted back to Cordelia. There was no doubt that she was magnificent. He was slowly and irrevocably falling for her. But what in *hell* was he doing? He drank his brandy and searched his mind for some kind of rational answer.

Suddenly he laughed into the wind. What an ass he was. A supermodel was bad enough, but Cordelia spent her days on a submarine. Talk about a pathological need to seek out unattainable women.

It was clear she was in a lot of pain. That crying on the dance floor nearly tore his heart out. Poor kid. He sighed again.

Hell, when it comes to pain, we're all in that boat, baby.

Some nights he could barely get through. Three a.m. was the time he usually awoke, and from then on it was hell until dawn. He hated the dark almost as much as he hated the claustrophobia.

He had a theory that if he went back in his mind, over and over, to that horrible day of the accident, it would lose its power over him. He didn't believe in shrinks. He knew he could heal himself. A few times a week, sometimes every day, for years now, he made himself go through the events one by one, allowing for the full impact of the emotion to come up. He hoped to diminish the power of the memory by pure repetition. It was a rough exercise, but he could take it.

First, he would picture loading the skis on the roof of the Volvo. He would snap the locks in place, stiff in the frigid Vermont afternoon. Their car had been the last to leave the parking lot at Killington. Beth was sitting in the front passenger seat and had opened the picnic basket and started to unpack their sandwiches.

"Do you want me to drive?" she had asked.

"Would you? I'm starving. I'll take over after I eat," he had said. How he regretted those words.

"OK, I need to warm up before I eat, anyway," Beth had said.

He could see her sliding over to the driver's seat, lifting her legs over the gearshift. She had been wearing a red Fair Isle sweater and black ski pants, and she had looked like the essence of Christmas. Her strawberry-blond hair was pushed back by her red knitted earmuffs. She had been beautiful.

In his mind, he made himself taste the ham sandwich and the coffee from the thermos. He made himself watch the snowflakes in hypnotic swirls dancing across the interstate in the headlights. He made himself see the grille of the tractor trailer as it came toward their windshield, suddenly appearing out of the darkness. His muscles still remembered bracing for the blow. The truck had smashed full force into Beth's side of the car. They had tumbled into the ditch, rolling over and over. He knew she wasn't going to make it out; she could never survive the impact. He had let himself go limp, giving up, wishing to die. Then something had hit him and he had lost consciousness.

Sinclair took a taste of his brandy, but it turned sour in his mouth. He poured it over the rail into the ocean. Only a few more steps now and he would be finished with his self-imposed therapy.

That night, he had come to with a flashlight beam in his face. He was upside down and trapped. He couldn't feel any part of his body, but he was conscious and could hear the squawking of radios as emergency workers moved around outside the car. Beth was moaning.

This was the hardest part to remember, and Sinclair decided he needed to walk around the deck—physically move, to be able to deal with the intense emotion.

"John," she had been moaning. "John, it hurts. John, where are you? John, help me."

He had shouted her name over and over. She was so hurt, she didn't seem to hear him. He couldn't help her. He couldn't do a damn thing. Even his rudimentary training as a medical student for one year was useless. He couldn't touch her. He couldn't even see her. He was encased in the twisted steel. He lay there, trapped, in the dark, listening to her bleed to death, and he lost his soul.

Cordelia sat in her beautiful white gown, curled up on the sofa in her stateroom reading the journal. She needed family now, especially after tonight. She found several entries that were written from the ship the *Mauretania* in 1908.

THE MAURETANIA, NOVEMBER 2, 1908

I AM BESIDE MYSELF WITH JOY AT THE DISCOVERY THAT ISABELLE V. IS ON BOARD THE *MAURETANIA* AS WE DEPART NEW YORK. IT MUST BE

PROVIDENCE THAT CASTS SUCH TEMPTATION INTO MY PATH. WAS THIS MEETING ACCOMPLISHED BY ANGELS INTENT ON MY HAPPINESS, OR DEVILS ENGINEERING MY DESTRUCTION?

A few pages later she found

THE MAURETANIA, NOVEMBER 3, 1908
MISS ISABELLE V. HAS RAPIDLY INVADED MY THOUGHTS AND CAUSES ME GREAT ANGUISH. MY MARRIAGE HAS LONG BEEN OVER, YET I REMAIN BOUND BY LAW TO MY LOVELESS SITUATION. IS IT WRONG I SPEND SO MANY HOURS WITH ISABELLE? SHE EMBODIES ALL THAT IS VIRTUOUS. SHE HAS KINDNESS, INTELLIGENCE, AND SPIRIT. I AM AFRAID, ONCE HAVING VIEWED THIS PARAGON OF WOMANHOOD, I SHALL BE FOREVER DISCONTENTED WITH MY DOMESTIC LIFE.

Fascinated, Cordelia kept going.

THE MAURETANIA, NOVEMBER 4, 1908
MISS ISABELLE AND I WALKED ON THE DECK AFTER BREAKFAST. SHE HAS TOLD ME ABOUT HER WORK FOR THE IMMIGRANTS IN THE TENEMENTS OF NEW YORK, AND HER VIEWS ON THE EMANCIPATION OF WOMEN. I CANNOT HELP ADMITTING THAT MY ADMIRATION FOR HER GROWS EVERY DAY, AND I REGRET THE PASSING OF EACH HOUR, FOR SOON I WILL BE DEPRIVED OF HER COMPANY.

Although Cordelia knew the end result of this courtship, she was hungry for the details. She skimmed ahead.

THE MAURETANIA, NOVEMBER 5, 1908
MISS ISABELLE V. CAUSED A SENSATION UPON HER ENTRANCE INTO THE FIRST-CLASS DINING SALON THIS EVENING. A FALL OF SILENCE DREW MY EYES TO HER STANDING ON THE STAIRS COSTUMED IN THE LATEST DARING FROCK FROM FORTUNY. VENUS HERSELF COULD NOT HAVE LOOKED SO ALLURING IN HER RISE FROM THE SEA. I IMMEDIATELY TOOK TO MY FEET TO ESCORT HER TO HER SEAT, MUCH TO THE DISAPPROVAL OF MANY OF THE LADIES PRESENT.

The romance turned serious.

THE MAURETANIA, NOVEMBER 6, 1908
I AM STRICKEN WITH DEEP REMORSE OVER WHAT HAS HAPPENED THIS
EVENING. MISS ISABELLE V. APPEARED AT THE TEA DANCE THIS AFTER-
NOON. I AM AFRAID I LOST MY GOOD JUDGMENT. I URGED HER TO JOIN
ME ON THE DECK AFTER TEA AND, THERE IN THE LEE OF A LIFEBOAT, I
EMBRACED HER PASSIONATELY.

Cordelia couldn't help but turn to the next page.

THE MAURETANIA, NOVEMBER 7, 1908
MISS ISABELLE V. APPEARED AT BREAKFAST, WAN AND SUBDUED. I
BEGGED HER FOR A FEW MOMENTS IN THE WINTER GARDEN, WHERE AT
THAT EARLY HOUR WE COULD CONVERSE IN PRIVATE. WE SPENT A GOOD
PORTION OF THE MORNING SITTING AMONG THE POTTED PALMS, WHERE I
KNELT ON THE SPOT TO DECLARE MY LOVE TO HER.

When Cordelia turned to the next page, she read what she had known
all along.

THE MAURETANIA, NOVEMBER 8, 1908
MY DEAREST ISABELLE AND I ARE LEAVING THIS SHIP AS NEAR TO THE
STATE OF MAN AND WIFE AS NATURE PERMITS. WE PLAN TO MARRY ONCE
I OBTAIN MY DIVORCE, AND WILL SPEND THE REST OF OUR LIVES IN THE
COMFORT OF EACH OTHER'S COMPANY, NOT CARING FOR SOCIAL CONVEN-
TIONS IN THE LEAST.

Cordelia closed the journal and looked out at the dark water, and
thought about Sinclair.

London

Paul Oakley woke at 3:00 a.m. in a panic. What if his package had been misplaced? It could break open and spread pandemic flu. What was happening to the patient in the Royal London Hospital? How did he get so sick?

The 1918 flu was arguably one of the most contagious diseases the world had ever known—as many as fifty million people died during the pandemic, as it made its deadly circuit around the globe. Some scientists argued that by the end, the disease had taken a hundred million lives. There was no way to know. Record keeping in 1918 was not what it is today.

But unlike any disease before it, the 1918 influenza targeted the young and healthy. One bizarre aspect of the disease was that once it struck, a person's immune system was triggered to attack its *own* body. The younger and stronger you were, the harder it hit you.

That was also happening to the patient right now. If this was the 1918 virus, and it got loose again, the population of London would be decimated by millions. Oakley couldn't bear to think about it.

He tried to sleep, but his head ached and his eyes were hot. The pillow was too hard, and the sheets suddenly felt like sandpaper. The alarm clock said 3:30 a.m. He thought he would go mad with anxiety. Why couldn't he get Miles on the phone?

The flickering television painted a blue glow over his bed. He switched off the set with the remote and shuffled over to the closet to collect his clothes and shoes. Within moments he was dressed. It was cool when he stepped outside the front door. His Bentley was still in the shop, and a rental car stood in the drive. What a hell of a day yesterday had been, and today didn't look much better.

There weren't any cars on the road at the early hour, and the traffic lights were regulating the night with pointless colors. Nearer the hospital, the harsh glare of the emergency-room floodlights hit his eyes. He pulled in and parked. The lot was empty. All the way up to the ICU, Oakley didn't meet a soul. The seventh floor had been evacuated of all patients except one. Even so, when the lift doors opened the hall was entirely too quiet. As he walked, his sneakers squeaked on the linoleum. A nurse was doing paperwork at the administrative station.

"Good evening," Oakley said.

"Good evening, Doctor," she said, barely looking up from her work. "I am afraid your patient expired at 1:26 a.m. They've taken him to the morgue. The Health Protection Agency doctor is there now." She looked at him with curious eyes and professional silence.

"I'll head down there now," he said carefully, without emotion.

"Do you want to check the other patient first?" she asked. Oakley turned back in surprise.

"What other patient?"

"Seventy-year-old male. Indigent. No identity documents. He walked into Emergency this evening with the same symptoms. He's in ICU now. Do you want to take a look?"

Oakley felt his heart start to pound in panic.

"Yes," he said. "Yes, I'd better."

Queen Victoria

On deck 7 of the *Queen Victoria*, the cabin attendant had propped open the door to the suite and was stripping the bed linens. As Bob walked by, he could see clearly into Cordelia's room. The journal was in plain sight, right on top of the coffee table. He suddenly got a great idea. If he could read the journal himself, he might be able to figure out where the deed was. That way he could beat Vlad and Anna out of the reward money.

Bob quickly tried to think of a trick to divert the room attendant's attention. All he needed was to entice him to leave the suite for a moment. There was a laundry bin in the hallway, just outside the room. Bob rolled the bin down the corridor, then came back and knocked on the open door.

"Could I get you to change the towels in cabin seven fourteen? I noticed you haven't done that yet."

The steward came out, his arms full of sheets.

"Certainly, sir. As soon as I finish up here." He looked around for the laundry bin and saw it at the other end of the corridor. He sighed and started down the hall to unload his laundry.

"How'd it get all the way down there?" Bob heard him grumble under his breath. Bob quickly stepped into Cordelia's suite and slipped the journal under his jacket. He emerged from the stateroom seconds later. By the time the attendant turned around, Bob was waddling down the corridor behind him.

"Thanks again, son. Much appreciate it."

"My pleasure, sir," the attendant replied. "Have a good day."

Marlene was spooning clotted cream onto a scone when Bob walked into their suite. She added strawberry jam and took a large bite, holding it gingerly over the plate.

"Yum. You really should try some of this, Bob."

"I got it, Marlene," he said, ignoring the scones and tossing Elliott Stapleton's journal onto the coffee table.

Marlene nodded, her mouth full. She swallowed and ladled more clotted cream on the other half of the scone as she talked.

"Won't she miss it?"

"Sure she will, but what can she do about it—call the police?"

"What about Vlad and Anna?"

"They don't need to know. And she won't tell them. It's not like she is going to be blabbing her business all over the ship."

Marlene took another bite, and part of the scone fell, landing on her pink sweater.

"In the meantime," Bob said, "we can read it. No use sitting around here waiting. She isn't going to do much reading with her boyfriend hanging around."

"You're right about that. Did you see the way he was looking at her?"

"This is a wild-goose chase, anyway. This girl isn't going to talk to us about anything important. We need to look for any reference to a deed."

Bob thumbed through the journal, fanning the pages.

"Jesus H. Christ, the writing is so small it's gonna take years to read this thing."

Marsaxlokk, Malta

Lunch had been over for a half hour, and still they lingered in the café. The scene was so lovely, they hated to move. Sinclair had pushed his chair back, propped his feet up, and closed his eyes to the sun. Cordelia was picking at the remains of the grilled fish on her plate. She looked at Sinclair lounging and sunning himself, and found herself once again thinking how incredibly attractive he was. His crisp white shirt, rolled to the elbow, set off his tan. And the rumpled khaki shorts exposed impressive and well-muscled legs.

It had been a romantic morning. They had ended up on the southeastern side of the island of Malta, in the fishing village of Marsaxlokk. The restaurant had been perfect: simple and local, far from the tour groups. The old quay seemed timeless; generations of people had sat, just like this, enjoying the afternoon sun and watching the colorful boats bob in the harbor.

Originally Cordelia had planned on taking the group tour of the island, but when Sinclair heard about it, he had offered her a personal tour instead. He knew Malta well, and had kept up a flow of fascinating comments as they walked through the ancient fort of the Knights of Saint John.

He made an effort to be especially charming. She had delighted in taking his hand as he helped her up and down the steep ramparts of the fort. Of course, she hadn't really needed his assistance, but was happy to accept. Up until now she had gone out only with men with large egos and casual manners. Sinclair's courtliness was a refreshing change.

But as intoxicating as Sinclair's attention was, every cell in her brain told her that he was out of her league. She should not get romantically involved. There were danger markers everywhere. His was a world of supermodels, fast cars, tabloid press, and public fights. Even the cavalier way he had just hopped on the *Queen Victoria* as if it were a crosstown bus was astonishing.

"What are you thinking?" he said without opening his eyes.

"How beautiful it is here, and how happy I am right now."

"Are you?" He opened his eyes.

"Yes, I am."

He looked at her and then closed his eyes again. She watched the boats in the harbor, and a few minutes went by.

"Now what are you thinking?" he asked.

She smirked.

"I'm wondering why someone like you doesn't have women crawling all over him."

"Who says I don't?"

"Then why are you here with me?"

"Because you happen to be great company," he said, still not opening his eyes.

"So are you," she said. "Thanks for a wonderful morning."

"I had fun too," he said, and shifted his frame lower in the chair. He tilted his head back more.

"Why do you live part-time in Turkey?" she asked.

"I like the heat."

"Why else?"

"I love the dig."

"What are you digging?"

"Gladiators."

"That's what you're digging in Ephesus? Gladiators?" she said, surprised.

"Yes," said Sinclair, opening his eyes. "I was digging antiquities at first, but since we found the gladiator graveyard I haven't been able to do anything else. We're finding out so much about how they lived."

"Who is 'we'? Who's helping you?"

"A pathologist from Turkey, and two archaeologists from the University of Vienna, Karl and Fabian. They're brilliant. We've been able to piece together exactly how the gladiators fought, died, even what they ate."

"That sounds so interesting," she said.

"You really should come to Ephesus," he said, and once again closed his eyes to the sun.

Queen Victoria

The guard motioned for her to come forward on the gangplank. All passengers had to undergo a security check every time they went on or off the ship. Cordelia inserted her cabin card into the machine, and her picture flashed on the screen. The guard waved her on as Sinclair went through the same procedure.

"Thanks," he said to the guard, and followed Cordelia to the elevator banks.

"Are you going up to your room?" he asked her as they walked into the lift.

"Yes. I'll meet you for dinner in about an hour?" Cordelia said. The elevator doors closed, and they were alone. Cordelia pushed the button for deck 7, and then realized he hadn't responded. She turned to look and found him staring at her, his face inscrutable.

"I'll meet you at dinner?" she repeated.

He still didn't reply, still looking at her with a very intense expression.

"What's wrong?" she asked.

He stepped toward her, pulled her to him, and kissed her. It came as a complete surprise! She had thought about kissing him many times over the past few days, and she wondered what it would be like. But now she discovered his kiss was even better than her fantasy. It was delightful!

He paused after the first kiss, his mouth inches from hers. It was as if he were expecting her to pull away. But she didn't, and instead turned her face up to him and closed her eyes, willing him to do it again. He pulled her close, this time kissing her more deeply. She melted into him, letting him know she liked what he was doing. And as she surrendered to the pleasure of it, she realized that her desire for him had been building all day, with every touch of his hand and every smile.

Just then the elevator chime announced their arrival on deck 7. Sinclair let go and backed away from her, assuming a decorous expression. The doors opened to reveal an elderly man waiting to get in. They all nodded politely, and Sinclair and Cordelia stepped out.

"Have a nice evening," the older gentleman said as he hobbled in with his cane. The elevator doors closed and they were alone in the main corridor.

Cordelia looked up at Sinclair, wondering what he would do. His stateroom was to the starboard side, and hers to the port. Normally they would part company right here. He walked up to her, brushed her hair back from her forehead, and spoke quietly.

"That was nice."

She looked up at him. "Mmmm." She nodded.

"We should try that again, only somewhere more private."

Without a doubt, he was inviting her to his room. She met his eyes, knowing that his suggestion demanded an immediate response. She hesitated. Her mind was flooded with reasons why she should refuse, but part of her wanted to go with him. It was harder for her to resist him than she had anticipated. There was an awkward silence as she struggled with the decision.

"Just so you know, I don't generally kiss girls in elevators," he explained. His eyes were still devouring her, waiting for her answer. She nodded.

"That's good to know," she said lamely. Again there was an uncomfortable pause. She just couldn't decide, so he finally spoke.

"Well, it's been a long day," he said. "I expect you want to get ready for dinner."

There was still a hint of hope in his voice. But she realized he was being a gentleman by giving her an out. She stepped back, looked at the floor, and then gazed back up at him. Their eyes connected.

"Yes," she said with regret. "I should get ready for dinner right now. That's really what I should do."

He smiled, ruefully, but there was humor and affection in his eyes.

"Okay, Cordelia," he said. "I'll see you later."

After he left her in the hall, Cordelia had started to her cabin, but suddenly she realized she hadn't checked her e-mail all day. Jim Gardiner had probably sent her an update, and she had a sudden urge to write to Susan and let her know the latest developments with Sinclair. Susan was so sensible when it came to things like this.

The computer room was empty. Even the attendant was gone, and at this hour most of the guests were dressing for dinner. Cordelia had a choice of consoles, so she took the nearest one and logged in. Susan had written to her already.

Delia, glad you are having fun!

Before I forget, a letter came for you from the government of Norway. Joel and I figured you were on such a roll, you were going to get the Nobel Prize or something. We opened it in case it was important.

They want you to contact them ASAP about some land in Svalbard. Jim Gardiner has all the details. Sorry we opened your mail, but we figured you were too busy to actually get back here anytime soon.

XX Susan

P.S. We miss you so much. Joel says Hi.

"We" miss you? Cordelia thought. Susan's relationship with Joel must be progressing rapidly. Cordelia clicked on the next note.

Dear Cordelia,

Sorry to interrupt your cruise, but I am receiving a good deal of correspondence about the deed to the Arctic Coal Mining Company land and I wanted to keep you informed.

I have done some research on the deed to the property in Svalbard. You will need physical possession of the deed to claim your rights to the land. But we cannot seem to locate the deed.

We are currently looking through Elliott Stapleton's papers. Solicitors in London are entrusted with a search of the London town house. We may also look into the estate of your great-great-grandfather's business partner, Sir James Skye Russell, in Oxfordshire, England, if need be. The deed could be there.

Percival Spence III, silent partner, is listed in later documents. But very little is known about him. We know he died during the great influenza epidemic of 1918 because his name appears on mortality records for Svalbard that year.

In any event, I will continue to pursue this matter. It would be a shame
to let that land go without a real effort to claim it. Try looking through the
journal to see if there is a reference to it.

Have a lovely time on the ship. Have a glass of champagne for me.

All my love, Jim Gardiner

There was one more message.

Cordelia Stapleton,

Give up the deed to the land in Svalbard or YOU WILL DIE. The seed
vault is the property of the world and cannot be owned by any one person. Give up your claim or you will regret it.

Citizens for World Survival

She stared at the words "YOU WILL DIE." Cordelia couldn't believe
the message was meant for her. *Why would someone want to kill her?* It
just didn't make sense. She had done nothing to harm anyone! Her first
impulse was to delete the message and make it go away. Instead, she kept
her head and forwarded it promptly to Jim Gardiner.

Back in her room, Cordelia was dressing mechanically, laying out a
black lace cocktail dress for dinner, but she was not concentrating on her
clothes. The threatening message had shaken her badly. Her hands were
trembling, and her nerves were jittery. She couldn't dispel the feeling of
danger. Even though she knew the ship was secure, she still felt terribly
vulnerable. What if the person who wanted to harm her was already on
board!

Of course, that was unlikely. The e-mail could have come from anywhere. In fact, she was probably *safer* on the ship. Only Joel, Susan, and
Jim Gardiner knew where she was. No one else knew she had been invited
on the cruise. She froze, staring at her own reflection in the mirror. No
one *except Sinclair*!

She sat down, her head spinning. What a horrifying thought! Could
she trust John Sinclair? After all, she had just met him and here he was,
with her day and night, watching her every move. Could *he* be involved in
this business with the Arctic Coal Mining Company? She shook her head

and tried to breathe away the fear that was rising in her. She closed her eyes and filled her lungs. But she felt as if she were suffocating.

She really didn't know him at all! Yet she had trusted him, telling him everything. She had even kissed him! But who was he, really? He had a terrible reputation as a womanizer, a real carouser. Why was he interested in her? She was nobody. She was not even that pretty. Well, not as pretty as a supermodel, anyway. What did he want from her? He never said. But he kept asking her to go with him to Ephesus. Wasn't that dangerous? Nobody knew that Sinclair was with her. She hadn't even mentioned him to Jim Gardiner.

She stood up and started pacing. *Stop being ridiculous!* Sinclair had nothing to do with this. This e-mail was a death threat. *A death threat!* How could it be possible that someone would want her dead? Cordelia sat down again to think, her knees wobbly.

She looked at her watch. Dinner was in an hour; she had to get dressed. She took off her robe and she stepped into the shower. The warm water didn't soothe her. She was too agitated. She reached for the shampoo, but washed her hair with bath gel by mistake. Then she dropped the shampoo and the conditioner, one after the other, and spent minutes groping around the bottom of the shower for them trying to keep the soap from stinging her eyes.

She was a nervous wreck. How would she get through dinner without dropping all the silverware and knocking over her wine? Sinclair would surely notice if she didn't calm down.

She walked to the mirror, pulled the towel off her head, and combed out her wet hair. Turning on the blow dryer at full volume, she could not stop thinking about the threatening e-mail. She tipped her head sideways and caught sight of the room reflected in the mirror. Something was wrong. She looked in the mirror again, whirled around, and turned off the dryer. She stared at the coffee table in disbelief. *The journal was gone!*

Cordelia abandoned drying her hair, put the cocktail dress back into the closet, and pulled out a navy blue jogging suit. She had to report the theft. Should she go to the purser? She dressed quickly, found her card key, and left the suite.

But standing in the corridor, she knew that there was only one course of action. She started down the narrow hall to John Sinclair's stateroom. Face your fears, she told herself. You need to get this straight, once and for all!

She walked to the starboard side of the ship and knocked on Sinclair's door and waited. Her stomach was in a knot. She could hear the shower running inside. Cordelia pounded on the door, harder. A steward came by and wished her a good evening, but she barely responded. Finally she heard footsteps and a hand on the inside door lever. Sinclair opened the door a crack to look out, and his eyes flashed surprise. When he pulled the door open wide, he was dressed only in a terry robe with a towel around his neck. He started to smile, but it faded quickly.

"*Cordelia!* What's the matter?"

"Can I come in? It's important," she said grimly.

"Absolutely," he said, stepping aside, holding the door open for her.

"I have to talk to you," she said.

"Yes, of course, but would you excuse me a second? I'll be right back," he apologized, retreating to his bedroom.

She could hear dresser drawers opening and slamming as if he were looking for his clothes in a hurry. She took a seat on the couch and looked around; his suite was much larger than hers. Out on the private balcony, rain hit the deck in a real squall. A bottle of champagne stood in an ice bucket, and there was a basket of fruit with a red BON VOYAGE ribbon on it. She leaned forward to sneak a peak at the card: *Have a great trip. All the best, Charles.* Two large white orchids were on the coffee table, along with a photocopy of an article on archaeology and a tan ostrich-skin-covered appointment book. She looked at the book but didn't touch it.

The door opened and Sinclair came out of the bedroom wearing a pair of jeans and a blue oxford shirt. His feet were still bare. He walked over to the couch and sat down, looking at her.

"You're upset," he said, staring at her. "Are you upset about . . . what just happened in the elevator?"

She couldn't meet his eyes, looked down at the floor, and found herself focused on his bare feet. Once again it crossed her mind that she hardly knew him. His feet were long and he had high arches. He had beautiful feet. Aristocratic feet. Nothing else came into her head, except here she was, sitting in the stateroom of a man she hardly knew, and he had bare feet. She had met him only a few days ago.

"What's the matter? You look absolutely spooked."

He was staring at her in puzzlement, buttoning the single-button cuffs. He smelled of soap and shampoo, and there were damp marks on the sleeve of his shirt where he hadn't dried off properly. His eyes moved quickly to her wet hair, the jogging suit, and her trembling hands.

"Cordelia, *what is wrong?*"

She stared at him.

"Why did you come on this ship?" she demanded.

His eyes widened.

"What do you mean?" he asked quietly.

"What do you want from me? *I need to know.*" Even to her own ears she sounded upset and angry.

Sinclair looked at her, perplexed.

"I thought I already told you. I wanted to get to know you better. I'm sorry. It was presumptuous of me . . ." He looked disturbed. He was still slowly buttoning the cuff of his shirt.

"Is that all?" she demanded.

He hesitated.

"I thought maybe we would spend some time together. And I was hoping that we would . . . get to know each other better. I realize it's all very sudden, but . . ." He shrugged. "I just thought I would take a chance on the remote possibility that you would be . . . interested in me."

His eyes were intense, troubled. Somehow that unhinged her even more, and she felt herself panic.

"I got an e-mail from someone threatening to kill me. And now the journal is gone. Did *you* have anything to do with it?" Her voice cracked.

His eyes widened.

"*Threatening to kill you?*" he said, deeply shocked. "I don't understand. *What* e-mail?"

Then she told him, blurting out her suspicions in a rambling tirade. Finally she stood up and stalked over to the glass doors of the suite and stood there with her back to him, staring out at the sea, trying to get control of herself.

"*I don't know what to do,*" she said out loud.

"Cordelia! *Stop this!*" His voice was horrified.

She turned and looked at him. He was watching her with shocked eyes, not moving, not speaking.

"How do I know that I can trust you?" she flung at him.

"Delia, be *reasonable!*" His eyes searched her face in bafflement. Somehow the use of her childhood nickname broke through to her. She saw how utterly paranoid she was being. She felt a flood of remorse. He must think she was insane! She faced him and tried to explain.

"John, don't you understand that I *had* to ask. *I had to know if you have anything to do with this.*"

"But how could you suspect *me?*" he said quietly, his eyes filled with hurt.

"John, I just panicked. I'm . . . *scared* . . ." she admitted, and her lips began to tremble.

His face softened, his eyes infinitely kind. He extended both arms to her in a mute gesture of reassurance, his eyes begging her to come to him. She couldn't resist. She flew into his arms, and he closed them over her in a tight hug.

"You poor darling, you poor darling." He held her, murmuring into her hair, "I know you're frightened. But you're *not* alone. I am here to help."

She finally broke down and cried into his chest, soaking his shirt, as he held her.

"*Shhhh. Shhhhhh,*" he coaxed. "It's all right."

Later, as she thought about it, this was the exact moment, when he held her and comforted her, that she began to rely on him. Not just trust him but *count* on him, the way she had never, ever counted on anyone before.

He didn't hesitate. He took charge without a word. He handed her a towel to dry her hair, called the ship's security, contacted the technology center to get the e-mail traced, ordered a pot of chamomile tea from room service, checked the name of her cabin steward and asked for an immediate interview, and inquired about security tapes from the corridor outside her room.

Within moments, a Cunard official in a very reassuring white uniform with blue braid was asking Cordelia for a complete accounting of what had happened. Sinclair said very little, but kept his arm around Cordelia's shoulders as she sat on the couch and gave her account. Half an hour later, it was over. They would report back with what they had found. The Cunard official left, and as the cabin door shut she slumped against Sinclair.

"My poor Delia, are you feeling better now?" he asked tenderly, tightening his arm around her. She sat up and looked him in the eye.

"John, that journal was so important to me. I just feel so . . ."

How could she explain how utterly bereft she felt? And now she was more than a little embarrassed about her tirade.

"I'm sorry, I don't think I was very fair to you earlier," she apologized.

"Don't mention it, perfectly understandable," he assured her, with a wry smile. "After all, I'm a *very* sinister guy."

She laughed, in spite of herself.

"Cordelia, I hate to ask this, after all we have just been through, but could you have misplaced it? In the library or on deck?"

"No. I know it was on the coffee table. I was reading it on the couch before bed."

"I see. But sometimes when you travel things get a bit disorganized."

"John, you don't understand. I have lived on a ship for the last ten years. I put things in the same place, out of habit, from living in close quarters. I don't misplace things," she said defensively.

"I understand," Sinclair said levelly. "We'll get the journal back."

"It's not *just* the journal. Someone wants to kill me."

"I know, Cordelia. No one is going to hurt you. They will have to get through me first," he said as if he meant it. "I won't let anyone near you. But if you don't mind, I'll have to keep you in my sight this evening."

"I won't mind that a bit." She smiled. "I shouldn't have accused you—"

"Don't . . ." he said, looking at her with great tenderness.

"I feel like a fool," she admitted.

He put his arm around her and didn't answer. He looked at his watch.

"How about this? It's nearly nine o'clock. We can order room service. You'll feel better if you get some food in you. Forget the fancy dress. You need to relax a bit."

Moments later, watching him order dinner on the phone, she felt calm. She sat on the couch, marveling at herself for letting him take charge. He was so totally in command of himself, he had brushed off her accusations without a second thought.

She watched him on the phone, in his jeans and blue cotton shirt, pacing, as he ordered entirely too much food. And suddenly she realized she was falling in love with him.

London

Paul Oakley sat with a cup of flavored coffee he had selected from the machine. It tasted like plastic with the artificial creamer, and he didn't really want to drink it, but he needed to think. It was eleven o'clock in the morning and he had been at the hospital all night.

The man in the ICU was unresponsive, and the autopsy tests on the first patient hadn't come back yet.

Should he come clean about the missing package? Miles still hadn't phoned back. That was strange. Miles had communicated frequently while he was excavating. He had even called to say the package had been sent.

But today nothing. No package, no Miles. The courier company was useless. Oakley had been on the phone with them all morning, and the electronic signature device had an illegible scrawl on it. They kept asking him for the tracking number on the receipt. And today he found out there was no receipt from the airport in Longyearbyen, although the desk clerk remembered a package going out. It was a goddamn mess.

Oakley stood up and dumped his coffee in the trash. It *was* possible these patients were dying of something else. He would just have to tough it out for another twenty-four hours until the lab tests came back and he knew for sure what they were dealing with. If the package hadn't turned up by then, he would alert the Health Protection Agency and the World Health officials. He hoped it wouldn't come to that; he didn't want to admit to breaking every law in the book by sending a live virus through the mail.

LuEsther T. Mertz Library,
New York Botanical Garden

Thaddeus Frost looked out the window of his office and could see the sparkling glass dome of the Victorian greenhouse over the tops of the trees. His office was at the top of the Beaux Arts building that housed the New York Botanical Garden's vast collection. The solid brick structure with twin towers was set into the rolling landscape. With all the architectural embellishments of the late Victorian era, the focal point was the beautiful bronze fountain, circa 1905, a cascading, sculpted panoply of sea nymphs and goddesses.

Frost loved looking at the fountain from his second-floor office window. He had chosen botany as his life's work, and was perfectly contented. Not only did he have access to a herbarium of thousands of specimens, but his real passion—the rare-book library—was just a few steps away. Any day of the week he could hold in his hands the original prints of Pierre-Joseph Redouté and Carl Linnaeus. He could peruse at will the full collection of hand-painted plates of Sir Joseph Banks, the botanist who sailed with Captain James Cook on his first voyage of exploration to the Pacific region in 1768.

On winter mornings, with the cold outside and the sun pouring through Frost's window, life was sublime. His office became as warm as a tropical jungle. Once a week, he would soak his orchids and feed them. And then he would make his own coffee, hand-grinding the extremely rare Indonesian *kopi luwak* beans and steeping them in a French press. With that kind of start, he figured, a week spent in the effort of saving the world's nearly extinct species of flora constituted a worthy and satisfying life.

But things were about to change. He walked to the door of his office and closed it, so no one could overhear. He dialed a cell phone on the other side of the world and waited for the connection. As he waited, he examined the Vanda orchids hanging in their pots. The deep purple flowers floated in the bright light from the window. It was a notoriously delicate variety and not everyone could grow them. But Frost had the touch. He sat up straight as the call connected.

"Mr. Sinclair, this is Thaddeus Frost of Bio-Diversity Trust," he said. "You don't know me but I got your number from your Monaco office."

"What can I do for you?"

"Do you know the whereabouts of Cordelia Stapleton? We have been trying to reach her. Your office said you might know how to get hold of her."

"What do you want with her?"

"We need to speak to her about a serious matter."

"What about? If I may inquire," said Sinclair belligerently.

"The International Seed Vault."

"Surely that is a matter for her lawyer."

"No doubt. But we need to talk about the deed to the land in the Arctic."

"Look, I can't speak for her. I would be happy to pass along a message."

"She is in grave danger. We need to speak as soon as possible. What is your next port of call? I'd like to meet up."

"What makes you think she would agree to meet you?" Sinclair sounded testy.

"If I know where you are, other people do too. Federal authorities have been in touch with me about a certain e-mail. She needs to take care."

"How do we know you have Cordelia's best interests in mind?"

"Feel free to have the FBI verify my identity. Come with Ms. Stapleton if you like. But we need to meet, and soon. Where are you putting in next?"

"It's no secret. You could look on the itinerary. We are in Kuşadası, Turkey, tomorrow."

"I'll be there. Can we all meet?"

"I have to think about it."

"Don't think too long. There are quite a few people on the ship who would like to have a conversation with Ms. Stapleton, and they are not as pleasant as we are."

"I'm going to check you out," Sinclair said cautiously. "If I agree, where do we meet?"

"I'll be in Kuşadası before you dock. I'll be in touch."

"That's tomorrow afternoon."

"I'll be there."

"Where are you now?"

"I'll be there tomorrow."

Thaddeus Frost hung up the phone. He picked up his duffel bag and walked slowly down the stairs, past the beautiful fountain, down the winding path to the exit of the Botanical Garden. He hated to leave his orchids, but it was time.

Queen Victoria

Cordelia sat down at the e-mail console while Sinclair loitered in the doorway of the computer center. He had insisted on dogging her every step since last night, even walking her back to her cabin and meeting her at her room before breakfast. Frankly, she was relieved. She still couldn't shake off the feeling of danger on the ship. She logged in and clicked on her e-mail account.

> Dear Cordelia,
>
> I have forwarded your last e-mail to the federal authorities and they are tracking it. In the meantime, be careful!! Do you want me to come and meet the ship at the next port of call? I am very concerned.
>
> Also, in regard to the deed, interest continues over the land rights in Svalbard. The government of Norway wants to set up a meeting. The Bio-Diversity Trust, a nonprofit organization that runs the seed vault, has also contacted us repeatedly.
>
> We still have not been able to locate the deed to the land. As you know, the physical deed is necessary in order to proceed on any of these offers. It has not turned up in the town house in London, nor with any known papers in the estate of Elliott Stapleton.
>
> Please take care. Let me know if you need anything. See you in London, if not sooner.
>
> With love, Jim Gardiner

Cordelia sat chewing on her fingernail. She read her first message, clicked on Reply, and wrote:

Dear Jim,

I have to admit the e-mail shook me up. But there is no need for you to meet me. I have been meaning to tell you that John Sinclair of the Herodotus Foundation is also here on the ship and has been helping me.

Bio-Diversity Trust actually contacted us yesterday, and we are meeting with the director, Thaddeus Frost, when we land in Turkey. I'll tell you about the meeting when I see you in London next week. And don't worry, I won't sign anything before showing it to you first.

I just can't believe all this interest in this land. I am beginning to think maybe it's better if the deed is never found.

Love, Cordelia

Cordelia opened her last e-mail. It was from Susan. The tone was distinctly sober.

Delia,

We have a big problem here: your cabin was ransacked by somebody. They broke in when we were out to dinner. We called the police immediately and they are investigating. I put everything back, and there doesn't seem to be anything missing. But the box with your parents' photos and papers was opened and the contents scattered everywhere. I'm sorry to have to tell you this upsetting news. I know how important these things are to you.

I called Jim Gardiner and told him about it. I figured you would want me to do that.

Call me if you need me. Joel sends his love.

Love, Susan

Grand Bazaar, Kuşadası, Turkey

The market square in Kuşadası was filled with tourists perusing the wares. The cacophony of Turkish street vendors was an exotic touch. Rugs were everywhere, a kaleidoscope of colors hanging from shop doorways. The open-fronted stores led off into cavernous back rooms, where stacks of carpets were piled waist high.

"Please, sir, come inside, sir." Sinclair looked at the man, who was clearly the proprietor of the shop. He looked respectable and prosperous, with a gold pen in his jacket pocket. Sinclair stepped into the store, holding on to Cordelia's arm.

"Give us a moment to look," Sinclair said. "We'll let you know if we see something."

The man drifted away. A young boy came by, holding a round brass tray with two steaming cups of apple tea.

"Compliments, sir, lady." They accepted the beverages and lingered in the store, looking over the carpets.

"We have a couple of minutes before we are supposed to meet Frost in that courtyard across the square," Sinclair indicated, sipping his tea. "I want to keep my eye on the entrance before we walk in there."

"All right," Cordelia answered. The pungent tea was restoring her. She had been feeling shaky all morning, worried about the scheduled meeting.

"We will be fine," he said. "It's broad daylight. We are meeting in the middle of a public space. I called the federal authorities in the States this morning. Thaddeus Frost checked out. He's legit."

She gave a tight smile.

The proprietor was back with two young teenagers. They began flinging the rugs on the floor and shaking them open. The man extolled the fine quality of each carpet as it was unrolled. Cordelia and Sinclair watched the performance. Carpet after carpet was laid at their feet.

"Pick one," said Sinclair.

"What?"

"Pick one. It's easier. I'll buy it and we can get out of here."

"I don't know which to pick."

"Pick any one. Pick the next one they roll out."

Cordelia pointed at a beautiful beige-and-persimmon prayer rug. "That one."

"Madam has excellent taste," said the proprietor. "I can give it to you for the special price—discount, you understand, discount."

He was punching numbers on a calculator and held it up for them to see. "Ten thousand dollars."

"That was an expensive twenty minutes," Cordelia said as they rushed across the square to the Garden Court.

"Well, I managed to haggle him down, so it wasn't that bad. Besides, I needed a rug for my place in Ephesus. Unless *you* want it?" he offered.

"On a boat? A five-thousand-dollar rug? You must be joking."

They walked through an archway and into a courtyard. Coming from the din of the bazaar, the plaza was an oasis of calm. Café chairs and tables were placed in the shaded spot, for lunch service. Palm trees stood in large stone containers and a small fountain burbled, the sound of running water creating a relaxing atmosphere.

The courtyard was empty at this time of the morning except for a tall, rangy man sitting at a table nursing a Turkish coffee. Extraordinarily striking, he had dark olive skin and blue black hair that was thick and tousled. He could have come from any part of the world. A perfectly cropped stubble hid his features. He was dressed in appalling taste, as if to conceal his stunning looks: baggy shorts and a mud-colored T-shirt. His Birkenstock sandals were an attempt to replicate the look of a classic expat.

But something countered the visual impression of the awkward clothing. This was no corporate middle manager living abroad. He looked entirely too fit. The way he raised his arm as he consulted his watch was graceful and powerful. He looked at them expectantly.

"Thaddeus Frost?" said Sinclair.

"Yes," the man replied. "Would you like to talk here, or shall we go somewhere more private?"

Vlad and Anna surveyed the entrance of the courtyard from the vantage point of the Kuşadası Grand Bazaar.

"Where are they going?"

"Wait here, I am going to check something," Anna said, darting into the carpet store.

"Excuse me," said Anna. "I am the personal assistant to Mr. Sinclair. I need to make sure his carpet is shipped to the correct residence."

The owner of the shop looked Anna up and down.

"You are Mr. Sinclair's personal assistant?"

"Yes, I am, and he just instructed me to make sure this is delivered properly. I need to see the shipping information."

The owner of the shop showed the bill of sale to Anna.

"He said he wanted it sent locally," the shop owner said defensively. "He just told me that himself."

Anna's eyes raked over the address.

"Excellent. See that you ship it out as soon as possible."

"No cause for worry," said the proprietor. "I have it written down."

"Thank you," said Anna briskly. "Mr. Sinclair appreciates it very much." She came out of the shop and pulled Vlad along the alleyway.

"He sent his rug to an address in Ephesus. Give me a pencil and paper so I can write it down before I forget it."

Vlad searched the inside of his jacket breast pocket for a notebook and pen, and Anna jotted it down quickly.

"Why would he buy a rug?" Anna mused.

"I want to know who they are meeting. That's a better question." Vlad lit a JPS cigarette and blew the smoke out in irritation. "We need to keep them in sight. I can't see a thing from here," he complained.

"The café over there will give us a clear line of sight to the entrance. We can wait there. Besides, I want a Turkish coffee." Anna clacked her way across the plaza on her high-heeled sandals.

✳

Sinclair settled into an armchair and looked around the office of the Bodrum Import/Export Company. The room smelled of new carpet. Thaddeus Frost said he had borrowed the office from a firm he was associated with. At least that was the story.

A ceiling fan whirred overhead and the rough plaster walls were newly whitewashed. Whoever put this office together had just done it. Everything looked new. There were beautiful kilims on the walls, carved wooden furniture, an antique brass lamp. The wooden shutters were open.

Outside in the courtyard, children were kicking a soccer ball around, creating the sound of normalcy. The noise of their play relaxed him. Sinclair hadn't realized how on edge he had been.

"Sorry about the carpet fumes," Frost said. "You know they've proved that the styrene-butadiene carpet adhesive can have toxic side effects. I kept the window open."

"It's fine," said Cordelia.

"Cigarette?" Frost offered an ebony box.

"No thanks," said Sinclair.

Frost took one for himself, lit it efficiently, and exhaled, blowing the smoke toward the window. His movements were controlled and deliberate. When he spoke he had a quiet voice, and beautiful manners, but underneath the polish he projected the clear impression he was a very tough guy—not someone to cross.

"What can we do for you?" asked Sinclair.

Frost barely looked at him; his attention was on Cordelia.

"You undoubtedly got our e-mails," Frost said.

"Yes," she answered.

"We wanted to talk to you in person. This deed is of vital importance."

"Well," interrupted Sinclair, "you are aware that Miss Stapleton has not committed to any course of action regarding the deed."

Frost looked sideways at Sinclair with some irritation.

"We would like to convince Ms. Stapleton that the best policy is to keep the vault in neutral territory." He turned back to Cordelia. "That is what I am here to do."

"I see," she said.

"Let me play devil's advocate for a second," said Sinclair, reaching forward to pick up the carved lighter. "Why not give the deed back to Norway?" He flicked the lighter open and the flame sprang up, blue. He put the lighter back. He picked up a pencil and began to doodle on the legal pad on the desk.

Frost's nostrils flared in anger and his eyes hardened.

"Norway, Russia, the United States, and Canada have been increasingly upping their stakes in the region. It's a land grab at this point." He turned to Cordelia again. "You must be aware that the Russians have claimed the pole."

"Yes," said Cordelia. "I followed Alexandrov's expedition."

She spoke firmly, but her body language relayed her nerves. Her shoulders were rounded and her hands were clutched together in her lap. Sinclair didn't look at her, and kept drawing circles, then dissecting them into eight parts with lines. He listened, seemingly absorbed in his task.

"You know the Russians are petitioning the United Nations for sovereignty of the pole. And that would involve control of the seabed," continued Frost.

"How can they do that?" Sinclair asked Cordelia.

"A UN Convention says no country can claim jurisdiction over the North Pole. It's an international site and the geological structure of the seabed doesn't match the continental shelf of any of the surrounding countries," she answered.

"So how can they claim the pole?" he asked.

"The Russians are making their claim based on Alexandrov's expedition to the seabed. The UN has agreed to review it."

Frost cut in. "By international law every country controls resources under its coastal waters for up to two hundred miles offshore. The Russians are claiming another million square miles of the Arctic, saying the underwater ridges are a continuation of Russia's continental shelf. They have made two expeditions to try to prove it: one to the Mendeleyev underwater chain in 2005 and another to the Lomonosov Ridge just recently."

"It's about the minerals and other resources," added Cordelia. "Natural gas, oil, tin, gold. When the ice cap melts, the seabed will become more accessible. In the next ten years this area may be all open water, and everyone will want the mining rights."

"Mining rights? In the Arctic?"

"Yes," said Cordelia. "Right now, commercial mining companies are trying to locate mineral deposits on the seafloor. It's a potentially lucrative source of all kinds of rare minerals as well as oil and gas."

"Which brings us to the seed vault again," said Frost, leaning back in his chair. "This property would be a foothold for Russia or Norway to claim more territory in the region."

"Forgive me, but if the seed vault was built by Norway, and Cordelia owns the land, it seems to me it's a matter between Cordelia and the government of Norway," pointed out Sinclair. He stopped doodling, his pencil poised as if to take notes on the answer.

"We believe she should give it to the Bio-Diversity Trust," said Frost. "That way it would be neutral."

"How neutral?" asked Cordelia.

"Bio-Diversity Trust helps all countries prepare, package, and transport their seeds for storage. The vault has three separate areas, and each one can store a million and a half seeds. They are being kept in case of a world catastrophe—to maintain biodiversity if there is some cataclysmic event. We don't take sides."

"Let's stop the fiction, shall we?" said Sinclair. "Bio-Diversity Trust may be neutral, but you don't really work for them. You work for the U.S. government."

Frost coolly blew smoke toward the window.

"We believe it's important to keep the vault politically neutral. As a scientist, I am sure you can understand that," Frost said to Cordelia.

Cordelia started to answer, but Sinclair cut her off.

"We understand more than you think," he said.

"We especially feel it's important to keep this property away from the Russians, because of their territorial ambitions in the region," Frost explained to Cordelia, ignoring Sinclair's outburst.

"Other than their undersea expedition, how else could they claim the land?" asked Cordelia.

"That is where the deed comes into it. If your deed is lost, they will file for sovereignty based on the claims of Russian miners who were there as early as 1890," explained Frost.

"So I have to produce the deed to prove the land belongs to me?" said Cordelia.

"Yes. The original land records were destroyed in a fire in Oslo in 1954. So your deed is the document of record."

"And if I produce it that proves I own the land and can do with it what I want?" asked Cordelia.

"Yes. And if you *can't* produce it, Norway will reassert its sovereign right to the land under eminent domain. And the Russians would fight it in court," added Frost.

Sinclair realized Thaddeus Frost was talking as if he knew the deed was missing.

"Anybody else in on this?" asked Sinclair.

"Sure. You have the crazies," said Frost. "There is a doomsday cult that thinks God will punish the world if it stockpiles seeds."

"You *know* about them?" asked Sinclair angrily. "Is that who threatened Cordelia?"

"*Of course* we know about them." Frost was acidly polite.

"So the answer is, according to you, we just get the deed and give it to Uncle Sam," Sinclair said flatly.

"My advice is to give the deed to Bio-Diversity Trust," said Frost emphatically, looking Cordelia in the eye. "But I am authorized to say certain U.S. government organizations would greatly appreciate it if you could see the issue from our point of view."

Sinclair threw his pencil down. He looked at Frost with open hostility. Cordelia tried to answer, but Sinclair cut her off.

"The *hell* she will! I won't have her pressured like this." Sinclair's voice echoed loudly in the sparse office.

"*Look!*" Cordelia burst out furiously. "I'm not going to sit here while you treat me and my land like a bargaining chip! I'll do what I *want* with my land, when I make up my mind."

There was tense silence. The sound of children playing filled the room. Sinclair took a deep breath and spoke more reasonably.

"What assurances of safety can you give her?"

Thaddeus Frost took another cigarette out of the ebony box and lit it, squinting his eyes against the smoke.

"Assurance of safety?" he said thoughtfully. "Yes, I think it can be arranged."

Cordelia was walking rapidly across the street, ignoring traffic. Two cars swerved to avoid her, both blasting their horns. Sinclair stood on the curb, helpless, cut off by traffic, watching her run away from him. She had a good lead and kept going, toward the bazaar, her strides abrupt and angry. He watched her disappear down the crowded street, her dark hair flapping as she moved. Sinclair found an opening in the traffic and sprinted across.

"Cordelia," he shouted. "Wait. Stop!"

He saw her turquoise shirt moving among the shoppers, weaving in and out of the tourists. Clusters of people blocked his way as they looked at the carpets and brass goods in the alleyway.

"Cordelia!" Sinclair dodged like a soccer player. He finally caught up with her and grabbed her arm.

"Wait," he said. "What is wrong?"

She turned, furious.

"How *dare* you!"

"How dare I *what*? What did I do?"

"How dare you speak for me! I can handle my own affairs."

Sinclair stepped back, stunned.

"I was trying to help," he explained. "Cordelia, how can you think I was doing anything but acting in your best interest? *I was protecting you!*"

"You were not. You were taking over."

"I *wasn't* taking over," Sinclair said. "I just wasn't letting that guy bamboozle my girl. That's all."

"Your *girl*?" she spat out, wrenching her arm away from him. "Your *girl*?"

"OK, I'm sorry. That didn't come out right."

"You're damn right it didn't!"

"Cordelia," he said in frustration, "one minute you want me to help, the next minute you are angry when I do."

She glowered and didn't respond.

"Let's take a minute to calm down, shall we?" Sinclair pleaded. "Can we just get a coffee and talk? There is a café there, just beyond that square."

They walked across to the tables. She sat in icy silence as he ordered. Then she spoke.

"I don't want you to push people around on my account," she said. "I have been taking care of my own business for a long time."

"I'm sorry," said Sinclair. "You're perfectly right."

"*I understand* what is going on here, I am not a child," she fumed.

"Of course," he agreed.

"Just because that guy in there thought he was being slick doesn't mean I was buying it. You never let me open my mouth!"

"That was wrong of me," Sinclair admitted.

"You kept cutting me off. Don't *do* that, John, I am not going to stand for it!"

"Understood, you are perfectly right," Sinclair said.

She sat there for a moment, her face set. She was still fuming, but then, inexplicably, her mouth cracked into a wobbly half smile.

"Did you just say, 'I'm sorry. You're perfectly right'?" she asked.

He nodded, puzzled.

"Whoever trained you did a good job. Hats off to that woman."

He smiled back in relief.

"I learned a long time ago, in certain circumstances it's better to just shut up and agree."

Finally she smiled. They sat quietly for a moment while the waiter served the coffee in little china cups. When he left, Cordelia leaned forward, taking a sugar packet and tearing it open, but she didn't pour it in. She held the sugar, suspended in thought. Sinclair stirred his coffee and let her think.

"John," she said after a few moments. "I'm sorry."

"I didn't mean to come off as controlling back there," he replied.

"The truth of the matter is, I *don't* know what to do," she admitted.

He reached for her arm to stop her.

"I know, Delia. It's a very complicated situation."

She poured the sugar into her cup and started stirring.

"John, that guy gave me the creeps."

"Thaddeus Frost? Yes, your instincts are right. He's a spook. But the good news is, he's on our side and is looking out for us now."

"Spook?"

"Undercover, for the U.S. government."

Cordelia sipped her coffee, still thinking. "I just *hated* the fact that we had to make this sort of devil's bargain with him."

"For the moment, it seems like our only option. But we didn't promise him the deed. We just asked for protection from his agency."

Sinclair sipped his coffee, watching her face. She sighed deeply.

"John," Cordelia said, looking up at him. "It's hard for me to rely on people. I fight it. I fight closeness and drive people away when it gets too . . . I really have never been able . . ."

"That was a tough meeting. Your nerves are raw. You've been threatened."

She took a sip of coffee and closed her eyes.

"This tastes *great*. I really needed this. I'm sorry we fought."

Sinclair smiled. He began to drink his coffee, more relaxed now.

"Listen, if that is the best you can do in a fight, forget it," he joked. "That doesn't count as a real fight. I'm more used to talons. You know, real hand-to-hand stuff. If you want to fight with me, you need some serious combat training."

She finally laughed. "What kind of girls do you date, anyway?"

"A bad lot," he said jokingly. "A bad, baaaaad lot."

They sat for a moment, but the silence was different now. A companionable feeling settled over them.

"Try to let me in, Cordelia . . . I want to be here for you."

"Being alone all these years, I needed to rely on myself."

"I'm sure it took a toll on you," agreed Sinclair.

"It did. The other kids had their parents when they got the sniffles, or if a teacher was mean to them. I had to work it all out on my own."

Sinclair ventured to put his hand over hers on the table. She let it stay there for a moment and then moved away, on the pretext of picking up the spoon. He pretended not to notice.

"Of course, I could always call Jim Gardiner. But for emotional things, I just learned to wall myself in. It's hard for me to break out."

"Well, you've come a long way if you can recognize that. Few people can admit it to themselves."

"I believe in being honest with myself . . . and with others."

"Thanks for warning me," he joked.

She gave him a smile.

"Come on, have you finished that thimble of coffee there?" Sinclair asked. "We have a half hour before all the shore excursions return to the ship. Let's shop a bit. Women tell me shopping is good therapy for stress." She smiled. He held her chair for her as she collected her purse.

"Let me buy you some earrings to go with that pretty shirt," he said. He took her by the hand and led her over to a jewelry shop window. "What do you like?"

"I don't need jewelry," she said.

"Sure you do. What woman doesn't need jewelry?"

"I never really shop for jewelry. It always seemed like such a tough thing to do—to walk into a jewelry store and buy yourself something. So I never wore any."

She looked in the window as she talked to him.

"After my parents died, all the family jewelry was sold," she explained. "Mom had a red Moroccan jewelry box embossed with gold." She continued looking at the display. "She had a necklace that she would always let me try on—a family heirloom from my great-great-grandmother Isabelle. She said I could wear it for my wedding."

Her tone was bleak. Sinclair turned to look at her.

"So that's gone too?"

"Sold."

"Oh, Delia," he said. He took her hand and led her into the jewelry store.

Queen Victoria

An hour later, Cordelia was fast asleep on the aft deck and Sinclair was stretched out on a lounge chair next to her. He looked at her curled up in the warm Turkish sun. Her feet were bare, her sandals on the deck next to her. She had dropped off quickly, but he found it impossible to nap after the nerve-shattering day.

She seemed so fragile—clearly the loss of the journal was bringing up new emotions. And then there was the death threat. Imagine her thinking he was stalking her, and meant to harm her. She must have been completely out of her mind with fear.

Where was all this going, anyway? He was crazy about her. That much was obvious. He just turned his life upside down, abandoned everything, and she still seemed so reserved. Maybe she was smarter than he was, and didn't want to get involved too quickly. But his feelings for Cordelia were growing by the day. He looked over at her and sighed. What a wonderful girl.

She wore her white jeans and turquoise tunic, but now, nestled in the hollow of her neck, was a delicate gold necklace with the beautiful enameled "evil eye" symbol so popular in Turkey.

The salesman in the jewelry store had explained that it was a *nazar*, an amulet from ancient mythology that protects against envy, the covetous "evil eye" of others. In the store, she had suddenly turned to Sinclair.

"John, I think I could use one of these."

"Great idea!" he had agreed.

Together they had selected a beautiful 18-karat chain and hanging from it a small enameled blue, black, and white oval charm—a stylized image of an eye.

"Turn around," he had said. "Allow me to put this on you. For luck."

She held her dark hair up so he could fasten it around her neck. He fumbled a bit with the clasp but managed to get it eventually, fighting the urge to bend forward and kiss the nape of her neck.

London

At the Royal London Hospital, Oakley fired up his computer and checked his e-mail. There was a message from his secretary, along with a clipping from *Svalbardposten*, Longyearbyen, Norway's weekly newspaper. That was unusual.

Was it an article about the dig? Oakley was still deeply concerned that Miles had not been in touch. There really was no explanation as to why he wasn't back yet, unless he had found something incredible. Yet why no phone call? And the package of samples was still missing.

Oakley opened the e-mail and froze.

"Oh my God," he said in horror. *"Oh my God."*

The headline seared across his brain: "British Scientist Killed by Polar Bear." Miles had been attacked by a polar bear and was dead! It happened in the graveyard in Longyearbyen. Paul doubled over, groaning in anguish. He put his hands over his mouth and rocked back and forth, moaning, staring at the screen, unwilling to believe it. He could not comprehend the horror of it.

Miles was his dearest friend and colleague. Dead. Oakley pushed away the mental picture of what it would be like to meet that kind of death. The image of his friend's face kept flashing through his mind. When was the last time he saw him? He had been smiling, confident of their expedition. That was the last impression he had of him.

How many years had they worked together? Their real connection came when they had worked on SARS in 2003, and avian flu in 2004. But they really bonded, and spoke daily, after the first human-to-human transmission of bird flu in Thailand. It was then they both realized it was a race against time. After that, Miles had had a major breakthrough, cultivating the SARS virus in a containment laboratory in London. He was brilliant.

Miles was dead, but with that knowledge came a new certainty. It was now clear why the samples had not turned up—because Miles had been killed by the bear. The samples probably were never sent. But if they had not been sent, where were the samples now? And that still didn't explain the patients at the Royal London Hospital.

Queen Victoria

Cordelia floated in the hydrotherapy pool of the *Queen Victoria* spa and let the power jets massage her neck and shoulders. The bubbles in the immersion pool tickled as they passed over her limbs. Suddenly, suspended in the water, she was reminded of the time she used to spend swimming in the ocean, after work. It was a nice memory. She lay back and relaxed.

When she looked up, Anna was coming toward her. Her voluptuous figure was barely covered by a hot-pink sequined bikini. Cordelia didn't know a lot about sequined bikinis, but this one didn't look seaworthy to her. Anna lowered herself by the ladder into the bubbling pool and bounced over to Cordelia.

"Hello, dahling."

Cordelia smiled a quiet hello. Anna lay back and let the bubbles massage her neck.

"This is great. Almost as good as sex."

Cordelia let the comment pass. There was an awkward silence between the two of them until Anna spoke again.

"This man is sexy, Cordelia, this John Sinclair."

Anna's angular face was grinning above the foaming water.

"He's a good friend," Cordelia said, edging away.

"He's only a friend?" asked Anna. "That's too bad. I see the way he looks at you. He wants more."

"He's a friend," said Cordelia again, pointedly.

"Have you known him long?" asked Anna. "When did you decide to take this cruise with him?"

Cordelia swam over to the ladder. She'd had about enough of this line of questioning.

"He's a friend of my family," she lied.

Cordelia climbed out of the pool and headed to the eucalyptus steam room. She pulled open the wooden door and the smell of the eucalyptus wafted out. It was heavenly. As she entered into the dense steam, there appeared to be only one other person in the steam sauna. Cordelia walked deep into the tiled room and sat on the warm bench. Her muscles relaxed in the heat, and the eucalyptus opened up her sinuses. She closed her eyes and gave herself over to it. After a moment, the other person stood up as if to walk out, but then turned and stood in front of the door. Cordelia opened her eyes, and through the steam she could barely see the lumpy shape of Gjertrud, in a floral swim suit.

"Oh, hello," said Cordelia. "I didn't recognize you at first."

"I need to talk to you," said Gjertrud quickly. "I'm from the government of Norway. I came here to ask you to meet with us over the deed to the land in Svalbard."

Cordelia stood up. What was this! Gjertrud was a government agent? The shock hit her. *She was being followed on the ship.* Suddenly she felt very vulnerable. Then anger flared up. How *dare* they pressure her like this!

"I don't want to discuss it. Especially in here," said Cordelia firmly. She flushed with anger. In the tiny closed sauna, her breathing became constricted. She was dripping sweat, and she wiped her face with a towel.

"We know there are other people on the ship who are trying to steal the deed. We only want to protect you," said Gjertrud. Her manner was completely changed, and her tone was much more forceful than she had ever sounded before.

"You might have a good reason for wanting the deed," said Cordelia. "But I don't think this is an appropriate place to discuss it."

"We'll set up a meeting. Name a time. We can do it here on the ship." Gjertrud's tone softened to a plea. She was still blocking the door.

Suddenly the room was intensely close and entirely too hot. Cordelia felt like she would faint. She pushed past Gjertrud and flung open the door. Rushing out into the cool air, she nearly knocked Anna over.

London

The ICU at the Royal London Hospital was assembled in full force. Patient number two was dying, lungs filled with blood, foaming at the mouth. In the enclosed room, severe respiratory distress sounded like a freight train.

The Health Protection Agency doctor stood back in weary resignation. He had been there for nearly forty-eight hours, and now *two* patients were fatal.

"Get Oakley on the phone. I want to talk to him about these lab tests. I can't figure this thing out."

"We called him already, Oakley is on his way," the nurse replied.

"Human-to-human transmission of H5N1 is very, very rare. It requires close contact, people in the same family living together."

The doctor looked at the nurse as if she had the answer.

"How do a young prosperous Russian man and a vagrant contract the same disease? It couldn't be human-to-human transmission. It defies logic."

The doctor riffled through his clipboard charts. "Oakley better get here quick. This looks *just* like the 1918 pandemic. And *that's* been extinct for nearly a century."

Queen Victoria

Sinclair sat in the main lounge waiting for Cordelia. He watched the cruise director shaking her hand in farewell. As of this morning, there was no sign of the journal. They hadn't stopped looking for it since Cordelia reported it missing two days ago. They were turning the ship inside out. Yesterday they had gone through every piece of dirty linen in the laundry in the hope that it had been scooped into the laundry cart when the bedding was changed. Sinclair couldn't imagine the logistics of sorting through the used sheets of a thousand passengers.

Cunard had also been incredibly efficient about the e-mail threat. The electronic message had been forwarded to the police in the States, and a full investigation was under way.

Sinclair mentally reviewed his plan for the next few days. Cordelia needed to get off this ship; she was too visible. He had decided Ephesus was a good hideout until they were scheduled to meet Jim Gardiner in London.

He envisioned the steep road leading up to his house and concluded that the place was perfectly situated. The countryside near it was almost impassable, so it was very defensible. People could not easily approach on foot. The steep incline would require hand-over-hand climbing, and even then it involved dangerous footholds on uncertain terrain. As for vehicles, the narrow road was clearly visible from his front veranda. Any vehicle could be heard from at least a mile away, as its motor would reverberate off the cliffs all around. There was no way anyone could approach without being noticed.

Cordelia came over, putting her passport in her bag.

"All done. We just leave our luggage outside the cabin door after midnight, and it will be delivered to the quay in the morning."

Sinclair didn't move. He stayed hunkered down in the armchair. Sitting there for a moment, he just wanted to enjoy the sight of her.

"Aren't you hungry?" she asked. "It's almost seven. We need to dress for dinner."

"You really like all this formal dressing for dinner, don't you?"

"After tonight I won't get much chance to dress up. Soon I'll be back on the Alvin, in a T-shirt and jeans all day."

As she said it, her voice caught in midsentence. Their eyes met. She quickly looked away, and there was a moment of strained silence. He ignored the implication of her comment and began gathering up his things. She took him by the hand.

"Let's see what's on the menu tonight," she said, dragging him to his feet. He came willingly.

As coffee was being served, Sinclair looked at the group around the table. Who knew who these characters were? The seat for Gjertrud was empty. Now Sinclair knew why. She didn't dare show her face after the sauna incident. But Norway was not about to give up on the deed. He was sure Gjertrud would be the first of many to try to talk Cordelia into giving the land to Norway.

Sinclair looked at the others with new suspicion. Who were these Russians, anyway? Anna was eating escargots with an obscene voluptuousness. Vlad was in the process of ordering a bottle of astronomically expensive cognac. Joyce Chin was spooning up flan from the spa menu, very smug in her brittle New York self-confidence. Was she trying to get the deed for financial gain? All she ever talked about was money. Sinclair even had suspicions about Bob and Marlene. Of them all, however, the Texas couple seemed the most innocuous—almost like legitimate vacationers.

Tomorrow he and Cordelia would be getting off the *Queen Victoria*. But they were not going to tell anyone about their plans. There was no way to guess who else was on Cordelia's trail.

As they were walking out of the Britannia Restaurant, Sinclair leaned close to her ear to pose a question.

"Want to take a walk on deck?"

Cordelia turned, delighted. "Of course!"

Sinclair took her arm and started toward the elevators.

"I have to say, I'm going to miss the ship when we leave tomorrow."

Cordelia looked at him with a rueful smile. "To think I was angry with you for coming."

"Were you? I had no idea," Sinclair deadpanned.

Cordelia smiled affectionately at him.

"Give me a moment to go back to my room; I want to change into flat shoes. I'll meet you on deck three."

"Nothing doing. I'm not letting you out of my sight."

"Then come with me. I really don't want to have someone creep up on me again."

"I won't let *that* happen, don't worry."

"I have to admit, I was pretty unnerved by Gjertrud in the spa," she said as she carded her door and pushed it open. "But nothing is going to happen to me in my own cab—"

She stopped suddenly.

He was standing behind her and couldn't see into the room. But he saw her back stiffen. She didn't speak, just stepped aside and pointed to the coffee table. The journal had been returned!

Izmir, Turkey

Malik was parked on the quay at Izmir when they disembarked the *Queen Victoria*. Sinclair spotted his skinny arm waving out the window, and directed the porter over to the ramshackle van. As they approached, Malik looked at Cordelia in surprise.

"Malik, this is Cordelia Stapleton," Sinclair said while he paid the porter. "Cordelia, this is my assistant, Malik."

Malik reached across to open the door for her, but a dog bounded into the front seat.

"And my dog, Valkyrie," added Sinclair.

"Kyrie, get in the back," said Malik.

The Norwegian elkhound looked at him and back at Cordelia.

"Kyrie, in the back," commanded Sinclair, but the dog shot out the door. Sinclair tried to get a hand on her collar without success. The dog was running circles around him. He heaved the bags into the car, raising a cloud of dust.

"Malik, do you ever clean this thing?"

"No sir."

Sinclair climbed into the backseat, dusting off his pants. The dog followed and sat on his lap, and tried to lick his ear. Cordelia watched from the front seat, laughing.

"She missed you."

Malik turned and gave Sinclair a wink, clearly referring to Cordelia.

"Let's get going," said Sinclair pointedly, pushing the dog off again. "Yes sir."

The van lurched forward and they bounced around on the cobblestones of the dock. Cordelia put her arm over the seat back to talk to Sinclair, the wind from the open window blowing her hair.

"Why do you think they returned the journal, John? Do you think there was any chance the cabin steward took it by accident and was too embarrassed to admit it?"

The dog was now panting into Sinclair's face. Sinclair gave up trying to clear himself of the animal and rested his arms on her back.

"I don't think so, Delia. I think someone else traveling on the ship stole the journal. And didn't find what they were looking for."

The air was getting more arid, and the roads were steeper now, winding up into the hills. Dust wafted in the open windows of the van. Cordelia started coughing, but waved her hand at Sinclair to let him know she was OK.

"Malik, do we have any bottled water?"

"No sir."

"The dust is bad," Sinclair apologized. "I think I'm used to it. You can rinse off when we get there."

"How long will we stay?"

"A few days. It's so remote nobody will look for you here. I want to get you out of sight."

He reached forward and put his hand over hers.

"We'll stay in Ephesus while we go through the journal, word by word."

"I have it right here," said Cordelia, opening the flap of her shoulder bag to show him. "I just wish I knew what we were looking for."

"I don't know," he said. "But clearly someone thinks the information about the deed is in there."

The battered truck followed Sinclair's van at a distance. There was no need to push it. Thaddeus Frost knew where Sinclair was headed; they had spoken earlier. After about twenty minutes, Sinclair's vehicle turned off the main highway and started up the laborious winding road to the summit, where the house was located. Frost followed. The road trailed up through the olive groves, with little else in sight. Frost kept his eyes on the rearview mirror as he drove, and there was no one following. He continued up the mountain behind Sinclair. At the summit, Sinclair's vehicle turned into a courtyard. As Frost drove by, he glimpsed a small house behind the stone wall. Good, that place would be easy to patrol. Frost drove past and took the next left to head back down the mountain. His surveillance would start this evening.

"Malik, would you please wait here a moment," Sinclair said as he got out of the van. The dog bounded ahead and pushed the door of the house open with her nose.

Sinclair walked Cordelia to the door and stood looking into the room. Kyrie was already nosing in the corners, searching for new scents. Now that Cordelia was here, Sinclair saw his bachelor quarters with new eyes. The large room was furnished with only the most rudimentary things. He hadn't thought of that when he invited her.

"It's not much, but it's more comfortable than you might think," he apologized.

"It's just this one big room?" she asked, looking at the bed pushed against the wall.

"That's pretty much it. I'll sleep on the couch. You can have the bed," he said, just to make things clear. "There's a bathroom through that door. Why don't you rinse off the dust, and I'll be right back after I get the bags."

Sinclair went back out to the van.

Malik had brought the two suitcases to the veranda. He now handed Sinclair a bag of groceries.

"Sir, it seems you have a problem."

"What kind of problem?"

"People coming after you. I heard much of what the lady says."

"Malik, who in hell is going to find us up here?"

"I am still worried," Malik said, shifting from foot to foot and looking around. Sinclair also surveyed the courtyard of the isolated house.

"There isn't anyone for miles. Besides, we are only staying for a few days."

Malik went to the van, opened the passenger door, and started digging around in the glove compartment.

"Sir, please take this."

He handed him a gun. Sinclair recognized it as a Glock 19. Solid and serviceable, it was used in most countries by law-enforcement officers. Its small size also made it perfect for concealed carry.

Sinclair, still holding the groceries, weighed the gun in his free hand and then gave it back.

"Thanks, Malik, I appreciate it—I really do—but I don't think we'll need it."

Malik looked uncertain.

"Sir, you need to protect your woman."

"I will protect her with this," he said, touching his temple.

"With all respect, sir, you are very clever, but you cannot outsmart a gun."

"Malik, if anyone touches that woman, I won't need a gun. I'll tear him to pieces with my bare hands."

The *Udachny*

Vlad, Anna, Bob, and Marlene all sat on the white leather couches and Evgeny was pacing the floor of the yacht. The *Udachny* was now anchored at Kuşadası, near the *Queen Victoria*.

"How could you let her get off the ship *without noticing*! I have never seen such a bunch of *idiots* in my whole life. Did you think you were on vacation? You were there *to do a job*."

Evgeny was red in the face and breathing hard. He inhaled deeply through his nostrils, with his eyes shut. He appeared to be gathering his thoughts.

"This is what we are going to do," he said, in a low menacing tone, opening his eyes.

"Bob, you go to London. Cordelia Stapleton has got to turn up there soon to check on her town house."

"Yes sir," said Bob.

"You can take *her* with you," Evgeny said, gesturing with disgust at Marlene. "And I want you reachable on that phone at all times."

"Yes sir," Bob repeated.

"Vlad," Evgeny said, pointing at him. "You will go to Ephesus and see if you can pick up her trail. Sinclair lives nearby and you can start nosing around and find out where."

"OK," Vlad said.

"And another thing, dress like you live there. Is that understood? I don't want to hear you wore some gold Rolex and blew your cover."

"Yes sir."

"And you," he said to Anna. "You are staying here with me."

There was a long pause as Vlad stared at Evgeny.

"If you think she can blend in in Turkey, you are out of your mind," Evgeny added. "She's going to sit here and wait for you to come back."

Vlad just nodded curtly.

"Now get going—and don't screw this up or you will all answer to me."

As they filed out of the salon of the yacht, Anna looked after them with a hint of trepidation. When they had gone, Evgeny turned to her, his fleshy mouth contorted into a sadistic smile.

"Your husband is a highly incompetent man, and I am thinking of killing him. Unless you persuade me not to. Do you think you know how to persuade me not to kill your husband?"

Cordelia stepped out of the shower. The stone floor was cool to her feet. The bathroom in Sinclair's house had a large window that looked out over the hillside, and brilliant sunlight was pouring in. A carved wooden table held a stack of white towels, olive oil soaps, and bottles of herbal shampoos and conditioner. There was aftershave in an unmarked bottle. She picked it up, uncapped it, and smelled deeply, remembering Sinclair's distinctive scent. She wondered who made it, putting it back quietly, feeling a bit guilty to be snooping in his things.

Then she pulled on a pair of jeans and a light blue sweater, and walked barefoot into the other room. Puccini's *"O mio babbino caro"* was playing at full volume. The dog trotted over and pressed against her legs, her tail whipping the air.

The house had an appealing simplicity—open plan with a high peaked ceiling. The kitchen stood at the back of the main room, with a counter and stools for eating. Near the front window, a couch and two armchairs were grouped around a low table. The large bed was pushed against the far wall, covered with a silk woven fabric in rust and ocher. Sinclair's writing desk stood before the other window, with a view into the valley below.

The scent of food wafted through the room. Cordelia walked over to Sinclair and looked over his shoulder as he stood at the stove, preparing lunch. It was some kind of grilled fish and braised chopped eggplant, peppers, tomatoes, and onions. A round of crisp peasant bread was sliced on a wooden cutting board. He took no notice of her, totally engrossed in what he was doing.

Cordelia took a slice of bread and chewed it as she walked around the room. The rug from the market in Kuşadası was now on the floor, and the persimmon-and-beige tones suited the room perfectly.

"You weren't kidding when you said you hadn't decorated."

He looked up from the stove.

"I don't require much. I'm just here by myself," he said.

"It's lovely," she said, curling up on the couch.

"Really?" he asked. "I thought you liked getting dressed up for dinner, and all that. Where has my princess gone?"

"She jumped ship with an archaeologist, I hear."

"Good for her," he said, smiling to himself, and turned back to his cooking.

"*Voilà*," he said a few moments later. He turned around, holding two plates of food, and joined her on the couch. He put the plates down on the low table and smiled at her with his intense blue eyes.

"Would you like a little wine?"

Ephesus, Turkey

Sinclair drained his glass and leaned forward.

"Can I tempt you to come with me to the site this afternoon?"

His eyes were shining with anticipation. Cordelia nodded. How could she refuse? By her count this was his sixth invitation to visit Ephesus since the day she met him.

Within moments the BMW Adventure was speeding down the hillside road, taking the curves at an angle. Cordelia clung to Sinclair's back and looked farther out, over the valley below.

It was a good, warm day, and the silver olive trees were shimmering in the afternoon sun. The landscape was timeless, with nothing to distinguish it from the way it would have looked centuries ago—lots of rock, scrubby vegetation, and sky. After a while, they were riding through more populated areas, and passing little farms and houses with chickens in the garden.

"Look there," Sinclair said above the motorcycle's roar, and pointed off to the left.

"It's the Temple of Artemis, one of the Seven Wonders of the World."

"It's just a few broken fragments and a pillar," she said in disappointment.

"I know, there's not much left. But *wait* until you see the dig at Ephesus."

Sinclair had explained that the structure of the ancient city was still there, its beauty very visible, just a little blurred by time. It had been one of the most important cities in Roman antiquity, and a major trading port for the civilized world. As Sinclair put it, Ephesus was the New York City of the ancient world.

Sinclair pulled the bike into his usual parking spot under a tree and unsnapped his helmet. Cordelia had already climbed down.

There were only a few tourists, and she could easily picture how grand it had once been. The archaeological site was overwhelming—the size of a real city. Walking down the marble street was like stepping back into ancient Roman times. Painstakingly excavated over the past few decades, the streets were nearly intact. Along the side of the main thoroughfare was a jumble of enormous marble fragments, the remains of buildings that had once been there. But much of the city was almost untouched: shops, houses, baths, and fountains. It was possible to pass through original columns, archways, doorways, and sections of the various temples. Neither of them spoke. He held her hand and walked with her as she took it all in.

The wide avenue wound down between two hills into several large spaces. There was the old marketplace square and, at the bottom of the hill, the colossal edifice of the famous library, one of the most celebrated of its time. Ancient steps remained there, and the façade with large columns stood about four stories high. They climbed the steps and surveyed the broad plaza in front of them. It was the central meeting place of the city. Next to the square was the huge amphitheater—so well preserved it could have been used for a gladiator match that very afternoon. When they stood at the center of the amphitheater, Sinclair finally spoke.

"This arena could hold almost three thousand people."

"Oh my goodness, it probably looked exactly the same when he was here. I remember Saint Paul's Letter to the Ephesians, from the Bible."

"Exactly. Saint Paul preached here in Ephesus," said Sinclair, sweeping his arm across the stands of the amphitheater as if it were full of people. "And these are the Ephesians."

Sinclair led her back out onto the marble street.

"Look at this," he said, bending down over an irregular piece of paving. There, carved in the marble, was a circle the size of a manhole cover, divided by lines that made it look exactly like a pie sliced into eight pieces.

"This is the ancient secret symbol of the Christians who were persecuted in Ephesus," said Sinclair, tracing the circle with his hand.

"I remember you were drawing this when we were talking to Thaddeus Frost," said Cordelia. "You were doodling it."

"I often sketch it. Its symmetry appeals to me."

"So this symbol was carved back in Roman times?" Cordelia knelt down and traced her finger around the circle.

"Yes, you have probably seen the fish symbol the Christians used as an underground way to identify other followers. Well, this was a secret signal for the Christians in Ephesus. It's called an ichthus wheel. The Greek letters make up the word *fish*: ΙΧΟΨΣ, which forms the acronym for *Iesous Christos Theou Uios Soter*. It's translated as 'Jesus Christ God's Son, Savior.' If you superimpose the letters inside a circle, you get this symbol."

"How interesting."

Sinclair knelt down and studied it with her. He was so close, she could feel his body heat. The scent of the sun and the rocks and the vegetation all around them mirrored the scent he wore. She enjoyed being so close to him, and listening to his voice.

"At first glance it looks pretty innocuous, like a cartwheel, or some kind of design. We believe the Romans were unaware of its symbolism."

Cordelia continued to trace the circle with her finger. The white marble was warm in the sun.

"It is astonishing that it's still here."

Sinclair looked pleased. He stood up, holding out his hand to pull her to her feet.

"Incredible, isn't it? Now, I want to show you my gladiators."

A short distance away, the ground had been subdivided into plots. He swept his arm to encompass the entire area.

"We've found sixty-seven gladiators so far. As you can see, they're near the amphitheater, for ease of burial after the games."

"It makes sense that it's close by the amphitheater, but how can you be sure it's a graveyard for gladiators?"

Sinclair led her along a dusty lane lined with shallow pits on both sides.

"We found two gravestones depicting gladiators, like this one here." He pointed out the stone. There were two carved figures clearly engaged in armed combat. "But the bones also tell us a lot. The men who were buried here were all between the ages of twenty and thirty. Many of the bones show evidence of multiple healed wounds."

"That could also be soldiers," suggested Cordelia.

"Yes, multiple wounds could be military," Sinclair agreed. "But the fact that they had *healed* wounds suggests they were prized individuals, treated with very elaborate medical attention. Common soldiers were allowed to die."

"Did they all die in the arena?"

"Yes, some died during the contests, and some were slain after the combat. We found a stone relief showing gladiators being killed. According to the rules of the game, if they didn't fight well or revealed some kind of cowardice, the crowd would yell 'Iugula!' which is roughly translated as 'Lance him through!' "

"How horrible."

"It was a ritualistic slaying," said Sinclair. "The gladiator was expected to remain motionless and die 'like a man.' The bones actually show evidence of how they were killed. Many of the bones have nicks in the vertebrae. A sword would be rammed through the throat and down into the heart."

"*Really!*" Cordelia was horrified.

"We also see a lot of caved-in skulls. We think the wounded might have been killed with a mercy blow, hitting them in the head with a hammer."

"Which is the most interesting gladiator you've found?" asked Cordelia, changing the subject away from death.

"I like this retiarius," admitted Sinclair. "He was lightly armed, wore no helmet, and carried a net that he would throw over his opponent to tangle him up. Then he would attack with a sword."

"I see."

"See the three holes right here in the skull? He was killed with a trident. A trident was one of the standard weapons of gladiators. It was used as often as a sword. Marine archaeologists found a trident in the harbor that matches this wound exactly."

Sinclair pointed out the three clear holes through the forehead section. As he did it, Cordelia felt a deep shiver, even though the warm sun was shining.

The taverna was situated high in the hills above Selçuk. It was clearly a local place, with stucco walls and rough beams. There was the faint tang of charcoal and the scent of spicy food. The two dozen or so patrons were clustered in small groups, talking. Outside on the terrace, the view was breathtaking. There were a few tables by the railing, and Sinclair moved to sit on the same side of the table as Cordelia, so they could both enjoy the view of the valley. Evening was falling, and the light was soft. The proprietor put down complimentary glasses of raki mixed with water—a drink that looked like diluted milk. Cordelia took a sip and made a face.

"It's an acquired taste," said Sinclair, and tossed his off. "Try this."

He picked up a dark olive from the dish and fed it to Cordelia. It was marinated in a spicy oil and had a dense, raisinlike texture.

Sinclair insisted she try everything. There was *ezme*, finely chopped pepper, onion, sun-dried tomatoes, and walnuts, eaten with sesame-topped bread. Then *köfte*, char-grilled spiced ground lamb.

"It's *manti*," he said when the next dish was placed in front of her. She dipped her fork in and sampled it. The combination of hot dumplings and cool yogurt was delicious. Sinclair poured her a glass of Yakut wine, a dry red that went well with the spicy food. They finished with honey-dipped baklava sprinkled with the light green gratings of pistachios. The dark sweet coffee had a rich aftertaste.

By the time they finished, night had nearly fallen on the valley. The sky was navy blue, and a few stars were starting to dance around a three-quarter moon. They sat in silence. He picked up her hand and held it, resting his arm on the table, not saying anything.

"Cordelia," he began. "I want to be fair to you—"

"You've been more than fair," she interrupted. "You have been wonderful to me. I feel guilty, getting you into this mess."

He kept holding her hand, looking into her eyes.

"A couple of greedy people think they can take advantage of you. I am happy to help, but don't think I'm being some big hero or anything."

"Well, I am grateful to you nevertheless."

He sighed. "I don't want you to be grateful to me."

"What do you want, John?" she asked. He didn't answer. He kept holding her hand.

The ride back on the motorcycle in the dark was exhilarating. The night air brushed her skin, cool and invigorating. They climbed higher and higher, flying through the darkness. The headlamp of the bike painted their path in advance. He pulled into the dark courtyard, and when he cut the engine there was utter stillness.

"It's a beautiful place," she told him, handing over her helmet.

"I love it here," he said.

He put the helmets on the bike and walked with her over to the edge of the terrace. The valley lay before them. Then he pulled her to him and crushed her in a deep embrace. His mouth found hers and she lifted her face and kissed him back. It was long and hungry and incredibly sweet. He ran his hand down her back and pressed her against his body. She leaned into him with her whole weight. He was strong and powerful, more muscular than she had realized. When he finished kissing her, he stepped back, breaking body contact, but he still held her hand.

"Don't, if you don't want to," he said.

"John, I know exactly what I am doing," she said, and turned and walked into the house.

Cordelia woke at dawn and looked at the light coming in the window. There were no curtains, and the sun reflected a bright pattern on the stone wall on the other side of the room. She felt the delicious ache. Her lips were slightly sore, her mouth was tender from his beard stubble. She felt good and healthy and strong. Her movement caused Sinclair to open his eyes. His legs were still tangled in hers, and he moved his heavy limbs off her.

"Good morning, Delia." His sleepy voice was incredibly sexy.

Her heart soared. Having him here beside her, saying good morning, took her breath away. How utterly wonderful to be with him like this. She was so absorbed in the moment, she didn't respond.

"Are you *sorry*?" he asked, propping himself up on one elbow and squinting at her. His hair was falling into his eyes, and he looked very tan against the white sheets. The sheet dropped away as he moved, revealing his sculpted chest. In the daylight, his unshaven face showed his age; fine lines were just starting to crease his eyes.

"Absolutely not," she answered, smiling.

"Good," he said. He reached over with one arm, scooped her up, and pulled her on top of him.

Cordelia was sitting on the couch by the window with her legs curled up, leaning back against Sinclair's chest. Kyrie was seated by the door, looking out into the courtyard, one ear tilted to listen to their voices. They were taking turns reading the journal aloud. The beautiful handwriting had turned sepia with age, fine and spidery, and reading was difficult. By reading aloud they could look and listen for some hidden message. As Sinclair read, Cordelia looked out the window into the sunlit morning.

My colleague Robert Peary's ship *The Roosevelt* is docked in the East River, in final preparation for an expedition to the North Pole. He is well funded. I yearn for such patrons but have had little success here in America. However, I remind myself that the largess of the Prince of Monaco has given me much, and I have enjoyed more than a dozen voyages because of his generosity. I will not tempt providence by complaining, but the luxuriousness of Peary's vessel is enviable. On board is every possible comfort, including a two-hundred-volume library. As I stood on the quay, I noted his sled dogs were prostrate on the deck in the July heat. He departs tomorrow for Long Island Sound and will meet with President Roosevelt at his home, Sagamore Hill, before continuing to more northern regions. How I envy him.

Sinclair handed the journal to Cordelia and she read:

Nothing can describe the glory of the polar region, which has captured the imagination of the Empire. Although my voyage to Spitsbergen is months away, in my mind I can see the sun reflecting on the frosted silver of the icebergs. I picture those towering edifices, their white bulk a high contrast to the deep blue of the Arctic sky, and the identical hue in the water of Advent Bay below. Some are suffused with a faint pink glow, and others are colored in surprising rainbows, from the most intense lapis lazuli and malachite green to the palest celadon.

Cordelia leaned her head back against John's shoulder.
"He really loved the Arctic."
"He certainly wrote enough about the land disputes at that time," said Sinclair. "He must have been very aware of the importance of hanging on to that deed. Listen to this.

This land in Spitsbergen is truly terra nullius. It has, up until this moment, been a vast wasteland, claimed by none. I

FIND IT IRONIC THAT TWO AMERICAN CAPITALISTS COULD RECOGNIZE THE VALUE OF THE LAND AND GENERATE SUCH COMPETITION FOR THE ISLAND. NOW OUR LITTLE MINING OPERATION HAS BROUGHT OUT THE AVARICE OF GREAT POWERS: ENGLAND, SWEDEN, RUSSIA, AND GERMANY. NORWAY IS THE MOST AGGRESSIVE AND IS TRYING TO CLAIM OUR SMALL ENTERPRISE AS ITS OWN. BUT THERE HAS NEVER BEEN AGREEMENT AS TO WHO SHOULD EXERCISE SOVEREIGNTY OVER SPITSBERGEN. NO COUNTRY CONTROLS IT, AND WE STILL RETAIN THE DEED TO THE LAND UNTIL SOME GREATER POWER SHOULD TRY TO WREST AWAY THE FRUITS OF OUR HONEST LABOR.

"How amazing that everyone is still fighting over the same land," said Cordelia.

They sat for a moment in silence.

"It's possible we won't find the deed, Cordelia," he cautioned.

"We'll find it," Cordelia said, picking up the journal. "I can feel it. He loved this place too much to have let the deed be lost. I am sure he hid it."

"Keep reading. I'll go pick up some things for lunch," said Sinclair. He scooped his keys out of the earthenware bowl above the sink and walked over to give her a lingering kiss. "I'll be right back."

Gabriel Fauré's "Cantique de Jean Racine" filled the room with angelic choral music. She looked up after a while and surveyed the beautiful little house, suddenly aware it would take very little to make her happy if John Sinclair was with her.

She sighed to herself, and Kyrie looked over, thumping her tail on the floor. Suddenly the dog pricked up her ears and looked hard out the door. She emitted a deep growl, scanning the courtyard.

"What's wrong, Kyrie?" asked Cordelia. She walked to the door and looked outside. There was sunshine in the courtyard, and the sound of a gentle wind. Nothing else. The terrain dropped off precipitously after the terrace, and she could see for miles: scrub brush of the arid land, olive trees, and a few ramshackle buildings down the slope. A figure far off on the adjacent hillside looked like a local farmer. That was all.

Cordelia closed the door and pulled the dog by the collar back to the couch.

"Come on, Kyrie, we need to read this journal." The dog snuggled up to her on the couch and put her chin on Cordelia's knee.

Twenty feet below the terrace of John Sinclair's house, Vlad crouched behind the stone wall. He had heard the dog growl and stopped moving. He checked his Windbreaker pocket for the gun and put his hand on it as he climbed over the three-foot wall into the courtyard. He stood up and looked into the empty courtyard. The BMW motorcycle was gone. Hanging on the hook near the door was only one helmet. Sinclair had left. The girl was still here. He didn't see the man standing behind the stone pillar at the entrance to the courtyard.

The man had been there since sunrise, so long he looked like part of the stonework. As Vlad climbed over the wall and started toward the door, he never heard the man come up from behind. He was unconscious with the first blow. Frost caught him before he fell, and dragged him out to the road. A pickup truck pulled up, and two farmers silently lifted Vlad into the back and stretched him out on the flatbed before driving away.

No one was there to see any of it. If they had, they would have noticed that the Turkish farmers had the pale skin of Anglo-Saxons, tinged with pink sunburn after only a few days in Turkey. Frost walked back into the courtyard and looked at the twin tracks Vlad's heels had made in the dirt as he dragged him toward the road. He scuffed the marks away, vaulted over the stone wall, and was gone.

Sinclair's phone rang just as the woman was packing the goat cheese into the paper bag.

"Sinclair," he answered, expecting Charles to be on the other line.

"Go back to the house now," said Frost. "We caught somebody outside. It's fine, we got him in time, but you need to get back there."

Sinclair grabbed the bag from the woman at the farm stand, thanking her in Turkish, and ran toward his motorcycle. Five minutes away was too much. As he drove, he found himself wishing he had taken Malik up on that gun.

✳

When Sinclair pulled into the courtyard, Cordelia was pacing the veranda of the house. She ran out to meet him.

"What's wrong?" His heart was pounding.

"John, I found something!"

He surveyed the courtyard. Kyrie was wagging her tail. Cordelia was grinning now. Everything was fine. He quelled his panic and forced himself to smile.

"I found a reference to the deed." Cordelia was beside herself with excitement and grabbed his hand. "Come look."

"Great," he said, taking off his helmet. "Now we're getting somewhere."

They read the journal together.

SEPTEMBER 13, 1908

GLORIOUS DAY. THE EXPEDITION TO SPITSBERGEN HAS BEEN COM-
PLETELY FINANCED AND OUTFITTING HAS BEGUN. ALL IS READY TO GO
AS SCHEDULED. THE MAY 1909 DEPARTURE DATE FROM TROMSØ IS FIRM.
BECAUSE I WILL BE ON THIS EXPEDITION FOR AT LEAST EIGHT TO TEN
MONTHS, I MUST PUT THE DEED IN A SAFE PLACE. THERE HAS BEEN TOO
MUCH CONTENTION OVER THE LAND, AND I DARE NOT RISK LOSING THIS
DOCUMENT. I WILL BRING IT TO JSR. AS HE IS LEAVING FOR THE MID-
DLE EAST, JSR MAY AGREE TO ENTRUST IT TO BRADFORD—IS AS GOOD A
CHOICE AS ANY FOR SAFEKEEPING.

"What do you think?" asked Cordelia.

"It seems like his partner, James Skye Russell, would have 'entrusted it to Bradford,'" said Sinclair. He put the bag of groceries down on the counter.

"I wonder who Bradford is?" said Cordelia.

"Maybe Mr. Bradford was his lawyer, or a business associate. Would *your* lawyer have any idea?"

"Jim might know. He's been looking through all the family papers."

"My cell phone is there on the writing desk. Call him. But before you do that, let's talk lunch. How does lamb shish kebab with okra and onions and rice pilaf sound?"

"John Sinclair, are you trying to impress me?"

"No, darling, just feed you," he said. "I'll impress you later," he added, and winked at her, starting toward the kitchen.

They were just finishing up lunch when Sinclair's cell phone rang. He picked it up quickly, on alert.

"Sinclair." He relaxed when he heard the voice. "Sure, she is right here," he said. "Let me get her for you." He handed the phone to Cordelia. "It's your lawyer."

"Hello, Jim. Yes, I am fine. I'm at John Sinclair's house in Turkey." She rolled her eyes at Sinclair. "Yes. Yes. I'll tell you all about it when I see you in London. Did you find anything about someone called Bradford? Oh. That's too bad. Well, we'll keep reading. See you on Monday. Right, four o'clock." She hung up the phone.

"Jim says there is no mention of Bradford anywhere."

"Then we will just have to go see the family of James Skye Russell. Where are they?"

"England. Just outside London. But, John, I don't want to leave here yet."

Sinclair kissed her on the top of her head.

"I'm afraid we can't stay. We need to go, and soon."

Kyrie was leaning against her legs, as if she knew this was good-bye. Cordelia patted the dog as she looked outside. It was so beautiful: the view from the stone veranda overlooking the hills, the coolness of the night, the taste of the wine, crisp and delicious, and the wonderful time in bed, learning about each other, memorizing what it was like to be held, caressed, and loved. Now it was over. She looked back into the house.

Sinclair was talking on the phone with Charles Bonnard, filling him in on their schedule. The van pulled up in the courtyard and Malik rolled down the window

"Good evening, lady. Hello, sir, your flight is at seven. We should go quickly."

London

Cordelia sat in the central dining room of Claridge's, drinking tea and eating cucumber sandwiches. There were all kinds of pastries on the beautiful green-and-white-striped china, and Cordelia was examining them as Sinclair appeared.

"We're all set," Sinclair said, taking a seat and pouring himself a cup of tea. "We have a rental car and will drive out to Cliffmere tomorrow, first thing in the morning."

Cordelia consulted her watch, dabbing her lips with a napkin.

"Quarter after three. After your tea, we'll head out to meet Jim Gardiner at the house."

"Where are we going?"

Cordelia looked up at Sinclair with a laugh.

"I have to check the address. Jim Gardiner says it's nearby, but I've never been there."

In the exclusive Mayfair district of London, Grosvenor Square was a luxurious green oasis with flower beds and wrought-iron benches. The park was filled with people walking their dogs, and nannies chatting as their infant charges slept in Silver Cross prams. Schoolchildren were riding bikes along the symmetrical paths. The day was balmy, and a half dozen office workers sat sunning themselves, unwilling to go back indoors.

Cordelia walked around, enchanted. Stately buildings rimmed the edge of the square. A brass plaque said Grosvenor Square was once called "Little America," because the second American president, John Adams, lived there in 1785. She noticed the American embassy at one end of the square, enormous and modern. The Canadian embassy flanked it at the other end. All around were town houses that had been preserved from the late Georgian era, with classical pilasters and pedimented doors and windows.

A few steps from the square proper, Cordelia found her new home, a solid testament to the affluence of Elliott Stapleton. It was a beautiful brick town house with white columns. The four-story building had a slate roof and multiple chimneys, and was silhouetted against the bright London sky.

"I can't believe this is mine," Cordelia said in awe as she crossed the street and walked toward it.

Sinclair looked the building up and down. "It's a beauty."

The door opened, and filling the doorframe was the form of Jim Gardiner.

"Delia! Welcome home," he said with a big smile. "By God, it's good to say that, honey."

She flew up the steps to hug him.

Inside the town house there was a quiet elegance. The rooms were clear of clutter, and the beautiful heirloom furniture was showcased by subtle colors on the walls, opulent silk drapes, and the rich patina of parquet floors.

"I *love* it," said Cordelia, looking around.

Jim Gardiner handed her a bulky envelope.

"Here are the keys. But you can't stay here until next week. The police want you to keep clear until they finish the investigation of the break-in. We think somebody was looking for that deed."

Cordelia took the keys and walked into the large dining room. A beautiful mahogany table was flanked by twelve Hepplewhite chairs. An antique silver bowl stood in the center of the table. Just visible through the heavy drapes was the traffic of Grosvenor Street and the park beyond.

Cordelia continued out into the foyer and started up the carved marble staircase, moving as if in a dream, quiet and thoughtful.

"I'm going to go upstairs to see the rest," she called back.

Gardiner and Sinclair exchanged a look, as if to signal to each other not to follow. When she was out of earshot, Gardiner turned to Sinclair.

"I'm glad you are with Delia. Until we can get this mess cleared up, she really needs some looking after."

"It's my pleasure."

"She doesn't know this, but the break-in last month triggered Peter Stapleton's heart attack. That's how he died. He interrupted the intruder."

"Oh, that changes the picture, doesn't it?" said Sinclair.

"All the locks are new," Gardiner assured him. "And the London police have the town house on surveillance."

"Don't worry, I'll stay with her as long as she needs me," he promised.

Paul Oakley was seated at his desk. The mail had piled up, and there were four research papers to be read, to say nothing of the Hong Kong findings on avian influenza to be written up. He had just settled down to work when the phone rang. It was one of his oldest friends in the world, Tom Skye Russell.

Not a day went by that he didn't miss Tom. Sometimes he was halfway down the corridor to his office when he remembered that Tom had retired last year—packed his desk and gone off to run his estate, Cliffmere, north of London, near Oxford.

"Tom, nice to hear from you."

"Paul, I tried to call you two weeks ago, but I guess you were traveling."

"I just got back from Hong Kong. I'm working with the Chinese on avian flu," said Oakley.

"I suppose you heard about Miles?"

Oakley could barely answer. He cleared his throat. "Awful, just *awful*," he managed.

There was an uncomfortable pause on the other end of the line.

"Paul, I wanted to get back to you about your request to exhume the grave site on our property. I think I have all the red tape cleared."

"That's just great, Tom. That is fantastic. I really appreciate it."

"If you think the tissue samples would be useful, I see no reason why we shouldn't do it. It's a family grave site, and I don't think my great-grandfather would have minded. He was a man of science, after all."

"I'm just hoping that the lead in the coffin is intact. If that seal is still solid, we have a very good chance of getting a viable sample."

"Well, the permits are approved for next week, if that's not too soon."

"Oh, that's excellent," said Oakley. "I can't thank you enough. I'll be down to secure the area and talk to the local police. I work with a company called Necropolis. They'll be doing the site survey. Should they call you directly?"

"Yes, certainly. Anytime is fine. I have a young American woman from the States who is going to be visiting. But that won't interfere with your work."

"We'll just keep to ourselves over by the chapel. You won't even know we're there."

"Right. See you next week, then."

Jim Gardiner and Sinclair were at the Coburg Bar in the Connaught Hotel drinking single malt and deep in conversation. Cordelia sat across from them, sipping her Campari and looking around the room. The décor was sophisticated yet cozy: gray green walls; deep velvet wingback chairs upholstered in shades of plum, gray, and persimmon; and flickering amber candles on each table. To think this place was just a few blocks from her new town house.

When the waitress came over, Sinclair and Gardiner stopped talking. She placed a bowl of hand-cut potato chips, a dish of green olives, and some spiced nuts on the low table. She dallied, fussing over the exact placement of the dishes and glancing sideways at Sinclair, looking him over. Sinclair ignored the woman, gazing out at the town houses of Carlos Place. Cordelia rolled her eyes at Gardiner, who pressed his lips together to hide a smile.

When the waitress left, they resumed their discussion. The jazz music drowned out their conversation to the rest of the room.

"The way I see it," said Gardiner, "this deed *does* exist. Otherwise we would have had claims against the property. No one has legally contested the rights since Norway ceded them to Elliott Stapleton in 1906."

"Why the big rush to claim it now?" asked Sinclair.

"I think the construction of the seed vault raised a hornet's nest of competing interests."

"Competing interests of the Norwegian government, the Russians, the Bio-Diversity Trust, and some old Russian miners," Sinclair said, counting them off on his fingers. "Anyone else?"

"There is also a group called Citizens for World Survival. The Department of Homeland Security told me they're some kind of domestic terrorist group, survivalists or some such thing," said Gardiner.

"It seems to me Norway has a pretty good claim on it, if we can't find that deed," said Sinclair.

"Correct," said Gardiner. "The land rights will revert to Norway if we can't find that deed in a reasonable time."

"Revert? Why?" Cordelia asked.

"The mine hasn't been in operation for more than thirty years. Norway will try to argue that the land is not being used for its original purpose, which was commercial mining. Without the deed, they would say the land is 'terra nullius,' no-man's-land, and under law it belongs to Norway."

"What about the Russians?"

"They are doing a modern version of claim jumping by bringing up the historical rights of the Russian miners."

"Would that fly in court?" cut in Sinclair.

"Probably not. But a private Russian company is offering ninety-seven point six million dollars for the land."

"Ninety-seven point six million dollars!" Cordelia slumped back in her chair.

"Yup, you find that deed, you could just sell it to the Russians and walk away," said Gardiner.

"Norway would contest it," Sinclair pointed out.

"You bet they would, but it wouldn't be her problem. She would be sitting pretty," said Gardiner to Sinclair.

"What about donating it to the Bio-Diversity Trust?" asked Cordelia.

"You *could* do that," agreed Gardiner. "But there is one problem."

"We don't have the deed," said Sinclair.

"Bingo," said Gardiner, and drained his whiskey.

Bob walked into the Coburg Bar and everything about him—his expression, his clothes, and his manner—screamed he was out of place. He scanned the room, as if looking for someone.

"Well, hello! Who do we have here? It's my friends from the *Queen Victoria*! Small world."

Cordelia could read Sinclair's annoyance in the subtle shift in the line of his mouth. He reluctantly stood to greet Bob.

"Well, I'll be damned if it isn't our lady oceanographer and Mr. Sinclair," Bob continued, beaming down at Cordelia. "Nice to see you again."

"Why, hello, Bob!" said Cordelia, surprised.

"Howdy do," said Bob. "How've you been?"

"What brings you here?" asked Sinclair tersely.

"Marlene and I got off the ship in Athens and came up to London for a few days of shopping. She's over at Harrods right now."

"Are you staying here at the Connaught?" asked Jim Gardiner.

"Nearby. I heard this was a good place for a drink."

He eyed their glasses. "I see you've started the cocktail hour already."

There was an awkward pause. Sinclair looked at Gardiner.

"Please join us," invited Cordelia reluctantly.

Sinclair gave Bob a cool smile and sat back down. Their conversation would have to wait.

"Why, thank you, mighty kind," said Bob, pulling up a chair. "I'm gonna need a drink before I see that bill from Harrods."

Bob walked quickly along the mews of Adams Row and in the back door of the Millennium Hotel. He would call Evgeny from his room. Evgeny answered on the second ring, and sounded so irritated, Bob was glad to be delivering good news.

"Listen, I just tracked Sinclair and Cordelia. Marlene found out they are staying at Claridge's."

"How did she find *that* out?" asked Evgeny.

"We had the address for her town house. Marlene just went around to all the nice hotels in the neighborhood, asking to leave a message. Sure enough, Claridge's took a message for her. You gotta love the service at five-star hotels."

"You didn't tip off anyone, did you?"

"No, Marlene said she was a real-estate agent," said Bob.

"Are you at the same hotel?"

"No, I thought that would be too suspicious. We're right nearby, at the Millennium. It's about a block away from the town house. I just pretended to bump into them having drinks."

"Good," said Evgeny. "Don't let them out of your sight."

Lounging back in the comfortable wing chair, Cordelia watched the two men she loved most in the world. Sinclair and Gardiner were laughing together, their faces happy and relaxed. They were getting on so well. She swirled the watery remains of her Campari in the glass and thought about how radically her life had changed in the past few weeks. Sure there were some bumps, but things were turning out OK after all. Just then the waitress brought over their tab, trying to catch Sinclair's eye again. He stood up to go.

"Time for some real food," he said, holding out a hand for Cordelia.

"I'll get this," said Gardiner, reaching for the drinks bill.

"Thanks, Jim. I'll handle dinner," Sinclair agreed.

As they left the Connaught, the top-hatted doorman wished them a good evening. Sinclair and Gardiner stopped to ask him directions to the restaurant.

Cordelia, still lost in thought, started walking slowly along Carlos Place toward Grosvenor Square. Her new neighborhood was gorgeous. The quiet street was lined with beautiful trees. She wandered down the block, leaving Sinclair and Gardiner to catch up.

Now that she had a house in London, she could come here whenever she wasn't working. After all, she had a generous vacation allowance, but until now there was no reason to use it. Now that was all changed. Think of it, a new place to call home, a new life off the ship!

But when could she and Sinclair be together? Weekends? Monaco wasn't that far away, was it? She needed to talk to him. They had been avoiding the subject, refusing to make plans beyond a few days in advance. They would have to face a separation sooner or later.

She walked on ahead. When she heard the rapid footsteps behind her, she assumed Sinclair and Gardiner were catching up.

Without warning, a violent force hit her from the back, knocking her nearly to her knees. A strong arm slipped around her stomach and she was lifted off her feet. Her breath was constricted by a viselike hold around her waist.

She was being held tightly. She couldn't see her assailant, but whoever he was, he was dragging her to the curb. She yelled at the top of her lungs, but the wind was knocked out of her, and not much sound came out.

Struggling wildly, she looked around and the street was empty. Out of the corner of her eye she could see a white panel van draw up, its door gaping open like a dark cave. Her adrenaline kicked in. She knew if she went into that van she would have no chance of getting free.

She flailed her arms at her captor and, reaching back, she felt her fingernails gouge his face. She tried to scream again, and this time managed to make it louder. She contorted wildly to twist her head around to see if Gardiner and Sinclair were nearby. If their backs were turned, she could very well vanish without a trace. It would take only seconds.

That horrible thought gave her new strength as she struggled, screamed, and kicked against her captor. Her spine nearly cracked as he tightened his hold. She could feel his chest heaving with the effort of dragging her backward. She knew she was giving him a pretty good fight. She was stronger than she looked, from years of swimming, and her long limbs gave her the ability to trip him. She tried to crush his feet with her high heels. Each time she could connect one foot with the sidewalk, she dug her heel in. The assailant was having a hard time of it. But no matter how hard she struggled, he was making progress toward the curb.

He pivoted, facing the van now, trying to push her into the gaping hole of the vehicle. On the filthy floor, she glimpsed a tool kit, some oily rags, and other refuse. He pushed her forward and she was nearly inside.

As a last desperate move she swung both legs up in an arc. Using his grip around her waist as leverage, she planted her feet on the aluminum siding of the van. She bent her knees and then pushed off with both legs, knocking her captor back a few paces. He staggered to recover his balance, but never lost his grip. That was her best move, and she knew he would not allow her to do it twice. He spun her around and began dragging her backward again.

But now she caught sight of Sinclair and Gardiner a long way down the street. As they turned around toward her, they finally saw what was happening.

Sinclair was faster off the mark than Gardiner. He tore down the block in a burst of speed, his arms and legs pumping. But to Cordelia his frantic dash had the slow-motion quality of a nightmare. He wasn't going to make it. Again, she was just inches from the door of the van.

She needed to buy more time. She let her body go limp, slumping over her captor's arm, creating a deadweight, and dropped her feet low to the ground. With one foot she managed to connect with the pavement, and tried to push away. She felt the heel of her shoe break off as she tried to wrestle free.

Sinclair reached Cordelia and caught hold of her arm. He yanked it so violently, she thought her shoulder would dislocate. Sinclair realized immediately that pulling on her was not going to free her. He spun around and placed himself in the small space between the van and the assailant, and began pummeling the man fiercely. Cordelia felt her captor's body shake with Sinclair's violent blows. As Sinclair placed a solid punch to one of his kidneys, the arm around her waist weakened. Cordelia renewed her struggle, and the grip around her slackened enough for her to wrest herself free. She fell to the sidewalk on her hands and knees, gasping in pain as she hit the hard pavement. Her hands had barely touched the sidewalk when she felt herself pulled to her feet again.

But this time she was being held in Sinclair's strong arms. As she clung to him, she was vaguely aware of the van tearing off behind them, tires squealing around the corner. She wrapped her arms around Sinclair's neck, burying her face in his chest. His comforting smell was mixed with the sharp scent of sweat. He held on to her tightly, still breathing hard from the struggle.

Just then Gardiner ran up, puffing heavily.

"Holy crow. Who in *hell* were they?" he demanded.

At the American embassy in Grosvenor Square, the young marine was impassive behind the bulletproof glass. Sinclair glared at him as he paced the waiting area. Twice, Sinclair had been told that Thaddeus Frost did not work in the embassy. But he was not to be put off. Sinclair repeatedly and politely asked that Frost be contacted. Finally a heavily perspiring junior diplomat came out into the lobby and talked to him. Sinclair was told to take a seat. No promises, but he wasn't being thrown out. He sat in a hard government-issue chair and didn't budge. About twenty minutes later, a steel door opened and Thaddeus Frost stood in the doorway. The expression on his face was not welcoming.

"Mr. Sinclair," he said coldly. "You should have called. I thought we agreed on that form of contact. I always answer my phone."

"I needed to talk to you in person."

"How did you *ever* know where to find me?"

"I took a wild guess," said Sinclair, rising. They stood eye to eye. The marine watched warily as Frost allowed Sinclair to pass through the secure steel door. They walked along an unadorned corridor and entered an empty office.

Frost took a seat behind the synthetic-wood-grained desk and waited for Sinclair to speak. In the first few seconds, Frost's eyes tracked from his rumpled suit to the slightly grazed knuckles on Sinclair's left hand. His gaze rested longer on a small triangular tear on the sleeve of Sinclair's glen plaid suit, the kind of rip made by something sharp. Sinclair still wore a tie, but it was loosened, and the silk fabric was water-stained right below the knot, from Cordelia's tears. Frost looked at the spot and then up to Sinclair's eyes.

"What can I do for you?" Frost asked.

"I thought you people were keeping a security detail on Cordelia," Sinclair challenged. He found it difficult to speak calmly.

"We are," Frost replied coolly.

"Then where the hell were you when two goons jumped her about *an hour* ago?"

"Surveillance ends at six. You were supposed to watch her at night."

"It was five thirty. I guess that is good enough for government work," said Sinclair. "What kind of b.s. is this?"

"I told you," said Frost levelly. "I *can't* keep a twenty-four/seven detail on her."

Sinclair ran a hand through his hair. Sweat prickled his scalp. He resisted the urge to fling off his jacket. "They almost *got* her. Some thug nearly pulled her into a van right out there on Carlos Place."

Frost answered courteously. "Understood. I'll up the security."

"I guess you forgot to mention there are quite a few more people involved in this than the governments of Russia and Norway and a couple of nuts who are rooting for the end of the world. Who *are* these people? It looked like a professional job."

"It seems there are some independent actors involved now."

"Independent actors? You mean the mob?"

"That is a broad term."

"Which means?"

"We are not sure who they are."

"*Not sure!!!*" Sinclair slammed his fist on the desk. He shut his eyes for a moment against the overhead fluorescent light. He needed to communicate better than this. He couldn't lose control. It was urgent. He tried again. "She doesn't *care* about the deed. She just wants to live her life. Can't we just walk away from this?" he pleaded.

"No," said Frost. "There is no walking away."

"How do I get them off her back?"

"Find the deed," Frost said. "Somebody out there wants it badly enough to kill."

"But she doesn't *know* anything," objected Sinclair.

"Doesn't matter. They will still try."

"I don't suppose it would be worth going to the police?"

"Not unless you want to spend the next two weeks drowning in paperwork."

Sinclair sighed, defeated.

"Look, I'll keep you covered," Frost assured. "Keep searching for the deed. Where are you going next? What are your plans?"

"We are leaving tomorrow morning for a house called Cliffmere, in Oxfordshire."

"Why there?"

"The owners of Cliffmere are old friends of the Stapleton family. They are mentioned in the journal. They may know something about the deed. It should only take a day or so to go up there and back."

"OK, I'll put a detail on you for the trip. Are you staying at the house?"

"Yes," said Sinclair. "It's enormous, with lots of land."

"Here's what we will do—we'll stake out the house from six a.m. to nine p.m. The night shift is yours. I'll find a local inn and stay there myself. Does that make you happy?"

"No, it doesn't," Sinclair said. "What would make me happy is finding that damn deed and being finished with this business."

Cordelia was curled up on the dark red couch in her room at Claridge's. The beautiful tartan drapes of the Mayfair Suite were drawn, and Jim Gardiner sat in a straight-backed chair, right next to her. Sinclair could tell the moment he entered that she had been crying. A wad of crumpled tissues was in her lap, and her face was puffy. But now she was composed. A bottle of brandy stood on the coffee table, and the two balloon snifters were empty.

Gardiner turned to him with a look of relief.

"Here you are. Glad you are back. Have a brandy," he said.

"I never mix grain and grape. Any whiskey about?" asked Sinclair. He tossed his crumpled suit jacket on the chair and went to pour himself a drink.

"How'd your *police report* go?" asked Gardiner, pouring himself another brandy.

Both Sinclair and Gardiner knew he had not gone to the police. They had agreed that Cordelia did not need to know he was meeting with Thaddeus Frost.

"Good, I think we have things squared away," Sinclair lied.

Gardiner glanced up, and they exchanged a quick look. Sinclair walked back to the couch carrying his whiskey.

"Have you two eaten anything yet? What about ordering something?" Sinclair asked.

"I could use some dinner. What about you Cordelia?" said Gardiner.

She shook her head.

"Not really hungry," she said.

"Nonsense, you can't skip dinner," said Gardiner. "How about some soup and a nice grilled cheese?"

She smiled at him and turned to Sinclair. "Jim thinks a grilled-cheese sandwich is always the antidote to anything bad," she said.

"Probably is," agreed Sinclair. "Listen, Cordelia, I think we should still head out to Cliffmere tomorrow if you are up to it. The faster we get this deed, the faster we'll be done with all this."

"Excellent plan," said Gardiner.

"I'm up for it," she assured them.

"You feel OK?" asked Sinclair.

"I'm not really hurt, just a little bruised. And I *would* like to get out of town for a bit," she admitted. "Especially with *those* people on the loose."

"I agree. We'll call and confirm with Tom and Marian Skye Russell for tomorrow. They were expecting us sometime this week."

Sinclair moved over to the couch to sit next to Cordelia and hold her hand. Gardiner looked at the two of them and cleared his throat.

"You know, I better be going. You kids make sure you eat something."

Sinclair nodded.

"And make sure you lock that door. Call me anytime, day or night. And let me know what you turn up at Cliffmere."

✳

At eight the following morning, Cordelia and Sinclair were huddled over a map at the main reception desk of the hotel.

"It looks fairly straightforward. It's only about ten miles north of Oxford," said Cordelia.

"Ms. Stapleton." The desk clerk was before her. "Sorry to interrupt, but did Mrs. Jones get hold of you?"

"Who is Mrs. Jones?"

"Mrs. Jones was inquiring for you yesterday morning when you were out. I told her to leave a message for you on your room voice mail."

"I didn't receive a message."

Sinclair was suddenly alert.

"What did she look like?"

The desk clerk began to look uncomfortable.

"I couldn't tell you. Average-looking woman. Middle-aged. Oh, yes, she was an American," he said.

"Did she say what she wanted?" asked Cordelia.

"She said it was something to do with real estate and a town house in London."

"Oh, I see. Thanks," said Cordelia, turning away.

Sinclair looked at her but said nothing.

Oxfordshire, England

There were rain showers on and off, and then fields glowed far into the distance. The hills alternated green and yellow with a patchwork of crops, and little sheep with black feet and muzzles stood like toys in a play-school farmyard. Sinclair lowered the windows and breathed in the rich air.

"It's beautiful here." He smiled. "I'm glad to get out of London."

"It's *gorgeous!*" agreed Cordelia, looking down at the map. "Take the next right. We're almost there."

After the turn, hedges on both sides of the lane obscured the view. They were in a narrow alley of green. Sinclair checked the rearview mirror. This was not a good place to be followed. They were all too visible, and vulnerable. But there had been nothing suspicious for the whole trip. Clearly they had escaped unnoticed.

"What did Tom and Marian say?" asked Cordelia, folding up the map.

"They said they've always wanted to meet you. They want us to stay for a day or two, to get to know you."

"Did they say anything about the Arctic Coal Mining Company?"

"We didn't talk about it," said Sinclair, concentrating on passing a slow-moving car. "I just explained we were interested in meeting them. They reacted as if you were a long-lost daughter."

The hedges parted and Cordelia gasped. A beautiful stone house stood in the middle of acres and acres of green parkland. This had to be one of the loveliest country estates in England. Sinclair pulled up to the elaborate wrought-iron gates. A polished brass plaque read CLIFFMERE.

"Here we are," said Sinclair, turning into the drive. "Ready to meet them?"

"I'm not sure," said Cordelia. "Just *look* at all of this."

Sinclair drove slowly down the lane. Shaded by ancient oaks, it went on for at least half a mile.

"My *goodness*, this is very grand," said Cordelia. "I had no idea."

"Impressive," agreed Sinclair.

They pulled into the cobbled courtyard in front of the house. Several dogs came up to the car and began to sniff the tires and alert the household. Within moments the enormous front door opened and a couple in their late sixties came out to greet them. The woman carried a basket on her arm, as if she had just been in the garden.

"You must be Miss Stapleton," she said, putting her basket down on the step and coming forward. She kissed Cordelia on the cheek. Marian Skye Russell had beautiful, clear skin, light blue eyes, and snow-white hair pinned up in a loose chignon.

Her distinguished husband stepped forward.

"A pleasure to meet you, Miss Stapleton," he said. "Welcome to Cliffmere. And you must be Mr. Sinclair. We spoke yesterday. Do come in."

Cliffmere, England

The main salon of the house was sumptuous, the windows hung with heavy red silk damask. There were enormous oil paintings and mahogany doors with their original gilt bronze hardware.

They all took seats on the formal settees facing one another near the central fireplace, where a small fire crackled. Marian began to pour coffee out of a silver pot into delicate Sèvres cups. It was chilly in the large room, and Cordelia snuggled deeper into Sinclair's vicuña coat she had borrowed and draped over her shoulders. Marian handed her the steaming coffee, indicating the cream and sugar on the low table next to her.

"Thank you," Cordelia said, taking the cup.

"I didn't get into this on the phone," Sinclair said, "but we are looking for the land deed for the Arctic Coal Mining Company in Svalbard."

"Surely that was with the Stapleton papers," said Tom.

"I'm afraid it wasn't," said Cordelia. "But there was a mention in Elliott Stapleton's diary saying it would be left with a Mr. Bradford."

Tom and Marian looked at each other, perplexed.

"I'm afraid I've never seen any reference to a Mr. Bradford in any of Sir James's papers," Tom replied.

"There were only two original partners, Sir James and Elliott Stapleton," added Marian. "I don't know of any Bradford."

"There *is* a lot of documentation about the land dispute for that period," said Tom. "The rights clearly went to your great-great-grandfather and Sir James. But when Sir James died, in 1918, it was discovered there was another silent partner listed—a Mr. Percival Spence."

Tom stretched out his legs. He still wore his walking shoes, wet with morning dew.

"It would be interesting to look at those documents," said Cordelia. "My lawyer says we need the *original* deed to claim the land."

"Well, then, we *have* to find it," said Marian. "We'll search through everything again."

"I am pretty sure the original deed is not here, and there is no one named Bradford," said Tom thoughtfully. He looked at the fire and appeared to search his memory. "None of the solicitors was named Bradford. And to my recollection there was no one with the first name of Bradford either."

Cordelia looked at the fire in the grate.

"We'll just have to keep looking," she said. "I know we can find it."

"Of course we will, dear," Marian said briskly. "We just have to put our minds to it."

Moscow

The man in Moscow was angry. Why were they chasing an American girl all over the world for the deed to some godforsaken mine? In the old days he would have gotten the information out of her after ten minutes in a cold, dark cell. His country was full of women, old women. Nobody had the balls to do what was necessary anymore. The phone rang.

"Hello." The assassin didn't need to identify himself. "I think I may have found the deed," he said quietly.

"Where?" The politician was immediately alert.

"I am at a place called Cliffmere, in Oxfordshire. It's a couple miles outside of London. I am staying at the local inn—the Golden Horn."

"And . . ."

"There seems to be some of the girl's family living at Cliffmere. She is visiting. I got into the house yesterday posing as a repairman and bugged the room. From what I am hearing, the deed may be here."

"Good, so get it."

"Not so easy. The house is huge. Ninety rooms. Too big to search. I'm going to keep the girl under surveillance and see what she turns up."

"Don't let her out of your sight."

"Believe me, I won't."

"By the way," the politician said, "the package from Longyearbyen never turned up anything. It was medical supplies of some kind."

"I see."

"You shot that scientist for nothing."

"I assumed he had dug up the deed and was sending it to Paul Oakley."

"No, he sent something else."

"But he was *standing* over the grave. The clerk in Longyearbyen said they found documents in the coffin the last time it was excavated. He was digging them up."

"No, you idiot, he was digging for samples. He did some exhumations in Barentsburg the day before."

"Well, I made a mistake. But it's no problem, dead men can't talk."

"You were lucky the bears ate the evidence. The police never knew," said the politician.

"Must have been a polar bear from United Russia," the assassin joked.

Cliffmere

The beautiful dining room was suffused with light. Cordelia admired the hand-painted china and the heavy silverware. The centerpiece, an antique Imari bowl, was filled with an arrangement of peonies and ranunculuses. There were cut-crystal finger bowls after the fish course, and beautifully monogrammed hand towels. It was all so elegant.

Venetian mirrors surrounded the small room, and Cordelia surreptitiously looked at Sinclair's reflection as he was talking to Tom. He looked younger, more relaxed than he had when she first met him. She knew the lines of his face now, and could read his moods by his changes of expression. She watched him sitting there, and loved him more than she had loved anyone in her life.

She was absolutely sated by all the courses: the cream of broccoli soup with Stilton, lamb shanks with saffron mashed potatoes, and finally the apple-and-walnut phyllo pastry with fresh whipped cream. During coffee Cordelia felt her eyes grow heavy.

"My dear, you look a bit fatigued," said Marian. "Why don't I show you to your room now for a bit of a rest before tea."

"I do need a rest, it has been a very stressful few days," admitted Cordelia.

"There is something we have to tell you," said Sinclair, looking at Tom and Marian. "Some pretty shady characters have been trailing Cordelia, and they tried to kidnap her yesterday."

"Oh, my *heavens!*" exclaimed Marian, but her expression changed to determination. "You will be safe here, my dear. I will see to it."

✢

Cordelia had never seen a bedroom so beautiful; it was like a museum. The furnishings were a mixture of French and English; a four-poster canopied bed was draped in pale blue damask silk that matched the color of two Wedgewood jasperware vases on the mantel. A pair of paintings, depicting cherubs, hung on the wall. Cordelia looked at the brass plates on the frames and read that the painter was François Boucher. The carpet was a blue-and-cream French Savonnerie, and a crystal chandelier hung overhead.

Yet for all its formality the room was also luxuriously comfortable. An upholstered satin divan, draped with a cashmere throw, was placed near the window that looked out over the lawn. On the low table next to it were several British novels, some European fashion magazines, and a box of Belgian chocolates.

The only thing missing was Sinclair. Tom and Marian had very decorously assigned them separate rooms. Neither she nor Sinclair had wanted to be rude by objecting to the sleeping arrangements. But as Marian was showing him the way down the hall, Sinclair had looked back at Cordelia and given her a wink that told her he would find her after they had retired for the night.

After a brief tour of her new bedroom, Cordelia began to get sleepy. The bed had been turned down, and the sheets had the pearly sheen of the finest Egyptian cotton. Her body ached from the assault yesterday—her ribs were sore, and her shoulder where Sinclair had pulled was stiff.

She wanted to sleep more than anything in the world. She took off her clothes and folded them neatly on the chair. Clad only in her bra and panties, she slipped between the silky sheets. The bed smelled of lavender. She smiled to herself and fell asleep.

Golden Horn Inn, Oxfordshire

The clerk at the desk of the inn was clearly not charmed by the gregariousness of the man checking in.

"Your room key, sir," he said as he handed over the key to room 116.

"I'm looking forward to seeing a bit of the countryside around these here parts," said Bob as he took the keys.

"Thank you, sir. Have a nice stay." The crisp British tones could not have been more chirpily dismissive.

"Thanks, son, mighty kind of you."

Bob and Marlene headed to the lift.

Room 117 of the Golden Horn Inn was a tangle of equipment. The Russian leaned over his computer and listened carefully to the bugs he had placed in the dining room, study, library, and kitchen of Cliffmere. This morning, it had taken only a few moments to place them, and now conversations were recorded directly into his media source program. It looked like an electrocardiograph machine. He could see when people were speaking from the undulations on the screen. He scrolled through, looking for the vibration lines. It was going to take hours to listen to everything. But there was nothing else to do in this rainy British dump.

Room 118 of the Golden Horn Inn was barely touched. The man who had checked in hadn't stayed long. Neither had the man in 119. They had left together to "see the countryside." They were now taking turns standing in the shrubbery on the property line of Cliffmere. One sat in the car while the other got soaked to the bone in the rain. Then they switched. Thaddeus Frost turned up the collar of his raincoat, longing for the sunny afternoons he had just enjoyed in Turkey.

Cliffmere

Cordelia came down the main staircase as the clock was chiming eight. She had slept through tea and felt completely refreshed.

"Here you are. I thought you would never wake up."

Sinclair was waiting for her at the bottom of the stairs.

"I ache all over from yesterday," she admitted.

"You poor darling. I'll give you a massage later. That will help."

He took her hand and lightly lifted it to his lips. He brushed the back of her knuckles with a kiss, and then turned her hand over and kissed her wrist, looking into her eyes. The touch of his lips on her skin made her pulse race.

"I missed you during my nap," she said.

"We can see each other tonight," he assured her, taking her arm and moving toward the main wing. "My room is just down the hall."

The study was a cozy box of a room, off the library, paneled in the very dark carved oak of the Tudor era. The room was well worn, with high-backed armchairs grouped around the fireplace. Marian's gardening catalogs were in a stack, along with several mystery novels. The fireplace had attracted a hunting dog and a large calico cat. The animals eyed Cordelia with curiosity when she came in. Sinclair walked over to pat the dog, who tilted its head so Sinclair could fondle its ears.

Tom poured two glasses of amontillado sherry and handed them to the ladies. He offered a cut-crystal tumbler of whiskey to Sinclair and then took a seat by the fire. Sinclair let the rich taste of the whiskey warm him on the way down, settling his soul.

"We need to talk about Bradford," said Tom.

"And Sir James Skye Russell," said Cordelia.

"Do you think the deed could be here in the house?" asked Sinclair.

"I think it's pretty much impossible. I know this may seem like a big house," Tom said, "but we have inventoried all the historical documents."

"And you couldn't have missed anything?" asked Cordelia.

"Probably not. The library is extremely rare and we have had it appraised. The curators went over all the books and papers about four years ago. We certainly would have found a deed at that time."

"No desks with secret compartments, no hidden rooms or hollow panels?" asked Cordelia.

"Oh, there are plenty," assured Tom. "A house this old is *filled* with hiding places. But I grew up here. I have been over every inch of the place."

"Where would you even *start* in a place this size?" asked Sinclair. "It would take years."

"Well," said Marian with brisk practicality. "We can't think clearly on empty stomachs. We had better go in to supper."

The main dining room was wood-paneled, and to Cordelia it looked at least the size of an indoor tennis court. The enormous dining table could accommodate forty people. As they dined, they all sat at one end, around a circle of candlelight, as if huddled over a campfire.

By the end of the sumptuous meal, Cordelia was utterly contented. She leaned back in her chair and sipped her coffee. She loved Cliffmere. Tom and Marian were treating her like family, and she had never seen Sinclair so relaxed. He and Tom had spent the afternoon touring the estate. As the two men sat there discussing their day, they could have been father and son; they had similar physiques and the same tall, rangy strength. Marian sat quietly, listening. She looked very lovely in her rose silk blouse and long black moiré satin skirt. Her pearls had the luster of several generations of wear.

The food had been superb: lamb confit terrine, slow-roasted rack of pork with wild mushroom ragout, and scallion potatoes. The lemon-blackberry tart was light and delicious.

"How we wish we had known about you all these years," Marian said warmly, squeezing Cordelia's hand. "We *do* consider you family."

"That means so much to me," Cordelia replied, her voice husky with suppressed emotion. "You have no idea how much."

Tom looked over at Cordelia and Marian, both of whose eyes swam with tears. He glanced at Sinclair, clearly uncomfortable with the emotional turn of the conversation.

"Shall we retire to the library?" he asked.

They left the table and walked into the next room. The library table had been set with a crystal decanter and delicate port glasses. They helped themselves to port, and started a slow amble around the enormous book-lined room. Soaring bookcases stood twenty feet high. About twelve feet up, a brass-railed catwalk gave access to the higher shelves. As they toured the magnificent collection, Tom pointed out his favorite volumes to Sinclair. Marian waited until the men were a few steps ahead before she turned to Cordelia.

"I *do* like your young man. Have you known him long?"

Cordelia flushed. "I'm afraid not. I just met him about two weeks ago."

Marian started in surprise. "Oh! I had no idea. I am sorry; I didn't mean to pry. I assumed you were—"

"No, it's no problem. I don't mind talking about it."

"You seem very close," observed Marian.

"Yes, things *have* moved along very quickly," Cordelia admitted. "We met at an award ceremony in Monaco."

"Were you accepting an award?"

"John's foundation was giving an award to Elliott Stapleton. In a funny way, I feel like my great-great-grandfather introduced us."

"That seems to me to be a *very* good introduction," said Marian soothingly.

"He invited me to lunch the next day, and then after that there was this problem with the deed. He kept helping me. And, of course, I started falling for him. . . ."

"He seems lovely."

"You should have seen him yesterday when they tried to kidnap me. He was incredible."

"I am sure he was magnificent," said Marian warmly, patting her hand. "Tom told me he seems to be a solid young man."

"I'm glad you approve." Cordelia smiled.

"And he certainly is *good-looking*," Marian added.

"You know, at first I was a little afraid he was a *too* good-looking."

Marian laughed. "There is no such thing as *too* good-looking. Besides, you are beautiful yourself, my dear. He might say the same of you."

"Thank you," said Cordelia. "Actually, he has never commented on my looks."

"He probably thinks you are tired of compliments, and he wants to impress you in other ways."

"I wonder . . ." mused Cordelia.

"Well, the way he was looking at you during supper tells the whole story," said Marian. "He is quite in love with you."

Cordelia blushed, and tried to recover her composure as they approached Tom and Sinclair.

"I would love to show you some of our pictures," Tom was saying to Sinclair. He turned to his wife. "Marian, shall we go into the gallery?"

They walked through a large archway into the next room. Tom switched on the ceiling lights to reveal a beautiful old wood-paneled picture gallery with twenty-foot ceilings. About two dozen paintings were exhibited along the sides. Some of the canvases were so large they measured the entire height of the room. They walked slowly along the gallery, inspecting the paintings and sipping their port.

"Here is a Constable," Tom said, pointing, "and another pastoral by Jean-Baptiste-Camille Corot. But the real centerpiece is this sailing scene of Antwerp Harbor by J. M. W. Turner."

Tom then went over to a pair of portraits.

"Now to the Skye Russells. *These* are the portraits of the first Lord Andrew Skye Russell and his wife, Mary, painted by Sir Joshua Reynolds in 1755."

The tall man had a determined chin, and wore an ermine-lined red coat. His wife was pale and aristocratic, her lapdogs cavorting around her brocade skirt.

Tom proceeded a few more paces.

"And *here* is the ancestor that should interest both of you. Sir James Skye Russell, painted by Mr. James McNeill Whistler in 1902."

They looked at the full-length portrait of a pale young man dressed in black. He carried a pair of gloves and wore what appeared to be an opera cloak. His face was interesting, sensitive.

"And this is his wife, Anne," said Marian.

She wore a pink frilled day dress, and faced a quarter turn away. Her skirt was embroidered with peonies. Cordelia noticed a softness in her expression.

"It's like *meeting* them! We have been reading about them in the journal all week," Cordelia exclaimed, looking at the beautiful soft brown eyes of the woman in the portrait.

They continued down the gallery.

"Here we have a Venice scene by Luca Carlevaris, painted in 1709. *View from Bacino di San Marco.*"

As they walked to the far end, a large painting drew Cordelia's attention. It was an Arctic landscape. A ship appeared to be moored among the ice floes. The snow was cast with a rosy glow, and in the beautiful light the icebergs loomed in opalescent splendor all around the ship. On the surface the ice had the look of mother-of-pearl, but underneath its color ranged from deep blue to celadon green. It reminded Cordelia of her great-great-grandfather's description of the Arctic.

"What a beautiful painting," she said admiringly.

"Yes," said Tom. "It is quite special. These kinds of Arctic landscapes became very popular in Queen Victoria's day."

"I guess in the tradition of the Victorian explorer," commented Sinclair.

"Exactly. In fact, an American painter, Frederic Church, set the fashion for romanticized Arctic landscapes when he exhibited *The Icebergs (The North)* in 1861. There was so much enthusiasm for these kinds of paintings, many of the polar explorers brought along a photographer and a painter."

"Is this painting by Frederic Church?" asked Cordelia.

"No, it is a little later than that, 1871, but the Frederic Church painting may have been the inspiration for it. This artist was also American. It's called *An Arctic Scene: Among the Icebergs in Melville Bay.*"

"Incredible," said Sinclair, stepping back to admire it.

"Who painted it?" asked Cordelia.

"William Bradford," said Tom.

They all froze, staring at the painting.

"*Bradford,*" they said simultaneously.

In a country lane in Oxfordshire, the two fat Americans in the rental car were clearly lost. They pulled up to a car parked next to a hedgerow. A bearded young man in a tweed cap was smoking a cigarette, standing next to the car. His companion sat in the driver's seat.

"Are ya'll from around here? Can you tell us where Cliffmere is?" asked Bob.

Thaddeus looked at the couple with interest.

"Yes, I believe it's right there, through the trees," he said in a credible British accent.

"Much obliged," said Bob. "I wanted to check out the farm. I hear Cliffmere supplies some of the best restaurants in London."

"I couldn't tell you," said Frost, tossing his cigarette and moving toward his car. He glanced down at the couple's license plate and memorized it. These tourists didn't seem like a threat, but you never could tell. He was jumping at shadows these days. In his entire career, he had never had a worse feeling about a case.

Sinclair finally broke the silence in the picture gallery.

"I hate to suggest the obvious, but shouldn't we check to see if a deed is taped to the back of the painting?"

Tom shook his head.

"This painting was cleaned two years ago. We took it out of the frame. There was nothing attached to it," he said.

"If William Bradford was a friend of Sir James's, maybe they gave the deed to him," suggested Cordelia.

"Not possible. William Bradford died in 1892. And the journal was written in 1908. I am not sure they would even have known each other. But in any case, Bradford would not have been around to receive the deed in 1908," said Tom.

Cordelia walked over to the red velvet settee in the middle of the room and sat down, staring at the painting.

"John, remember that description of icebergs we read about in the journal? Look at the color of the ice. This is *exactly* the scene Elliott was describing. I know we're on the right track."

"What did the journal say about Bradford?" asked Tom.

"We only came across one passage, and I have it memorized," said

Cordelia. " 'I will bring it to my partner JSR. As he is leaving for the Middle East, JSR may agree to entrust it to Bradford—is as good a choice as any for safekeeping.' "

They all stared at the painting.

" 'Entrusting it to Bradford is as good a choice as any . . . ,' " repeated Sinclair out loud.

"It *has* to be this painting! I know he was talking about this scene," said Cordelia again. "I *feel* it!"

Suddenly Tom slapped his knee in excitement. He leapt to his feet.

"*I know where to look!*" he exclaimed.

They stared at him in expectation.

"Come along to the library."

"Would you roll that ladder over here, John?" Tom requested, searching up into the dark regions of the bookshelves.

"Certainly."

Tom explained as he walked along the bookshelves.

"Bradford wrote a book; really, it was a folio of his photographs of the Arctic that he used as studies for his painting."

"Bradford was American, you said. Why is this folio in England?" asked Sinclair, rolling the library stairs over.

"The mania for all things Arctic was sweeping England, and his paintings and photographs found a richer market in London than they did in New York. Queen Victoria was a patron."

"But you say this folio is a book of *photos*?" said Cordelia.

"Yes, an enormous leather-bound folio. It was sold as a collector's item for the personal libraries of Victorian gentlemen and was very much in demand by high society. It was a great conversation piece, for after-dinner entertaining."

Tom started climbing the ladder. "Queen Victoria commissioned a painting from him, and he was the toast of London society. Push to the left a bit, would you, John?"

Sinclair rolled the ladder carefully, with Tom balancing on top.

"Here it is," said Tom. Sinclair braced the ladder with his shoulder as Tom lifted the heavy volume off the shelf. It was the size of a very large atlas, bound in black leather.

"This book is extremely rare. They published fewer than three hundred here in England, and plans for an American version were never completed."

Tom used both hands to swing the heavy portfolio around. Afraid he might drop it or lose his balance, he handed it down to Sinclair, then stepped down.

They examined the impressive volume on the library table. The leather cover was hand-tooled, with a relief of polar bears walking across the Arctic ice. Tom pulled open a drawer in the library table and handed out white cotton gloves.

"We have to put these on so the oils of our skin don't taint the antique paper," he explained.

They put the gloves on while Tom pulled out a long wooden spatula about two feet long.

"The paper is brittle. We have to turn the pages with this. I will slide it in between the paper, and, Marian and Cordelia, you support the corners when we turn the page."

Gingerly the three of them turned the first page.

The preface was signed "WB 1872." Page by page, they examined the book, turning the pages gently and exclaiming over the images as each appeared. Several dozen sepia photos were clearly the original studies for scenes Bradford later painted. The text was elaborate and dramatic, very much in the style of Victorian travel writing. Finally they came to the photo that inspired the painting *An Arctic Scene: Among the Icebergs in Melville Bay*. It was identical to the painting in the gallery.

"*That is your painting!*" exclaimed Cordelia.

Tom didn't answer. He put down the wooden page-turner and focused on sliding his gloved fingers underneath the cardboard plate. He lifted carefully, and as the old glue gave way it came up with a snap. He then put his fingers under the corners of the loose photo and raised it. There underneath was a small square of folded paper, coffee-colored with age.

They stood staring at it for a few moments, afraid to touch it.

"*Is that the deed?*" asked Cordelia.

"I don't know. We should see if we can get this unfolded without destroying it," said Tom.

"I have a good bit of experience with old documents," said Sinclair, "some much older than this. Last year I opened an Egyptian papyrus in Cairo. I am sure I won't damage it."

He could barely suppress the excitement in his voice. He turned to the others. "We need a bright light, a clean surface, in case it crumbles, two pairs of tweezers, and a pane of glass to put over it when we are finished unfolding it," he explained.

"I have tweezers for my crewelwork, and we can take a pane of glass out of one of the picture frames on the piano," said Marian.

"I'll go get a bedsheet to cover the library table," said Tom, "And, John, why don't you bring that floor lamp over for some extra light."

Within minutes they were reassembled.

"Let's have a look at this," Sinclair said quietly as they crowded around him. He removed the square of paper from the folio with the tweezers and bent over it. He was infinitely patient in unfolding the document, giving it his full concentration and not speaking. It didn't crumble, but the old paper looked very brittle. As he opened it, they could immediately see it wasn't a legal deed or any kind of official document. There was some writing and a series of numbers. When the paper was fully extended, it read:

THE CAPTAIN OF THE *NAUTILUS* HOLDS THE KEY. ELLIOTT STAPLETON 1918

42 ,15,		2	55, 51, 4, 68	9, 24	17, 80, 5, 63,
73, 71	1, 45, 90, 79				
33, 8	49, 41, 34, 27, 13, 38, 60				

"It's some kind of code," said Tom.

"Look at the date," said Sinclair. "It's 1918—that's ten years *later* than the journal entry. I wonder why?"

"That *is* curious, isn't it," said Marian.

"Who is the captain of the *Nautilus*?" asked Sinclair. "Is that the name of the ship in the painting?"

"No," said Tom thoughtfully. "The ship in the painting is Bradford's ship, and it was called the *Panther.*"

"It's not Stapleton's ship either. Elliott Stapleton went on expedition with Prince Albert on the *Princess Alice,*" Cordelia added.

"Wait. I have a historical record of all registered ships in any given year. Maybe we can find the *Nautilus* there." Tom rolled the ladder over to the corner of the room and came back with a large ledger. He began looking through the index.

"I see in 1800 there was a human-powered submarine designed by Robert Fulton, called the *Nautilus*," Tom said.

"The same Robert Fulton of steamship fame?" asked Sinclair.

"Exactly. It says here he was commissioned by Napoleon in France to build one of the first submarines, named the *Nautilus*."

"Would that submarine have a captain? Unless he means Fulton," Sinclair said.

"That would have been too early for this. It was in 1800," added Tom.

"The *Nautilus* was also the name of the first nuclear-powered submarine that went under the North Pole in the 1950s," Cordelia interjected.

"But again, not the right historical period for this code," observed Tom.

"It has to be some kind of ship, because the paper says there was a captain...." Cordelia trailed off.

"I think there were some British naval ships named *Nautilus*," Tom said, skimming through the book.

Marian was sitting quietly, staring at the paper. "I know this may sound silly," she said, "but I think these numbers could be a book cipher."

They all looked at her in surprise.

"I read a lot of mysteries," she explained. "Tom usually thinks I am filling my head with all kinds of nonsense. And he is probably right...."

"She always has a mystery on her bed table," he affirmed. "But, Marian, I wouldn't *dream* of criticizing what you read."

They exchanged a tender glance as Marian continued. "I don't know if you have heard of a 'book cipher.' It was popular in Victorian literature."

"How does it work?" asked Cordelia.

"There is usually a key text. It's the basis of the code. For example, it can be a passage in the Bible or any other classic book, like *David Copperfield* or *Moby-Dick*."

"Marian, I had no idea..." Tom was looking at her in astonishment.

"Sir Arthur Conan Doyle created this type of code in the 'The Adventure of the Dancing Men.'"

"Could this be that code?"

"No. I was just using that as an example. There are thousands. It's called cryptoanalysis. Edgar Allan Poe's 'The Gold-Bug' also uses a cipher text. Poe was an expert at ciphers and codes. The hero in that story uses it to find the buried treasure of Captain Kidd."

"It sounds very plausible, if codes were popular at the t—" said Sinclair.

Cordelia broke in. "*Wait!* If it's a book code . . . when was Jules Verne published?"

They all stopped to consider, but nobody answered.

"In Jules Verne," Cordelia continued, "the captain of the *Nautilus* is Captain Nemo in *Twenty Thousand Leagues Under the Sea.*"

"*Of course,*" said Tom and Sinclair in unison.

"I haven't read it since I was a child. But that book is what started my interest in submarines," Cordelia explained.

Tom had pulled down a volume of the *Encyclopaedia Britannica,* and looked up the entry for Jules Verne. He read silently for a moment.

"Verne was at the peak of popularity in the 1870s," Tom said, snapping the book shut. "That was right in the middle of the Victorian era. The book would have been very well known when your great-great-grandfather was writing this code."

"It was published when he was a child," observed Sinclair. "He probably read it when he was young, just like Cordelia did."

Sinclair and Cordelia exchanged a look of suppressed excitement.

"Do we have a copy of *Twenty Thousand Leagues Under the Sea?*" asked Marian.

"As a matter of fact, we do," said Tom.

"Let's see if I can remember this," said Marian as she took the novel in her hands. "It's actually pretty simple, as far as codes go. But, of course, I have never decoded anything, so let me think a moment. John, why don't you write down the letters as I call them out. There is a pen and paper over there on the writing desk."

"How do you begin?" asked Cordelia.

"Is there anything that looks like a page number or a line number on the note?" Marian asked.

Cordelia bent over the scrap of paper.

"Yes! It says P-thirty-five, L-sixteen!" said Cordelia.

"Page thirty-five, line sixteen reads: ' "I have hesitated for some time," continued the commander, "nothing obliged me to show you hospitality," ' " read Marian.

Sinclair wrote out the sentence, assigning each letter a consecutive number. Cordelia looked over his shoulder and caught a glimpse of the cipher.

I-1 H-2 A-3 V-4 E-5 H-6 E-7 S-8 I-9 T-10 A-11 T-12 E-13 D-14 F-15 O-16 R-17 . . .

"That looks fairly complicated," she observed.

"Not necessarily," Marion reassured her. "You will see how simple it really is."

They turned back to the paper under the glass. Tom read off each number, and Sinclair wrote down the corresponding letter. The whole exercise took about five minutes.

"So what do we have?" asked Marian.

"It makes no sense," said Sinclair, showing them the paper. It read:

AFH BIVW IM RIETOU IEL ES TMDOECD

"Something is wrong," puzzled Marian. "The numbers must be off."

"Are you sure we have the right page and line?" asked Tom.

"Yes, it says P-thirty-five, L-sixteen. It couldn't be more clear," said Cordelia.

"That's what I have," said Marian, recounting the lines on the page. "What could be the problem?"

They all sat for a moment, thinking.

"Hold on now," said Tom. "What *edition* is that copy of the book? The original book was in French. That means many translations, many different editions."

"We need the edition Elliott Stapleton used," agreed Sinclair.

Marian flipped over the book she had in her hand and looked at the cover page.

"This edition is 1941."

"He would have used a 1908 edition or earlier. He was on the steamship from Boston when he wrote the journal entry," said Cordelia.

"Where can we get a copy of Jules Verne from 1908?" asked Sinclair.

"And a copy from an *American* publisher," added Cordelia. "He was coming from America at that time."

"How do you *find* something like that?" asked Marian.

"We can call Jim Gardiner," assured Cordelia. "He knows how to do *everything.*"

Cordelia took the robe from the back of the wardrobe door and folded it around herself. It was cold in her room; her bare feet were freezing on the wood floors. She supposed she had been spoiled by American central heating, and too many expeditions to the Bahamas.

She opened the door of the blue bedroom and tiptoed out. If anything, the hall was even colder. A dim light burned on the table, and the corridor disappeared off into cavernous darkness. The paintings were softly illuminated, and there wasn't a sound. Sinclair had said he was three doors down, in the Chinese bedroom. She counted carefully, and knocked on the heavy door.

Sinclair opened it immediately and pulled her in, wrapping her into his robe against his warm body. It was heaven.

"I thought you would never get here. What *took* you so long?" he demanded, but didn't bother to wait for an answer. He just kissed her deeply.

"Delia, it's so *good* to hold you," he murmured into her hair. "Come to bed."

He slipped off her robe and her nightgown and pulled her, naked, under the covers of the enormous carved bed. She no longer had to worry about freezing. Within minutes, she was throwing the blankets off.

It seemed like years since she had been with him, and his every touch set off a ripple of pleasure. He caressed her tenderly, aware of her every tremor. They merged immediately, unable to wait, and it went on and on. All sense of time was lost. Her arms stayed wound around him as they lay across the bed until she fell asleep.

Much later, she woke and roused him. "John, I'm *cold.*"

He stirred, and without a word reached back and pulled the heavy coverlet up around them, gathering her close to his warm body in a private cocoon for sleep.

Outside Cliffmere, in the back-entrance service lane, two men sat in a truck. Thaddeus Frost was smoking out the window, trying to overpower the cologne the other man was wearing. Frost filled his time picking apart the components of the scent. It was a game for him. The first aroma was citrus, woods, and amber. The lemon was initially sweet but then there was a more vegetal undertone, a stylized violet with cloves, and then the powdery whiff of carnation. He threw away his cigarette butt and thought about it more. It was the sweet notes that bothered him. The deeper notes of sandalwood, birch tar, and the woodiness of orris were all good. Frost looked at his watch. Midnight.

"Why don't we head back? It's not likely anything will happen at this hour."

"Right," the other man answered. "The house is dark. I'm picking up the signal that the alarms are activated."

"It's about time," observed Frost. "I could use some sleep."

"I have a hunch whoever is out there will strike soon."

"I agree. I think they will see plenty of activity once they find that deed," said Frost.

"Well, we better get there first," the other agent said as Frost started the truck.

Cordelia opened her eyes to see Sinclair looking at her.

"Good morning, my love," he said.

"Good morning." She smiled. "What time is it?"

"Eight o'clock."

"That late!" said Cordelia, sitting up and looking for her nightgown and robe. Sinclair reached for them on his side of the bed and handed them to her.

"Do you have an appointment?" he asked with amusement.

"No, but how am I going to sneak back to my room in broad daylight?" she countered, pulling her nightgown over her head. When her face emerged, he kissed her hard on the mouth.

"Who says you're going back?"

The breakfast room was empty when they arrived downstairs. They found chafing dishes on the sideboard, and racks of toast set at each place along with the famous Cliffmere butter, apricot jam, and English marmalade.

They helped themselves to eggs, sausage, bacon, and grilled tomatoes. The housekeeper came in to ask if they would like juice or fruit, and put a carafe of coffee on the table for them.

"Do you think we can get hold of Gardiner today?" Sinclair asked, pouring her a cup of coffee. "We need to find that book."

"Yes, I will call this afternoon," said Cordelia. "I also promised Marian I would help her repot the begonias in the conservatory."

Sinclair was smiling at her. "I can see you love this place," he observed.

"You know," she admitted, spreading marmalade on her toast. "I feel so at home here. Tom and Marian are the closest thing to family I have in this world."

"You have me," he said softly.

She smiled at him, chewing her toast happily.

"And that makes me the luckiest woman in the world."

Sinclair dialed Charles in Monaco and got his voice mail.

"Charles, we will be staying for another week at Cliffmere. You can get me on my cell if you need me."

Sinclair looked at his watch. It was already a quarter to ten. Tom had asked him to meet him at the stables right after breakfast. Sinclair opened the French doors and set out across the lawn.

He cut through the kitchen herb garden, down the grass terrace on the east side of the house, past the maze, through the eighteenth-century rose garden, to the woodland park. A dog bounded out of the underbrush and came up to lick his palm.

"Hey, fella," Sinclair said. "Want to tell me which way to go?" The beautiful hound looked at him expectantly. Suddenly Sinclair saw Tom come out from behind the yew hedge.

"I gave up on you," he said.

"Sorry. Late morning. I sort of overslept," apologized Sinclair.

"Let's go to my office at the stable. It's a good place for a talk."

Tom's land-management office was spacious and comfortable, with deep leather chairs and a large window looking out over the lawn. The room was lined with wooden cabinets for all sorts of historical documents, many of which dated from the Elizabethan era. Modern records for the organic farm were in file cabinets and online: produce yields, animal registration and sales documents, land-maintenance schedules, and purchase receipts. On the wall behind Tom's desk were reproductions of the estate's historic garden plans—among them one for the original Elizabethan knot garden—and diagrams for the landscape park by Lancelot "Capability" Brown.

"Since I retired, the farm has been pretty much a full-time job," Tom announced, sitting back in his leather chair behind the desk. "I never knew it would be so successful."

Sinclair stayed silent. Clearly something else was on Tom's mind.

"I guess you want to know why I brought you here?" Tom said. "Marian wanted me to talk to you about Cordelia. We feel we need to look out for her."

"I couldn't agree more. She really doesn't have anyone looking out for her except her lawyer, Jim Gardiner," said Sinclair.

"Well, she has us now. And I want to make that clear."

"That will be a great comfort to her, I am sure," Sinclair affirmed.

"Yes," continued Tom, shifting uncomfortably. "In that vein, I wanted to speak with you because somebody has to ask you, and I believe in all decency the job falls to me."

"Ask me what?"

"What are your intentions in regard to Cordelia?"

Looking back on the conversation, Sinclair realized it was one of the best he had ever had in his life. He told Tom about his previous marriage and the fatal accident that had claimed his wife.

Tom had listened sympathetically, but then broached another subject.

"Forgive me, but I am a bit concerned about some recent press reports about you."

"You mean the tabloids, about Shari?"

"Yes. It's all over the Internet."

"Shari and I are finished. It's not an issue."

"Marian tells me you and Cordelia have been together for less than two weeks. Is that true?"

"Yes, it started quite suddenly," Sinclair admitted.

"These things always *start* suddenly. What's more important is how they end," said Tom.

"Are you telling me to end it?" Sinclair asked, aghast.

"No, what I am telling you is that Cordelia is a very vulnerable young lady."

"Tom, I know. I will do the right thing."

Tom sat silently for a moment.

"I am counting on you to do just that," Tom said.

After an hour of transplanting begonias, Marian told Cordelia to take a nap. But Cordelia usually couldn't manage it in the middle of the day, so she sat on the divan next to the window reading the journal.

> IT HAS COME TO MY ATTENTION THAT NORWAY HAS BEEN ENCOURAG-
> ING THE LAND CLAIMS OF ALL AND SUNDRY MANNER OF INHABITANTS OF
> THE ISLAND OF SPITSBERGEN. A SWARM OF NEW CLAIMANTS HAS SPRUNG
> UP AND IS TAKING POSSESSION OF IMMENSE TRACTS OF LAND ON THE
> ISLAND, AND NEARLY ALL CLAIMS ARE FILED BY FISHERMEN AND HUNT-
> ERS WHO HAVE NO COMMERCIAL INTEREST IN POSSESSION OF THE LAND.
> THERE SEEMS TO BE NO ACKNOWLEDGEMENT THAT THE ARCTIC COAL
> MINING COMPANY BENEFITS NORWAY AND, MOST SPECIFICALLY, SCORES
> OF NORWEGIAN STOCKHOLDERS. I HAVE BEEN ALERTED TO THIS BY MY
> AGENT IN SPITSBERGEN VIA OUR VERY DISCREET METHOD OF COMMUNI-
> CATION.

Cordelia put a bookmark in the spot, got up, stretched, and went out to find John.

Sinclair walked across the terrace with Cordelia. The light was soft, and the west garden was verdant and glowing. It was a pleasant day, just cool enough to require a light jacket. The trees were tinged with color, and he could feel fall coming.

Sinclair was glad to have Cordelia all to himself, if only for an hour or so. At Cliffmere, until now, they hadn't had much time alone. This afternoon, under a bright blue sky, they walked through the garden, their strides matching perfectly. Sinclair linked his fingers through hers and thought of nothing but the feel of her hand in his—skin against skin, one of the most elemental pleasures in the world.

They began exploring the garden nearest the house. The immediate vicinity was deserted, but the activity of the farm could be heard in the distance. There were many formal flower beds in final bloom. The kitchen garden, with its rows of herbs, was still thriving, and Cordelia bent down to read the markers: THYME, BASIL, MARJORAM, CAMOMILE. Farther along, the rose parterre had gone dormant, and the bushes were pruned and wrapped in burlap for the winter. They went down the stone steps and started across the broad expanse of lawn.

Sinclair had every intention of keeping to the open areas, in full view of the house. It would not be safe for Cordelia to wander on the wooded paths or in the fields. There were plenty of places they could explore without taking risks.

At the end of the lawn, they came across the boxwood maze. Together they stood and read the plaque that said it had been planted in 1760. Even this late in the season, it was green and dense with leaves. The monolithic hedges loomed eight feet tall and spanned at least an acre.

"Let's go in," said Cordelia. "I have always wanted to see one of these."

Sinclair hesitated. The entrance looked like a dark green cave.

"I'm not so sure. It's too hidden," he cautioned. "Someone could be watching us right now."

"Don't be silly. Who would be hiding in a maze?" she scoffed. "John, that's really *too* melodramatic."

Sinclair pulled her toward him and kissed her lightly on the lips. "I just want to be cautious," he explained.

"John, it's *fine*. Come on, I really want to see what it looks like."

"Listen, darling. Let's not be reckless," he pleaded.

"*Reckless?*" she replied, and broke away, laughing. She sauntered into the hedge-lined alley that served as the starting point.

"Delia, seriously, I don't think we should," Sinclair said, following behind her. His better judgment told him to stop her immediately, but that might come across as too controlling. She was very sensitive about that. And why curtail her fun? She had been through so much in the past few days.

He would stay right with her, and make sure they did not get separated in the labyrinth. After a few yards, it was too narrow to walk side by side, so they went single file, with Cordelia leading. He relaxed a bit and started to enjoy the challenge of finding the center. Together they followed serpentine routes that led around the blind corners and ended in cul-de-sacs of greenery. They looped around paths that put them back where they started. Within minutes, they were lost.

"I *love* this! It's so much fun. Come on, John."

Cordelia stepped quickly ahead and turned right. She disappeared from view. He turned twice to the right, once catching a glimpse of her, but then lost sight of her. He could hear her calling to him. She sounded close.

"Come this way, John." Her voice was muffled by the hedges.

"Cordelia! Where are you?"

It was dim in the narrow path. There was the scent of earth and vegetation. The thick boxwood formed walls on either side of him, and the sun was blocked except for the small piece of sky above. He called for her again. There was no answer.

A sudden fear welled up in him. What if someone really *was* hiding in the maze, waiting for her? He knew it was unlikely, but he still couldn't shake off the irrational fear. His heart began to pound—a stress response to losing control. He needed to find her quickly. He started to run down the alleys, calling her name. Once or twice he thought he could hear her movements, but he couldn't be sure.

Suddenly it felt very claustrophobic in the narrow path. Disorientation came in a sickening wave. The old feeling of terror had welled up so fast, he was stunned. He fought the sensation and forced himself to breathe. He closed his eyes and tried to remain calm. But it wasn't working.

"*Cordelia!*" he shouted.

It was too much. He looked at the impregnable hedges. He was losing his capacity to control his anxiety. The claustrophobia was crushing him. He sat down on the damp path and tried to force air into his lungs. His hands were shaking, so he pressed them down on the cool earth. His knees felt weak. He looked up at the sky overhead and saw that it was bright. But looking up made the hedges appear taller and closer.

Deep down he could feel the knot of anger at himself for being so weak. Panic was like a stone on his chest, crushing his will. If he could calm down, he might be able to push the panic away. He started to concentrate on breathing, and focusing on his inner strength. He stood up and got a good lungful of air. That was better. He tried another. The green walls of the maze were still bothering him, but when he was standing up they didn't seem so tall.

Just then Cordelia came around the corner, laughing. Her hair was flying all over and there were leaves stuck in it. She looked so vital and pretty, the sight of her cleared his head.

"John, what *are* you doing?" She reached to take his hand. "I got all the way to the middle, and you didn't follow," she complained.

He pulled his hand back because it was so grimy.

"I got lost. Let's get out of here. I find it a bit confining," he replied, surprised his voice was so even.

"Are you angry with me?" she asked, hearing his somber tone.

"No, not at all. It's just that it's getting late," he said, brushing his hand off on his trousers. "Any idea how we came in?"

"Yes," she said, looking at him curiously. "It's two turns to the left."

"Good. It's nearly teatime. Let's go in."

"OK," she agreed. "I could use a cup of tea. And I want to see if they have any of that incredible gingerbread they make for the London shops."

From the back courtyard, the Russian watched them go into the maze. He was dressed in the hunter green coveralls worn by the workers at the Cliffmere Organic Farm. Any good observer would have noticed the pocket of his Barbour-waxed coat was listing to the right, weighed down by the Beretta 92. The Russian would have preferred his usual Glock 19. The thirty-four-ounce Beretta was damn heavy. Unfortunately it was the only gun offered by his contact, so he had to take it.

The Russian pushed the wheelbarrow across the lawn to the west terrace, just in front of the study. The French doors were ajar. He slipped carefully through the long window, removing his wellies at the doorsill, and padded noiselessly through the study into the library. There, in the middle of the library table, was the code they had been talking about, under a pane of glass. He took out his camera and photographed it four times. Then he slipped out the way he had come in. He was just crossing the stable yard when Sinclair and Cordelia came back across the lawn, hand in hand.

⊛

The fire in the Tudor study was warm and comforting. A tray held a silver teapot, two cups, and a plate of homemade gingerbread. Cordelia bit into the dense cake and let the spicy flavor melt on her tongue. The Earl Grey tea, with its light taste of bergamot, was perfect with it. Sinclair stood, warming his feet on the brass railing of the fireplace.

"How did you know?" he asked, looking into the fire.

"John, your face was frightening."

"I thought I could hide it."

"How could you think I wouldn't notice?" She took a sip of her tea.

"I'm glad you know now. It's enclosed spaces. I can't take them," he admitted.

He looked miserable. She wanted to stand up and put her arms around him, but there was something in his stance that told her it wouldn't be welcome.

"Cordelia, I *wanted* to tell you about the accident. But I didn't want to put too much on you. You have your own problems."

"I don't have so many problems that I can't help *you*."

She reached out her hand to him. He took it, gave it a quick squeeze, and then dropped it. He turned away and looked out the window. Her heart froze at the gesture.

There was a long silence as he looked at the lawn. Finally he turned to her, and when he spoke his voice had the heavy tone of resignation.

"Cordelia, I might not be right for you. I am not good at relationships. I can barely manage my own private hell."

"John! What are you saying?" she cried out in dismay.

He turned to her, frowning with anxiety.

"Why would you need two hundred ten pounds of trouble?"

He paused, as if bracing for her response. She stood up and walked over to him.

"Don't do this, John. *Don't,*" she pleaded.

He said nothing. His expression was blank; he was trying not to show any emotion. She scanned his face and her eyes narrowed in suspicion.

"Is it Shari?"

His eyes opened wide in surprise, but he didn't respond.

"It's not like it's a secret, John. I read *Paris Match* on the ship," she said.

"You *did*? And you still wanted to go ahead with me, after *that*?"

"I did. I didn't believe that was the real you. That man in the photos was not the John Sinclair *I knew*."

"I never behaved like that before in my life," he vowed.

"I wonder if you want a supermodel?" she challenged. "Or somebody who is real?" Cordelia walked away and picked up her teacup, and took a sip to compose herself. He came over and took the cup away from her, put it on the table, and clasped both her hands.

"Cordelia, I want *you*."

"You do?"

"Yes. I want you to know that things with Shari weren't serious."

"And this is?" she asked.

He sighed heavily. "Yes. Although I have to admit I'm worried about where this is headed."

"You are?"

"Of course I am," he said. "Cordelia, look at our lives. We live on different *continents*. What are we going to do in a couple of weeks? Quit our jobs? Move? Or do we just e-mail each other from time to time?"

Cordelia pulled her hands away and put them behind her back.

"I know it's going to be tough. But even so, I want to give it a try," she said, tears filling her eyes. "I don't know how this is going to work out. But I am *not* going to just give up on it."

He looked at her for a long minute and then shut his eyes. He opened them and reached for her, and pulled her to his chest.

"OK, Delia. That was your chance to put the brakes on. If you want to stop this, it's *your* call. But if you want to make this work, I'm willing."

"I want this *so much,* John," she said. "I've never felt like this before. I know it's soon, I know it's complicated, but I want it."

"I want it too, you know," he said, kissing her lightly on the forehead. He pulled back with a rueful smile. "But don't say I didn't warn you."

New York City

The manager of the rare-book store came to the phone. Twice in one week was too much of a coincidence. He needed to know what was going on. He took the phone from the salesgirl.

"Bauman's Rare Books, may I help you?"

"Yes," said the assassin. "I am looking for a certain copy of *Twenty Thousand Leagues Under the Sea* by Jules Verne. None of the other American booksellers seem to have one."

"Yes sir, we can help you. We actually located that volume for another customer just yesterday."

"I am looking for a 1908 edition, printed in America. It can be a slightly earlier date."

"I have a 1906 copy—we found it when we were doing the search for our previous customer."

"I will take it."

"Very good, sir. Would you like it leather-bound? That will take an additional three weeks. I can recommend a burgundy calfskin—it looks quite handsome."

"No. No leather binding. Just the original book. I will send someone to pick it up at your store. Is four o'clock good? I want to get it right away. It's a birthday gift."

"Certainly, sir, we will set it aside. Who will be calling for it?"

"Mr. Jones will be coming by at four," the man said, and hung up.

The manager stood holding the phone, wondering why the customer had never asked the price.

Cliffmere

The setter was moving at a brisk trot down the wooded trail. It was a handsome animal, larger than a traditional gundog. This one stood twenty-seven inches at the shoulder, an excellent bird dog with the distinctive black and tan markings of a Gordon setter. Sinclair let the animal set the pace and increased his speed to keep up.

The trail was a mossy track through the woods, a cross-country bridle trail. It was just on the verge of dusk, and dense foliage on each side of the trail nearly obscured the sunlight. It was damp and cool—very soothing to Sinclair after the tension of being indoors so much of the time.

As Sinclair inhaled the fresh air, he began to feel better. It was good to get out of the house and move a bit. He needed to think on his own. The strain of being vigilant day after day was getting to him. Even when he slept, he wound his fingers through Cordelia's hair so no one would be able to capture her without waking him.

He had been on edge for days. Today he was at the breaking point. So when an opportunity for a moment's respite had turned up, he had seized it. Right now he had no worries about leaving Cordelia. She was in the kitchen, flanked by three men: the head chef, the assistant cook, and the pastry chef. They were teaching her how to make a traditional English game pie. The interior kitchen of the house was secure, and the men were armed with sharp knives. All that seemed safe enough.

Sinclair had watched for a while, and then, realizing he was not needed, he kissed her cheek and went out for a quick walk. She barely noticed when he slipped out through the kitchen door.

The path wound down through the woods to the river. He had been moving at a fast clip, but suddenly he stopped, on alert. Something was wrong. The dog halted and growled. There wasn't a sound; the forest seemed empty. But he knew something was there; he trusted dogs more than he trusted people. Charles had taught him that. The dog growled again as Thaddeus Frost stepped from behind a tree.

"You had me worried there," said Sinclair, coming up to put a hand on the dog's collar.

"I didn't mean to startle you. But I saw you coming out of the house."

His eyes were hard, and for the first time Sinclair saw how utterly dangerous Frost would be as an adversary.

"What's going on?" Sinclair asked.

"We picked up another Russian. This one was inside the house."

"*Inside the house, here?*" Sinclair stared, aghast. "When?"

"This afternoon."

"You got him?"

"Yes, we got him. He's out of commission," said Frost.

"I can't believe this!" Sinclair exclaimed.

"He's Russian, just like the one we got outside your house in Ephesus. We're not sure if they're connected."

"Connected or not, they tracked us here."

"Yes. The one we got today actually photographed the document in the library. It was nice of you to put it under glass for him. He got a good picture."

"Oh, no." Sinclair groaned.

"You *know* they are trying to kill her. You realize that, don't you?"

"Yes."

"Be extra careful at night," Frost cautioned. "Don't let your guard down. We're not here after the alarms go on at eleven p.m."

"We? How many. Two?"

"And you make three."

"OK, so what do we do now?" Sinclair asked.

Frost walked over to a tree to examine a fan-shaped fungus on the trunk. In the wooded setting, dressed in his tweed jacket and tan slacks, he was halfway camouflaged. Frost bent low to examine the underside of the shelf of fungus. It was bright yellow orange. He broke off a chunk and sniffed it.

"I *said*, what do we do now?" Sinclair said forcefully.

Frost turned back, as if he had just noticed him.

"Can't we hide somewhere?" Sinclair burst out. "I *hate* having to sit here just waiting for these bastards to go after Cordelia."

Frost walked soundlessly over to Sinclair, the pine needles cushioning his footsteps. His voice was low, as if he were concerned about being overheard.

"No. It's a good setup here. Much better than in London. There is a lot of activity during the day, with the farm. A lot of people are around to keep their eyes open. And at night the house is Fort Knox with the alarm system on."

"So how'd he get in?" Sinclair was careful to keep the accusation out of his voice.

"Disguised as a farmworker. He walked in through the French doors by the library. We saw him immediately. We were watching him the whole time. We bagged him the second he came out of the house."

"That still makes me nervous. What should we do?"

Thaddeus Frost turned back to the growth on the tree. He snapped off a larger section of the fungus. Holding it gingerly, he took a ziplock bag from his pocket and sealed the sample inside.

Sinclair watched the whole process without comment. Frost turned back.

"You need to decode that book and find the deed. After you find it, sell it, or give it away. Once it's out of your hands, they will leave you alone."

"You still want it, don't you? That's what you're really here for," said Sinclair.

Frost sighed and looked at him with contempt.

"When they start slicing up your girlfriend with a box cutter, right in front of you . . . you won't think *I'm* the bad guy. You'll get your priorities straight. Now I strongly suggest you get back into that house."

Thaddeus Frost turned and slipped behind the rhododendron and was gone.

Sinclair, Cordelia, Tom, and Marian all sat in Tom's private study. The upstairs room, just off his bedroom, was clearly a sanctuary for deep thought. Medical volumes lined the shelves and research papers were neatly stacked on the desk. They were taking turns reading passages from the diary out loud. Marian had, in her very practical manner, suggested that they get through it as quickly as possible. Tom was bent over his desk, reading steadily, his silver hair shining under the bright light of the brass accountant's lamp.

NORWEGIAN STOCKHOLDERS IN THE ARCTIC COAL MINING COM-PANY HAVE REQUESTED THAT THE NORWEGIAN GOVERNMENT CONFIRM THE UNDISPUTED POSSESSION OF THE ADVENT BAY TERRITORY BY THE ARCTIC COAL MINING COMPANY SO THE MINING OPERATIONS CAN CON-TINUE. THE MAJORITY OF LABORERS EMPLOYED BY THE MINE ARE OF NORWEGIAN NATIONALITY. THEREFORE, IT SHOULD BE IN THE INTEREST OF THE NORWEGIAN STATE TO UPHOLD THE LIVELIHOOD AND FINANCIAL INTERESTS OF ITS CITIZENS.

Sinclair stood up to take over the reading, taking his place at Tom's desk to continue.

I HEAR FROM MY MANAGER IN SPITSBERGEN THAT NORWAY HAS REFUSED UNDER ANY CIRCUMSTANCES TO CONSIDER GRANTING THE RIGHT TO ERECT A WIRELESS COMMUNICATION STATION. WE HAVE OFFERED TO INSTALL IT AT OUR OWN EXPENSE, AS IT IS CRITICAL DUR-ING THE IMPASSABLE WINTER MONTHS, WHEN ADVENT BAY IS CHOKED WITH ICE. THIS WOULD GREATLY BENEFIT THE COAL-MINING OPERATION, WHICH EMPLOYS SO MANY NORWEGIAN CITIZENS. MY ONLY CONCLUSION IS THAT NORWAY IS POSITIONING ITSELF WITH THE INTENT OF EVENTU-ALLY TAKING OVER THE TERRITORY.

Marian took the book from Sinclair and read in her clear voice.

EVEN ON THE MOST WORTHLESS PART OF OUR GREEN HARBOR PROPERTY, THE NORWEGIANS AND RUSSIAN TRESPASSERS HAVE FILED MULTIPLE CLAIMS. THEY FILE A CLAIM NOTICE WITH THE NORWEGIAN GOVERNMENT, AND THE MORE CUNNING OF TRESPASSERS BUILD CAMPS OF ONE OR TWO MEN, WHO STAY PART OF THE TIME. IT IS A MYSTERY TO ME WHAT THEY EXPECT TO DO WITH THE PROPERTY. THEY PROBABLY HAVE A VAGUE IDEA THAT SOMEONE WILL COME ALONG AND PAY THEM FOR IT, BECAUSE THEY ONCE WERE SQUATTERS AND DROVE SOME STAKES ON THE LAND.

Marian stopped reading and looked up and caught Sinclair's eye. He nodded at her, instantly understanding the implications of the passage. "Even back then, this land was being fought over. *Plus ça change, plus c'est la même chose,*" he said. "The more it changes, the more it stays the same."

Jim Gardiner hauled his vast bulk out of the tiny rental car. A half dozen dogs swarmed around him in the courtyard of the house. He started swatting them away.

"Down, boys, down."

They went into a frenzy of playfulness, dodging and rushing him, pulling at the hem of his raincoat. To Cordelia, Gardiner looked like a large bear, beset by hounds. He held a paper-wrapped parcel high above his head, protecting it.

"*Delia,* get rid of these beasts!" he called.

Cordelia flew out of the house and down the steps, and the dogs scattered. She gave Gardiner a hug. He stepped back and surveyed her.

"Honey, you look great. This country life is doing you some good."

"I feel great. But Tom and Marian are feeding me way too much. They grow organic gourmet food on this farm."

"Wow," said Jim. "Very fancy."

"The scones and jam at tea are *to die for*. But we walk it off. We have been spending at least half the day outdoors. I have never felt healthier in my life."

"That sounds great. Glad I came," he said, laughing. "By the way, how's your fella?"

"Oh, Jim, I love him. He's so perfect."

"Glad to hear that, honey. I get a good feeling about him."

"Tom and Marian have practically *adopted* him."

"Good. Now *you* should too," he joked, winking. "Well, here's your book," he said, presenting her with the brown paper package. "I had to turn London and New York upside down to get it."

"Thank you so much, how wonderful!"

"I got it from a rare-book dealer in New York. Sorry it took so long, they had to overnight it from the States."

"A 1908 edition of Jules Verne's *Twenty Thousand Leagues Under the*

Sea. Printed in America," Cordelia marveled, opening the brown wrapping and looking at the cover.

"Now that I found your book, are you going to tell me what is going on?" asked Gardiner.

It was nearly dusk and the light reflected on the pane of glass covering the book cipher. Sinclair was bent over it with great intensity.

Cordelia read the key text aloud: "Page thirty-five, line sixteen reads, 'We were lying on the back of a sort of submarine boat, which appeared, as far as I could judge, like a huge fish of steel.'"

"Oh!" Marian exclaimed. "Cordelia, a *submarine*! How lovely!"

"That sounds like a good omen," Tom said encouragingly.

"Submarines were pure fantasy at this time," observed Sinclair. "Elliott Stapleton would be surprised that his great-great-granddaughter actually ended up working on one."

"He would be so proud of you," Marian said, smiling at her.

Sinclair wrote the text out, assigning a number consecutively to each of the letters. When he finished, they examined the document.

They began with Cordelia calling out each number of the sequence and Marian writing down the corresponding letter of the alphabet.

"The last letter is *R*," said Marian, sitting up and rubbing her neck.

"Read what it says," said Sinclair.

Cordelia took the paper from Marian with shaking hands.

"THE DEED IS BURIED WITH MY PARTNER."

They all sat looking at one another.

"Well, I'll be damned," said Gardiner.

"The deed is *buried* with his partner?" said Sinclair.

"Would that be Sir James Skye Russell?" asked Marian.

"It would *have* to be Sir James," said Cordelia.

"But why would the deed be *buried* with Sir James?" mused Marian.

"Where is his grave?" asked Cordelia.

"Right here. Next to the family chapel—about half a mile away from the house."

"So we need to dig up the grave?" asked Sinclair.

"It would appear so," said Tom.

"That's *horrible*," said Cordelia.

"Not really," said Tom. They all looked at him. "This couldn't have happened at a better time."

Tom's voice took on the scholarly cadence that replicated the tone of an academic lecture.

"Sir James died in Paris in 1918. He was a British diplomat who was sent to prepare for the Paris Peace Conference after World War One. But while he was in Paris, he was hit suddenly by a flu that killed him in less than twenty-four hours.

"His body was immediately sealed in a lead-lined coffin," continued Tom.

Sinclair had his arm around Cordelia's shoulder and watched her reaction. She was listening very carefully.

"There was a very great fear of this disease," Tom was saying. "A person could go from the peak of health to his death overnight. It was a horrible, gruesome death, and the corpses were highly contagious, which is why they buried the victims so fast."

"So Sir James's body was shipped back to England to be buried?"

"Yes."

"Wait, there is something missing here," interjected Sinclair. "The 1908 journal led us to the Bradford folio. But the note saying 'The deed is buried with my partner' was not written until 1918. Why the ten-year gap?" asked Sinclair.

"Why would Elliott Stapleton have buried the deed in that grave?" Cordelia puzzled.

"Everything we have discovered would seem to suggest that he did," assured Gardiner.

"Why would he have *buried* the deed?" asked Sinclair. "They sure wouldn't have opened up that coffin to put it inside."

"True, but it may not be in the coffin. It may be in another container next to the coffin," suggested Tom. "Lots of people were contesting the land. Elliott and Sir James were often away on expeditions. They probably would always put the deed in a safe place before they left."

"A safe place, like the Bradford folio. Clearly in 1908 they left the deed there," said Marian, quoting, " 'to entrust it to Bradford is as good a choice as any for safekeeping.' "

"So why isn't the deed in the Bradford folio now?" asked Jim Gardiner.

"It was their usual hiding place. But Elliott must have decided that their usual hiding place wasn't secure in 1918," said Sinclair. "What was different?"

"Sir James's death," said Tom. "The house changed hands in 1918 and went to his cousin."

"Elliott would have had to find a hiding place other than the library!" Cordelia agreed.

"So he buried the deed but took the extra step of leaving a coded note in the Bradford folio to indicate where it was hidden?" Marian ventured.

"Wait," said Cordelia. "Where was Anne Skye Russell, Sir James's wife? Why couldn't he just give it to her?"

"She died the year before, in childbirth. The child survived and was raised by Sir James's sister in Yorkshire."

"The house was off-limits, so he buried it. But why was he hiding it in 1918? Why that year specifically? Did Elliott Stapleton go on expedition that year?" asked Sinclair.

"Yes, he did," said Cordelia. "He made an attempt on the North Pole that year."

"If Elliott buried the deed, how do we know he didn't dig it up again?" asked Gardiner.

"He couldn't have. He died in 1919," said Cordelia. "He never came back to England."

"And the code was still in the Bradford folio. No one found it. And *he* didn't remove it. So the deed must still be buried," said Tom.

"Tom, why do you say this couldn't have happened at a better time?" Cordelia asked.

"As it so happens," said Tom, "the grave is being exhumed next week."

"*What!*" said Sinclair and Cordelia together.

"I gave permission to my former colleague, Paul Oakley, to dig up Sir James's grave. Oakley is looking for a good sample of the 1918 virus."

"For research?" asked Cordelia.

"Yes, it's critical. There are only a few places to get samples now. Most remains have been destroyed by time. Traditional wooden coffins break down—the tissue becomes so badly decomposed that the virus is lost. But in a lead coffin there is a chance the lungs are still intact. Even after all this time."

"I can't believe you would *let* them dig up your great-grandfather's grave," said Gardiner.

"This pandemic killed possibly fifty million people. More people died than in World War One, World War Two, or even from AIDS. But the

1918 virus is extinct now. And anything we can find out about it will be helpful in developing a vaccine for the *next* pandemic."

"So they are digging up Sir James to do genetic decoding?" asked Cordelia.

"Yes," said Tom. "When I was still at the Royal London Hospital, we were already linking this virus with avian flu. It may be that the two viruses are related. The swine flu we recently experienced was just a scare, but this virus is really deadly. So when Oakley asked me about finding victims of the 1918 pandemic, I volunteered Sir James."

"And I agreed," affirmed Marian. "I think it is the only responsible thing to do. It may save lives."

"What if you spread another pandemic?" asked Jim Gardiner.

"We believe the virus is no longer able to infect people, but we are taking all kinds of measures to prevent an accidental release if we are wrong."

"So it's safe?" asked Gardiner.

"We can't be a hundred percent sure. So we will use a secure biocontainment tent over the grave," said Tom. "Marian and I will be watching the whole thing from inside the house on closed-circuit monitors."

"Will monitors be good enough to see if the deed is buried?" asked Cordelia.

"Probably not, but you will need to stay inside," said Sinclair.

"What about you?" Cordelia asked Sinclair.

"I'll be standing there watching every shovel full of dirt. We simply *must* find that deed," Sinclair said with such finality, no one argued with him.

Sinclair watched Cordelia and Marian cross the lawn to the east terrace. Three dogs were running wild circles around them. Cordelia was wearing a shooting sweater for warmth, and it swamped her figure, falling well below her hips. Her legs were clad in jeans and rubber wellies. Unobserved, Sinclair enjoyed watching her elegant grace as she walked. What a beauty she was!

He was glad they had decided to stay at Cliffmere until the excavation. For one thing, Cordelia's town house was off-limits until the investigation could be concluded. And as Thaddeus Frost had said, Cliffmere was infinitely safer and more secure than a London hotel and they both were beginning to feel very much at home with Tom and Marian, who would not hear of them returning to London.

The extra week had done Cordelia good. Tom and Marian's support was therapeutic. They had kept her busy and productive. She was less jittery and almost appeared to forget her danger.

Sinclair had stayed vigilant, but with the farmworkers about and Thaddeus Frost monitoring the house, he had felt relatively secure during the day. So much so he actually started to relax and enjoy Cliffmere. He shadowed Tom as he went about the daily review of the free-range poultry operations and livestock. Tom was particularly proud of his cattle.

This morning, Sinclair and Tom had stood at the five-barred gate looking over his English longhorns.

"These Dishley longhorns are quite in demand," Tom had explained. "One of the chefs in London has said ours is the best beef in Britain. Now all the finest restaurants want to buy our organic grass-fed beef."

To Sinclair, they looked a lot like American longhorns except their coronet of horns swept forward and not up like handlebars.

"That is fantastic," Sinclair had enthused. "You must be so proud of your operation here."

"So much to do, my boy. So much to do. No time to gloat quite yet."

Sinclair had a wonderful time learning about the farm. Tom spoke to him at length about free-range poultry farming and the threat of avian flu. Sinclair learned more than he could ever have imagined. Tom's expertise extended well into the virology of the disease.

While the two men spent the day together outdoors, Cordelia and Marian stayed closer to the house and the outbuildings. Together they helped inventory the produce: eggs, cheeses, meats, and organic fruits and vegetables. They also packed the famous baked goods: gingerbread, shortbread, and scones, stacking them in the hunter green Cliffmere boxes, tying them up with grosgrain ribbons.

This afternoon Sinclair watched from the library window as he caught up on Herodotus Foundation business. He could keep an eye on Cordelia, sitting on the terrace with Marian, her feet in green wellies propped up on a stone wall. Marian was leaning forward, speaking earnestly. The two women looked relaxed and happy. But this could not last forever. They had to make plans about what to do next. Sinclair picked up his phone and dialed Charles.

"Hi, Sinclair. Still in England?" Charles answered.

"Yes, it's going well. But a lot has happened."

"Anything wrong?" asked Charles.

"I'm in a little over my head. We had some trouble in London. When we go back, I could use some help."

"Certainly. I'll meet you at Claridge's as usual?" asked Charles.

"Yes. In a day or so. I'll let you know when."

The special biocontainment tent had been erected and inflated over the work site at the family chapel at Cliffmere. Necropolis, the grave excavation company, had come and prepared the ground, carving up the lawn into oblong rectangles and rolling it up like carpet. Now three men in space suits were clearing the uppermost layer of soil, careful not to strike anything that offered resistance.

It was his imagination, but Sinclair thought he could smell the damp earth rising from the open grave. Of course, that was ridiculous; his air was filtered. He chafed inside the sealed suit and tried to breathe normally, but there was a slight feeling of suffocation. He fought it.

Sinclair was used to open-air excavation, and all this felt very claustrophobic. To quell the feeling, he had to keep telling himself that excavation was excavation; it was all the same. After all, what was the difference between digging up old bones in Ephesus and digging up the remains of Sir James Skye Russell? About a couple of thousand years, he mused.

In front of him the three gravediggers were perspiring inside their sealed hoods. Their shovels struck resistant earth.

Again Sinclair tried to concentrate on something else. Breakfast with Cordelia. She had looked luminous as she drank her chocolate. How could she eat all those croissants and stay so slim? Butter and marmalade too.

This morning he had decided to skip eating. Too risky. As he had left, Tom and Marian's faces reflected the green glow of the closed-circuit monitors. The library had been dim and quiet.

He had crunched up the gravel path to the chapel a half mile away. A local official had stood at the gate. An orange containment fence circled the church and the cemetery. Sinclair had produced his letter of admission, and endured the squint of the uniformed officer as he peered suspiciously at it. The guard was being especially officious, telling him to stay on the gravel walkways and not cut across the lawn. Only after multiple directives had he reluctantly waved Sinclair through.

The large vinyl enclosure looked like a wedding tent at first glance, especially because it was so near the chapel. It was huge, inflated, and sealed with a double air-lock door. Sinclair had dressed in the vestibule, with help from the assistants, who made sure he was sealed into his suit before entering.

Professor Paul Oakley—thin and intense—had greeted him.

"Mr. Sinclair, a pleasure to meet you. I know your work at Ephesus. That gladiator graveyard is spectacular. Incredible work there, if you will permit me to say so."

"Thank you."

"If you would stand just to my left, we will avoid any mishaps. Gently now, lads," he said to the diggers.

"It won't do to contract this stuff," he said in an aside to Sinclair. "It's deadly."

"No worries, I've had my flu shot."

Paul Oakley snorted behind his mask.

"A flu shot? That won't be much help. They estimate this disease killed twenty-five million people in the first month."

"Just goes to show, you shouldn't skip that flu shot."

Sinclair's nerves were making him crack jokes. Oakley didn't have an ounce of humor about him.

"No joke, Sinclair. Most influenzas kill the young and the very old. This pandemic killed the strong and those in the prime of life—because of cytokine storms. You are a prime target."

"What is meant by 'cytokine storms'?"

"They trigger the overreaction of the immune system. The stronger the immune system, the stronger the reaction," Oakley explained. "People would contract the disease and collapse within hours, attacked by their own body fighting the disease."

"That fast?"

"At best, they'd be dead by the next day: bleeding from the nose, ears, coughing up blood, losing bowel control, bleeding from the intestines—a real horror show."

Sinclair checked his mask to make sure it was secure.

"The majority of deaths were from bacterial pneumonia, a secondary infection, but the Spanish influenza of 1918 also killed people directly, causing massive hemorrhages and edema in the lungs. They called it the Spanish influenza because they originally thought it came from Spain."

"This flu is an old one—extinct. Why the interest?" Sinclair asked.

"This is a version of H1N1. The recent swine flu was H1N1 also, a different strain. One of our chief goals is to see if it is in any way related to the H5N1—the avian flu we are seeing around the world today."

"I see."

"One theory is that the 1918 flu started with birds also, although it has never been proven. We are looking at human-to-human transmission of present-day avian flu. If we can find the link to the 1918 flu, it may put us one step ahead if another pandemic hits."

"I think I'll stick to my Greek and Roman inscriptions. You can handle the pestilence."

Oakley didn't hear; he was leaning over the grave. "Will you look at that. . . ." Oakley said in awed surprise.

Ten hours later, they were all seated around the long wooden table in the kitchen of the estate. The remains of steak-and-mushroom pie were before them, and they were drinking mugs of hot sweet tea with milk. Fruit and cookies had been brought out, and the staff had retired. Tom, Marian, Cordelia, Paul Oakley, and Jim Gardiner were all still talking about the exhumation.

Sinclair was silent. It had been a long day and he was exhausted. There had been no sign of a document in or around the coffin, and that had been a big disappointment. Sinclair reviewed in his mind the procedures he had witnessed. He kept telling himself there was no way he could have missed it. After the topsoil had been removed, the diggers had worked steadily until they stood chest high in the trench. They had to dig much wider and longer than the coffin, to give the scientists room to maneuver and to avoid putting any foot pressure on the coffin. Hours later, the coffin had become visible. Sifting the layers of soil from the lead-lined coffin was painstaking. Sinclair had remained alert, looking for anything else that might have been buried in the soil.

Over the years, the coffin had split, probably due to the extraordinary depth of the interment. For flu victims, the burial was twice as deep as usual, for fear of contagion. Oakley had decided to leave the coffin in the ground because of the split in the lid. There had been a discussion over whether to take samples through the split, but in the end the heavy lid had been raised and samples were taken directly from the corpse. They had been expecting to find a well-preserved cadaver, but it was heavily decomposed due to the cracked coffin.

Oakley had explained that they hadn't expected to find the virus intact, but that it should have left its "footprint" in the lungs. He said there were opportunities using molecular biology to re-create the virus, or at least look at its genetic makeup. A full sequencing had not been achieved so far because only fragments of the virus had been recovered from other exhumations.

Sinclair had half listened to Oakley's discourse on influenza. He had examined the grisly contents of the coffin as the team biopsied the lungs. There was no sign of a deed, or of any kind of box or container.

Now, hours later, in the kitchen, Sinclair was only half listening to the chatter. He was slicing up a pear and wondering where the deed was. Tom, Marian, and Cordelia had all exchanged a look of disappointment when he and Oakley had come in from the day's work. Sinclair gave them a small shake of the head. *Nothing,* he mouthed silently. But no one mentioned it. Out of deference to the exhumation project, they were all waiting until after Oakley left to discuss the deed.

"This could give us a little more to go on," Oakley was saying with enthusiasm. "The samples were not great, but I think they are usable."

Sinclair observed Oakley with interest. Clearly his dedication to his work was fierce. Oakley was whippet-thin and highly energized. His conversation displayed a rigorous mind, and there were flashes of impetuousness that often came with real genius. In his early forties, he was still almost boyish, with a tweedy kind of rumpledness about him. His sandy hair had no trace of gray, and his face was yet unlined.

"When did the first influenza appear in civilized society?" Cordelia was asking.

"No one knows. These diseases are ancient, prehistoric. The word *influenza* is from the Italian *influenze di freddo,* or 'influence of the cold,' " said Oakley. "The word first appeared in the English language in the 1700s."

"How much genetic data did you get from your exhumation last year in the Arctic?" asked Tom.

"Not all that much. We expected the bodies to be buried in the permafrost. But that wasn't the case."

"What happened?" asked Cordelia.

"Well, the coffins had risen gradually over time. Or another possibility is that they hadn't been buried deep enough in the permafrost to allow the virus to survive."

"Where did you do the exhumation?" asked Jim Gardiner.

"Svalbard, on the island, in the town of Longyearbyen. The people were miners in the Arctic Coal Mining Company. Actually, there were seven young men who were signed on to work in the mine, but they contracted Spanish flu on the ship and died when they got to the mining camp. They were buried in the company cemetery."

Cordelia, Sinclair, Tom, and Marian all looked at one another.

"The company cemetery? Did you say the *Arctic Coal Mining Company*?" asked Cordelia.

"Yes, why? What's the matter?" asked Oakley.

The story came together at a rapid pace. If Oakley had not been there, they never would have found the answer.

Sinclair leapt to his feet and started to pace. "I can't believe the coincidence of this!" he said. "Perhaps we're looking in the wrong grave!"

"Didn't Elliott Stapleton go to the Arctic in 1918?" asked Jim Gardiner.

" 'The deed is buried with my partner'—the partner in Svalbard!" said Cordelia. "He didn't bury it *here*. He buried it *up there*!"

"Percival Spence," said Jim Gardiner.

"The *other* partner!" said Cordelia.

"The *silent* partner," said Gardiner.

"Silent as the grave? *That* kind of silent partner?" asked Sinclair.

". . . who died of Spanish flu, just like Sir James!" said Cordelia.

"There *is* a Percival Spence buried there," said Oakley. "At least that was the name on one of the gravestones we found."

"*That's it!!*" said Gardiner. "*By God, that's it!!*"

"There were no remains in the grave," said Oakley. "When we dug up the coffin, it was empty."

"Empty!" said Sinclair.

"Yes, it was an empty coffin," said Oakley. "Except for some document we found inside."

They all froze in shock. Oakley looked around at them and his face lit up.

"Oh my goodness, it's your deed!" he said, finally understanding.

There was not a sound in the kitchen. No one breathed. No one blinked.

"Where are the papers now?" Sinclair asked quietly.

"We put them back where we found them. They were in a leather folio. We just closed up the coffin and buried them again."

It was past midnight by the time Oakley had the sample cases loaded into his beautiful vintage Bentley. He and Gardiner would ride back to London together. Gardiner gave Cordelia one of his trademark bone-crusher hugs and climbed into the passenger seat. Then, just before they pulled away, Gardiner turned the hand crank, rolling the window down.

"I'll only need a day or so to get that paperwork together. You can claim the deed in Norway by Friday."

"Thanks so much for everything, Jim."

"God, I hate leaving you. Are you sure you'll be all right?" He had already asked that twice, but he still looked concerned.

"I'll be *fine,*" she assured him. "Besides, John won't let me out of his sight."

He nodded and waved as the car pulled away. Cordelia stood on the front steps of Cliffmere watching the red taillights of the Bentley disappear down the long drive. She watched as the car turned onto the main road. Then it was quiet. She stood outside a few more minutes, in the cool of the night. There was always a twinge of sadness watching Gardiner go.

But this time she walked back into the house with the comfort of knowing that her family was waiting for her. It was the first time she had ever felt that way.

The small Tudor study was aglow with the fire in the grate. Tom and Marian were sitting in the armchairs, while Sinclair paced up and down.

"Well, I don't see a choice. We *have* to go to Svalbard," Sinclair was saying.

Cordelia entered and perched on the arm of Marian's chair.

"If we let the Norwegian authorities dig up the deed, they could try to claim it, or the Russians could steal it from them," Sinclair said. "We have to be there when they open the coffin."

Tom spoke up with authority. "I really don't think it's a good idea for Cordelia to go."

"She should stay here with us," added Marian.

Marian took Cordelia's hand, an unconscious gesture of protection. Sinclair looked down at them.

"Marian, she can't stay here," he said kindly. "Don't you see that?"

"We wouldn't let her out of our sight," assured Marian.

Sinclair took a chair next to them.

"I know you would do your best to protect her," Sinclair said, "but it's so dangerous. Someone got into the library just the other day."

"What about asking for police protection for Cordelia while you go to Svalbard?" suggested Tom.

"No police," said Cordelia. "I'll go. It's *my* land. It's *my* deed. It's *my* problem!"

"How can you get there safely? People have been following you all along," Marian pointed out. "They will come after you and you will be putting yourself in danger, especially in an area as remote as Svalbard."

"We could go quickly and quietly and nobody would know," suggested Cordelia. "A two-day trip, just up and back."

"Hold on, you need to talk to Oakley first," Tom spoke up. "You need to find out about what kind of contagion risk you are taking by digging up that site."

"But the coffin is empty! There is no risk," said Sinclair.

"You should *not* go, Cordelia," said Marian. "John can go, but you should stay here."

Marian looked to Sinclair for agreement. Sinclair stood in the middle of the library as they all stared at him.

"I would feel better knowing that she is with me," he said honestly. "I want to watch out for her myself."

Cordelia spoke up firmly. "That decides it. I am going with John."

London

Charles Bonnard was waiting in the lobby of Claridge's when Cordelia and Sinclair came into the hotel.

"Sinclair!" he called when he saw them. "Over here."

Charles looked as handsome as ever, but there was a pinched anxiety to his face and a nervousness to his movements. He rushed up to Sinclair, clasping him in a quick hug. Sinclair hugged back, slapping Charles's back affectionately.

"Thank God you are here. I was worried," Charles said.

Cordelia was quiet, but Charles broke the ice and rushed over to give her a quick squeeze. She hugged him back, a bit awkwardly, and stepped back. He was beaming at her with unrestrained delight. Then he was in motion again, grabbing her bag and rushing over to press the lift button.

"Good to see you, Charles," said Sinclair.

"How was the country?" He looked them both up and down as they waited for the lift.

"It was absolutely wonderful. I finally went home to Cliffmere," Cordelia said, and looked over at Sinclair with a smile.

There was no hiding the love that passed between them. Charles looked up at the lift light and pretended to follow the progress of the floors. But when they were alone in the lift, he shifted to a conspiratorial tone.

"What's up?" he asked Sinclair.

"Let me get Cordelia settled and then we can talk about the foundation."

"Right," said Charles. "I'm just down the hall in room five twelve when you are ready."

"Give me a few minutes," said Sinclair, as he opened the door to his and Cordelia's room. He dropped the suitcases in the middle of the room and turned to her.

"I'm going to talk to Charles for a moment. Do *not* open this door for anyone. If the maid service knocks, just tell them to come back later."

Cordelia nodded.

"I'll double-lock the door when you leave," she said. "And then I'm going to have a nice bubble bath."

"In that case," Sinclair said with a smile, "I won't be gone but a minute."

Charles was at the window, looking out at the darkening street, when he heard Sinclair knock.

"It's open," Charles called.

Sinclair came in quickly and shut the door. There was something furtive about his movements. Charles noticed but said nothing. Sinclair would tell him in his own time.

"You seem well," Charles lied.

"It's been a little rough," admitted Sinclair. He hesitated a moment and then went on. "You know, Charles, first of all, I have to thank you. . . . Cordelia . . . well, she's wonderful."

"I am so glad to hear that. When I met her at the gala, she seemed like the kind of girl you would really get along with."

"Well, your instincts were perfect. Thanks for pushing me to go on that cruise. I was pretty cut up over Shari, and I really wouldn't have done it."

"I never push you, I just suggest." Charles smiled. "So tell me what is going on."

He walked over to the couch and sat down. Sinclair continued to stand, restless and agitated.

"Let me see . . . well, we decoded the note, and it said, 'The deed is buried with my partner.' So we figured it was buried in Sir James's grave."

Charles looked at him in astonishment.

"You're making this up."

"No, I swear. So we exhumed the grave to see if it was inside."

"Sinclair, I am starting to worry about you. You can't go two weeks without digging up dead people."

"I guess you have a point." Sinclair forced a laugh.

"So what happened?"

"There was no deed in the coffin with Sir James."

"So what now?" asked Charles.

"Now we *think* we know where it is. But it's turning into a scramble. A lot of people are looking for the deed."

"Like who?"

"At first we thought it was a handful of governments—you know, the Norwegians, the Russians, and now the U.S."

"The U.S. cares about land in Norway? What for?"

"The International Seed Vault—a repository for all kinds of plant seeds. Each country keeps its own seeds in the vault. It's sometimes called the Doomsday Vault; if there is a catastrophe, there will be seeds to replant all the different species in the world."

"Like what kind of catastrophe?"

"Pandemic," suggested Sinclair. "Or some other situation where there is some kind of world collapse that wipes out populations or agriculture in certain areas."

"So this thing is built on Cordelia's land?"

"Yes, and we are now attracting what my spook friend is calling 'independent actors'—probably the Russian mob."

"Your *spook* friend? You mean a spy?"

"Thaddeus Frost is . . . well, not really a spy. We checked him out— or Cordelia's lawyer did. He's some kind of undercover operator for the American government. I called him after they tried to kidnap Cordelia."

"Kidnap Cordelia!" Charles leaned forward in surprise.

"Yes—last week in London. Which is why I called you."

Charles sat staring at him. "I feel like a fool for asking, but what can I possibly do?"

"I need you to help me persuade Cordelia to lie low and disappear for a week or so while I go to Norway to get this deed. We think the deed is buried at another grave site."

"You going to dig *that* up too?"

"I might have to. But Cordelia can't go; it's too dangerous. She needs to stay with you."

"*Of course* she can't go. Are you *insane*? After someone tried to kidnap her?" said Charles heatedly.

"That is what I am saying. But I am terrified to leave her alone."

"Shouldn't she stay at Cliffmere?"

"No, it's not safe. Someone already broke in there. And her lawyer, Jim

Gardiner, normally would take care of her, but he is going to have to go up to Norway with the paperwork to claim the deed."

"So you want me to stay with her," Charles concluded.

"Yes. If you would."

"All right, I can do that," said Charles. "Where should we stay? Here? Her town house?"

"No. You have to be completely out of sight. Where nobody can find her. I would say that you should stay at my place in Ephesus, but even that isn't safe. They caught a Russian mobster staking it out."

Charles got up and started pacing.

"John, this is really serious. You are way out of your league. No offense, but these people are professionals."

Sinclair stood in front of Charles.

"Let me put it this way: I need you to do this. I just don't trust anyone but you."

"What about the police?" asked Charles.

"If I had trusted law enforcement last week in London, she'd be gone right now." Sinclair looked distraught.

"Look, I am happy to help. But where do we hide her?"

"What about your place in Capri?" suggested Sinclair.

"The Villa San Angelo?" Charles considered for a moment. "It seems good. It's remote, that's for sure, but the local people always talk. If I show up with Cordelia, it won't be much of a secret for long."

"Right," said Sinclair. "I hadn't thought of that. Especially with Brindy just down the road from you. It would be all over town by lunchtime."

"Isn't that the truth," admitted Charles.

"Well, how about you two stay with your mother in Paris? Nobody would look for her there."

Charles considered that for a moment, sitting down again.

"That is a great idea!"

"Your mother wouldn't mind? It could be dangerous."

"Are you kidding, she would *love* it. What drama—a beautiful young American on the run."

"She would have to keep quiet," Sinclair cautioned.

"Oh, no problem. We'll tell her it's top secret, all very hush-hush," assured Charles.

"Great," said Sinclair. "Great! It will take some convincing to get Cordelia to agree. We can work on that later."

"So what's the plan?" asked Charles.

"I've been thinking," Sinclair said. "You could take the train from London to Paris."

"That's easy enough," agreed Charles. "But won't she be recognized if they are hanging around looking for her?"

"We would put her in disguise—change her hair, that kind of thing. It would be a bait and switch. The two of you would leave together, just like a normal couple staying at the hotel."

"If you say so," said Charles.

"After you leave, I'll head up to Norway. They will follow me instead of Cordelia."

"That should work. When will we tell her?"

"Tonight we have to meet Paul Oakley, a virologist at the Royal London Hospital. Let's go out to dinner afterward and suggest it to her. I definitely need backup. Cordelia can be very stubborn."

"Then you are well matched," shot back Charles. "So when do Cordelia and I head to Paris?"

"Tomorrow morning."

"OK, I will call my mother, and then I'll hop out to Selfridges to pick up some kind of disguise. It's just down the block."

"Nothing too flashy, Charles. She has to look different, but also blend in."

"Don't worry. I have some ideas."

"I hope Cordelia goes along with this scheme. She really can't come with me to Norway."

"There's only one problem," said Charles.

"What?" Sinclair looked concerned.

"If I show up at my mother's apartment with that girl, my mother will have us married within a week."

"Then your mother is considerably more dangerous than I thought," Sinclair said, laughing.

Thaddeus Frost made a face with the first sip of canteen coffee at the Royal London Hospital.

"I know, it is god-awful," Paul Oakley apologized.

"I usually don't drink commercial coffee. I prefer to drink my *own* brew. *Kopi luwak* beans from Indonesia."

"What's that?"

"If you haven't tried it, you really should. *Kopi luwak* beans are the rarest coffee beans in the world. They run a couple hundred dollars a pound, *if* you can find them."

"What on earth can they do to coffee beans to make them *that* expensive," Oakley demanded.

"They are hand collected in the wild. They are beans that have been eaten by an Asian palm civet."

"I don't understand. If the Asian palm civet *eats* the beans, how do you make coffee from them?"

"The beans pass through its system undigested and are collected in the forest after the animal eliminates them."

"That is disgusting!" Oakley looked at Thaddeus Frost in disbelief.

"Not at all. They are purified and roasted. The fragrance is unbelievable. You can get them commercially only in London and New York. But I buy mine from a private vendor in Asia."

"My God!" Oakley broke in. "You don't want to be drinking *that* kind of coffee. You *must* know that SARS was connected to the masked palm civet."

Thaddeus Frost cut him off. "We'll talk about it later. Here they are."

Sinclair walked in, his raincoat drenched. Cordelia's hair was wet from the downpour outside. Sinclair put his sodden umbrella on the floor and pulled back two chairs. The overhead fluorescent light was unflattering; Sinclair looked tired, and Cordelia was sallow from stress.

Frost stood to greet them. "Nice to see you again," he said politely.

Cordelia looked at Sinclair. "I didn't realize that . . ."

"Thaddeus is helping us find the deed," Sinclair explained.

"I see," said Cordelia coldly, as they all took seats around the cafeteria table.

"We were just chatting," said Frost, "and Professor Oakley was telling me about the grave site in Svalbard."

Oakley looked startled.

"The excavation you did *last year*," prodded Frost. "We will talk about *this* year's dig with Miles in a minute."

Oakley blanched, but recovered and began to explain.

"Last year we were up there in Longyearbyen collecting tissue samples for research on the 1918 pandemic. As you know, the permafrost is great for preserving human remains. When we dug up the grave of Percival Spence, we found a set of documents in the coffin."

"Describe them," said Frost, taking notes in a small notebook.

"They were in a leather case, the size of a business envelope but thick. It was tied with a bit of string."

"And you told us the other day that you put the papers back," confirmed Sinclair.

"Yes. They're still there."

"Good. We can recover them," said Frost, and then suddenly changed the subject. "Now, speaking of Longyearbyen, what do you know about Miles? I assume you two were in it together." His pen was poised over the notebook.

Oakley began to squirm and looked at the notepad. Cordelia and Sinclair exchanged a puzzled look.

"Who's Miles?" asked Sinclair.

There was an awkward silence.

"I only know what is in the newspapers," Oakley replied to Frost. "They say he was eaten by a bear."

"No, he was shot." Frost looked grim. "That was what the forensic report concluded."

"What do you mean?" Oakley demanded.

"When they first examined the remains the Norwegian police drew the conclusion it was a polar bear attack. But the autopsy turned up other evidence. His skull had been shattered by a bullet, not crushed by a bear."

Oakley was staring at him, horrified. "You mean he was—"

"That is why I am involved. If it were a simple accident, it would not be of interest to me," Frost said.

"*What in hell are you people talking about?*" asked Sinclair. He reached over and took Cordelia's hand.

Frost turned to both of them. "It's a sad story. A scientist decides to do a little research in Svalbard about two weeks ago. Funded by Dr. Oakley here. The first dig is in Barentsburg to get some tissue samples. But the next day he goes to the cemetery of the Arctic Coal Mining Company."

"Where *we* are headed," said Cordelia.

"Exactly," said Sinclair, looking uneasy.

Frost continued. "But poor Miles had a little mishap."

"He was attacked and eaten by a polar bear," Oakley said, without conviction.

"*Shot* and *then* eaten by a polar bear," corrected Frost, still looking grim. "Go ahead, Oakley, tell them where."

Oakley looked at Frost uneasily. He replied in a low voice.

"At the grave of Percival Spence."

"Now isn't *that* a coincidence," said Frost sarcastically, and lit a cigarette.

Cordelia was staring at Oakley, wondering what he was hiding. He seemed nervous—his posture was very stiff. A mop of hair fell over his eyes, and some strands were plastered to his temple with sweat. He was clasping and unclasping his hands on the plastic tabletop.

Cordelia looked sideways at Sinclair. Something was not right with him either. He was leaning back, looking straight ahead, not saying much, clearly keeping his own counsel. She could see he was very uncomfortable with the entire conversation. Why hadn't he mentioned that Frost was involved in tonight's meeting? She couldn't stand Frost and had made it clear to Sinclair that she was uncomfortable with him from the beginning.

Cordelia was fed up with the whole meeting. She leaned over and placed two hands flat on the table, trying to cut into the conversation. Frost and Oakley were both talking. They didn't stop, even though she tried several times to interrupt. She decided stronger measures were needed. So she brought her fists down on the table with a bang. Startled, they all turned to stare.

In the glare of the harsh cafeteria lighting, she scrutinized the three of them. Sinclair looked wrung out, Oakley was as pale as marble, and Frost had narrowed his eyes, as if preparing for combat. They were *supposed* to be meeting tonight to talk about going to the grave site to recover the deed.

"Gentlemen," she said with controlled anger, "it seems to me you are all hiding something. There is something you are not telling me. What is it?"

Simultaneously their mouths opened to protest. She shook her head and pushed back her chair.

"I will not be played for a fool," she said, seething. "I need to know everything there is to know before I can make any kind of decision. If I am going to go chasing up to Svalbard, I need to know the whole story.

I find it utterly *inconceivable* that you would withhold any information, especially after the shooting up there. Now either tell me what is going on, or I'm leaving."

She turned to look at Sinclair, who seemed as guilty as the others. He was staring down at the tabletop, not meeting her eyes. There was a full ten seconds of silence.

"Miss Stapleton, I believe I can shed some light on some of this," Oakley said. "May I suggest we go to another, more private spot in the building to continue this conversation."

Cordelia gave him a curt nod. They all stood and silently gathered their sodden umbrellas and raincoats. Cordelia marched out of the hospital canteen. The three men followed.

At the bank of lifts, Oakley turned to the group. "I'm going to have to sign you into a secure facility, if you wouldn't mind taking out some form of ID. There are a few things you need to know before you go to Svalbard."

They all wordlessly reached for their wallets. As they stepped into the lift, Oakley punched the floor B-4, for the fourth level down in the basement. He simultaneously slid his ID badge into the card-key slot to access a restricted area.

"We are going to the underground lab, where we store samples and do most of our work on pathogens," he said. "It's perfectly safe; we keep security very tight because of the threat of terrorism."

The lift door slid open and they could see a glass booth with a security guard sitting behind a gray metal desk. "Good evening, Sean," Oakley greeted him. "I have some people I need to bring in this evening. I'll vouch for them."

The guard eyed the group and nodded. "Very good, Dr. Oakley."

One by one, Oakley signed them in as the guard scanned their ID cards with an electronic record device. When they had finished, Oakley pushed through the inner door. They proceeded to a gray concrete hallway, lit by overhead fluorescent lights.

"Come this way," said Oakley. "I want to show you something."

Oakley scanned the lock on a steel door with his ID badge and pushed it open. The storage facility had a damp, musty smell, layered with a faint odor of lab chemicals. He flicked on the lights, revealing a large room with row upon row of steel shelves. It was clearly a storeroom for samples. Some amorphous blobs of pink and gray were floating in old-fashioned formaldehyde jars. The shelves also held age-stained, sepia-colored card-board boxes with faded fountain-pen writing on the labels. Oakley walked down the narrow aisle in front of a ten-foot-high shelf. Reaching about shoulder height, he pulled down an old cardboard file box. Supporting it with both hands, he walked to a conference table and metal folding chairs at the back of the room.

"Please take a seat," he said, his voice echoing. "This might take a moment to explain."

Once they all settled down, Oakley lifted the lid and extracted a small plug of wax about a half inch thick and the size of a postage stamp.

"This," he said, holding it up between his thumb and index finger, "is a razor-thin sliver of lung tissue embedded in paraffin. It was taken from a soldier who died in the 1918 pandemic. Back then, medical officers would sometimes take lung samples and soak the bit of tissue in formaldehyde and then embed it in paraffin."

They all unconsciously leaned back.

"No need to be alarmed," Oakley assured them. "It's not a live virus. We have to dissolve the wax away with a solvent before we can examine it. Then we extract the genes from the cells. Primarily we can look at the genes of the victim who died, but if we are lucky, we may also find some of the genes from the virus as well."

"Why the science lesson?" Frost demanded impatiently. "Get to the point." His face was closed, unreadable.

Cordelia looked at him with intense dislike and turned to the scientist. "I expect the point you are making is that it is dangerous to dig up the grave," she prompted.

"Actually, no," Oakley said, replacing the square of wax in the box as if it were the most precious thing in the world. "It won't be dangerous to dig up Percival Spence's grave in Svalbard. There is no body in the coffin. Just your deed." He looked up at them somberly.

"I am about to tell you why we have been digging up in Svalbard in the last month." His eyes went to Frost, but he elicited no response. So Oakley took a deep breath and plowed on. "There are only about fifty of these 1918 flu samples in the entire world. Each one is so small, it has only a few thousand cells. That may seem like a lot, but none of them have the entire sequence of the flu virus. These samples were our *only* source of 1918 genetic material. This is all we had to work with to sequence the virus."

"So *what?*" said Frost. "Get to the point."

"The *point* is millions can die if we don't find out more about this virus as soon as possible. We think it has similarities to another virus that we are seeing emerge."

"What virus? I haven't heard about any pandemic," Frost said.

"We believe that the strain of avian flu that is in Asia right now could be the next global pandemic. Millions of birds die every year. They used to simply cull the bird populations to keep it somewhat under control. But in the last decade or so we discovered that humans can contract the disease. And, most important, humans can now sometimes pass it to each other."

"So it jumped species?" Sinclair asked.

"We believe it did. Human-to-human transmission is entirely possible. And that makes it dangerous."

"So why don't the individual countries work to eradicate it?" asked Cordelia.

"They are trying, but there is no real way to stop it. Infected birds carry the disease and spread it wherever they fly, and they cross borders. Most of the time the infected carriers just infect other birds. But now people who live around the birds have become infected. The disease has appeared in rural areas of China where people live with their chickens in the household. And there was a severe outbreak in the live-poultry market in Hong Kong. A half dozen people died."

"I remember reading about that," Cordelia admitted, "but it didn't seem all that serious to me."

"Well, it is. We're working round the clock to decode the genome and find out more so we can develop a vaccine. Potentially, this avian flu could kill millions of people, the way the 1918 pandemic did. This strain of H5N1 is *highly* pathogenic. In recent years, outbreaks have killed two out of every three people who have contracted it. There have been at least four hundred known cases of human infection in Asia, Africa, the Pacific, Europe, and the Near East."

"Still, compared to the common flu, that is a small number of cases," Sinclair interrupted.

"Yes, but if this strain mixes with the common flu it will be a disaster."

"How could that happen?" asked Sinclair.

"If a person became infected with the avian flu and the common flu at the same time, a superbug could develop that would be virtually unstoppable. It's only a question of time before that happens. That is my theory.

I believe avian flu is the next global catastrophe, on a scale you cannot imagine." Oakley looked stricken. Breathing hard, he was now perspiring freely.

"Why is that not happening?" Sinclair demanded. "If avian flu is already infecting people, why isn't it spreading more rapidly?"

"Good question," said Oakley. "We don't know. But we do suspect that the 1918 pandemic may have the key. One theory holds that the 1918 flu was initially an avian flu, carried by birds. Some scientists think it then went on to infect other animals, such as pigs, and then ultimately became deadly to humans. That's one theory, anyway. But we just don't know."

"Now I get it," Cordelia said. "I was so focused on finding our deed, I never paid much attention to your exhumation at Cliffmere."

"We dug up Sir James Skye Russell's grave site because we hoped to get another viable sample. The key to preventing the next pandemic is to study the victims of the past." Oakley rested his hands on the box of samples, as if protecting them.

"Did you get a sample from Sir James's grave?" asked Cordelia.

"No, the body was too decomposed," Oakley said. "And our theory about a lead coffin preserving the remains was erroneous. The virus had been destroyed."

"Sorry to hear that," said Sinclair.

"And your point is?" Frost prompted. "Why did you drag us down here? You could have told us that without the show-and-tell."

"I believe we may have found a live virus up in Svalbard," said Oakley. "My colleague went up there a few weeks ago to exhume some grave sites in a remote area called Barentsburg. He found a perfectly preserved, frozen cadaver, took samples, and sent them to me."

Frost glowered. "Where are they now?"

"That's just it," Oakley said, his face crestfallen. "The samples are missing, and I find it hard to tell you this but . . ." Oakley dropped his voice, and they all leaned forward. "I believe the samples were lost in the mail. I never received them, and then Miles was . . . killed." There was complete, stunned silence.

"What does all that mean?" asked Cordelia, confused.

"I have come to believe the people who are after your deed may have misunderstood what Miles was digging for and stolen the samples, thinking the package contained the deed."

"So where are the samples!" Frost demanded.

Oakley's face was sallow, and his mouth barely moved as he spoke. "I don't know. But if the vials with the samples were opened, they could have infected someone. Now keep in mind, the virus would be transmissible for only a few hours before the sample would break down in the sunlight and the heat," Oakley explained, wiping his forehead with a handkerchief. "So no one would be infected *unless* they opened the vials and handled the samples right away. That's the *good* part."

"And the *bad* part?" Cordelia asked, almost in a whisper.

"I think two people *were* infected and died right here in this hospital," Oakley said. "Both patients tested positive for an unknown strain of H1N1 flu that I have never seen before this. They died within hours. They had all the symptoms I have been reading about in the eyewitness accounts of the 1918 pandemic."

"If they died of the 1918 flu, you may have your sample after all, in those two cadavers," observed Sinclair.

"Yes, ironically, we may," Oakley admitted to him. "Although it was not my intention to unleash the virus."

"So should we be worrying about a pandemic in London right now?" Cordelia asked, dry-mouthed.

"No. I think they are the only victims," Oakley assured her. "It's been over a week and no other cases have turned up. The sample must have degraded shortly after it was opened. And no one else came into contact with it."

"Jesus H. Christ," said Frost, leaning back, stunned. "What a goddamn nightmare."

The doorman at Claridge's observed the attractive young couple as they came out of the hotel. The man's arm was around the woman's shoulder and she was murmuring something. He was leaning toward her to listen, half shielding her face from view. They looked very much in love.

She was blond, young, and pretty, and wore a pink silk skirt and a neat little white Chanel jacket. Her high-heeled sandals were flimsy and impractical for traveling. She carried a very large shapeless purse, the latest in fashion, and wore dark Chanel sunglasses with rhinestones on the sides.

At the curb, three vintage Louis Vuitton suitcases were lined up with a rather serviceable large blue L.L.Bean rolling suitcase. Black duct tape had been pasted over the monogram of the nylon suitcase.

The couple quickly moved to the taxi. The woman entered first, and turned her back on the street-side window. The man blocked the view from the hotel by standing in front of the open door and holding a folded raincoat over his arm.

"*Chérie*, have you brought everything?" Charles said, leaning into the taxi. He gave her a wink. Then he stood up and, speaking in French so the driver could hear, added, "I hope you have everything. I checked the room twice."

The woman didn't respond. Cordelia had absolutely no idea what he was saying. But if she didn't reply, there was no way anyone could tell she wasn't French.

Charles and the driver got into the car.

"Saint Pancras Station," he told the driver with a heavy French accent. "We are taking the Eurostar home to Paris."

"Right you are, sir," the cabdriver said as he looked in the mirror at the couple. The woman was tall and slim, dressed very stylishly. He couldn't see her face clearly because the man was leaning over to caress her blond hair. They were clearly Parisians. The French sure knew about romance. He averted his eyes and took on the snarl of London traffic.

Cordelia and Charles walked into the historic St. Pancras Station in the heart of London. The majestic train depot had been refurbished, and now functioned as the hub for the high-speed trains that traveled under the English Channel to Paris.

The soaring structure dated to 1868—the height of the Victorian era, and only seven years after Queen Victoria lost her beloved Prince Albert to typhoid fever. The original design of the famous train shed by William Barlow was a giant steel rib cage of arches, towering and distinctive, one hundred feet high. This morning, dozens of trains were running in and out under the historic dome. The streamlined Eurostar, with its characteristic aerodynamic nose, was ready for boarding. Charles and Cordelia found their way to coach 17 and settled into their assigned seats.

"I'm sorry we are traveling standard class," Charles apologized. "The full-service car has meals and drinks. But there are stewards. Back here no one will pay any attention to us."

At that moment, two college students took the seats across from them and began stowing their gear. A woman with a baby sat down in front of them.

Cordelia looked around. "This is very comfortable. It's like business class on a plane."

"I like the Eurostar so much better than flying," said Charles. "This train goes a hundred sixty miles an hour. We'll be at my mother's house in Paris in two and a half hours."

Cordelia sighed. "Thanks for doing this, Charles. I'm sorry I argued with you and John so much last night. I know it wasn't pleasant. But it made me so angry that he was leaving me behind."

"We *have* to play it safe, Cordelia. John is right. You need to disappear until he can find the deed."

"I know, but I *hated* leaving him this morning. I'm so worried about him."

"Sinclair can take care of himself. You have no idea how tough he is."

"I do, actually. I got a glimpse of what he is made of in London," Cordelia said.

"Well, just to make things clear between us. I'm counting on *you* to save *me* if things get ugly," Charles said with a wink.

"I will." She smiled.

"Now if you don't think I'm getting too fresh, I am going to sit a bit closer to you. Then I am going to put my arm around you." He moved to cradle her with his left arm, turning her toward the window and blocking the view of her face from the aisle.

"We don't want anyone getting a look at you. Why don't you put your head back on my shoulder and take a nice little nap."

She adjusted her position to keep her face turned away from the aisle. But she felt awkward leaning on Charles. She giggled with embarrassment.

"This is so weird, playing at being a couple like this. I hope you don't mind. Tell me if I am crushing you."

"I never had it so good," said Charles, "and you are not crushing me, you are light as a feather."

"By the way, your shoulder is not nearly as comfortable as John's, I'll have you know," teased Cordelia.

"Oh, go ahead and complain, why don't you? I'm totally outclassed by that guy all the time. You'll just have to put up with me until he gets back."

He gave her shoulder a squeeze.

"Charles, why is your French so good?" she asked.

"I'm French," he said.

"You *are*?" she said, nearly turning around. He pushed her back into place.

"Yes, my mother is French. She lives in Paris, remember."

"Oh, right, I hadn't really focused on that. Your accent in English is so perfectly American. I would have guessed you were from New England."

He laughed. "You would have been half right. I went to boarding school in Connecticut."

"Why?"

"My father is American."

Cordelia felt him shift uncomfortably. "Where does he live?"

His voice was strained as he continued. "I actually never met him. He never acknowledged me. Officially, that is. But he set up a trust fund for my education and insisted I spend my teen years in the States."

"I don't understand."

"I am what is commonly referred to as a bastard."

She winced in embarrassment. Luckily he could not see her face. There was a long silence.

"Well, aren't we a pair? I'm an orphan," Cordelia said, and patted his arm. "Anyway, I would *swear* you were American."

"I'll take that as a compliment," he said, and lapsed into silence.

Within minutes, the train glided out of the station. They sped through the London suburbs, flying past gleaming modern towers and then clusters of apartment buildings. By the time they were skimming across the verdant English countryside, Cordelia was fast asleep in Charles's arms.

Sinclair sat in the lobby of Claridge's. He was packed, checked out, and ready to go. A tall, dark-haired woman walked in wearing a neat little Burberry raincoat, low-heeled navy blue pumps, and carrying the same quilted Dior bag Cordelia had. She also had a green Harrods shopping bag on her arm.

She walked right up to Sinclair and kissed him on the cheek.

"Sorry to keep you waiting, darling. I'm ready to go."

Sinclair stood up and put an arm around her waist.

"Cordelia, thank goodness you're here. The bags are already in the limousine. We have to hurry if we want to make our flight."

They walked out of the hotel together and slowly started toward the limousine. As she reached it, the woman paused and looked up and down the street. Sinclair made himself conspicuous tipping the porter and the doorman. Any observer would have gotten a good look at both of them. They got in and the car pulled away into traffic. Sinclair leaned forward and asked the driver to put up the glass partition. Then he turned to his companion.

"Thaddeus did a great job. You look just like her," Sinclair said admiringly.

The woman smiled. "I'm really a redhead. This is a wig. We copied the picture you gave us, for the hair and makeup. And there were a few surveillance photos of her clothes."

"You have her to perfection. By the way, we also came up with a pretty good transformation for Cordelia. She looks totally different."

"How so?"

"She's a blonde. And she's wearing a pink dress and those high-heeled shoes with the straps—you know the kind I'm talking about?"

"That is quite a change."

There was an awkward pause. She shifted in her seat, looking at Sinclair. She seemed to be assessing him.

"I should introduce myself," the woman said. "I'm Erin Burke."

"Nice to meet you, Erin. If you will forgive me, I will avoid shaking your hand just now, as the driver might notice and find it odd."

"You'll have to settle for this," Erin said, leaning forward and kissing him lightly on the lips, running her hand down his chest, inside the lapel of his suit.

"Watch it, lady, I'm taken," Sinclair said to her in a low voice.

"Maybe so, but for the next couple of days we have to pretend," Erin said flirtatiously.

"Pretend away," said Sinclair. With a faint smile of amusement, he turned away and looked out the window.

Paris

It was gray and raining when the train pulled into the Gare du Nord. Charles shook her gently, and Cordelia woke feeling tired and achy.

"Did I miss going under the Channel?" she asked in disappointment.

"I'm afraid you did," he said. "We're in Paris."

She sat up. "Oh, Charles, I was so tired, I just crashed. I am so sorry."

"I rather enjoyed it. I like women who don't talk much."

She laughed and straightened her skirt, pulling down her jacket. She must look like a real mess. The wig was itchy, and her eyes burned.

"I'll grab a porter. Why don't you wait here?"

"Okay," she said, glad for a moment to pull herself together. Why did she feel so sluggish?

She pulled out her compact and looked at herself. Her eyes were unnaturally bright. The wig was a fright. No use trying to comb her hair, but she found lip gloss in her monstrous snakeskin purse and applied it.

The only thing she was wearing that she actually liked was her necklace. In her compact mirror she reviewed the lovely amulet Sinclair had bought her in Turkey.

Cordelia thought of Sinclair, and felt a jolt of fear. She hoped he was safe. Suddenly she looked around and the train was empty. Why was Charles taking so long?

She looked around nervously, and caught sight of Charles coming back along the aisle. Dear Charles, no wonder Sinclair was so fond of him. He really was adorable.

"Ready to go meet my mother, Delia ? I'm sure she is going to *love* you."

Cordelia smiled at him.

"Something tells me you are going to play this one to the hilt."

"You bet," he admitted. "It's not every day I get to take a gorgeous girl like you home to the family cottage."

Of course, his home on the rue de Vaugirard was hardly a cottage. It was located in the 6th Arrondissement—one of the central sections of the city, on the left bank of the Seine. The apartment was in the grand style she had seen only in glossy magazines such as *Architectural Digest.* The Bonnard household took up the second and third floors of the large Haussmann-style building. The classic *immeuble* had a façade of cut stone, topped by a slate mansard roof—typical of much of the architecture of Paris. The second, or "noble," floor had balconies looking out over the adjacent Luxembourg Garden.

Cordelia walked into the entrance hall and saw that there were high ceilings with plaster moldings. Beautiful carved oak doors opened to the entrance hall. That was where Charles's mother chose to greet them, in a gracious but formal way.

She was a tiny woman dressed in a mauve skirt and a cream satin blouse, pearls, and hair upswept in a classic French chignon. As Cordelia approached she noticed the older woman's face was high-cheekboned and patrician. But it was her bearing that defined her as aristocratic.

Suddenly Cordelia felt nervous about meeting Madame Bonnard, especially in her disguise. But her anxiety was dispelled instantly as Madame Bonnard clasped her hand.

"Charles has told me so much about you, my dear. Please come in. I am delighted to have you here in my home."

Her greeting was suddenly interrupted by a massive wolf bounding into the hall. All gray fur and long limbs, he launched himself at Charles. Charles grappled with giant paws as he tried to prevent the animal from jumping on him.

"Watson, down," he said, ruffling the dog's harsh coat. "Sorry, Cordelia, I should have remembered to tell you about Watson."

Cordelia had realized by now it was a dog.

"That is the biggest dog I have ever seen in my entire life. Is it a Great Dane?" she asked.

"Watson is a wolfhound. An Irish wolfhound," Charles said. "Although Mother just calls him 'the animal.' " He pronounced it with a French accent.

Madame Bonnard laughed. "When Charles calls me on the phone, I always tell him how much trouble the animal is causing."

As if he knew the word *animal,* Watson fell back down on all fours and seemed chastened. He looked at Cordelia speculatively, but she was too intimidated by his size to pat his head.

"Don't be afraid. He's a big baby. He will grow on you. You'll see," assured Charles.

"Do come in. I'm keeping you standing in the foyer," said Madame Bonnard.

They walked past the grand curved marble staircase into the main salon of the apartment. A row of floor-to-ceiling windows looked out on the Luxembourg Garden. The view of the formal flower beds and verdant lawns gave the illusion that the apartment was on a country estate, yet Cordelia knew the Eiffel Tower was only a few dozen blocks away.

Madame Bonnard sat in one of the upright chairs and indicated that Cordelia should sit next to her. A housekeeper in a white smock came in and offered tea, coffee, or chocolate. She told Cordelia her room was prepared; the front bedroom to the right of the stairs.

After a moment Charles excused himself, saying to his mother, "I'll just pop in on Clothilde to say hi."

The housekeeper returned.

"Madame is wanted on the telephone."

Madame Bonnard left the room to take the call, saying she would be right back. The room became absolutely quiet.

The wolfhound sat regarding her, as silent as a sphinx. He blinked at her but didn't move.

"Good boy, Watson," she said.

She started looking around the room, decorated in a classic French style. The chairs and furniture were delicate and formal, with a beautiful gold Aubusson on the floor that looked antique. Small bombé chests lined the walls, over which hung gilded mirrors. Cordelia noticed the three crystal chandeliers were sending fireflies of reflection on the ceiling and walls in the afternoon sun.

She wondered where Sinclair was and what he was doing.

Oslo, Norway

Sinclair walked arm in arm with Erin Burke through the airport in Oslo, Norway. He hated everything about this operation. He hated leaving Cordelia behind, and the gnawing fear that he was exposing her to some kind of danger. He hated the subterfuge of being with this woman. He especially hated that he'd had to lie to Charles.

Well, he hadn't exactly lied, but Charles and Cordelia had no idea he was traveling with an American agent. They thought he was just going up to Svalbard to talk to some Norwegian officials to try to locate the deed. What he was doing now was probably the most dangerous part of this whole affair. Thaddeus had explained that any "independent actor" who was after the deed would trail them. That was why Erin had to go, and not Cordelia. This operation would require a serious agent who could defend herself.

Thank God Cordelia had agreed. The less she knew about what he was going to do, the safer she was. A nice quiet stay in Paris with Charles's mother would be perfectly fine.

Sinclair had no compunctions about making Erin a target. Her role was to draw out the aggressors and force them into the open. Erin not only expected a dangerous encounter, she was hoping for it. And she was physically perfect for the job; she could pass for Cordelia, even at close range.

He knew it was trivial, but he hated having to playact an affectionate relationship with her. He was not attracted to her in any real way, and her proximity was starting to wear on him.

He had observed her on the flight from London. She had reclined in the airline seat on the first leg of the flight reading the *National Geographic* magazine that Frost had provided as a prop. Her legs were stretched out on the leg rest, alongside his. She wasn't really reading. She was lying in wait for any sign of interest. He could feel the tension in her body as she sat next to him. He resolved not to speak to her.

He had run his eyes down the muscles on Erin's legs; they were strong and lean. She was a beautiful woman, but he also had a suspicion she could break his neck at the slightest provocation. Her arm under the raincoat had been pure steel; this was no woman, this was a fighting weapon. He laughed at the thought that Thaddeus should think he needed this kind of protection. He didn't need Erin to protect him; he needed protection *from* Erin.

Now, on the last leg of the trip from Oslo to Longyearbyen, she had removed her shoes, and Sinclair had noticed her toenails were painted a most provocative bloodred. Cordelia would never wear that color. But that was not the only false note; Cordelia would never kick off her shoes and sit with bare feet on an airplane. It was a mistake that only Sinclair would have detected. He sat thinking about Cordelia; she was refined and elegant to every fiber of her being. And he missed her.

How were she and Charles getting on? He did not dare call for fear his phone transmission would be intercepted. If he needed to call Charles, they would pretend to talk about foundation business, using the code words *environmental project* to indicate the deed. And Sinclair had also promised not to call until he got to Longyearbyen, the small town on the island of Svalbard. It was just a speck of land high above the Arctic Circle—in the northernmost region on planet Earth. And when they landed, he knew, he had very little time to find the deed.

Paris

Madame Bonnard was seated next to Cordelia and pouring tea. The blend was a special mix by Fauchon, and the madeleines had just the right amount of lemon zest. Madame Bonnard lifted the lid of the teapot to check its strength and added a small amount of hot water.

"May I offer you a little more—you must be tired from your journey."

"Yes, thank you," said Cordelia. "I can't thank you enough for letting me hide here."

Madame Bonnard did not reply as she poured.

"Where is Charles?" asked Cordelia.

"He mentioned he wanted to take some photos. It's very foggy and he thought he might get some nice shots of the Seine. He will be back later."

"I didn't know he was a photographer," said Cordelia. "I have only just met him, but I think he is great."

His mother smiled. "I am afraid I had quite the wrong impression about you when you arrived. I thought you were a friend of Charles's—a romantic friend."

Cordelia blushed. "Oh, no, not at all. He just agreed to help John Sinclair protect me for a while."

"And this John Sinclair, have you known him long?" asked Madame Bonnard gently.

"Actually no—just a few weeks. But he has helped me so much."

"A few *weeks*! Are you aware of his reputation, my dear?" asked Madame Bonnard. She passed Cordelia the plate of madeleines.

"I know he was dating a fashion model. But he told me it's over. Charles did too. So I'm not too worried."

Madame Bonnard looked down and fussed with the edge of the table-cloth. She folded it to her satisfaction, and then looked up.

"One must not leap into these romances," said Madame Bonnard. "I speak from experience, my dear. Very hard experience."

"Usually I can tell right away if someone is good for me," said Cordelia stubbornly, putting down her teacup.

Madame Bonnard looked doubtful. "I think one becomes infatuated easily. If an older man makes a fuss over one, it is easy to lose one's head."

There was a long silence. Cordelia didn't know what to say. Finally Madame Bonnard spoke again. "I understand you lost your parents when you were young."

"Yes."

"I wish you would allow me to give you some advice. Not as a parent—I would not presume. But accept this advice from an older woman. I know you will make up your own mind. But the experience of a previous generation may be helpful."

Cordelia was leaning back in her chair. She didn't want to hear whatever Madame Bonnard was preparing to say.

"If you will indulge me by listening to a personal anecdote. This story has some relevance to the dangers of quick romances."

Cordelia nodded.

"I fell in love with Charles's father in a matter of days. He was twenty-eight, I was seventeen. He was American and had come to Paris for a few months after graduating from law school. His visit was to be an introduction to European culture."

Cordelia drank her tea and listened.

"Paris is a dangerous place for young men. They feel that they deserve to have a great love here, that the Parisian experience would not be complete without it, and the reputation of the city demands it."

"Paris is very romantic," Cordelia agreed cautiously, taking a bite of her madeleine. She was glad the topic had shifted away from John Sinclair.

"Charles's father was the son of an American senator. He was being groomed for political office. And it is not good for American politicians to have a foreign wife."

"What happened?" asked Cordelia.

"His family heard about me and demanded that he come back to Savannah. He was summoned home. But after he left I realized I was *enceinte*—you know . . . carrying Charles."

Cordelia looked at the woman, fascinated. She hadn't expected this kind of revelation.

"Of course, this was many years ago. When Charles was born there was no chance of him being acknowledged by his American father. The pregnancy was a personal and political inconvenience. And, of course, Charles's father *did* go on to public office, just like his father before him. He became a very famous American senator."

"How awful for you," said Cordelia in sympathy.

"My own family was horrified, but then they helped me in my 'embarrassed' condition. I was married quietly to a very good man, a family friend, Alphonse Bonnard. He was willing to do this for me. And all of Paris society thought that Charles was born prematurely."

"Why did you have to get married?" asked Cordelia.

"It was out of the question to have Charles on my own. I come from one of the oldest families in France, and so did Alphonse Bonnard; so Charles, despite the rejection of his real father, has a heritage to be proud of."

"And there was never any reconciliation with his real father?"

"No, Charles has never met his birth father. He knows who he is, but he has never spoken to him or written to him. In fact, his father has not spoken to me since the day he left Paris. I was contacted by a lawyer after I wrote to tell him I was carrying his child."

"It's a sad story," admitted Cordelia. "I can't help feeling that his father is the only one who lost out. Charles would make a lovely son for anyone."

Madame Bonnard smiled. "I certainly think he is very special. I tell you this not to catalog the charms of my son but to give you a word of caution. The few weeks you have known John Sinclair are insufficient for you to see all the nuances of his life."

"It is true, I don't know a lot about him. But he has been so utterly . . ." Cordelia paused, looking for just the right word.

"John Sinclair may find you enchanting one moment and inconvenient the next. It *can* happen, my dear."

Cordelia stared at Madame Bonnard and swallowed hard.

"I *have* been worrying . . . John and I had a discussion in England about the future. He said we live very different lives, and we may *not* end up together in the end."

Madame Bonnard looked grave. "What else did he say?"

"He said we live worlds apart, on different continents. We have different lives. He didn't see how it would work."

"My dear, what did you do?"

Cordelia sat upright, suddenly very anxious.

"I made him stop talking, and promise to give our romance a try."

Madame Bonnard reached over and patted Cordelia's hand again.

"Charles tells me you are a smart girl. An accomplished girl. And you are at the top of your field. I advise you to also be cautious until you know John Sinclair better."

Cordelia flushed. "Thank you for your kind advice, Madame Bonnard." She stopped for a moment and then added with sudden energy, "I feel I am very much in love with John Sinclair. And he has been very, very kind to me in my difficult situation. And Charles thinks the world of Sinclair."

"Charles is a *man*," said Madame Bonnard simply. She picked up a little silver bell and rang it to have the housekeeper come and clear the tea tray.

"Cordelia, I hope with all my heart that John Sinclair is the love you have always dreamed about. But you should make him prove that he is worthy of your love. And that will take some time."

Longyearbyen

Sinclair stood at the window of the Spitsbergen Hotel and surveyed the Arctic landscape. The refurbished miners' lodge, located halfway up the mountain, gave him a clear view of all the surrounding landscape. At this time of year, the light was still bright late into the evening, and the scene in front of him had all the beautiful desolation of the moon. The original name of the place, Spitsbergen, meant "jagged mountain" in Dutch. The peaks formed a ring around the town of Longyearbyen. Most of the houses were nestled along the main street, and the lights were beginning to glow faintly against the uncertain dusk.

Sinclair was awestruck at the intrepid spirit that prompted people to live here. While the summer months were blessed with long days of light, in the winter, the town was plunged into total darkness. The sun never rose from the horizon, and the moon alone circled overhead in the sky, tracing a single orbit each day, illuminating the snow with ambient light. But hiding in that vast whiteness was man's single most deadly predator: *Ursus maritimus,* the polar bear.

Sinclair marveled at the courage of Cordelia's great-great-grandfather to come here to explore, and in subsequent years to establish the first settlement of miners, in the hope of building his Arctic Coal Mining Company into a thriving operation. Sinclair fully understood how valuable the journal really was. He was glad Cordelia could read it and understand her great-great-grandfather better.

He looked out at the landscape that Elliott Stapleton had loved, and made a silent vow to protect Cordelia's legacy. He would find the deed and restore this land to her. Then it would be up to her to decide what to do with it.

As he looked across the land, Sinclair silently asked Elliott Stapleton a question. There was no one else to ask, and he felt it was fitting to do it here. Sinclair asked Cordelia's great-great-grandfather for permission to marry her. It seemed the thing to do, somehow respectful and proper. She was, in essence, the polar explorer's true daughter, even if the generations didn't quite match up.

Sinclair listened inside his head. There was no psychic answer—only the silence of the desolate mountains that now lay before him. He hadn't expected any answer, really; it mattered only that he, in his own mind, had stated his intention honorably and sincerely. He would ask Jim Gardiner later. But the only answer that mattered now was Cordelia's. That question and answer would have to wait.

He heard the bathroom door open. He turned, and Erin came out wearing only a towel. She hadn't bothered to take the large one, so there wasn't much Sinclair could not see. He was irritated. Her intrusion broke into his thoughts and disturbed him in more ways than one. He felt his body react in a way he could not control. He surveyed her openly, unable to stop himself.

At first he told himself he was looking at her like an inanimate object, taking in the lines of her. But that was a bald-faced lie; his sexual attraction to her was intense. Previously, under the soft drape of women's clothing, she had managed to look alluring. But now, nearly naked, her body was almost irresistible. He could imagine it under his fingertips. What would it be like to grasp those strong legs and make love to her? Her breasts were soft, the nipples large. As she turned around, he could see her buttocks were full and round. Her long red curls cascaded down her back and ended halfway to the cleft in her buttocks. Sinclair broke out in a slight sweat. He didn't think he could take it much longer. Then it got worse.

Erin abandoned the pretense of the towel and began to ransack her Harrods shopping bag. She scooped up fistfuls of lacy white lingerie and piled them on the bed. She began cutting the sales tags off with a pair of nail scissors. After she had stacked the frothy lingerie on the bed, she dug back into the shopping bag and began tearing the cellophane off boxes of creams and cosmetics. Then, as she reached one more time into the shopping bag, she took out a red package containing a bottle of perfume. The mere sight of the box nearly tore the breath out of him. He stared. Of all the perfume in the world, why in God's name did it have to be Aphrodite?

She turned to him, fully naked.

"When I got this assignment, I didn't have time to pack."

She was challenging him. It was a clear and open invitation. His eyes were riveted by her body, and she seemed to be silently demanding his homage.

Sinclair mustered his strength. He wanted to walk over to her—he really wanted her—but the price was too high. There was no going back on the promise he had just made to Cordelia in his mind. Any justification of a last fling would only cheapen it. He met Erin's eyes.

"Let's keep our minds on the mission, shall we?"

She twisted her beautiful mouth into a smirk.

"Finding it difficult?" she countered. "Frost said you would be a real challenge."

"I presume you were talking about the assignment," Sinclair retorted. "And speaking of difficult, I don't exactly find Frost an easy guy to deal with."

"Thaddeus Frost is a *national treasure*," Erin snapped. "He is the *best* there is. You are damn lucky he was assigned to handle this case."

"I'm glad to hear it. Let's hope *you* live up to his expectations."

"Don't worry, I won't disappoint you," she purred.

He turned back to the window. Behind him he heard the rustling of cellophane, a box being opened, and the cap of a bottle being popped off. At the sound of light spritz, he shut his eyes. Slowly drifting toward him was the scent of the perfume Aphrodite, which in the past had signaled his destruction.

Sinclair woke up early, with the light streaming in the window. The Arctic morning was full upon the town. At this latitude and longitude, 78°13′0N, 15°38′0E, the sunlight was intense, but a quick look at his watch on the bedside table told him it was only five o'clock in the morning. There were another eighteen hours of daylight to go in this day, and he was glad of it. He had a lot to do.

Erin was sprawled on the other side of the bed, still deeply asleep. Her red hair covered her face. Last night she had put on a tiny pair of panties and a minuscule T-shirt, and slid into her side of the bed. Sinclair had ignored her, keeping his long limbs well away from her and putting a pillow in between them. They had to share the bed to maintain their cover as lovers. He couldn't have the hotel staff talking about the couple who slept in separate rooms. Everyone had to believe that Erin was Cordelia; it was the only way to keep Cordelia safe.

But it was torture to sleep with a woman like this. And he had to hand it to her, she had an impressive repertoire of feminine wiles: hair tossing, stretching languorously, slathering her legs with body cream right in front of him. But when they retired he had turned away and faced the window to sleep.

The light coming in from the window hit him in the eyes. He sat up cautiously, making no noise. If all went well today, and he found the deed, he could drop this charade and send Erin packing. But for now he wanted her exactly where she was: asleep. He had work to do and he didn't need this woman around. He didn't need her protection. He didn't care what Frost had said about teamwork. He could handle it by himself if anything turned up.

Sinclair quietly got out of bed, and moments later he was dressed and slipping out the door. The desk clerk looked up, startled to see him in the lobby so early.

"Good morning," Sinclair said, greeting the clerk. "It's so light outside I couldn't sleep. This takes some getting used to."

"You'll adjust after a few days," the young man replied. "I just made fresh coffee if you would like some."

He indicated the self-serve coffee bar near the large picture window. Sinclair walked over to fix his coffee and survey the town. Not a creature was moving about in the entire landscape.

"What time does the town clerk's office open?" asked Sinclair.

"The town clerk?"

"Yes, you know—where all the official paperwork is done, permits and things like that," he said.

"It's in the center of town. Right across from the general store."

"I was thinking of applying for a marriage license," lied Sinclair. "It's a romantic place to get married, don't you think?"

"It certainly is," agreed the hotel clerk, looking out at the barren landscape. "I think the office opens sometime around ten o'clock."

"Could I get out and roam around a bit before that?" asked Sinclair. "Rent a vehicle or something?"

"Sure," the young man replied. "I could get you a Land Rover for about two hundred dollars for the week. That wouldn't include petrol, of course, but they do throw in the rifle for free."

"Rifle?"

"For bears." The man pointed to the large sign behind the desk illus-trated with the silhouette of a polar bear and listing several safety rules. The poster cautioned: VENTURING OUTSIDE THE SETTLEMENTS WITHOUT A RIFLE IS PROHIBITED.

"Oh, I'll be careful," assured Sinclair. "How soon could you get a vehi-cle here?"

The young man looked at his watch. "My dad owns the company that rents Land Rovers to tourists. I figure in about half an hour."

Sinclair drove down the rutted track, off the mountain, and through the middle of town. It was the same route Miles had traveled the day he met his fate in the graveyard of the Arctic Coal Mining Company. Sinclair was headed to the exact same spot, only he was making certain to keep his rifle loaded and ready. After what Frost had told him about Miles and the polar bear, Sinclair was ready to shoot almost anything that moved.

The road snaked behind the town buildings and headed out along the coast of Advent Bay. In this season, the ground was gray and patchy with coal dust. The grimy residue and lack of vegetation made the landscape stark. A coating of snow would have turned it into magic. He should come back during polar night and see this place during its most fiercely beauti-ful season.

The road curved, and Sinclair could see the spire of the old miners' church, and the filigree of the wrought-iron fence that hemmed in the sev-eral dozen headstones. As he pulled up, he noticed the gate listed drunk-enly on one hinge. Sinclair parked his vehicle, keeping the engine running while he surveyed the graveyard. He reached back for the gun.

He walked along the rows of stones reading the names. They were quaint and formal, and the majority of them not Norwegian names: Jer-emiah, Samuel, Nathaniel, Benjamin, Thomas. And then suddenly there it was: Percival. PERCIVAL SPENCE. An empty grave that held the deed.

Sinclair squatted down and looked at the headstone. After a long dis-cussion with Tom and Marian Skye Russell, they had pretty much con-cluded that there was no such person as Percival Spence. No records existed except his listing as "silent partner" in the Arctic Coal Mining Company documents. Was this silent partner silent as the grave? Did it make sense that Elliott Stapleton would bury the deed here if he were headed farther north, to the pole? Sinclair's mind turned over the possibilities as he looked at the headstone.

He leaned closer and examined the ground. It had been dug up not too long ago. He picked up some soil. It was soft, and the dirt had pebbled a bit from moisture. But the topsoil had an entirely different look from that of all the other grave sites. Sinclair stood up and put a boot onto the corner of the grave site and pressed. His foot left a clear depression of about six inches in the soil. The other sites had hard-packed soil that had settled for many seasons. This one did not.

Oakley's expedition was a year ago, wasn't it? The ground would have settled by now. And Miles never got a chance to start excavating. But this grave had been dug up recently—certainly well after the snow had melted for the summer season.

Sinclair stood and looked around rapidly to make sure he was alone. As tempting as it was, he could not unearth the coffin at this moment. He would need permission. It had to be official. The deed had to be valid for Cordelia, and if he broke any laws acquiring it they might be tied up in court for years.

He started back to the truck, cradling his rifle in the crook of his arm. With any luck, he would find the town official in charge of this when the municipal offices opened.

He wanted to do it before Erin caught up with him. She must be stirring by now, and would come looking for him. Finding the deed this morning would shut down this whole cursed operation, and not a moment too soon.

Paris

The sun was streaming through the silk drapes in the bedroom at 40 rue de Vaugirard. Cordelia woke feeling as if she had been asleep for centuries. She stretched her limbs and felt new energy flow through her. She checked her watch—7:30 a.m.

Suddenly she was ravenously hungry—and it was the kind of hunger that would not be quelled. She needed some solid food. She showered and dressed in the charming little boudoir off the bedroom.

Cordelia opened her door and walked into the upstairs hall. All was silent. She felt like a stranger in this place, and didn't know which way to turn. But then there was a voice. Charles was speaking farther down the long corridor, his voice echoing back to her.

She walked toward the sound—along elegant crimson carpet, past a hall table with fresh flowers. The corridor was softly lit. To her right was an elaborate private elevator that connected the two floors of the apartment. Charles could be heard clearly now farther along. A paneled door was partially open and she knocked.

"Entrez!" said Charles.

She pushed the door open wide and stood absolutely still. The room was a collage of fashion sketches and photos. Every surface was pasted with cuttings from magazines: fashion shoots, glossy magazine covers, clippings from catalogs and art books.

Then Cordelia saw Charles and a young woman with blond hair seated at a drawing board. They appeared to be looking at a sketch. The windows beyond framed them in a charming cameo, their heads together. Charles was medium blond, and the woman had the same coloring but slightly lighter. There was something similar about them, in the way they were seated, the postures identical. Charles stood immediately.

"Cordelia! You are up?" he said.

"Hi, Charles," she said, hesitating. Surely she was interrupting.

"No, come on in," he said, immediately drawing her forward by her hand. "Meet my sister, Clothilde."

Cordelia looked at the young woman and was struck by her beautiful gray eyes and soft blond hair. She was very pale, almost ethereal. But what surprised Cordelia was the way the girl moved to greet her. She glided forward in a wheelchair.

The kitchen of 40 rue de Vaugirard faced the inner courtyard of the building. Looking down at the cobbled square from the kitchen window, Cordelia had the perfect vantage point to observe all the comings and goings. She watched a small European car zip into its spot in the enclosed parking area.

"Keep an eye out for a white Peugeot," said Charles. "Maman is out; she hates us messing around in her kitchen."

"Can you believe we are still scared of our mother?" Clothilde laughed.

Charles was slicing bread with a long serrated knife. Clothilde was wheeling expertly around the kitchen in her chair, collecting orange juice from the refrigerator and making coffee. The counters had all been built low to accommodate her.

"Maman wants Annette to do everything around the house, but Clothilde and I like to do things for ourselves," Charles explained.

"Maman lives in another century," added Clothilde.

Charles walked by and squeezed his sister's shoulder in a gesture both conspiratorial and affectionate.

Charles began breaking eggs for an omelette. He cracked them with one hand, effortlessly, as he kept his other hand on Watson's collar. The dog could reach anything on the low counters, but appeared to be content to stand by Charles as he cooked.

Cordelia surveyed him quietly. Charles did everything with such style. He was turning the simple preparation of breakfast into an art. She could see Clothilde was amused by his rebellion against the domestic dictums of Madame Bonnard. Cordelia suspected the whole exercise was Charles's way of empowering Clothilde to be more self-sufficient.

Cordelia felt a great surge of warmth for him. Did he simply fly through life making it all better for everyone? Smoothing out the rough spots? He certainly had helped her without a qualm. She thought about the long trip on the train from London to Paris; sleeping in the shelter of Charles's arms, she had felt so safe. He had such a gentle, caring nature.

Standing in this kitchen, she was conscious of something that had been pulling at her for many years. She suddenly knew that there was an intangible thing hovering in the room. Looking at Charles and Clothilde, she had a glimpse of what she had been missing since childhood. This was a real family. There was a closeness she had experienced only fleetingly, where each unspoken need was answered without the necessity for verbal exchange. That kind of interaction had eluded her ever since her parents died. Yet here in this kitchen they were treating her as one of their own.

Clothilde held out a cup of coffee to her.

"Try this. Charles makes the best café au lait in the world."

Longyearbyen

The main street of Longyearbyen was lined with large barnlike structures. The roofs of the buildings sloped steeply, so in winter the snow would slide off the eaves. But now, in early fall, without the softening effect of snowdrifts, the architecture had a squat, hunkered-down appearance. The commercial district of the town extended only about four blocks and then ended abruptly. From there on, the barren wilderness took over. But within the cozy confines of the main street, it was possible to envision a life of reasonable comfort and safety. The village had its own kind of rustic charm, with shops and offices to handle the necessary business of the community. There were also ornamental touches, such as sculptures commemorating Longyearbyen's heritage: a lifesize bronze polar bear and a statue of the founder of the town, John Longyear.

Sinclair entered the first building—a massive shedlike structure, approximately the size of an airplane hangar. A sign read SVALBARDBUTIKKEN, which meant nothing to him. But when he entered through the sliding glass doors, it was immediately obvious it was a general store, stocked to the rafters with food, household goods, outdoor gear, clothing, toys, electronics, and every possible necessity for the climate. He noticed several aisles of whiskey, gin, vodka, brandies, and other kinds of alcohol—all staples to make polar night, or even polar summer, more enjoyable.

Sinclair turned and walked back out into the deserted street. A second official-looking building was across the way. This one seemed more promising.

He walked into the main hall and found a wall board listing various offices. The Office of the Director of Public Construction and Property was up a flight of steps on the mezzanine level. That seemed a likely place to start. Sinclair headed up.

The door was open, and a lovely young blond woman was seated at the reception desk. Her thick sweater did nothing to hide her spectacular figure, Sinclair noted.

"Is the director in?" he asked.

She looked up and did a double take when she saw Sinclair.

"Yes, sir—who may I say is waiting for him?" She was instantly all smiles and attention.

"John Sinclair."

"Please have a seat, Mr. Sinclair."

She walked away, down a corridor and out of sight, to announce his arrival. Within moments, she returned, followed by a rotund fellow with a white beard and a big smile. The man's resemblance to Father Christmas was striking, and rather amusing given the town's proximity to the North Pole.

"Hello, I am Anders Olaussen. What can I do for you?" he asked, shaking Sinclair's hand.

"Might we adjourn to your office?" Sinclair suggested. "I am afraid it's a bit complicated."

"Please." Olaussen swept his arm back to indicate Sinclair should go first.

"The graveyard?" said Olaussen, rummaging through a paper file. "Sorry, some of the documents are not on computer yet."

"No problem," said Sinclair.

"Here we are," he said, extracting a file from a metal cabinet next to his desk. "This is from the Historical Preservation Society. Let's see . . ."

He was flipping through documents, and Sinclair noticed they were written in Norwegian.

"Here we are, just as I thought. There was a death there last month."

"The polar bear attack," said Sinclair.

Anders Olaussen's head snapped up. "You heard?"

"Yes, the victim was a friend of a friend."

"I'm terribly sorry."

Sinclair nodded and said nothing.

Anders Olaussen looked down at the paper again.

"Well, I'm afraid I have bad news. The document is no longer there. It was removed from the coffin," he said.

"You mean the Arctic Coal Mining Company deed?" asked Sinclair.

"Yes. I'm afraid someone has beaten you to it."

Sinclair's heart skipped a beat. "Who?"

"The curator of the Svalbard Museum. He dug up the deed to preserve it."

"Where is it now?" asked Sinclair, not believing his ears.

"I assume he's keeping it at the museum. If you follow Main Street, you'll find it about halfway up the mountain."

"Thank you," said Sinclair, getting up. "I am very obliged for your help."

"I wouldn't run up there so fast," said Olaussen.

"Why?"

"You can't access that deed unless you have a legal right to it."

"I see," said Sinclair. "Well, that's easily remedied. The owner of the document is coming to Longyearbyen."

"Well, you'll have to wait anyway. The museum is closed right now," he added. "The curator is on the mainland until Thursday."

"Are you sure?" asked Sinclair.

"Yes, I am. Nils Edgeland is in Tromsø, working at the Polar Museum. I'm taking care of his dog while he's away."

"So there is no way to get inside and see the deed?"

The man shook his head. "No. You will have to wait for Nils to come back."

"I can't wait that long."

"It's only two days from now," he pointed out. The tone said it all: outsiders were in too much of a rush. And the rules could not be bent.

"Fine," said Sinclair, summoning all his patience. "Here's my card. Would you be kind enough to have Mr. Edgeland give me a call if you hear from him? I am staying at the Spitsbergen Hotel."

"I would be most delighted," Olaussen said, brightening and accepting the card. It was clear he did not want to argue about it.

Sinclair was on the verge of leaving, but then hesitated a moment. He thought about what he was going to say and then plunged ahead.

"This deed is the property of my fiancée," he confided. "She is the great-great-granddaughter of Elliott Stapleton. For reasons of privacy, I would ask that you not discuss this with anyone."

"Certainly," Anders Olaussen assured him.

Sinclair shook his hand and walked out into the street. It was going to be two very long days. But that would give Cordelia time to come to Longyearbyen and claim her legacy.

Paris

Charles was singing a song in French and pushing Clothilde along the gravel path of the Luxembourg Garden. Clothilde was laughing, suggesting alternative lyrics in French, each of which sent Charles into peals of laughter. Cordelia understood little of what they were saying. She was walking Watson on a leash, looking out over the park.

They arrived in the central garden, just in front of the Luxembourg Palace. The formal flower beds edged by boxwood were bright against the blue sky, pink snapdragons in one bed, yellow and orange in another. Charles settled down on one of the park chairs and Cordelia drew one up next to Clothilde's wheelchair. Watson remained standing, looking at Charles.

"OK, Watson, I get it," Charles said, getting up again. He turned to the women. "I'm going to take Watson for a proper morning run. I'll be right back. Will you be all right?"

Cordelia looked around at the empty paths of the park. "I'm sure it's fine, Charles. No one is anywhere near us."

"I'll only be a second," Charles said. "I give you full permission to gossip about me while I'm gone."

"Good. We will," Clothilde answered.

Charles and the dog headed off toward the symmetrical rows of chestnut trees. His sister watched him go.

"I'm so glad you've come to Paris. We never see Charles."

"Thank you for having me. I'm enjoying myself so much, I almost forgot I'm supposed to be hiding."

They sat for a moment in silence. Clothilde looked off at the trees. After a few moments, she turned back to Cordelia.

"Sorry, I was thinking of how funny life is," she said. "It takes some interesting turns."

"It certainly has," agreed Cordelia. "I hardly recognize my own life at this point."

Clothilde nodded in agreement and glanced down at her own legs. "I have been through quite a few changes myself," she said quietly. A moment of understanding flashed between them.

"I love your necklace," Clothilde said, changing the subject. She leaned closer to look at the evil-eye charm.

"Thank you. John bought it for me in Turkey. It's supposed to protect me."

"It's so pretty," Clothilde said. "I noticed it immediately when I met you."

Cordelia touched the blond wig Charles had insisted she wear for the excursion.

"I feel ridiculous in this. It seems so long ago since they tried to kidnap me, but Charles and John insist I stay in disguise until the deed is found."

"Charles told me about the attack."

"Yes, it was terrifying."

"Maman is worried about you," Clothilde added, her eyes troubled.

"I am so touched by her concern. You have all made me feel like part of the family. I don't have a family of my own."

"Yes, Charles told me."

"I'm sure you realize that you are very lucky to have each other," Cordelia said, looking around the Luxembourg Garden, with its beautiful symmetry. The historic Palace of Marie de Médici stood behind them.

". . . and to live in this beautiful place."

"Yes," Clothilde agreed. "I love it here. And it's great for Watson; he needs the space."

"Watson is so adorable. In fact, your whole family is wonderful," Cordelia said. "Your mother is a great lady. I am in *awe* of her elegance. And Charles is so charming. I am quite smitten with him."

"Are you?" wondered Clothilde speculatively. "And what about John Sinclair? Are you smitten with him also?"

Cordelia blushed. "I love John Sinclair," she said simply.

Clothilde arranged the fringed cashmere shawl on her lap. She didn't look up, but said, "You are so beautiful, it probably doesn't matter to you about John Sinclair's other women."

Cordelia's heart stood still.

"What other women?"

"The contessa Giorgiana Brindisi and Shari. I know there have been many others," Clothilde said.

"I have read about his relationship with Shari," admitted Cordelia.

"Shari made a spectacle of herself. That affair was in the papers all over Europe," Clothilde added, shaking her head.

"He told me it ended," Cordelia objected.

"Yes, it blew up. Did you see those pictures in *Paris Match*! Wasn't that horrible?" Clothilde exclaimed. "That woman is detestable."

"She is?"

"*Completely*. I hate her. Even when she's drunk, she still looks fabulous." Clothilde laughed, and Cordelia couldn't help but laugh along with her.

"Who is the other woman you mentioned?"

Clothilde leaned forward. "They call her Brindy. The contessa Giorgiana Brindisi. She's an Italian countess, and comes from a very distinguished family in Italy."

"I've never heard of her," said Cordelia.

"Sure you have. She's the famous fashion designer. You've heard of Brindisi luggage, haven't you?"

"Oh my goodness, of course I have! Also the clothes. I saw the shop on Fifth Avenue when I was in New York," exclaimed Cordelia. "How long did they date?"

"About five years. It was very much the talk of Capri. She had a house there, and so does Charles. They all used to hang around together."

"I supposed the contessa is beautiful too," said Cordelia.

"She is much older than you are," said Clothilde kindly.

"Do you know what happened with that relationship?" asked Cordelia.

"I really don't know. I think it has been over for several years now."

"I see," said Cordelia with relief.

"Brindy was pretty bitter about the breakup. When she was trying to hang on to him, she invented a perfume just to drive him wild."

"She did?"

"Yes. She named it after the ancient Greek goddess Aphrodite."

"I suppose John liked that," Cordelia said, laughing.

"Actually, his work inspired it. About seven years ago he was involved in an archaeological excavation on Cyprus. They uncovered the world's oldest perfume flasks—about four thousand years old. According to legend, Cyprus is the birthplace of Aphrodite."

Cordelia gasped. "Wait, I just realized! *Aphrodite!!!* That's a world-famous perfume!"

"Yes, well, she made it specifically to seduce Sinclair. She analyzed the remnants of the herbs he found in the ampules on the island—things like extracts of anise, pine, coriander, bergamot, almond."

"How incredibly clever," observed Cordelia.

"And then she mixed in some modern scents also," added Clothilde. "And believe me, Sinclair went wild for it. Charles told me he found it irresistible."

"I tried it in the department store," Cordelia admitted. "It *is* very sensual."

"It worked. Sinclair and Brindy were together for several more years after that," concluded Clothilde.

Cordelia stayed silent.

"Maybe I should not have told you all of this."

"No," said Cordelia firmly. "My eyes are wide open. Your mother warned me about John's reputation."

"Did you mind?"

"Not really. She also told me about Charles's father."

"She *did*!" exclaimed Clothilde. "Well, she must like you a lot. I didn't find out until I was thirteen."

"She told me Charles's father is a senator in the States. But Alphonse Bonnard was *your* father, wasn't he?"

"Yes. He died in a plane crash," Clothilde said. "I survived." She looked down at her legs again and said no more.

Just then Charles came sprinting up with Watson. They were running so fast they both looked as if they were flying.

"Sinclair just called. He has found the deed!" he said, breathless.

"He did! That is great!" Cordelia cried out. "Can I speak to him?"

"He couldn't talk," Charles said. "Anyway, he doesn't want to say too much on the phone."

"He didn't ask for me?" asked Cordelia, disappointed.

"He did. But he had to go," Charles said. "Anyway, there's no *time* for this! We have to leave immediately to get a flight to Longyearbyen, *today*."

She looked at Charles's face. He was flushed from the run, his collar was crooked, and his hair was mussed. He was smiling broadly at them both. How young, handsome, and full of life.

Charles was talking to the SAS ticket agent at Charles de Gaulle Airport. There was a three-hour flight to Oslo with a good connection for another three-hour trip on to the Arctic town of Longyearbyen. They could be there by late that afternoon.

Charles handed over both of their passports, taking Cordelia's from her in a very proprietary way. He was playing the part of her lover to perfection. She would swear he was enjoying this charade immensely.

She had discovered a lot about Charles during their time together in Paris. For one thing, she now knew why he was always dressed to perfection; Clothilde picked out his clothes. Cordelia looked down at her own hunter green suede, three-quarter-length princess-cut coat. It had been Clothilde's, but she had insisted Cordelia take it.

"It's perfect for the Arctic," she had explained. "I don't wear it anymore. I used to wear it for après-ski in Gstaad."

Cordelia tried to protest.

"I insist. You will need something warm to wear, and it goes with your beautiful green eyes."

Cordelia reached down to squeeze her hand. "Thank you so much, you have been so kind."

"We hope to see you again sometime," Clothilde had said.

Cordelia saw the hope in her eyes. Clothilde wanted her to take a romantic interest in her brother. Cordelia had to admit there was nothing that Charles Bonnard lacked in terms of charm, intelligence, and humor. But he was not Sinclair.

She missed Sinclair's quiet strength. She missed the way he narrowed his eyes when he was thinking, and the way he absently stroked her hair when they were lying together. She loved his incredible mind, and the way he made love to her.

She even adored the things he *didn't* do: he would never keep up conversation just to fill the silence. He let so much go unsaid, yet never failed to *do* the perfect thing. Despite all the warnings about him, she loved Sinclair with all her heart.

Charles turned back to her and took her arm. "We're all set, it's gate four."

By the time they reached Oslo, Charles agreed it was perfectly safe for Cordelia to shed her disguise. After all, she would have to resume her real identity in Longyearbyen in order to claim the deed. In the terminal, between flights, she headed to the ladies' room to take off her wig.

"Don't be too long. The plane boards in five minutes," he cautioned.

When she returned, he glanced up at her and smiled. "You look a lot better."

"I threw it in the trash," she said. "I never want to see it again."

Just then his phone began to chime.

"*Oui?*" he answered.

Charles listened for a moment, and then looked at his watch. He paced in front of the gate, apparently uncertain what to do. Cordelia heard him telling the other person in French that something was *impossible*. The way he was saying it also needed absolutely no translation. He was angry.

He held his hand up to her in the signal of "give me a moment," and walked farther away. The conversation became more heated as he paced and argued with the caller. Finally he snapped the phone shut and walked back to her.

"Let's go," he said, his voice harsh.

"Is everything OK?"

He barked a bitter laugh. His mouth clamped into a stubborn line; he was clearly not going to respond. He began to gather up the bags in an irritated way. She stepped closer to help, but he waved her off, struggling to get all of them by himself. She stood back, perplexed.

"Life can be *merde*," he said, hoisting the strap of a bag onto his shoulder. "Let's go."

He set off to the gate, carrying all the bags, and Cordelia followed along behind.

Longyearbyen

John Sinclair walked around the perimeter of the Svalbard Museum. The wooden structure was halfway up the mountain—a beautiful vantage point of the village and the sea beyond. Even at this time of year, white chunks of ice were visible in the water in the bay. The museum was locked—as the town clerk had told him it would be—and a handwritten sign in Norwegian and English promised a reopening on Thursday.

Sinclair walked up the wooden steps of the building again and peered in through the glass panes on the door. He could see a small wooden vestibule, a polar bear skin hanging on the wall, and an antique dog sledge propped in the corner. The main room of the museum was through a doorway on the left and out of view. No sense in trying to force his way in. Cordelia needed to claim the deed formally, legally, and in a manner that was above reproach and would stand up in court if challenged. Jim Gardiner would be here by tomorrow, and Cordelia and Charles would be arriving later today.

Flight SK 4414, Oslo to Longyearbyen

Charles sat across the aisle from Cordelia and looked out the window. The whine of the jet engine cut off all conversation. His face was drawn and he was staring straight ahead. The engine revved to full throttle and the plane glided up into the cold Norwegian afternoon. When they attained altitude, she turned to him.

"Charles, is everything OK? Is Sinclair all right?"

"Yes, *chérie*," he said. "I'm so sorry to have worried you. Yes, everything is going well with Sinclair. He is meeting us at the airport."

"Oh, good," said Cordelia, relieved.

"Sinclair also told me that Jim Gardiner is coming tomorrow, with all the legal documents we need for you to claim the deed. He couldn't get a connecting flight from London today. There is only one scheduled flight in and out of Longyearbyen every day."

"Charles, you seem upset. Is there something I can . . ." She faltered, uncomfortable intruding into a personal matter.

Charles sighed and shook his head. In the bright northern light from the window, Cordelia could see that he was still very angry.

"Charles! *Tell me*. What is the matter?"

The seat next to him was empty, so she unbuckled her seat belt and slid in beside him.

"What is wrong?" she asked quietly.

"That was Mother on the phone. My father—my *real* father—has just sent for me, and she wants me to fly to Washington to see him."

"What for?" Cordelia asked.

"He is in critical condition. He had a car accident, and he finally wants to talk to me."

"Charles, *you should go*! Why are you on this flight?"

"It's too late. It's too late in many different ways," he said.

"But he is your father."

"Yes, but he is doing this for himself. For his own conscience. Well, damn him to hell. It is selfish, and I won't make him feel better, even if he is on his deathbed."

Charles was now flushed with anger, sitting stiffly, looking straight ahead.

"Charles! I'm so sorry."

"I learned a long time ago one must do what is *right*, not what is *easy*. I have always tried to have that quality of character that was so lacking in my father."

Cordelia nodded, not knowing what to say.

"The right thing to do is to make sure you—who have been cheated out of your legacy—can recover the deed to your great-great-grandfather's property."

"Charles . . ."

"The *wrong* thing to do would be to get on a plane to pander to a selfish old man who suddenly has a crisis of conscience thirty-six years too late."

There were bright pink patches on both his cheeks—a flush of anger. She desperately wanted to hug him, but knew enough not to try.

"Charles, I cannot thank you enough."

"You do not have to thank me, Cordelia," he said with dignity. "I do it for you. But I also do it for *myself*."

Longyearbyen

The clerk at the Spitsbergen Hotel desk saw Cordelia and turned to take a brass key out of a slot behind him. There were only about twenty old-fashioned slots and the brass keys were dropped off at the desk.

"Here you are, Miss Stapleton."

"Thank you," Cordelia said, surprised he would know who she was. "Is Mr. Sinclair back yet?"

"No, he hasn't been back since this morning."

Charles finished signing the registration slip and took his key.

"Cordelia, shall we?" he asked, moving toward the stairs with Cordelia's bag.

"Funny, the desk clerk knew it was me," Cordelia remarked.

"Sinclair must have told him to keep an eye out for our arrival," said Charles.

"Where do you suppose he is?" asked Cordelia. "I find it very strange he didn't meet the flight."

"I have no idea," said Charles. "If the key to his room was at the front desk, he must be out."

The long corridor had a half dozen rooms marked with numbers. Cordelia found room 12 and started to unlock the door. Charles continued down the hall.

Cordelia opened her door and called back over her shoulder.

"See you in a half hour in the lounge, Charles."

She turned around and opened the door. Once inside the room, she stopped in embarrassed confusion. This room was certainly not his. She looked at the number on the door and the key in her hand. The number 12 was clearly marked on both.

"Charles?" she called down the hall after him. "They've given me the wrong key. This can't be John's room."

Charles came over, and they both stood in the doorway of room 12 looking around, perplexed. Cordelia stared at a bra hanging off the arm of the chair. Women's clothing was spilling out of a suitcase. Makeup and cosmetic jars were scattered all over the bathroom shelf. On the other side of the room, men's clothing was draped over the chair at the desk, and a large suitcase was on the floor.

"It's not the right room," said Charles uncertainly.

"This can't be John's room," agreed Cordelia. "I'll just go downstairs and tell them."

Just then she noticed a leather Gladstone bag with the initials JS in gold near the lock.

"*That's John's bag!*" said Cordelia in shock.

They both looked back at the white lace bra on the chair. The rumpled bed had been slept in. Both pillows were wrinkled and crushed. The sheets were in disarray.

Neither said a word. Cordelia looked at the dresser next to the bed. A bottle of Aphrodite perfume was clearly visible, and the discarded red box sat next to it. Charles saw it at the same time, and took action.

"Why don't you come along to my room for the time being," Charles said, pulling the door closed. "I am sure there is a perfectly reasonable explanation. . . ."

Cordelia mutely followed Charles down the corridor to room 15.

Sinclair looked at his watch and then did a double take. It was six o'clock in the afternoon! He had no idea it was so late. In the high Arctic, the light provided no time cues that the day was passing. With the light uniformly so bright all day, he'd simply lost track of the passage of time. Charles and Cordelia must have landed an hour ago! He was supposed to have met them at the airport. He cursed under his breath as he raced over to the Land Rover. It was at least a twenty-minute drive to the airport.

The airline official shook his head.

"No, they're gone. I saw them get into a taxi," he said.

Sinclair waved his thanks to him, and sprinted back to the Land Rover. It would take him at least thirty minutes to get back to the hotel.

Charles walked around his room, checking the heat and opening the drapes. Cordelia sat in the single armchair, hunched over, her elbows on her knees. Neither said a word.

"Let's go back out to the lobby," Charles said finally. "I think I saw some coffee out there. I could use some."

"Did you try his cell phone again?" asked Cordelia.

"I'll dial it again," Charles said.

Her mind kept going back to that lacy white bra. *Who is she?* She thought about the bed—rumpled and incriminating. He had been so insistent that she go to Paris with Charles. And in England he had tried to end the relationship. Was that a feeble attempt at letting her know he could not be faithful?

"His phone battery must be dead. It goes directly to voice mail," said Charles.

"Charles?" she began.

He looked at her resignedly. "Yes, *chérie*?" he replied, his tone dismal. His expression suggested he knew what she wanted to ask. His reticence was practically an indictment of Sinclair. Cordelia stood up and walked briskly to the door.

"Come on, Charles, we both need some coffee. Look at it this way; it can't get any worse for either of us. What else could *possibly* happen?"

Charles smiled mirthlessly.

Sinclair was driving the final leg of the mountain track to the hotel. He berated himself for being so negligent about the time. It was unthinkable that he had left Charles and Cordelia on their own in Longyearbyen.

The track was rough, and he had to reduce his speed. The narrow road wound back and forth, as steep and serpentine as any switchback he had ever driven in the south of France. There were large boulders on either side of the route, left by seasonal rockfall off the mountain. Large chunks of granite hampered his visibility, and he could see only the dirt track immediately in front of his vehicle.

The Land Rover labored up the incline. As he rounded a blind curve, a figure stepped out from behind a rock. He saw a woman in a green Windbreaker. It was Erin, standing directly in front of his vehicle, and she waved for him to stop. He pulled up abruptly. She came around to his window.

"Can you give me a ride back to the hotel?" she asked. To his surprise, she didn't seem at all annoyed that he had left her behind. He looked at her closely. Her Windbreaker didn't seem enough protection against the chill. He also immediately noticed that despite all warnings, she wasn't carrying a rifle.

"What are you *doing* out here? Hop in," he said, reaching across and pushing the passenger door open for her to climb up.

"I can't believe you aren't carrying a rifle. Erin, that's *dangerous*."

She hoisted herself into the front seat. Sinclair watched, registering subconsciously that there was something unnatural in the way she was moving. She looked tense; her gait was stiff. Something was wrong. He looked at her face. She returned his gaze, and her eyes signaled a warning.

"Erin, what . . . ?"

Out of the corner of his eye he saw someone dash out from behind the boulder. Another figure sprinted toward the car from the other side of the road. Before he could finish his sentence, two men were in the backseat, behind him.

"Turn around and go back down the mountain," a male voice said. "I have a gun in your back." His accent was Russian.

Sinclair flashed a dark look at Erin. "Lady, you are nothing but trouble," he said.

For the first time since Sinclair met her, she actually looked embarrassed.

In the lounge of the Spitsbergen Hotel there were only two guests. Charles was sprawled in a chair, and Cordelia was standing at the plate-glass window looking out over the landscape. She had been there for an hour without speaking.

Charles finally got up and walked quietly to the front desk, so as not to disturb her. Clearly she had a lot on her mind.

"Excuse me," Charles asked the young man. "When did you last see John Sinclair?"

"This morning. Is anything wrong?" the young man asked.

Charles took the clerk by the elbow and led him away to the back office, out of earshot.

"The lady over there by the window is Miss Stapleton," Charles explained.

"I know," said the clerk.

"What was the name of the woman who stayed in room twelve with Mr. Sinclair last night?"

The clerk looked confused. "Miss Stapleton," he answered.

"The same woman who is standing at the window?"

"*Yes,*" said the clerk. "What is this all about?"

"The woman by the window flew in to Longyearbyen with *me* this afternoon. Someone else must have stayed with Mr. Sinclair."

"Well, I don't know anything about that," the clerk said. "The woman who stayed here last night registered as Miss Stapleton. She came in with Mr. Sinclair yesterday. She showed me ID. I have the registration here."

The clerk went back to the desk, collected the registration book, and showed Charles the signature.

"And the woman by the window is the same woman who signed this?" asked Charles.

"Yes," said the clerk. "In fact, this morning Mr. Sinclair came down and asked me about going to talk to the town clerk for a marriage license."

"*A marriage license!*"

"Yes. He thought it would be romantic to get married here."

"Well, Miss Stapleton was with *me* last night in Paris. So Mr. Sinclair was clearly here with another woman," said Charles.

"Well, if that is the case, she looks just like *her,*" said the clerk. "But, hey, it's not my business. I think you have to sort this one out on your own. I don't want to get involved."

Suddenly a flash of inspiration hit Charles. Bait and switch, Sinclair had said. Sinclair must have come here with a decoy while he and Cordelia went to Paris. *Oh, the stupid fool! Why didn't he say so?* It must be someone from Frost's team trying to find the killers who were after Cordelia. It was so obvious now that he figured it out. Of course Sinclair and the other woman stayed in the same room, to give the impression that the woman was Cordelia.

"Did they go out together?" asked Charles.

"No, I told you, he went out early this morning, and she went out later. He said she was all worn out and would sleep until noon." The young clerk smirked a little, conveying the clear implication that Sinclair had kept her up all night in amorous activities.

"Did you see her go out?" Charles asked, willfully ignoring the innuendo.

"Yes, she went out about two hours ago. She was going to walk into town. I told her to take a rifle and stay on the road."

Charles patted him on the shoulder. "Keep all this to yourself," he said.

"Sure," said the desk clerk. "Believe me, I don't know what is going on. And I don't want to. I don't want any trouble here."

"Don't worry, there isn't any reason for trouble. Everything is *fine*," Charles assured him, realizing that he was truly turning into a champion liar.

Mine number 2 in Svalbard was normally used as an excursion for tourists. In summer, visitors could don helmets and descend a few hundred yards into the mine. The guides would point out where, in the early 1900s, miners used to cut black coal by hand from the ceiling of the shaft. The walk downhill and the tour usually took forty-five minutes.

This late in the afternoon, there were no tourists, and the mine was closed. A white sign with a clock dial pointed to 10 a.m. tomorrow as the next opening time. Only a flimsy plywood partition prevented anyone from entering the tunnel to the mine.

One of the gunmen kicked at the barrier and it fell away with one blow. Then he walked ahead carrying an oil lantern. Sinclair and Erin were in the middle, and the other followed. They made a tense little procession. Footing was uneven, and Sinclair could see only the small glow of light from the lantern, illuminating the black walls of the tunnel. The mine was already chilled from the night air, and there was only the sound of their steps as they stumbled along the coal-strewn surface of the tunnel.

Sinclair had to bend forward to avoid bashing his head on the irregular ceiling. His height was a handicap in the confined space, and his size substantially limited his movements. He could not, and dared not, turn around to check Erin. After walking for about twenty minutes, the lantern revealed a chain stretched across the pathway. The chain was meant to delineate the end of the accessible part of the mine. But Sinclair could see that the tunnel continued, and they all stepped over the chain and continued to walk deeper into the mine.

Sinclair had never seen his captors before, but he assumed they were both Russian. While he was walking, he spent his time calculating an escape. A hundred times, Sinclair thought about putting up some resistance, and the same number of times he knew that either he or Erin would end up dead in the scuffle. There was no room in the cramped tunnel for a real fight, and he couldn't risk it.

As they moved lower into the mine, the air grew even colder. Erin was visibly shivering in her light Windbreaker. Sinclair signaled a pause, and then took off his coat and put it around her shoulders as the two gunmen waited.

"Come on, Romeo," one growled in his harsh Russian accent. "Date night is just beginning." They both laughed.

Sinclair was glad to shed the clothing. As they headed lower, the confined space was beginning to bother him, and he struggled against wave after wave of claustrophobia. Sweat beaded his forehead, and his legs felt weak from the effort of fighting off the panic. He knew in another couple of yards he would start to feel the debilitating chest restriction and shortness of breath of a full-blown episode.

At the Spitsbergen Hotel, Charles walked over to Cordelia and took her by the elbow. Her face was set, and she looked exhausted.

"I just figured out what is happening," Charles said. "You know . . . about the room."

"Don't even try to make excuses for him," Cordelia said coldly. "I know you are his friend, but do me a favor—don't give me any stories about John Sinclair. I am *not* going to believe them."

Charles shifted to a conciliatory tone. He put his arm around her and squeezed affectionately.

"Honestly, Cordelia, I am not going to even attempt to try to explain what went on in that room. That is for you and John to sort out."

"I'm not sure I even *want* to sort things out at this point," she said angrily.

"Perfectly understandable," Charles assured her. "But I think we should do two things right now. One is get you fed—you look hungry. And two, we need to figure out where Sinclair and the female agent went."

"Agent?" A small flicker of hope passed over her face.

"Yes, it was a bait and switch. You were playing girlfriend with me, and he had a fake Cordelia with him. He and Thaddeus Frost were trying to flush out the Russians, or whoever they are."

"Are you sure?" She whirled on him, her face awash with relief. He nodded.

"Did you know about it all along?" she burst out.

"Of *course* not! Sinclair never told me about this part of the plan. And I was so focused on keeping you safe, I never thought to ask. I assumed he was coming here alone."

"So how do you know it's true?" she asked doubtfully, her hope wavering like a flag in the breeze.

"Why else would he be here with a woman who looks like you? The desk clerk thought it *was* you because she registered as you. No other explanation makes sense."

Cordelia stood suspended, tense, trying to believe him.

"They *had* to share a room," Charles explained. "He couldn't very well book two rooms when he was supposed to be here with you."

She nodded slowly.

"He never would have sent for you if he were cheating on you, now would he?" Charles asked reasonably.

"No, I suppose not," she admitted.

"You don't know this guy like I do. It's so typical of him—he knows what is going on, but he never bothers to explain it to anyone else."

"What do you mean?" she asked suspiciously.

"He just doesn't communicate. Believe me, he's been this way for years."

"You don't think they . . . slept together . . . ?" Cordelia asked, her voice barely audible. "Do you?"

"No, I don't. But I think you should ask him yourself. Just to clear up any doubt about it."

"Believe me, I will."

She turned to the window and looked out.

"I want to get this deed and get out of here."

"Me too," said Charles, looking out over the jagged mountains. "But where in *hell* is Sinclair?"

Sinclair was sweating heavily in the narrow passage and trying to breathe. The gunman prodded him forward, and suddenly the tunnel emerged into a large cavernous area. He could see the ceiling soared some twenty feet high, but the cave was dark and indeterminate in breadth. The extra height of the space quelled his attack. Sinclair wondered if there were other hidden pathways that could serve as escape routes, but it was too dark to see. The space appeared empty except for some old mining equipment scattered around.

A figure emerged from the shadows and greeted him with a demonic grin.

"Sinclair," he said. "How nice of you to visit. Have you found anything interesting we should know about?"

"Who the hell are you?" asked Sinclair.

"I've been tracking you since Monaco."

"Let me guess—you have a red Ferrari?"

Evgeny didn't answer. Sinclair scrutinized the man and took his measure. A bulky thug in his midthirties, he was muscular and powerful. But he had short legs, which were slightly bowed, and that feature alone marred his looks.

Sinclair figured he could fight him and beat him in other circumstances. But even with Erin they were outnumbered three to two, firearms not included.

The gunmen seized Erin and bound her hands in front of her with plastic restraints. Then they advanced on Sinclair, one holding a gun, the other tearing at his clothes in a rough body search. One gunman gave his testicles a deep jab when feeling between his legs for a weapon. Then he thumped Sinclair with an elbow between the shoulder blades and drove him to his knees.

"Nothing," he announced to Evgeny, who watched the process dispassionately.

"Too bad," said Evgeny. "Now the woman." He smiled at Erin in a lecherous way. "I look forward to our evening together, Cordelia."

She gave him a look that could sear meat.

One gunman held them in his sights while the other manhandled Erin in a thorough search. She set her face in a grimace.

"Nothing," said the man again.

"Well, I guess it can't be helped." Evgeny sighed. "Cordelia and I will have to have an intimate chat." His face held a strange expression of eagerness mixed with malice.

"Say good-bye to your girlfriend, Sinclair. Unless there is something you need to tell us. It might make it easier on her if you shared it with us now."

Sinclair looked at Erin for an indication of what to do. She gave the slightest shake of her head. Tell them nothing, she was saying. Sinclair felt sick, helpless. She was going to be the one they put pressure on, and there was nothing he could do.

"Wait, she doesn't know anything," said Sinclair.

"We shall see," said Evgeny, grabbing her by her upper arm. He stripped Sinclair's coat off her shoulders and threw it back to him.

"She won't be needing clothes," Evgeny said, leading her to the back of the cave. Erin looked over her shoulder as she was pulled off into the blackness.

They disappeared. One man sat on the mining tractor and kept his gun pointed at Sinclair. The other one took out a thin plastic strip similar to the type used by law enforcement. He bound Sinclair's hands in front of him and pushed him against the wall. Wordlessly the gunman waved his weapon at Sinclair to tell him to sit down on the floor of the mine.

Immediately Sinclair felt the tingle of restricted circulation. His hands would be numb in an hour if he couldn't get the thing off. He heard Evgeny beginning to question Erin—his voice punctuated by the sound of violent slaps.

The chef at the Huset restaurant was not at fault. Rave reviews from the *Financial Times* of London and the *New York Times* hung in laminated plaques on the wall. Charles and Cordelia had ordered the reindeer steak with cloudberry-apple chutney, but the food sat on their plates almost untouched. Charles looked around at the ultramodern Nordic décor, accented by Svalbard memorabilia: miners' hats, pickaxes, polar bear skins, and reindeer antlers.

"It's a pretty nice place, considering what's outside," he remarked.

Cordelia took a sip of her mineral water and managed a weak smile. The pall of anxiety had hung over the table all evening. They had left word at the hotel that if Sinclair turned up he should call them. But Charles's cell phone sat silently on the table as they both tried not to look at it.

The mine was freezing cold, and quiet, and Sinclair could no longer hear Evgeny. The interrogation had gone on endlessly, and then, just a few moments ago, all sound had died down after a few strangled gasps. The silence was ominous. He was furious with himself, and depressed. There was nothing he could do to help Erin.

In his area of the cavern, the oil lamp had burned low. The gunmen, increasingly obscured by the diminishing light, had not bothered to get up to trim the wick. The flame had finally gone out.

He wondered what was next. There was only the sound of a drip of water somewhere nearby. Perhaps Evgeny had led Erin somewhere else. Sinclair waited. He could sense both gunmen still sitting there. It was clear they had instructions not to move. But he couldn't understand why they didn't relight the lamp.

All of a sudden, Sinclair heard a sound that gave him hope—a snore. The guards were *asleep* in their surveillance positions. He started to get to his feet, trying to unbend his stiff legs and maneuver with the restraints digging into his flesh. But as he started to move he suddenly felt a hand close over his mouth. It was a woman's hand. He flinched. He had no idea anyone was that close to him. He couldn't see her, but he could smell the faint scent of Aphrodite.

A quick flick of a knife between his hands and the restraint was cut. The circulation started flowing again, burning and itching as blood coursed through his fingers. Erin sat next to him and whispered into his ear.

"You take the one on the left, I'll take the right."

Her voice was so soft it could have been a breeze. No one could have heard it, certainly not the sleeping guards. He nodded his head so she could feel his assent.

She tapped her index finger on his arm in a silent count.

One . . . two . . . three.

She was gone. He could hear her garroting the sleeping guard, his boots thrashing the ground. Sinclair was not as nimble, but managed to charge the other man, groping to find him in the dark. A shot went off, and it echoed eerily in the empty mine. He had no clear technique to his attack, simply smashing the man over and over against the hard floor until he no longer moved. Sinclair finally stopped, not sure if he had killed him or just knocked him unconscious.

"Sinclair," she said. "Help me light this."

She pressed the illumination dial on her watch to find the lantern. Sinclair rummaged through the gunman's pockets and found a butane lighter. He touched it to the wick and the lantern flared. In the light she looked a fright. The dark wig was gone. Her hair was matted with blood, and her face was a swollen purple mess. Her shirt was in shreds. She had lost her Windbreaker, and she stood there in her bare feet, the red nail polish on her toes a macabre match with the blood on her face.

Sinclair gasped. *"Erin, you're hurt! Oh my God I am so sorry,"* he burst out.

She ignored him, put down the oil lamp, and walked over to the dead man.

"I need some shoes." She began unlacing the boots from the feet of the man she had just killed.

"Where is the other . . . guy who was questioning you?" Sinclair asked.

"Dead," she said.

"How did you . . . ?"

"You know, Sinclair, raping a woman is terribly distracting. You tend to forget to defend yourself," she said grimly.

"*Rape*?" Sinclair gasped.

"You think I *let* him? He was dead before he could even—" She never finished the sentence. The boot came free in her hand. She calmly began putting it on.

"Still light outside," Charles remarked. "I can't believe it's nine o'clock at night."

"Yes, it's getting late," Cordelia agreed, nodding thanks to the waiter for her coffee. Where could he have gone? In every direction there was only wilderness, populated only by Arctic fox, Svalbard reindeer, and polar bears. People didn't venture far at night in this territory. He *had* to be in town.

"Let's head back," Charles said, pushing his half-eaten dinner away.

"OK," said Cordelia.

Back in the car, Charles said what had been previously unspoken. "If he doesn't turn up tonight, we should go to the authorities tomorrow.

Somebody would have noticed him in the village. With his height, he doesn't blend in easily."

Cordelia nodded. Charles started the Land Rover and put it in gear.

Back at the hotel, the clerk just shook his head. No messages. Charles took his key and hers, and followed Cordelia upstairs. They stood outside room 12.

"Do you want to stay in John's room, in case he comes back later tonight?" Charles asked.

In her mind Cordelia could still see the white lace bra and the bottle of Aphrodite perfume on the dresser.

"No, I want to stay with you. I would feel safer. Do you mind, Charles?"

"Of course I don't mind. Please. It's the least I can do. I will leave a note in Sinclair's room to let him know we are here. He'll see it if he turns up."

Charles let himself into room 12 with Cordelia's key, shutting the door.

Suddenly alone in the empty hallway, Cordelia felt nervous. All her senses were on high alert. As angry as she was with Sinclair, in her gut she knew something had happened to him. He would never leave her and Charles at risk like this.

When Charles returned to the hallway, her anxiety diminished. Charles would know what to do—at least she had him. As they entered room 15, Charles looked at the bed.

"Why don't you just lie down for a bit?"

"If you don't mind," she said. "Charles, I *know* John will turn up."

"He will, don't worry."

Cordelia lay down on the bed and pulled the long green coat over herself for warmth.

"I will just close my eyes for a moment," she said to Charles.

"Good. You should rest, *chérie*. Take a nap. I will sit up for a while."

He pulled up the armchair and hunkered down into it, propping his feet on the other corner of the bed and closing his eyes.

Cordelia watched him get comfortable, pulling his coat over himself. But even though he was supposedly in repose, his face was still tense and vigilant. She felt herself getting sleepy under her warm coat and let herself give in to it, secure in the knowledge that Charles would never let anything happen to her.

✳

The loud banging on the door frightened her awake. She lurched up, clutching at her coat. The lights were still on and Charles was now stretched out beside her on the bed, fully dressed with his shoes still on. He was also jolted awake, but she was the first to reach the door.

"Stop, Cordelia. Don't open it. Check who is there!" Charles burst out.

"Who is it?" she asked cautiously.

"Cordelia, it's me. John," came the muffled response.

She yanked the door open and he pulled her into his arms. He smelled of smoke, dirt, coal, and sweat. She breathed in his scent and clung to him.

"John, I was so frightened. We couldn't find you—"

Then, over his shoulder, she saw a woman with red hair. The woman was partially turned away, her gun pointing down the hall. Cordelia stopped hugging Sinclair and stared at her.

The woman reacted to the silence and turned around to look at them. Cordelia could now see her face was mottled with bruises, and her face, hands, and arms were scratched and bleeding. The woman, despite her long red hair, was the exact height and build as herself.

"Nice to meet you, Cordelia," Erin said.

"Who are you?"

"Erin Burke."

"Who did this to you?" Cordelia gasped.

Sinclair gave Erin a warning look. "Give me a moment, will you?"

Erin regarded them both, with their arms around each other. "Sure. No problem. Where should I go? I don't think I'm dressed for the lounge downstairs."

"Why don't you go to our room," Sinclair said. "I'll stay here with Charles and Cordelia and fill them in."

"I *could* use a shower," Erin said, and walked away.

Sinclair turned back to Cordelia.

"Oh, Sinclair," Erin called from down the hall.

"Yes?"

"Key."

Sinclair fished it out of his pocket and tossed it to her. Erin caught it and turned to open the door of room 12. Cordelia watched in silence.

"Sinclair, thank God you're back," said Charles. He looked at Sinclair's wrists, raw from the restraints. There was blood all over the front of Sinclair's jacket, and his face was smeared with black coal dust. He put a gun down on the dresser and sank into the chair.

Charles looked somber. "Who were they?"

"Russians. They took us down into a mine at gunpoint and beat Erin up pretty badly. They were trying to get her to tell them about the deed."

"Did she say anything?" asked Charles.

"She doesn't know where it is. I found it this morning without her."

"Why?" asked Charles. "Aren't you working together?"

"I wanted to dig around on my own. I didn't trust her," Sinclair admitted. "I see now what a mistake that was. She never said a word even though they were trying to beat it out of her."

Cordelia shuddered at the thought of it. "Will she be OK?"

"Yes, she says she just has bruises and a couple of cuts. No broken bones."

"We need to get more help," said Charles.

"I've already called Thaddeus Frost," said Sinclair. "Jim Gardiner will be here to take care of any legal complications. He'll be here in a few hours."

"Good," said Charles.

"So here's what we need to do," Sinclair said, and pulled his chair closer to begin outlining his plan.

London

Jim Gardiner got up at 5:00 a.m. to take the SAS flight out of Heathrow to Oslo. He was carrying his legal case filled with Stapleton documents. If the Norwegians wanted proof, he had the entire legal record of the Stapleton family going back three generations.

The day was rainy and starting to turn into typical London damp, a hint of the winter season to come. Gardiner easily found a taxi outside the Connaught Hotel. He would land in Svalbard in nine or ten hours.

He was distressed that Cordelia was up there without him, and without Thaddeus Frost. Sure, Sinclair and Charles were capable guys, but they were up against trained killers. The faster this was over, the better.

Thaddeus Frost had called him in the middle of the night with the news of the attack against Sinclair and the agent. He hadn't slept since. The Norwegian authorities would have to get involved now. Gardiner figured three dead bodies at the bottom of a coal mine was a genuine international nightmare, and was going to require all kinds of reports and paperwork. Hell, if it were up to him he'd bury them on the spot and call it a day. It's not like they would be missed. But they all had to play by the rules, even if the Russians didn't.

Gardiner sighed. Today was going to be a long one, and he hadn't had time for breakfast. Maybe he would get a donut at the airport before the plane took off.

In the SAS first-class lounge, a woman in a leopard-print blouse was hunched over her coffee. She smiled at Jim Gardiner when he walked in.

Gardiner gave her a polite nod. He was balancing his coffee and donut in one hand and his briefcase in the other, headed for the chairs across the room. He had barely settled in when she came tottering over, her stilettos creating serious ambulatory problems for her.

"Excuse me, do you have a pen?" she asked. "I need to write down a phone number."

"Sure," said Gardiner. He started digging in his jacket pocket. It wasn't there. Damn. He opened his briefcase and started looking for it among the documents.

As he was rummaging, Anna drew his attention away from his coffee like a magician, creating a distraction with her other hand. She pointed at the briefcase.

"Is it there? I think I see it in the bottom there."

He looked deeper into his case. She quietly opened a large topaz ring on her right hand by lifting the jewel. Underneath the stone was a small cavity filled with white powder. It was an antique poison ring—a surefire bet for assassins for centuries.

Gardiner was still rummaging as her right hand moved quickly. White powder fell into his coffee. He never saw it.

"Got it," he said, holding up the pen triumphantly. "You have good eyes, it was on the bottom."

Thaddeus Frost walked into the first-class lounge at Heathrow and spotted Jim Gardiner right away. He was wearing the red tie they had agreed upon as a signal. The American lawyer was having coffee and a donut in the far corner. He looked avuncular, easygoing, just the way he had sounded on the phone. Thaddeus scanned the room automatically. The only other occupant was female, middle-aged, blond—no threat.

He walked over to meet Jim Gardiner. Out of the corner of his eye, he saw the woman take a look at her watch and rush out of the lounge at a fairly good clip, clearly late for a flight. Why did people cut it so close?

Gardiner stood up to shake hands. Frost noticed immediately that the older man was sweating heavily. That was strange. The lounge was as cold as an icebox. Must be the sugar; donuts will do that to you. Come to think of it, that donut smelled as if it had been cooked in rancid, partially hydrogenated cooking oil. That was bad enough, but then Frost caught a whiff of the coffee. God-awful swill. Then he sensed a different kind of smell in the steam coming from the cup.

He reached over and picked up the coffee cup. It was half empty.

"Where'd you get this?" Frost asked.

"The kiosk just past the security gate," said Gardiner.

"Don't drink it," Frost said. He smelled it again, and put it back down on the table.

"It's not that bad," said Gardiner. "Not the best, but not terrible."

"There is something wrong with it."

"How can you tell?"

"I can smell it."

"Are you kidding me?" Jim Gardiner started to smile. "What are you, some kind of coffee expert?"

"Actually, yes."

"So where do the beans come from?" joked Gardiner, mopping his face with a handkerchief. "Kona or Sumatra?"

"There is a chemical additive in this. Did someone go near it?"

Jim Gardiner was sweating even more profusely; he started to wobble on his feet.

"Nobody."

His eyes rolled back in his head. He fell sideways and Thaddeus Frost caught him, staggering under the weight. He lowered him gently, and Jim Gardiner passed out cold on the floor.

John Sinclair was sleeping with Cordelia in the crook of his arm in room 15 of the Spitsbergen Hotel. His phone was still in his hand. The vibration had jolted him awake.

"Sinclair."

He listened, and was instantly alert.

"What can I do?" he asked.

He listened for a moment more and hung up.

Cordelia was starting to stir. On the far side of the bed, Charles was snoring lightly.

"John, who was that?" she asked, still half asleep.

Sinclair pulled himself up, disentangling his arm from underneath her.

"You better wake up, Delia, it's not good."

Cordelia sat up, her hair in her face, her eyes half open. On the far side of the bed, Charles stirred, pulled his coat over his nose and continued to sleep.

"What's wrong?" she asked, becoming alarmed.

"It's Jim Gardiner. He was at Heathrow and . . . well, he has had an . . . accident."

"An *accident*? A *plane* accident?"

"No, not that kind of accident. He's on his way to the hospital, but the paramedics got to him in time and he should be all right."

"What *happened* to him?" she cried out, now fully awake.

"Delia, he was poisoned."

Sinclair knocked on the door of room 12. Erin was the last person he wanted to bother, especially this morning. He figured she would be very badly hurt after her severe beating yesterday. Still, Frost had told him to rouse her.

When she opened the door, Sinclair recoiled. The entire surface of her face was blue-black with bruises. The antiseptic ointment she had put on them made the purple and black welts shiny and even more livid. Her features were swollen, nearly obliterated. Her eyes were slits, and her bottom lip was distended, split, and crusted with dried blood.

"Sorry to disturb you," apologized Sinclair.

"What's up?" she asked. She spoke through the broken lips carefully, trying not to move her mouth.

"We have a problem, can we come in?"

Erin looked out into the hall and saw Charles and Cordelia standing next to Sinclair. She opened the door wider to let them all in.

"Wow, Sinclair. A real party! Come on in. It's BYOB, so I hope you came prepared."

They all filed in and took seats as Sinclair began to outline the plan.

A half hour later, Charles was the first to arrive in the lobby. The lounge was empty and the check-in counter stood unattended. Through the picture window he could see the first rays of sunlight appearing over the jagged peaks, and within an hour it would be fully light. He heard Sinclair's footfall on the stairs and turned to confront him.

"You want to tell me what is going on before Cordelia gets down here?" Charles asked testily.

"What do you mean?" asked Sinclair, slipping on his light parka.

"Don't be dense," said Charles irritably. "You are going to have to explain to Cordelia why you were sleeping with that woman."

"She knows?" Sinclair looked surprised.

Charles gave him a dark look.

"Yes, she *knows*; we walked into the room."

Sinclair spun on his friend. "How'd she get in?"

"The desk clerk gave her the key. Cordelia looks just like Erin in disguise. Remember?"

Sinclair groaned. "I never thought of that. She saw the bed?"

"She sure *did*," said Charles. "It was pretty torn up. And lingerie was hanging from every piece of furniture. It looked like a bordello in there."

Sinclair sighed, and finally answered.

"Nothing happened."

"Well, my friend, it doesn't matter if *I* believe you. Cordelia is the one you have to convince."

Sinclair stayed silent.

"Why the *hell* didn't you tell me you were coming up here with an agent?" Charles demanded. "You don't trust me?"

"I didn't want Cordelia worried. And I figured the less you knew, the less you would have to lie about."

They stood silently, looking out at the daylight growing stronger behind the mountains.

"You can't do everything by yourself *all* the time, Sinclair."

Sinclair looked at him, puzzled. "I asked you for help, Charles, didn't I?"

"Yes. Babysitting. And you came up here to face down dangerous criminals on your own. Did it ever occur to you that these people are trying to *kill* you?"

"I am aware of that," Sinclair said. "Last night we were almost . . . well, it's over now. But don't think I was the hero; Erin was the one who turned that around."

"She doesn't *look* like she won," observed Charles darkly. "What happened?"

"I still can't forgive myself for what happened to her. But they're dead now."

Charles's eyes narrowed.

"*Dead?* Did you kill . . ." Charles scrutinized Sinclair's face.

Sinclair stayed silent.

"OK, look, John, we need to get help," Charles said quietly. "This is too much."

"We *have* help. Erin is a trained agent. Thaddeus Frost is on his way."

"Then why don't we just stay *here* and wait for him?"

Sinclair turned to face Charles. "Because I don't know who else is out there; they could be on the way here right now."

Charles turned away from him with irritation. "Let's forget the deed."

Sinclair turned to Charles and grasped his arm. His voice was urgent. "I need to get her out of here, right away. And she needs to claim the deed or they will never leave her alone. Can't you see that?"

Charles shook his head, perplexed. "I don't know . . ."

"Look, I can't just sit here and wait for somebody to come after her."

"All right," Charles said reluctantly. "But if we are going to do this, let's get going and get it over with."

"Thank you, Charles," said Sinclair. "We will just keep moving until Thaddeus Frost gets here."

The Land Rover headed out down the mountainside, with Sinclair driving and Charles riding shotgun. Literally. In the backseat, Cordelia looked over at Erin, silent and determined. Erin's pistol was in her hand, resting against her knee. Her bruised face was nearly buried in the hood of her parka. There was an alertness to her body that signaled there was danger in what they were about to do.

The day was bright already, but no one was stirring. The town set its own pace, independent of solar activity. This time of year, the inhabitants of Longyearbyen were inured to the early sunrise and got up much later.

The town was stretched out below, but the vehicle was not headed down into the valley. Sinclair had sketched out the details to them quickly and efficiently. They would drive farther into the mountains, follow the rim of the bowl, and take the narrow track roads along the top of the jagged peaks. It was circuitous, but it was the best way to avoid notice.

The next part of Sinclair's plan violated every Norwegian law and a couple of American ones too. It was called breaking and entering in *any* legal system in the world, but there was no other way. Sinclair and Cordelia would enter the museum and find the deed while Erin and Charles stood guard outside. With so many people looking for the deed, it was too dangerous to wait any longer for official permission to take it.

The Land Rover jostled along the bumpy track, and the trip seemed endless. When they finally pulled up to the museum, Sinclair surveyed the terrain. He wanted to park out of sight, but the back of the small building was flush against the cliff, and there was no place to hide the vehicle.

"I'm not so comfortable with this," said Sinclair. "Let's make it fast."

Sinclair and Cordelia got out quickly and walked up to the wooden steps.

"Ready?" he asked.

"Yes."

"Sure you are up to it?" he asked again. She looked up at him. He was rugged and handsome in the early Arctic glare. His eyes were intense blue, and the day-old stubble defined his strong jaw. How far they had come together in such a short time.

She gave him a brave smile. "Yes, John, let's go. I want to get back to London as quickly as possible to see Jim Gardiner. That's all I care about right now."

Sinclair went up the steps first and surveyed the entrance. The door was no problem. Most breaking and entering in this vicinity was done by polar bears, and they never bothered with locks, they just smashed down the doors. So while the wood of the door was sturdy enough to inhibit bears, the lock was ridiculously flimsy. Sinclair started in on it with an improvised pick—his folding field knife.

"How do you know how to do that?" Cordelia asked as he carefully probed the lock.

"I had some misspent teen years. The family liquor cabinet was my training ground," he replied. He twisted the knob and it turned easily. "After you."

The air in the museum hit them in the face: cold and very musty—like old hides that hadn't been cured properly. Their footsteps echoed hollowly on the wooden boards. They walked through the vestibule, past the polar bear skins and an antique dog sledge propped in the corner. The shedlike exhibition space was large, and a staircase led up to a second floor. The museum display was very rudimentary; all the objects of interest were either hanging on the walls or in freestanding cases in the middle of the room.

"You take the left side, I'll take the right," directed Sinclair.

They walked around scanning the glass cases for old papers, or anything that resembled a deed.

"Anything?"

"No," said Cordelia. "This is all about the whaling and mining operations in Spitsbergen at the turn of the last century. There are no real documents."

"Let's go upstairs," suggested Sinclair. "I'm sure the curator's office is up there. The deed may be in a desk drawer, or even a safe."

As they headed toward the narrow staircase, Sinclair felt an unaccountable prickle of anxiety. He stopped, alarmed. Subtleties of intuition were not his style, but something about this wasn't right.

"Let me go first," he said.

Cordelia let Sinclair squeeze past her on the narrow staircase. He walked up the first few steps and stopped.

Cordelia saw him hesitate, clearly uncertain what to do. He put a hand back to stop her from climbing up farther. Her view was blocked.

"Delia, go back down now. *Now!*" he said.

She turned and went down the steps quickly, nearly stumbling. She got to the main floor and looked back; Sinclair was not following her. He was standing on the stairs, immobile, looking into the room above.

"*What is up there, John?*" Her voice cracked in fear.

"Delia, please go outside with Erin and Charles," Sinclair said urgently. "Please, do it *now.*"

His harsh tone of voice was chilling. She turned and walked quickly across the ground floor of the museum and out the door.

Sinclair could only assume it was the curator: Nils Edgeland. He had been impaled by a whaling instrument in his back. His shirt was stained around the puncture wound and the blood had congealed around the shaft of the weapon in a dark burgundy gel. His body was slumped on the floor in a nearly fetal position, as if he were still writhing in pain.

Feeling a bit light-headed, Sinclair looked away from the body at the antique whaling implements on the walls. He had spent many a summer in Nantucket and was familiar with the function of nearly every tool on the wall: long-handled flensing knives with curved blades and blubber spades. Sinclair realized he was slightly in shock, because it suddenly seemed terribly important to find the right word for the weapon that had killed the man. He shook himself out of it. He had to think clearly.

Sinclair approached the body. Nils had been dead for a day or more. The blood was congealed. Only the cool temperature in the empty museum had kept the body from decomposing. But that explained the ripe smell that had hit them when they entered.

There was no way to help this man. Whoever had killed the curator must have been looking for the deed. But what if they hadn't found it? As callous as it seemed, Sinclair realized, he should continue to look for it.

He turned his eyes away from the gruesome sight and started searching. It was certainly worth a try, before the police came in and turned the place into a crime scene. Once that happened, they would never allow him near the place.

He walked around, being careful not to touch anything. His boots echoed on the wooden floorboards. All the exhibition cases were intact and nothing seemed out of place.

Sinclair scanned the walls and the glass cases, which were filled with historical documents: provisions slips for the Arctic Coal Mining Company, shipment order forms, coal-mining records, receipts for whale-oil deliveries, and letters from dignitaries and statesmen who had visited Spitsbergen.

He carefully scrutinized the document cases. There were handwritten records from a century ago, but nothing looked quite like a land deed. Just as he was turning away from a display, he saw the leather volume. It was exactly like Cordelia's journal. The case wasn't locked. He wrapped his shirttail around his hand to raise the glass lid of the case and gingerly lifted the volume out without touching anything else.

As he opened the leather-bound book, he saw the exact same handwriting he had seen in the journal: *it was another diary written by Elliott Stapleton!* He tucked it into his jacket pocket.

On the way back to the staircase, he glanced at the array of whaling implements on the wall. He lifted down the first whaling tool he could reach, a three-pronged blubber fork that was used to lift slabs of whale meat out of the kettle. He would have preferred one of the guns they had taken from the dead Russians, but Erin and Charles had them, as they kept watch outside.

Erin and Charles were seated in the vehicle, looking at the bright morning. They held their guns pointed out the side windows, resting on the windowsills. All was quiet; the town below looked like a toy village.

"Erin, how are you feeling this morning?" Charles asked.

He looked at Erin and admired her fortitude. It was clear she was in pain. All morning she had been putting on an admirable show of bravado for the group, breezily dismissing the deeply bruised face, black eyes, and cracked and swollen mouth. Even now, when she and Charles were alone, she didn't let down. She immediately bristled at his sympathetic tone.

"*Fine,* why do you ask?"

"Well, *you* may be feeling fine," he joked, "but *I* didn't get enough sleep."

Erin grunted and the small tilt to the corner of her mouth might have indicated amusement. They settled in for a wait, both comfortable with the silence.

There was nothing stirring in the landscape before them. Charles looked in the rearview mirror. Suddenly another vehicle appeared behind them, pulled into the parking area, and skidded to a stop in the loose gravel.

"Erin, watch out!" he called.

Erin looked in the side-view mirror and saw four men rushing their Land Rover from the back. She cursed and whirled around, leveling her gun out the window. But her reaction was slow. The combination of painkillers she took last night and lack of sleep dulled her response. One man wrenched the gun out of her hand. She turned to Charles, and he was also losing the struggle to retain his gun. She whirled around. They were being held at gunpoint by two men.

Cordelia was just coming out of the museum when the ambush started. In the flurry, none of the gunmen had noticed her standing there. Cordelia tiptoed down the wooden steps and crouched behind the second vehicle. The men were talking, and she realized they weren't Russians! They had *American* accents!

"Why don't we take them to the seed vault."

"Is the boss up there already?" asked another man.

"Yes. He's waiting."

Cordelia hid behind the back chrome bumper and tried to decide what to do. It would be too dangerous to try to go back inside the museum to warn Sinclair. Out here, there was no real place to hide. She immediately understood that she might have only a few seconds before she was discovered. They would certainly see her when they returned to their vehicle.

She knew that she should try to leave some sort of message for Sinclair. It might be her only opportunity to alert him. Kneeling down, she started writing the words *seed vault* in the rough dirt with her fingers. It was difficult to do without making any noise.

Suddenly one of the men grabbed her from behind. He hauled her to her feet and pressed a gun to her back.

"Look what I found," the man called to the others. "She was hiding behind the car."

"Bring her over," someone shouted.

Cordelia looked down at her half-formed message. She had only managed to scrape out the letters S E E in the dirt. Was that enough of a message for Sinclair to understand? Would he know what S E E meant? It was doubtful that he would even notice it. She needed to leave another sign; something that would call Sinclair's attention to the message in the dirt.

The gunman was prodding her in the back, and she barely had time to think. Reaching up to her throat, she put a finger through her necklace and pulled hard. The chain broke and it fell to the ground, a bright object, right next to the letters. She stepped over the necklace and walked toward the others.

"This is the one we are looking for," the man announced. "Cordelia Stapleton." He never looked down as he stepped over the message.

"Good," one of the others replied. "Let's get out of here fast."

Sinclair stood on the steps of the museum and looked out over the barren land. The Land Rover had simply vanished. No clouds of dust, no distant vehicles racing across the valley. Nothing. It was incomprehensible that they could have disappeared so fast. What had happened? They would never have left voluntarily. Perhaps they had been taken hostage, the way he and Erin were yesterday.

Sinclair looked down, searching for tire tracks. The soil was loose and mixed with fine gravel. Then he saw something light blue and gold on the ground, winking in the bright sunlight. It was near where the Land Rover had been parked. He walked over and looked at it. It was the evil-eye necklace he had bought for Cordelia in Kuşadası!

He picked it up and held it in his hand. The sight of it made him heartsick. He never should have left her, not even for a second. She must have put it there to tell him something. He looked down again, and his eyes focused on a pattern in the dirt. There were letters scraped there. He walked around in a full circle. They were easily decipherable: S E E. See. See what? He knew Cordelia had meant to give him a clue to their destination, or possibly to the identity of their abductors.

He ran a hand over his forehead to clear his brain. Panic was impeding his thought process. What had she been trying to write? He started through all the letters of the alphabet. SEE-A SEE-B SEE-C.

SEE-D. He stopped. SEED. The seed vault! How could he be so thick? He kept staring at the spot where Cordelia had written the letters in the dirt. How long ago had she done that, ten minutes? How long had he been in the museum? He didn't know. He had never hated himself more than at that moment. He was failing, and failing badly. And Cordelia's life was at stake.

Sinclair stood up and wondered if he could see the seed vault. He knew it was buried deep into the mountainside. The steel door of the vault was visible on the cliff face in the distance. From here he could just barely see a metallic glint against the mountain. To reach it, he needed to go down this mountain, across the floor of the valley, and back up the mountain on the far side.

The distance was enormous, and it was two miles into the village. There was no alternative; he had to run.

It seemed like a cruel joke, having to chase after them on foot. As Sinclair started off, he cursed his stupidity. He needed to keep running at a steady but sustainable rate. His brain raced ahead of his feet, and he began to form a plan.

He needed to get help. The only person he knew was the director of public construction and property. Anders Olaussen. Father Christmas. Olaussen would know how to access the seed vault.

The road was steep, and Sinclair used the pronged whaling implement as a hiking pole to take the pressure off his knees. The dry air burned his throat and rasped his breathing. He was parched long before he came to the bottom of the mountain. When he reached level ground, he felt like he had been running for hours.

He finally reached the outskirts of the town and located the Svalbardbutikken, the general store. On Main Street, he saw a few families out doing their grocery shopping. He walked more slowly, trying not to attract attention until he stood outside the office building. He entered and ran across the lobby and up the short flight of stairs to Olaussen's office.

The young secretary had just come in and was still standing with her coat on, setting a coffee cup on the desk.

"Is the director in?" asked Sinclair.

"Oh, hello, you are back," she said, startled.

"Is the director in?" Sinclair demanded.

"I . . . I don't think so, I just got here."

Sinclair pushed past her and headed down the narrow corridor to the back office. The door was ajar. Sinclair stopped, aware that something was amiss. With the toe of his boot, he edged the door open.

He was too late. Father Christmas was dead at his desk, slumped over as if asleep.

At that moment, Sinclair had the clarity of mind that comes with extreme fear. Nils Edgeland and Anders Olaussen were mere bystanders in all of this, but they been killed in cold blood. Cordelia, Erin, and Charles were in grave danger. He had to get to the seed vault!

Near the dead man's hand, Sinclair saw a bundle of keys on a key chain. He needed a vehicle, and here was an opportunity. Without any compunction, he scooped up the keys and dropped them into his coat pocket.

The young woman came into the room just as he finished pocketing the keys, but she didn't seem to notice. Her eyes were on the man slumped over the desk.

"He is dead," he told her.

She looked at him, her eyes round and frightened.

"What kind of car does he drive? Is his car outside?" Sinclair was moving toward the door. The young woman wasn't watching, absorbed in the grisly spectacle before her.

"He parks in back," she said. "I didn't see the car. He has a Volvo."

"Call the authorities," Sinclair said, standing at the door.

He watched her reach for the phone, and then he turned and slipped out of the office. Sinclair sprinted down the stairs and out onto the street. He took a quick left turn around the corner of the building and found the parking lot in the back. There were four vehicles, and three of them were Volvos. Which one? He looked at the keys. He pressed the automatic lock button, and heard the faint click of a door unlocking. He pressed it a couple of more times and located the vehicle.

He opened the door, threw the whaling fork into the back, and slid into the driver's seat. He pulled the leather journal out of his pocket and slid it under the passenger seat. The car was an old model; it started with a key. He sorted through the tangle, fingering several security fobs and two dozen keys of all sizes. Finally he located the ignition key and inserted it. Despite the cold, the car jumped to life. He didn't have much time.

London

Thaddeus Frost stood in the corridor outside Intensive Care at the Royal London Hospital. It was a damn good thing he had brought that poisoned coffee with him in the ambulance, or Jim Gardiner would be dead. He had saved hours of guessing. The lab test had been started as soon as Gardiner was admitted. It was a relief that he was going to live. But he might not be completely functioning ever again. The doctors had said the powerful nerve agent might leave him blind, or crippled, or mentally impaired.

Frost wanted to make sure Gardiner would pull through before he headed up to Oslo. After all, he was personally responsible for the incident. He should never have left Gardiner on his own in the airport. Only those few minutes late, and it had turned into a deadly mistake. Inexcusable.

Frost had immediately called Paul Oakley to come and help him. He knew the ropes at the hospital, even if this kind of toxic poisoning was not his specialty. True to his word, Oakley was there in a half hour. He hurried up the corridor, looking deeply upset.

"Thanks for coming so quickly," Frost said. "When I called you, I didn't realize you had met Gardiner. I was just hoping you could help cut through some of the red tape here at the hospital."

"Yes, I know Gardiner," said Oakley. "I met him when we were doing the exhumation at Cliffmere. We rode back to London together."

"I was at Cliffmere also," said Frost. "Although if you had seen me, I would not have been doing my job properly. I was in the shrubbery."

"I had no idea all this was so dangerous," Oakley said. "This attack is . . . well, I'm not sure Gardiner will recover."

He looked gray with worry and his wire-framed glasses were slightly off-kilter.

"These people are killers. I shouldn't have let him go to the airport alone. I was late," Frost confessed.

Oakley's eyes opened in surprise. He put his hand on Frost's arm and spoke gently.

"You mustn't blame yourself. In fact, you probably saved him. How in the *blazes* did you know the coffee was poisoned?"

"I smelled it."

"You *smelled* it?" Oakley echoed, in disbelief.

Thaddeus Frost smiled a rare smile.

"Yes, I am cursed with an extrasensitive sense of smell. I am practically a human bloodhound."

"What do you mean?"

Thaddeus nodded. "Mostly it's a curse. In an airplane, I can smell an overdue diaper change twenty rows back."

"How extraordinary!"

"Sometimes, for my botanical work, it's very useful. I can smell natural scents that others don't pick up."

"Like your coffee beans," said Oakley.

"And my orchids. Most people don't realize they each have a unique scent."

"That is absolutely *fascinating*," said Oakley, who was starting to stare at him as if he were a potential subject for study.

"Of course, food is a horrible ordeal," Frost went on to explain. "I can't eat much. If the chef uses day-old fish or slightly overripe cheese, it's awful."

"I have never heard of anything like it."

"I smoke to ramp it down, so I can cope. Smoking impairs your sense of smell," Frost explained.

"Smoking will kill you."

"I should be so lucky," said Frost, looking at his watch. "Listen, I hate to do this, but I need to leave right away. I may have already missed the flight with a connection to Longyearbyen."

"What about Gardiner?"

"Could you stay and monitor him?" Thaddeus asked. "There is a situation up in Svalbard."

"Cordelia and Sinclair!" realized Oakley, alarmed. "Of course. Are they all right?"

Thaddeus nodded. "For the moment."

"*Go!* I will tend to Gardiner."

Thaddeus Frost clapped Oakley on the arm and walked quickly to the elevator. His mind was already calculating what was necessary. He picked up his phone and dialed his contact in Norway. With this kind of body count, it was going to turn into a mess; he'd be up to his eyeballs in paperwork for months.

"I need an airlift to Longyearbyen today. I am getting in to Oslo too late to make the commercial flight," Frost instructed. "Be ready to go as soon as I call. We can't waste a moment. The situation is critical."

He hung up the phone. It would be only a matter of hours until he reached Longyearbyen. He flagged a taxi in the rainy London street and headed to the airport.

As he sat in the backseat, Frost brooded. He hoped Sinclair had his wits about him. He seemed like a capable guy. Actually, with a little course work, Sinclair could be a top-notch operative. Well, trained or not, he was in the game, and it was getting more dangerous by the minute.

SAS Flight SK 802

Anna settled down into seat 6B on SAS flight SK 802 to Oslo. Nobody was following her. The poison must have worked. Evgeny would be pleased. She reviewed her options. Now that Vlad was out of the picture, helping Evgeny had real benefits—full partnership in the deal. When Moscow paid up, she would get 20 percent.

The Americans had Vlad in custody, the stupid fool. He had been picked up outside the house in Ephesus not twelve hours into his surveillance. Who knew what would happen to him.

She should have left him long ago. What a miserable husband. Her mother always told her, never marry for love—only for money. Of course, Evgeny was a difficult man, but at least he knew how to get things done. Sure, he was sexually deviant. But she had seen worse at the government-run school in Russia, like that dorm matron who would come at night to fetch her. Besides, there was no real danger. She knew how to act to make Evgeny think he had dominated her.

She checked her cell phone before turning it off for the flight. No messages. That was strange. Evgeny was supposed to call her. Here it was nearly noon and she still hadn't heard from him. He should be at the Polar Hotel in Longyearbyen, as they had planned.

Her thoughts were interrupted. The stewardess was leaning over to ask her something.

"Coffee?"

Anna smiled and shook her head.

"No thank you, not right now."

Longyearbyen

Cordelia was wedged in between Charles and Erin in the backseat of the Land Rover; the gunman and the driver were in front. The gun muzzle was resting on the seatback, ready to pivot toward any one of them if necessary.

Erin sat stiffly next to her, not communicating, clearly planning an escape. But Charles reached over and took Cordelia's hand and gave it a squeeze. His grasp felt warm and reassuring, a source of comfort. They didn't dare speak.

The vehicle drew to a stop. Cordelia looked out the window. All around was barren mountainside and the glare of the Arctic sun. No sign of life or habitation. A steel door and a large industrial structure jutted out of the side of the mountain. It must be the seed vault.

"Get out," one of the men ordered.

They climbed out meekly, anxious not to provoke him. The other gunmen got out of their vehicle, and they all congregated near the door. After a brief muttered conversation, three of the men went into the vault. The steel entrance door closed, and a single gunman remained, his weapon leveled at them.

Within seconds, Charles and Erin decided to take advantage of the situation, and started edging toward the gunman. It was clear they were going to try to rush him.

"Get back or I will shoot," the man barked, swiveling his gun back and forth to cover the two of them. Charles and Erin, without a word, worked in tandem, and spread farther apart. That widened the angle he had to pivot to cover both of them. Cordelia watched as they moved with perfect teamwork, as if they had formulated a plan.

"Don't move or I'll shoot," the man said, but he sounded frightened.

Cordelia took a closer look at him. He was young, in his midtwenties. He didn't *look* like a criminal. He was an American kid—fairly clean-cut, dressed in a rough Carhartt canvas jacket, and chinos tucked into hiking boots.

"Get back!" he cried in panic.

Just then Cordelia had a flash of inspiration. She should leave another sign for Sinclair, in the hope that he was following them. Now was a perfect moment when the gunman was distracted. As Erin and Charles were closing in on the man, Cordelia stepped a few paces away and knelt down in the dirt, and picked up a sharp stone. She would draw the ichthus wheel Sinclair had shown her—the one carved in the marble in Ephesus. He would recognize it instantly. Scraping away at the dirt, she drew a circle, about a foot in diameter, and divided it into eight equal parts. Then she stood up, dusting her hands off on her slacks.

Erin and Charles were closing in, the gunman looking terrified, his back against the door of the vault. But just then the door slid open and the other men emerged from the vault with weapons drawn.

"Please don't shoot," Cordelia said, and stepped away from her symbol in the dirt.

The stolen Volvo was laboring up the mountain to the International Seed Vault. In his mind, Sinclair reviewed the message left in the dirt outside the museum: s e e. It *had* to be the seed vault.

As he drove, Sinclair dialed Frost's number and got his voice mail.

"It's Sinclair. We have a problem. Erin, Charles, and Cordelia were taken hostage. I think they're in the seed vault, so I'm headed up there now. Come as quickly as you can."

Oslo

Thaddeus Frost sprinted across the tarmac. The Norwegian Air Force jet was ready, its engine screaming. As he approached, a uniformed officer came down the steps to meet him.

"Good evening, sir, we're at your service."

Frost didn't break stride, and launched up the steps, shouting over the din of the engine.

"We have a hostage situation. Three people, maybe four. We believe they are being held in the seed vault. I need you to get me some backup immediately."

The man's eyes widened.

"And there are two casualties in Longyearbyen. Norwegians," Frost continued.

The military officer nodded. "I'll have the pilot radio the police at Longyearbyen at once."

Longyearbyen

The industrial thermostat at the International Seed Vault was permanently set to maintain a steady temperature below freezing, somewhere between -10 degrees and -20 degrees Celsius. That was the ideal range to preserve the seed packets. But even if the cooling system failed, the Arctic mountain was a natural refrigerator—the seeds would still be protected by year-round permafrost.

Cordelia, Charles, and Erin sat on the floor, their hands and feet bound with duct tape. They could feel the bone-aching chill through the concrete. High aluminum shelves towered over them, each stacked with hundreds of black file boxes containing the seed packets. Their captors had left them unattended, placed several feet apart and bound up tightly. Although they were immobile, they could converse freely.

"You didn't find anything in the museum?" Charles asked Cordelia.

"No, there was nothing on the ground floor. Just as we were going upstairs, John told me to leave."

"Why?"

"I don't know. He saw something; he was very upset," said Cordelia.

"Who *are* these people?" Erin broke in. "I can't figure out who they are. Last night the ones who got us were Russians."

"Judging by their accents, these are clearly Americans," said Cordelia. "But I don't know who they are. A group called Citizens for World Survival sent me a death threat when I was on the ship."

"Why?" asked Erin.

"They want the vault to be neutral. They say that no country has the right to own it."

"And the Russians?" Charles asked. "What did they want?"

"They wanted the deed," Erin said. "But they're out of the picture. They've been neutralized."

Cordelia stared at her. "You *killed* . . . ?"

Charles caught Erin's eye, frowning; he shook his head slightly. Erin understood his meaning.

Suddenly the door swooshed open and three gunmen came into the room. There was a long moment of silence as they stood at attention, as if waiting for someone to arrive. Then a large man entered.

Cordelia cried out in shock. *It was Bob! And Marlene waddled in after him.*

"Howdy-do, Cordelia," he said.

"What are *you* doing here?" she said angrily.

"Oh, honey, we're so sorry, but we *had* to do this," explained Marlene. "We had to stop you from giving the deed to anyone."

"Why? What business is it of *yours*?"

Bob walked around looking at the seed boxes with interest. He spoke over his shoulder, not bothering to turn around.

"Will you look at all these seeds! Isn't it funny, all these countries saving them up in neat little boxes."

Anna got off the plane in Longyearbyen and checked her cell phone again. No message. How odd that Evgeny hadn't called her. The last time they had spoken was sixteen hours ago.

She walked through the small airport in Longyearbyen and stepped outside. What a desolate place! Thank God there was a van waiting for passengers.

"Polar Hotel," she told the driver. He took her suitcase and flung it in the back, and returned to the driver's seat.

"You here for sightseeing?" he asked.

"Yes," she replied. "Such a beautiful spot. I just couldn't stay away."

The driver backed up, did a U-turn, and drove the short distance to the hotel.

※

"I'm joining my boyfriend. He arrived yesterday," Anna told the desk clerk, giving Evgeny's full name.

"That would be room four twelve," the clerk said. "He's already checked in."

"Is he there now?" asked Anna.

"No, he went out."

Anna took the key card to the room and wheeled her suitcase behind her. Room 412 was just off the main corridor. She knocked sharply on the door. No sound inside. She carded the door open.

The room was intact, the bed unused. All of Evgeny's things were in the bathroom, and his clothes were in the closet. Where was Evgeny? How far away could he go in this godforsaken place?

Inside vault number 2, the young gunmen were nervous. Cordelia noticed they were not used to handling weapons. Bob was walking around the vault.

"Lance here has been looking for that deed for weeks now," he said. "We even went through all your things in California."

"How *dare* you!" Cordelia shouted, furious. "Those things were personal."

Bob ignored her, glancing around at the vault. "Will you look at this place? Built right into the bedrock."

"What are you going to do?" asked Erin quietly.

"The elders of the church voted on it, decided the vault must be destroyed."

"Destroyed? How?" Erin demanded.

"You'll see." Bob walked over to Erin and looked down at her with contempt. "It was wrong of y'all to kill poor Evgeny. You should've given him the deed."

"Why were you working with Evgeny?" Erin asked.

"We were doing our thing, to try to destroy the vault. But we ran into Evgeny and made kind of a side deal, to work together to find the deed and split the money."

"So why do you need us? You didn't have to kidnap us to destroy the vault," Cordelia pointed out.

"Ya'll know too much."

"You won't get away with it," Erin snapped.

"Sure we will. Lance has just finished putting incendiary explosives in the seed boxes. The whole vault is going up, to burn out the seeds."

"Don't worry, it will be quick," assured Marlene.

"You sick sons of bitches," growled Charles.

"*What the hell?* What kind of freaks *are* you people?" Erin demanded.

"Now that is just not a nice way to talk," said Bob patiently.

"You goddamn bastards. You think you are doing what's right?" Erin shouted, "*I think you are goddamn nuts, that's what I think!*"

Cordelia looked at Erin. It was clear something had snapped and she was losing control. Possibly her pain medication had worn off and she was struggling to cope. Her red hair was wild, tumbling over her shoulders. Her face was contorted with rage, and her bruises were even more livid. The two black eyes gave her a ghoulish appearance, and her pupils were pinpoints of hate. Her mouth was contorted, swollen.

The three young men were looking at Erin uncertainly. They shifted their gaze to Bob and Marlene. Bob shook his head slowly, as if she were a naughty child.

"Lance, son. I don't think we can listen to this kind of talk."

"Yes sir," Lance replied.

"You are going to have to keep this little lady here quiet so we can get on with what we need to do."

"Yes sir," Lance repeated.

Bob turned and walked to the door, not looking back. Marlene lumbered out after him.

Lance strode over to where Erin sat on the floor. He stood above her—a tall, rangy man with a heavily lined face and flat reptilian eyes.

"May the Lord forgive you," he said in a kindly tone. Without any hesitation, he leaned over, put his gun to Erin's temple, and pulled the trigger.

The sound of the shot was a dull thud. Half of Erin's head, behind her right ear, dissolved into a mist of blood that spattered across the floor, staining the light gray concrete. Her body slumped over on its side. She lay staring straight at Cordelia with lifeless eyes. China-doll eyes, big and green. There were bits of skull and red hair near her face; her cheek was pressed to the floor in a pool of blood. She was dead.

The room spun and Cordelia thought she would faint. *Erin. Dead. Just like that!* Cordelia was unprepared for the shock of it. She kept staring at Erin's lifeless body, which just moments ago had been so vital and alive. Suddenly Cordelia could not feel her fingers and legs, and the concrete floor seemed even colder. She lost all sense of reality, and had the sensation of floating, looking down on the scene. Her mind was numb, and she was losing her ability to think. She realized that she must not go into shock; she had to stay alert. Then she heard someone talking. Someone was shouting.

"*How could you!*" Charles yelled. "*What kind of a man are you, to shoot a woman, tied up like that?*"

Cordelia looked over at Charles. She was still numb, but she was glad Charles was yelling at Lance. She didn't have the strength herself. She couldn't seem to speak.

Charles was fighting against his bonds with all his strength, desperate to break free. His contortions were fierce, his face purple with rage, his hair sweaty and plastered to his temples. The three gunmen watched him warily, their weapons drawn.

Lance started walking slowly toward Charles, his gun dangling at his side. Cordelia realized what was about to happen. It jolted her into action. She called out. And to her surprise, fear made her voice strong and commanding.

"*Leave him alone!*"

Lance turned to Cordelia with a hard stare.

"I'll *tell* you where the deed is, just leave him alone," she begged.

"*Cordelia, no!*" Charles burst out.

"You shut up," Lance told him, and looked back at Cordelia. "You know where the deed is? You need to talk to the boss."

"Fine, take me to him," Cordelia challenged.

Lance walked over, put the gun into his belt, and took out a folding knife. The lethal blade slid between her ankles, cold and frightening. He cut the duct tape, grasped her arm, and hauled her to her feet.

"*Cordelia, no. Please!*"

Cordelia looked at Charles as she was led away. "Charles, listen to me. It's not worth your life."

Lance gripped Cordelia by the upper arm and pushed her out of the room. The three gunmen backed out of the vault, keeping their weapons pointed at Charles. The steel door closed and the swoosh of the air lock sealed it. He was alone. Charles looked at Erin's lifeless body, lying in a pool of her own blood.

※

Sinclair stopped the car on the rocky road. He needed to park below the lip of the cliff so no one would see him. Luckily there was a small indentation in the rock face, and the Volvo fit neatly into it.

Before closing the car door, he remembered to take the whaling fork from the backseat. As preposterous as it was as a weapon, it was better than nothing. He started up the steep incline to the exterior door of the seed vault, leaning heavily on the shaft of the whaling fork for balance. Circling around the mountain, away from the road, he found he could go higher than the entrance of the vault and then descend without anyone on the ground seeing him.

As he climbed, he slipped a little on the loose shale and gravel. But despite the uncertain footing, the slope was not difficult. Finally he stood above the doorframe and calculated his approach.

There was no one guarding the entrance. Sinclair looked at the tiny town of Longyearbyen below: toy houses and cars, the long stretch of Main Street that ended in the beautiful blue of Advent Bay. The ribbon of road winding up the mountain was empty. There would be no immediate help from Thaddeus Frost. He was clearly on his own.

From his vantage point over the door he could see the vault without obstruction. He gave it the once-over and started to move. But then something registered. There was a pattern on the ground! He dropped down the cliff, sliding on the loose gravel, knocking pebbles down like a light rain. They clattered around the entrance to the seed vault. For the final drop, he found his balance and then jumped.

Just in front of the vault, a patch of earth had been disturbed. It looked like a scratched message. He approached. *It was an ichthus wheel!* There was no mistaking it. It was distinct and very clearly drawn. Either Charles or Cordelia had left the symbol for him. They were inside!

Sinclair examined the door of the vault. It was about eighteen feet high and made of blast-proof industrial-strength steel, with no visible handle. So it must open electronically. He looked around. Sure enough, on the right side of the door was a small black square the size of a deck of cards. It must be a scanner. But he didn't have the corresponding scan card, so there was no way to get in.

Sinclair paced back and forth in frustration. He jammed his hands into his pockets and his fingers came into contact with the bunch of keys. Of course! The director of public construction and property would have keys to the vault! It was a very important town facility. Sinclair examined all the electronic fobs and swipe cards. A small black toggle looked promising. He waved it in front of the panel, and to his utter astonishment the door slid sideways to reveal a long passage into the mountain.

In vault number 3, Cordelia stood before Bob, her knees quaking from fear. Erin had been so brutally killed; Cordelia fully realized the same thing could happen to her in an instant.

She tried to formulate a plan, but the symptoms of shock were making her mind fuzzy. The only thing she knew and clung to was that Sinclair was coming for her. She had to believe it.

Bob was watching her suspiciously. "You say you know where the deed is?" he asked.

"Yes, at the museum. We found it and left it there because we wanted to get official permission to take it."

Her voice came out cool and confident. It was a spectacular lie, but she managed to sound convincing.

Bob started to chuckle. "You really are a Girl Scout, aren't you? Official permission. Did you hear that, Lance? She wanted *official* permission."

Lance nodded, but his face was dour.

"Where is your friend, John Sinclair?" Bob asked. "Why wasn't he with you?"

"He's back in town, meeting with officials to claim the deed legally."

Bob cracked up at that one too.

"You hear that, Lance—he is meeting with the town officials about the deed."

Lance nodded.

"What kind of time you figure you need to set these charges?" Bob asked Lance. "Another half hour?"

"At the most."

"OK. You stay here and do that. We'll head on over to the museum," Bob said. "If it's easy pickings for that deed, we may as well grab it and sell it to the Russians after all."

Lance walked away and opened a metal box resting on one of the shelves. Bob started toward the door, but turned back to Cordelia.

"I figure this is a fitting place for you to die. Right here on your great-great-grandfather's property," he said.

Cordelia knew better than to answer. She'd seen what had happened to Erin.

Anna decided there was no use waiting for Evgeny. She put on her jacket and sauntered through the lobby. The desk clerk of the Polar Hotel smiled at her.

"I'm going out for a little stroll."

"You will need a rifle if you are leaving the settlement," he warned. "There are bears. Especially this time of year."

"Oh, I just want to walk around town," she assured him.

"All right, then stick to the road. You should see the first buildings on Main Street right up ahead. You'll be safe inside the confines of the town."

"Thank you," Anna said with her best smile, and walked out into the brisk afternoon.

As Anna strolled into town, she could see a cluster of people between the two main buildings. The dome lights of an ambulance flashed blue and red against the dullness of the landscape. A stretcher held a body bag; the form underneath was immobile. She looked to see if it was the size and shape of Evgeny. It wasn't. Why did she have the feeling Evgeny was dead?

She sidled up to one of the men who stood watching the medics. He was a good-looking man in his midthirties, rugged with nice Nordic blue eyes. She smiled at him and he smiled back.

"Has there been an accident?"

"Yes, the fellow there has been shot."

"Who is it?" she asked.

"Anders Olaussen, the director of public construction and property. A terrible tragedy."

"Why would somebody shoot him?" she asked.

"No one knows. There's no logical reason. He was a local official."

"In charge of property? Like, what kind of property?"

"The seed vault. The old mines. The museum. That kind of thing."

"Oh," said Anna. "The seed vault. Where is it, exactly? I'm up here as a tourist. I'd be interested in seeing it."

"Right there." The man pointed above the roofline of the tallest building in the town. "See that silver structure jutting out of the mountain? That's it."

"Oh, interesting."

"Don't let this accident put you off your vacation," the man said. "Longyearbyen is actually pretty safe."

"Oh, I'm sure it is," said Anna, as she walked away.

Thaddeus Frost climbed out of the military jet and onto the tarmac. Longyearbyen was bitter cold and very windy; his ears were freezing, his hair was blowing all around. Of all the godforsaken places! Why couldn't he get assigned to tropical climates?

He turned on his phone and listened, cupping his hand around it to cut the sound of the wind. Sinclair's voice message sounded rushed and muffled.

Frost snapped his phone shut. It was much worse than he thought: three dead Russians, two Norwegians, an agent beaten to within an inch of her life, a near fatal poisoning in London, and now three hostages in the seed vault. What a goddamn mess.

In vault number 2, Charles wormed his way over to the shelving and pushed his back against it. Using his feet as leverage, he inched his way up until he managed to stand erect. Then he began rubbing his wrists against the rough screws on the metal shelf, hoping to abrade the duct tape and break free. As he worked, the contents of the shelf shook and the black seed boxes rattled around. The sound was echoing loudly through the empty vault.

Charles looked over at Erin's body on the floor. He felt his throat tighten. She really had given her life for this mission, and she had never expected a word of thanks. He thanked her now, in his thoughts, and tried to pray for her. But he couldn't pray properly; he was too focused on getting free.

Suddenly the tape gave way. Charles tore it off his wrists and bent down and stripped the tape from around his ankles. The gunmen would be back. It was only a question of minutes. He began to search the room for some kind of weapon.

Thaddeus Frost jumped into the Norwegian police vehicle.

"We need to get to the seed vault as soon as possible."

The driver was young and in uniform. His response was negative.

"We can't go right now, sir. You are wanted in town; there has been a death."

"That can wait. I need a few dozen men to go with me to the seed vault."

"I have eight men. But they're in town. We'll have to go there anyway."

"Eight men?" Frost said. "That's all?"

"Yes, that's all I have. And they're not even officers yet, they're still in training."

Frost pulled on his gloves in irritation.

"I'll take anyone I can get," he said. "Let's go."

Anna saw the police car pull up on Main Street. Two men got out. The one in uniform was clearly a Norwegian policeman. The second one seemed familiar. He was wearing a trench coat—clearly a civilian. Then she remembered. He was the bearded man from the first-class lounge in London.

He gave her a cursory glance but didn't recognize her. She didn't change her trajectory, but walked past him. Then she blended into the large crowd, which had gathered to gawk at the body bag and the ambulance. There was no danger of her being recognized. He hadn't really had a good look at her in the airport lounge. The only man who could really identify her was dead from poison. Besides, her clothes were entirely different from those she had worn in London. Now her platinum hair was covered by a red ski cap. A parka hid her figure—and a woman's shape was all that most men noticed anyway.

She watched Thaddeus Frost approach the ambulance and start a conversation with the policeman on the scene. The Norwegian officer was on the radio, giving emphatic and repeated instructions. She walked casually over and stood near him to listen.

His language was a flow of fluid sounds, all long vowels and soft consonants. She had five languages at her command, but the Nordic tongue was incomprehensible. Then she heard the words "International Seed Vault"—the consonants of the English words crisply interrupting the flow of Norwegian.

Perhaps Evgeny was there. The town director was dead. That *had* to be Evgeny's work. She should check out the vault—it was her best lead so far. Anyway, there was no point in hanging around here. There were too many police.

In vault number 2, Charles was scrounging through everything he could find. There were about twenty shelves in all. They were all steel structures about eight feet tall, stacked full of black metal boxes that looked like small filing drawers. Charles put his hand on one of the steel shelves and it swayed back and forth. They were not bolted to the floor and could tip over with a good push. That was a start. It might come in handy as a diversion when the gunmen came back.

The middle of the floor was clear except for Erin's body. She seemed so small in death, and Charles moved his eyes away to avoid looking at her.

In the far corner, behind some shelves, he saw a small glassed-in office with a desk, chair, and some papers. When he turned the doorknob, he found the office was not locked. He flipped the electric light switch, and after a triple blink of the fluorescent overhead tubes the room was lit with a harsh glare. All around was a jumble of gear: parkas, boots, flashlights, snowshoes, and cross-country skis. Charles started sorting through the debris to find something to use to defend himself.

At first he grabbed the flashlight. But it was not heavy enough to use as a cudgel, so he threw it aside instantly. The snowshoes were light aluminum and not useful at all. He looked at the skis and the poles, stacked upright, jumbled in a corner. They appeared to be discarded equipment from decades ago. Suddenly he had a flash of inspiration. He grabbed a ski pole. It was made of light titanium, straight and long. *Yes, it would do perfectly!* He stripped the small basket disc off the bottom of the pole and turned it into an improvised rapier. Now *this* he could fight with.

✵

Bob had put on his heavy coat and was ready to go. Marlene stood at his side, carrying her oversized purse.

"When you set it off, just make sure *our* people are out, and then let it rip," said Bob.

Lance jerked his head in Cordelia's direction. "Do I shoot her first?" Cordelia sat on the floor, her feet and hands bound again with duct tape. Bob considered a moment. He looked over at Marlene. She seemed upset, and sure enough, she spoke up.

"Bob, I don't think we should shoot that girl . . . it just doesn't seem right," she said. Bob looked uncertain, shifting uncomfortably from foot to foot.

"The church elders didn't say anything about killing people. It's just not right," she wheedled.

"Oh, hell, you're right, honey. Let's just let 'em be, Lance. Lock each of them up in different vaults. The fire will kill them. I guess that will be good enough."

Lance nodded again.

"How long do you figure it will take?" asked Bob.

"Oh, another ten, fifteen minutes—not much longer."

"OK. Well, Marlene and I will be getting along. We booked a flight out of here in an hour or so. We'll see y'all in Texas."

"OK, Reverend, I will see this through. God bless."

"God bless you, son, and Godspeed."

Sinclair walked down the long corridor of the seed vault. He realized that if he encountered anyone he would be in full view; there was absolutely nowhere to hide.

He ran lightly along the corridor, trying not to make a sound, but the rasp of his breathing was magnified in the echo chamber of the vault.

Why was it so empty and quiet? Certainly they were all in here somewhere. Sinclair was sure he would encounter someone soon. He held the whaling fork in his hand, but he knew it was of no use against a gun. Still, it was better than nothing.

He came to a wide-open space with high ceilings and a round desklike structure in the middle. It looked like a guard post. Beyond it were three corridors that went farther into the mountain. There was no way to tell which way to go—he simply had to take a guess. He silently slipped around the central desk and chose the corridor straight ahead.

The corridor on the left rang with the heavy footsteps of Bob and Marlene. She was breathing hard as she struggled to keep up with him.

"Bob, are you sure this is all right?"

"Now, honey, we have been over this a million times. We have been planning this for the last year."

"Yes, I know, but I was not counting on killing people. We only wanted to destroy the vault. Evgeny was the one who wanted to trap Cordelia and her friend. They seemed like such nice young people."

"Well, that *nice* young man, John Sinclair, killed Evgeny last night."

"I know, but Evgeny was a very bad man, Bob. I'm sorry we got mixed up with him."

"I agree. Well, no use worrying about him, he got what he deserved."

"But Cordelia and her friend? They didn't do anything."

"They stand in the way of God's will."

"So they have to die?"

"We can only be thankful that we are chosen to do his work," Bob assured her.

Marlene nodded uncertainly. They reached the large exterior door of the vault. Bob hit the compressor EXIT button and the door slid sideways to reveal the brilliant sunshine.

Anna saw the young man on the motorcycle. He was wearing a helmet, and his body had the whippet-thin shape of a boy still in his early teens.

"Hello," she said to him. He cut the engine so he could hear her, and raised his visor.

"I'm a tourist here and was wondering if you would take me around," Anna said. "I could pay you to show me the sights." She kept her voice coquettish.

He looked at her with interest. "How much would you pay me?"

"One hundred dollars an hour," she said. "Cash."

"Sure, I could do that. But we need to stop for gas. That will be extra," the kid said.

"No problem."

"Where do you want to go?"

"The International Seed Vault," Anna replied and smiled.

Thaddeus Frost spoke quietly to the chief of police. The training station was only two miles away, and there were eight young recruits there at this time. Clearance from Oslo was necessary if he was going to commandeer them, but that could be done in a few moments. Together they walked over to the central police station of Longyearbyen and entered the small office. The knotty-pine paneling and the steel desk were the same as in any rural police department in any country in the world. How was it they all looked the same? The few mug shots on the bulletin board did not seem all that menacing.

The Norwegian officer phoned Oslo and spoke in a hurried and demanding tone. With any luck they would be on their way to the seed vault in a half hour. Thaddeus Frost glanced at his watch; it was getting late. He wondered how Sinclair was doing.

Sinclair had never seen a map of the interior of the seed vault. But intuitively he figured out the layout. The main corridor branched out into three separate tunnels, which led to three different vaults, deep in the mountain. It was going to take time to search all of them because he would have to double back to the central guard desk each time.

He looked at the exterior door of vault number 2 and noticed the same steel construction at the entrance, with the same type of black scanner panel. Each vault was locked separately. Sinclair took his set of keys with the black toggle and waved it in front of the door, and it slid open with a *pish* of the air lock. A blast of cold air brushed his face.

The first thing he saw was the dead body. The overhead fluorescent spotlighted the pool of blood, in bright contrast to the gray floor. The victim's face, now blanched marble, was without expression, the green eyes staring. Her red hair trailed into the blood. *Erin!*

Sinclair's heart sank, and a terrible guilt washed over him. He never should have left her. Then he realized that if Erin was dead there was little hope for Cordelia and Charles. In a panic, he scanned the floor for more bodies. As he stepped quickly into the room, some second sense told him he was walking into a trap. He saw out of the corner of his eye an eight-foot shelf tilting toward him. He sprinted forward rapidly as it crashed to the floor behind him, the black seed boxes dislodging and bouncing all over the floor. Some of the boxes opened and spilled plastic seed packets around the room. Sinclair whirled around ready to fight, and then froze.

"Charles!"

"Sinclair, thank God!"

"Where's Cordelia?"

Charles looked absolutely distraught. "They took her, right after they shot Erin."

"How many?"

"Three men with guns and a ringleader named Lance. He's the one who shot Erin."

"Are they Russians?"

"No. Americans. There's this religious guy, kind of a preacher who is going to blow up the vault, and a woman who I think is his wife."

"Hold on. They're *not* Russians?"

"No, Americans."

"Who the hell *are* they?" Sinclair wondered.

"They called him Bob."

Sinclair turned slowly to Charles, his face terrible. "Big guy, dyed blond hair, his wife very fat and kind of slow?"

"Yes, how did you know?"

"Bob and Marlene," Sinclair groaned.

"Yes, those were the names."

"How could I be so stupid?" Sinclair groaned. "How *could* I?"

Charles looked at him. Sinclair was pounding his fist into his forehead as if to knock some sense into his head.

"Sinclair, *what?*"

"They were on the ship," Sinclair explained, "*and* in London. How could I miss that?"

"They are still here in the vault. I think Cordelia is with them," said Charles.

"Good, let's go get them," Sinclair said, moving back toward the door.

"Wait! What on earth is that?" asked Charles, pointing to the whaling fork.

"It's a whaling fork."

"Oh," said Charles.

"It's the only thing I could find," explained Sinclair.

"I found a ski pole," said Charles, holding it up.

That was the last thing he said. A man in a black parka was coming in the door with his gun drawn.

Outside the seed vault, the afternoon light was still bright. Three gunmen stood looking at the circle that had been drawn in the dirt—a circle that looked like a cartwheel.

"It wasn't here before," one said.

"I would have seen it," said another. "I stood guard here all morning. And this was definitely *not* here."

"I don't think humans drew that," said the third. "It's a sign from God."

"Of course it is. It's an ichthus wheel!" one said, with the glowing eyes of someone who had seen a miracle.

"Why would anyone draw an ichthus wheel in the dirt here?"

"It *is* a sign," the first man declared definitively.

They all walked around looking at it from different angles.

"Its definitely an ichthus wheel. *Iesous Christos Theou Yios Soter—* Jesus Christ, Son of God, Savior. All the Greek letters are there. Superimposed. It's the real thing."

"It's a sign from the Lord," the tallest man said with utter conviction.

"What could the sign mean?"

"Think about it," the first man said, weighing his words carefully. "We are about to destroy this vault. I think this is a sign of divine protection."

"Protection of the vault?"

"Yes. It's right in front of the door, isn't it?"

"This is a clear sign from God," agreed the other man. "Who would draw an ichthus wheel in the dirt? Nobody. This is a sign from a heavenly messenger—an angel."

"We should stop Lance from blowing it up," said the tallest man, urgently.

"How can we do that? He's already setting the charges."

They fell silent.

"It's the sacred symbol. I don't think there is any question about what it means. We have to do *something.*"

"Let's tell Lance about it. He will know what to do."

One by one, they turned and walked back into the vault.

The teenager pulled into the fueling station and Anna slipped off the motorcycle. There was a single red pump, and a weather-beaten shack stood a few yards away. The teenager unhooked the nozzle and began to pump the gas.

"Is the seed vault far?"

"No, not really," he answered, changing hands to hold the cold nozzle. "Just up that road over there. I don't know why you want to see it. It's not much—just a door in the side of the mountain."

"So, we can't go inside?" Anna asked.

"No, it's locked."

The boy hung up the gas nozzle and put out his hand for the money. Anna slipped some bills out of her wallet and gave them to him. She put the wallet back into her shoulder bag, worn bandolier style across her chest. The boy looked at her breasts, outlined by the strap of her purse cutting in between. Anna smiled at him.

"I'll be right back," he said, walking to the shed to pay for the gas. She watched him retreating. When he reached the shed, Anna jumped on the motorcycle, revved it, and pulled it in a tight circle to face the road. In less than ten seconds she was headed straight up the road toward the International Seed Vault.

Lance approached the door of vault number 2. All the charges were ready to detonate. He didn't care what Bob had said about letting Charles die in the fire—that kind of thinking was just plain sloppy. He pulled out his gun and opened the door. But when he entered the vault there was no sign of Charles. Another man was standing there. He was very tall, tan, and looked very fit. Lance had no idea who he was.

"How did *you* get in here?' Lance demanded.

He leveled his gun at Sinclair, advancing a few steps. Suddenly Charles stepped out from behind a shelf. Before Lance could react, Charles swung his weapon. He cracked the ski pole with tremendous force down on Lance's wrist, and the gun fell skittering across the concrete floor. Sinclair stooped to pick it up.

Lance whirled to confront his attacker, but Charles already had the titanium ski pole pointed at his throat. Lance looked at Charles, surprised, off-balance. He tried to move his head to the side, but Charles, in a fencer's stance, kept the tip of the ski pole against his larynx.

"You killed Erin," Charles said quietly. "And now I am going to kill you." His voice was ice.

Lance looked down at the ski pole. "With *that*?" he jeered, derisively.

Charles stood as still as a statue, arm extended, the tip of the ski pole still pressed into Lance's larynx.

Sinclair closed his fingers around the gun. He was tempted to shoot the man on the spot and be done with it. But he didn't want to risk it; he hadn't fired a gun in a long time and Charles was standing too close. So Sinclair stayed immobile.

"You're too late," Lance said. "The whole thing is going to blow any minute, and everything's gonna be burned."

"Tell me how to stop it and I'll let you live," Charles replied. Lance just laughed and shook his head.

"Then I am going to have to kill you," Charles said.

Sinclair stared at the two of them, poised in a macabre tableau: Lance strong in a defiant stance, Charles light and lithe with his improvised weapon—gripped as easily as he held his fencing sabre.

There was a long moment of silence as Charles prepared to attack. Sinclair was familiar with that moment, an infinitesimal fraction of time drawn out and suspended. He had experienced it many times when fencing with Charles.

Lance was regarding the ski pole with derision, totally unaware of the mortal danger it posed. He moved as if to step away, but the point of the ski pole followed. The muscles in Charles's arm tensed. He was about to strike.

Sinclair knew that there were no halfway measures; Charles would have to strike to kill. Charles had the necessary skill; he was one of the finest sabre fighters in the world. But his fencing had never ended in death before.

Sinclair saw Charles narrow his eyes and a muscle in his jaw ripple in tension. It was an expression Sinclair had never seen. When he and Charles fenced each other, the wire masks hid all but the shadows of the eyes and face. The way Charles looked now was chilling.

He attacked. The movement was so fast Sinclair only saw the devastation on the man's face. Charles took out both eyes in less than a second, puncturing the corneas and leaving gaping holes. Blood wept down the man's cheeks. Lance's mouth opened, and he began to scream. After a moment his legs buckled, and he sank to his knees. His sightless eye sockets faced up to Charles as his mouth screamed in agony.

Charles stepped closer and placed the tip of the ski pole in the soft indentation between the two collarbones. He found the hollow of Lance's neck with the point. After he settled the tip, he reversed his grip. Charles rammed the pole down hard, with a brutal thrust. The blade of the ski pole punctured the esophagus and drove straight into the heart. Charles gave it an extra thrust, and then he pulled it back out again.

There was a moment of awful silence. Charles stood there breathing heavily, holding the bloody ski pole. Lance slumped to the floor, dead.

"For Erin," Charles said, and turned away. The ski pole clattered to the floor.

Sinclair stood immobile as he watched the carnage. There was silence in the vault after the last death scream. Charles was breathing heavily from his exertion and seemed spent, and mentally drained. He walked away, staring vaguely at nothing.

Sinclair saw the door open again. Three men came into the room with guns drawn, and his mind went on alert. He was terribly outnumbered. He stepped forward, his hand wrapped around the gun in his pocket.

For a moment, no one spoke, then one of the three gunmen said, "We need to stop this."

Sinclair hesitated.

"The Lord has given us a sign not to destroy the vault," another said.

Sinclair stood without moving. *What did they mean?*

"Do you know how to disconnect the explosive device?" Sinclair asked.

They all silently shook their heads no.

"Lance is dead," one observed. They all looked at his gruesome body on the floor.

"We wash our hands of this," the tallest man said. They laid their guns on the floor and walked out quickly. The door swooshed shut behind them.

Charles turned; his face was pale from shock.

Sinclair spoke quietly. "Charles, we need to move quickly. Where's Cordelia?"

The corridor was cold. As Sinclair and Charles ran back to the central guard post of the vault, they could feel warmer air flowing in.

"The outside door must be open!" said Charles.

"Could she have left?" asked Sinclair.

"I don't know. But we can't risk it, we need to check the other vaults first," said Charles.

"I'll take the one on the left and you look in the vault on the right," said Sinclair.

"No, let's stick together. I don't know who else is still here," said Charles, starting down the one on the right.

"Fine," said Sinclair. "I'm with you. Let's go."

Cordelia sat in the middle of the floor of vault number 3. She hadn't heard a sound for at least five minutes. She had struggled against her bonds, but she couldn't seem to loosen the duct tape. So she had started worming her way toward the door, making slow progress, sliding on her buttocks across the concrete floor.

Lance had set his charges and left, putting an electronic device on the shelf across the room. Cordelia could see red numbers flashing, but she had no idea when the explosive charges would go off. She was mostly worried that Lance had gone back to shoot Charles. She figured that no matter what Bob had said, Lance would kill Charles anyway. He looked like that kind of man.

She looked up and saw someone standing in the doorway. She gasped. *It was Anna from the ship!*

The woman before her was quite a change from the glamorous woman she knew. Anna was wearing a parka and a shoulder bag. She looked like a guerrilla commando. She advanced into the room smiling, as if they were meeting for afternoon tea on the *Queen Victoria*.

"Cordelia, we have been looking for you. Have you seen Evgeny?"

"Who is Evgeny?" asked Cordelia.

Anna didn't answer. She looked around the room, and suddenly noticed the black digital device on the seed shelf. She walked over and examined it.

"It says nine minutes," Anna said. "Is this thing set to go off in nine minutes?"

"I don't know," said Cordelia. "Please untie me so I can get out of here."

Anna shook her head. "Not unless you tell me where the deed is."

"I already told Bob and Marlene. The deed is at the museum," Cordelia said. "Didn't they tell you?"

"Bob and Marlene?" said Anna in surprise. "I had no idea *they* were here."

Cordelia was confused. Weren't they working together? They had all been at the same table on the ship. Was it possible they were all competing with one another to get the deed?

"Untie me and I'll help you find them," improvised Cordelia quickly.

"No, I don't think so," Anna replied. "I don't think so at all."

She walked out the door and left Cordelia sitting on the floor.

Sinclair and Charles were standing at the guard post in the central area of the vault when they heard footsteps running in their direction.

"Who's that?" whispered Charles.

"Whoever it is, they're coming fast," said Sinclair.

"Get down," said Charles, squatting down in the well of the central desk. Sinclair crouched next to him on the floor. They had a clear view of Anna as she ran by. She never even noticed them.

"Who's *that*?" asked Charles again.

Sinclair didn't answer; he was already on his feet. He overtook Anna in three long strides and tackled her to the floor. She fought him fiercely.

"Let me go! It's going to explode!" she shouted.

Anna was writhing, struggling with Sinclair, who held her easily with his superior weight and contained her with one hand.

"It's *you*! I should have guessed," he growled.

"Let me go! The vault is wired to blow up. We have less than nine minutes."

"Where's Cordelia?" asked Sinclair.

Anna didn't answer. But the inadvertent "tell" of her eyes flicked toward the corridor on the left. Sinclair was off her in a flash and headed in that direction. Anna scrambled to her feet and began racing toward the exit.

"Charles, leave her, come on!"

Sinclair tore down the corridor on the left. It was the only place they hadn't looked.

Thaddeus Frost watched the three figures walking down the mountain with an easy, relaxed quality to their gaits. As the vehicle drew parallel to them, the Norwegian policeman lowered the window. The three men looked benignly at the officer.

"Peace be with you," said one of the young men. He spoke English with an American accent!

"And also with you," Thaddeus replied, leaning across to the window. He didn't know where *that* response came from—probably the vestiges of childhood, and Mass with his mother, who had named him Jude Thaddeus after the patron saint of hopeless cases.

The three men smiled in beneficent recognition of his piety.

"I wouldn't go up there, brother," one of them advised. Frost looked at him. He couldn't have been more than thirty years old.

"Why not?" asked Thaddeus.

"It's the International Seed Vault."

"I know," said Thaddeus.

"It's about to blow up," the man said.

Cordelia wormed across the floor of the vault number 3, her hands and feet still bound. Across the room, the numbers were relentlessly ticking down. Anna had left the door open, but Cordelia's hands and feet were taped so tightly she couldn't even crawl.

Suddenly she heard the sound of feet running in the corridor. They were coming closer. Was it friend or enemy? She stared at the oblong of the doorway, her heart pounding.

A figure appeared. It was John Sinclair! She could scarcely trust her eyes. *He had come!*

He was totally disheveled, with blood smeared on his jacket, pants covered in dirt. He looked taller and more powerful than she remembered.

He didn't see her at first; his eyes scanned the room frantically. Then he noticed her, sitting next to the shelving on the floor. There was a moment of suspended astonishment as their eyes connected. He exhaled, shutting his eyes for the briefest second, as if in thankful prayer.

The split second flashed by, and he was moving toward her, his face grim. He grabbed her by the arms and hauled her to her feet. This was no tender embrace; he spun her around and began stripping the duct tape from her wrists.

"Sorry, Delia," he apologized. "I know this hurts, but we have to get out of here."

He bent down and was working the duct tape off her feet.

"John, there's a bomb!"

"We know," said Charles from the doorway.

She looked up and gasped. *He was alive!*

He looked ghostly, his face pale and his blond hair almost silver in the light of the vault. Charles, lovely Charles! Her eyes started to tear up.

"I thought he *killed* you," she said. Her voice broke with emotion. Charles came over and threw an arm around her shoulders, and kissed the top of her head.

"No, he didn't kill me, Delia," Charles said quietly. "I'm not leaving you quite yet."

Anna ran out of the seed vault at full tilt and plowed straight into the arms of a member of the Norwegian police. She wrestled with him, but he grabbed her and held her fast. Several of the young police trainees were standing attentively, with their weapons leveled at her.

Thaddeus Frost stepped forward.

"Who are you?" he demanded.

Frost looked at her face and knew he had seen her before. He had total visual recall; it would come to him in a moment. And then it clicked. His eyes widened in astonishment. He replayed the mental tape from the airport lounge at Heathrow: leopard shirt, cleavage, coffee, rushing out for a late flight. He saw Gardiner drinking poisoned coffee.

"Arrest this woman for attempted murder," he said coldly.

✳

The red numbers on the bomb read 6:00 minutes. Sinclair, Charles, and Cordelia ran out of vault number 3 and careened down the corridor toward the main door of the seed vault. Cordelia could feel the seconds ticking in her head.

Charles was the fastest, and kept looking back as he ran. She and Sinclair followed close behind, and Sinclair grasped her hand to pull her along. The sound of their footsteps echoed in the empty hallway. The corridor seemed so much longer than when she had first entered.

The gray tunnel stretched before her endlessly, and she couldn't help envisioning the fire that would blast through it, incinerating them if they didn't make it out. Suddenly the fresh air from outside started to brush her face, and she could see the glare of the open sky in the doorframe.

Charles was the first to burst out of the tunnel. He came face-to-face with the police and stopped. Sinclair and Cordelia drew up behind. They all looked in surprise. The entire Svalbard law-enforcement team was now assembled at the exterior of the vault.

Thaddeus Frost was standing by the vehicles, talking on the radio. He turned at the sound of their steps and sprinted over quickly, his trench coat flapping around him.

"*Get these people out of here!*" he called to the police recruits. They lowered their weapons and began to help Cordelia and Charles over to the vehicles. But Frost put a restraining hand on Sinclair's arm.

"Is it going to blow?" he asked quietly.

"Five minutes. Less. It's an incendiary device," said Sinclair.

"Where is it?" Frost demanded. "We need to defuse it."

Sinclair stared at him, uncertain what to say. There was no way to describe where to look for it. They both knew Frost couldn't find it by himself—at least not in time.

"OK, I'll show you. Let's go," Sinclair said without hesitation, turning back toward the entrance again.

"*Get back!*" Frost shouted to the others. He waved them all away. "Get out of here! *Now!*"

"*Sinclair!*" Charles yelled. It was a howl of outrage. Sinclair turned around and stood before the door of the vault, suspended.

"*Sinclair, no!*" Charles shouted, and threw up his hands to the sky as if to demand why. The possibility of death hung between them, acknowledged but unspoken.

"*There's no other way!*" Sinclair called.

Charles stared at him in disbelief. "*Sinclair, you can't!*" he howled.

"*Charles, please. Take care of her for me,*" Sinclair called.

Charles dropped his hands, defeated. He nodded, once. A commitment made. Cordelia turned back at the sound of their voices. She saw immediately what was happening and started running toward Sinclair. Charles caught hold of her, to stop her from following. She struggled to break free.

"*John!*" Her scream was frantic. "*No, please! Don't!*"

"*Cordelia, I have to!*"

"*Please, don't,*" she cried. "*Please, John.*"

"*I'll be back,*" he shouted. "*I promise.*"

Sinclair turned and ran back into the International Seed Vault. Frost followed.

For Sinclair, the run back into the vault was entirely different from the exit they had made moments before. He was immensely relieved that Cordelia was safe. But a heavy, oppressive feeling overcame him. Sinclair was conscious of the full weight of the mountain bedrock above. Tons and tons of granite rested on this small tunnel. And as he ran deeper and deeper into the mountain it felt as if the tunnel were narrowing, and he had to bend over to stop the terrible weight from crushing him.

Just moments before, when his sole focus had been on getting Cordelia out, he hadn't given the tunnel a thought. But now his mind was playing tricks. Now the situation had all the qualities of his most dreaded nightmare. In his mind, he met his old phantoms: the dark snowy night, the overturned car. He kept running in an effort to fight the attack of claustrophobia he knew was imminent. He needed to push the panic out of his mind, but suddenly the blackness and the sweating terror crashed in on him. He slowed his pace and stopped, barely able to breathe.

He and Frost reached the circular desk with the three tunnels arrayed in front of them. His eye was drawn to the corridor on the left, and suddenly it seemed even smaller and darker than he remembered.

He didn't want to go in there. It looked like death—the terrible fear of death had haunted him ever since the car accident. It was his grave. He knew it. He knew he would die in that little tunnel in this remote place. He would never see Cordelia again. He knew it more than he had ever known anything in his life.

"What's wrong," demanded Frost. "Did you *forget* which way it is?"

Sinclair lifted his hand and pointed to the corridor on the left, leading to vault 3. Frost cast him a curious glance and ran off into the tunnel.

Sinclair stood still. He begged his mind to let go of the fears that kept him a prisoner. He had tried so hard to get free of that horrible night when he was trapped in the car. He had relived the memory with relentless tenacity for years. Surely it was time to let it go. He had to be cured by now.

He took a deep breath, as if preparing to dive underwater. And then he followed the sound of Frost's footsteps.

Cordelia clung to Charles, tears streaming down her face. She had fought and struggled against him to go after Sinclair, but Charles had held her tightly.

"Charles, he is going to die!! *I have to stop him!*"

Charles kept his arm around her as sobs racked her slim body. Damn Sinclair and his heroics! Despite all odds, they had managed to get out of the vault safely, but Sinclair had to run back in to save the day. Didn't he know that his life was more precious to Cordelia than any other in the world? How could he do this?

Charles was absolutely furious. If Sinclair got out of there alive, he was going to kill him himself. He released Cordelia tentatively, ready to catch hold of her again.

"Delia, we have to move farther down the mountain. In case . . ." He couldn't finish.

She nodded passively. She seemed defeated. She offered no resistance as Charles took her hand. He kept an arm around her shoulders to steady her as they went down the steep road. She wound both her arms around him, crying so hard she could barely see.

A line of Norwegian police vehicles passed them going down the mountain. One van stopped next to Charles and Cordelia. There were two uniformed Norwegian officials in the back.

"Get in. You need to evacuate," the officer said in English. "The vault is going to explode in five minutes."

Charles winced. He would have given anything to have spared Cordelia that statement. He handed her up to the outstretched hands in the back of the vehicle, and then launched himself after her. The truck careened down the mountain in a cloud of dust, leaving the vault behind.

Sinclair found Thaddeus Frost crouched over the digital device. The red numbers glowed 3:00 minutes. For some reason, Sinclair was surprised they had that much time left. It had felt like an eternity as he had stood in the tunnel and tried to overcome his fear. But it must have been less than a minute.

Now his mind was focused and calm, and every object in the room stood out in crystalline clarity. Frost was working a small screwdriver into the back of the device.

"Do you know what to do?" asked Sinclair.

"*Quiet!*" said Frost. Then he looked up at Sinclair as if he had just noticed him.

"*Get out of here while you still can!*" Frost said urgently.

"No, I won't leave you," Sinclair replied.

Frost gave him a puzzled stare, then looked down again at the device and went on working. Sinclair squatted next to him. He couldn't let Frost die here alone. That much he owed him.

He had failed so badly. He had bungled almost every step of the way. Erin was dead. His utter incompetence had nearly gotten Cordelia killed also. He had promised to help her, and then he had failed. He didn't deserve her; he simply didn't deserve her.

But there was one thing he *could* do. He could stay here with Frost and not abandon him. This moment was still under his control. He needed to see it though—even if it meant death.

A bead of sweat worked down Frost's forehead and dripped onto the floor. The device read 2:00 minutes.

Sinclair looked around at the vault. Box after box of seeds had been labeled and placed in neat rows along the shelves. Imagine killing for this. Imagine wanting to destroy this so badly that human life was worthless to you. What kind of people were they?

Sinclair settled back and thought about his own imminent death. He had always heard that heroes can't imagine their own death, and that is why they could rise so easily to the moral heights of sacrificing themselves for a greater good. He wasn't that way. He imagined his own death every time he had a claustrophobic attack. And now he *knew* he was going to die in the godforsaken vault.

It was funny, having all this time to think about death. Sinclair had often assumed that his final moment on earth would end with what were called "bioscopic fantasies"—scenes of his life flashing before his eyes with vivid and incredible speed. It was a phenomenon reported by many who had been on the verge of death. But now he realized that for him the final moments were going to be calm and utterly under control. And, astonishingly, he could breathe, without any symptoms of claustrophobia. The attack had vanished. Wouldn't it be ironic if he were cured so late in life—just moments before he died?

Sinclair had one regret—that he had not been able to get the deed for Cordelia. Then, with a random flash, Sinclair remembered the journal tucked under the front seat of the Volvo. Perhaps the deed was folded in the journal. Why not? The book and the deed both belonged to Elliott Stapleton. Why hadn't he checked? Silly, really. No time now.

The device said 1:00 minute. Sinclair finally allowed himself to think about the fact that he would not see Cordelia again. His heart ached in his chest. The physical pain of loss was so intense he couldn't bear it. He could feel his spirit dying. It would be a few more seconds of hell. And then he would be gone.

Cordelia and Charles stood on level ground at the base of the mountain. The Norwegian police recruits were positioned in the middle of the road, blocking access to the seed vault. Everyone was looking up at the mountain, waiting. The entrance of the vault stuck out like an iceberg from the rugged bedrock—shining silver in the light. It would be only moments now.

Charles wondered if they would hear the blast. Or would it just be a fireball inside the structure? Would Sinclair feel anything? He hoped not. Charles tightened his arm around Cordelia's shoulder and vowed to protect her for the rest of his life. He had promised.

Sinclair had been a big brother, mentor, and friend—even a father figure, in a way. Who knew how deep the emotional bonds were? My God, he loved him.

Charles had a sudden image of Sinclair throwing back his head and laughing. He thought about Sinclair lounging on a yacht, joking about some thing or other. But that wasn't the real Sinclair. Charles had another image of Sinclair standing in his dig in Ephesus, covered in dust, looking up and smiling as he approached. How many times had that happened? More times than Charles could count. And for Charles that was the image that pierced his soul with sadness.

The device said :30 seconds. The moment had taken on a totally surreal quality. For Frost and Sinclair, only a few more seconds until death. *For eternity*.

Now, more than anything, it was important to hold on to the image of Cordelia. He wanted to cherish it until the very last second of consciousness. His last thought. As Sinclair conjured up and sorted through all his mental images of her, he came up with his favorite—Delia sitting on his couch in Ephesus, curled up with Kyrie, reading the journal. He had lived an entire lifetime since they met in Monaco. The gala. Her blue dress. Holding the award. Walking on the deck of the ship. Reading the journal together. What a waste. It was over.

Sinclair looked at Thaddeus Frost. His face was gray. Sinclair realized that Frost would "die trying," as the cliché went. His hand holding the screwdriver was steady, but his eyes were frantic.

Sinclair stared down at the device. Relentlessly the numbers continued their reverse progression of seconds, :19, :18, :17 . . . Suddenly the red numbers blinked twice, followed by— And the device went dead. *He had done it!!*

Frost looked up, his eyes deeply shadowed. Sweat ran down his temple. Although he looked at Sinclair, he didn't appear to see him. He had a faraway stare. Finally his eyes focused on Sinclair, squatting on the floor next to him.

"Thanks for staying." Frost's mouth quivered with the effort of speaking.

Sinclair looked back at him with nothing less than awe.

"It was the least I could do," said Sinclair sincerely.

Frost closed his eyes and slumped back against the shelf, exhausted.

Cliffmere

The lawn of Cliffmere had never looked this green. It was late fall, and Cordelia sat out under the oak tree with a cashmere throw over her knees. She had an approved grant proposal on her lap for a joint venture by the Oceanographic Institute of Monaco and the Woods Hole Oceanographic Institution. The paperwork was not urgent, as the project would not start until the spring. That was fine with her. She wanted some time off. After all that had happened. After all that had *not* happened.

Was it only two months ago she had seen him in London? It seemed longer. But the details were etched in her mind.

The London office of Bristol and Overton had exuded the gravitas of a century of documents, signed, sealed, delivered, notarized, and executed, and whatever else they did to documents in London. Cordelia had signed over the deed. Funny how it had turned up in the journal after all. Not the journal she had been reading, but the one Sinclair found at the museum. It had been tucked in there by the curator for safekeeping.

Jim Gardiner and Sinclair had watched Cordelia sign over the land deed. Gardiner had been weak as he sat in his wheelchair. He was still quite sick. But he was getting stronger now, and they said with physical therapy he might walk normally in another six months. No permanent damage, they had explained, but recovery would take time. It was lovely of Paul Oakley to take such an interest in Gardiner's recovery. They were becoming quite a couple, with their daily walks though the park—Jim in a wheelchair, Oakley pushing him along.

Cordelia was glad to sell the land to the Bio-Diversity Trust. They had insisted on paying market rate. It was more money than she could ever spend in a lifetime. Thaddeus Frost would run the seed vault for real, as he should. After all, he had nearly died protecting it. The trust was a non-profit organization, not affiliated with any government. Norway had been reasonable about the land, and the Americans didn't fight with them. Only the Russian government was annoyed. But, thankfully, the Russian mob was out of it now.

Cordelia had tried not to think about Sinclair. But she kept seeing him standing in the lawyer's office at the deed signing, dressed in the navy blue suit that made him look so tall and handsome. When he left, he had kissed her on the cheek. He smelled of sunlight and herbal lemon verbena cologne. The touch of his lips to her cheek seemed formal, but tender at the same time. She felt the kiss on her skin long after he left. Just after he kissed her, he had promised to call. That was two months ago.

Of course, Charles had come to Cliffmere. He had promised, and sure enough, he had arrived, with his dashing clothes and his impeccable manners. She had watched him talking to Tom and Marian Skye Russell and was so grateful he was there, even though he had come alone.

And then, when she and Charles had sat together in the study, Sinclair had been in both their thoughts. How was he? she had asked. Fine, working in Ephesus. After that, Charles didn't mention him and neither did she. But they were both conscious of *not* saying his name. They were *both* suffering.

Sinclair was gone. That was all she knew. Charles wouldn't speak of it. Out of loyalty. To her *and* to Sinclair. In the end, Charles had bent over and kissed her hand tenderly.

"Cordelia, we all need some time."

That was all he had said.

And now she sat on the lawn, unwilling to go back to California and the Alvin to resume her old life. She couldn't even face London and her town house. All she wanted to do was to stay at Cliffmere until spring. Family. She needed family. And Tom and Marian were there for her, insisting she stay. Sinclair was in her thoughts every day, all day. She clung to him, but never spoke of him aloud. Neither did Tom and Marian. She would go to Monaco in the spring. Yes, she would go to Monaco in the spring, and maybe Sinclair would be there.

Ephesus

Sinclair stood at the edge of his terrace and looked out over the dry landscape of Turkey. Kyrie was pressed against his leg. She had been keeping close since he came home. The dog sensed that something had changed in him the minute he walked through the door. Svalbard had changed him. Charles had always said, "A dog knows the truth."

Charles. He missed him. They hadn't spoken about that day in the vault. They would. He was sure someday they would, but it was too soon. Charles had visited only once, to beg him to call Cordelia. He had walked through the streets of Ephesus looking for him.

Sinclair had been glad to see Charles. He had climbed up from his excavation, and they had sat together on the warm marble slabs of the ruins and talked. It had felt normal until Cordelia's name came up. Charles had seen her. At first Charles had been polite, but underneath Sinclair could see he was angry.

How was she doing? Not all that well, Charles had explained. There was unspoken accusation at first. Sure, Sinclair knew he should not have disappeared like that after the deed signing. But wasn't that the honorable thing to do? Of course he loved her, he had explained. But he had done so much wrong, had put her in such danger. He had missed all the warning signs, and only by the grace of God had he managed to preserve her life. Only a few minutes later and she would have been dead. He couldn't forgive himself. He couldn't promise to love and protect when he knew he had failed her so miserably. She deserved better. She certainly deserved a man better than he.

Charles had replied in an angry tirade, and didn't hold back. He called Sinclair a fool and a stubborn egotist. Harsh words, but Sinclair could tell he meant well. He knew that Charles was trying to goad him into action. In the end, Charles had left angry and disappointed. They hadn't talked much since, only for business.

Sinclair heaved a sigh and reached to touch the dog's head. It was time to make something to eat. Another day alone. It was almost unbearable.

Sinclair walked into the stone house high above Ephesus, looked around the simple room, and thought instantly about Cordelia. He looked at the couch where she had curled up reading the journal. It was the last memory, the one he had chosen.

He walked around the empty room aimlessly. Was there never to be any peace for him? He walked to the front window and looked out at the empty courtyard. The sun was baking the earth and it was nearly noon.

Sinclair looked down. The evil-eye amulet he had bought her in Kuşadası was on the writing desk. He picked it up and held it in his hand. Weeks ago, he had sent it out to the jeweler to have the chain repaired, and now it just sat on his writing desk, day after day.

He reached for his cell phone. He didn't consciously make the decision, and even now he hardly realized what he was doing. It just happened.

He closed his eyes. Malik picked up on the other end.

"Malik, it's Sinclair. I need to get a charter flight. Yes, this afternoon. Leaving for London."

"Yes sir, is there anything else?"

"Yes, I am going to need a hired car when I get to London. I need to drive to the countryside."

"Yes sir. I will pick you up in half an hour?"

"Yes," said Sinclair. "Yes, I'll be ready."

Sinclair walked to his armoire to pack some clothes. On the way he turned on the stereo. The house was filled with the haunting music of Arcangelo Corelli's *La Follia*.

Acknowledgments

I would like to express heartfelt thanks to all who have supported and encouraged me in this endeavor. My deepest gratitude goes to Maurice Tempelsman, who provided humor, inspiration, and advice through every phase of this project. Thanks also to my lovely sons, William and Beau Croxton, who have faith in all my new undertakings no matter how ambitious or adventurous. Additional gratitude to my family for their support—Nan, Susan, Campion, and Ted Overbagh. The talented Tempelsman family for their encouragement—Marcy, Leon, Cathy, Julian, Audrey, and Marina. The awe-inspiring women of the Speisman family: Rena, Haley, Tara, and Brittany.

Much appreciation to those who read or discussed drafts of the book and made valuable suggestions, including: Nan Overbagh, Philippa Holland, Cathy Tempelsman, Jenny Rider, Marin Strmecki, Tom and Marian Cooper, Roman Pipko, Tristan Mabry, Marie Amaral, Peter Tedeschi, and Ben and Maria Batsch. And special thanks to my wonderful, supportive colleagues at CNN who cheered me on, as well as innumerable friends who encouraged me in my writing career.

Thanks to my agent, Mort Janklow, for faith in my ability to establish a career as a fiction writer after twenty-five years in the news business. This book would never have come to print without the exceptional team at Scribner: Roz Lippel, for incredible patience and guidance during the stresses of a debut novel; Kara Watson, for insightful suggestions on original drafts; as well as the dedication and support of art director Rex Bonomelli and copyeditor Katie Rizzo.

The visual team Carol Seitz and Kim Wayman for the author photograph. William Croxton for his invaluable contribution to still photography and video.

The scientific and technical details of this book are as true to life as possible. Any departure from what is scientifically possible stems from my own invention and the demands of a fictitious plotline. Many people helped contribute to accuracy, including the wonderful scientists at the Woods Hole Oceanographic Institution, including Dr. Susan K. Avery, president and director of WHOI; senior scientist Dr. Susan E. Humphris, for helping me envision the character Cordelia and also for invaluable help with the details about the Alvin submersible; Jane Neumann and all the WHOI marine scientists who took the time to answer my questions and provide inspiration for the book. Thanks also to Dr. Max Essex of Harvard University School of Public Health for his insight in helping me with the intricacies of the 1918 pandemic and influenza viruses, and for advice on what might be possible, or not possible, in terms of plot. Also my deep appreciation goes to the New Bedford Whaling Museum for their curatorial advice about the original Bradford folio. And last, thanks to Cary Fowler of the Global Crop Diversity Trust for insight into the Svalbard Global Seed Vault.